THE THREE MOST WANTED

CORINNA TURNER

unSeen

PRAISE FOR CORINNA TURNER'S BOOKS

LIBERATION: nominated for the **Carnegie Medal Award 2016.**
ELFLING: 1st prize, Teen Fiction, **CPA Book Awards 2019**
I AM MARGARET & **BANE'S EYES**: finalists, **CALA Award 2016/2018.**
LIBERATION & **THE SIEGE OF REGINALD HILL**: 3rd place, **CPA Book Awards 2016/2019.**

PRAISE FOR *I AM MARGARET*

Great style—very good characters and pace.
Definitely a book worth reading, like The Hunger Games.
EOIN COLFER, author of the *Artemis Fowl* books

An intelligent, well-written and enjoyable debut from
a young writer with a bright future.
STEWART ROSS, author of *The Soterion Mission*

This book invaded my dreams.
SR. MARY CATHERINE BLOOM OP

Margaret, Bane, Jon and the Major have stayed with me
long since I finished reading about them.
RACHEL FRASER

One of the best Christian fiction books I have read.
CAT CAIRD, blogger, 'Sunshine Lenses'

PRAISE FOR *THE THREE MOST WANTED*

I cannot reiterate enough how much I am enjoying these books
and how talented this author is.
TIFFANY, blogger, 'Life of a Catholic Librarian'

The I AM MARGARET Series

Brothers *(A Short Prequel Novella)**
1: I Am Margaret*
2: The Three Most Wanted*
3: Liberation*
4: Bane's Eyes*
5: Margo's Diary*
6: The Siege of Reginald Hill*
7: A Saint in the Family *(Coming Soon)*

The YESTERDAY & TOMORROW Series

Someday: A Novella*
1: Tomorrow's Dead *(Coming Soon)*

The UNSPARKED Series

BREACH! (A Prequel)*
1: DRIVE!*
2: A Truly Raptor-ous Welcome
3: PANIC! *(Coming Soon)*

STANDALONE WORKS

Elfling*

Mandy Lamb & The Full Moon*

Secrets: Visible & Invisible (I Am Margaret *story in anthology)**

Gifts: Visible & Invisible (unSPARKed *story in anthology)*

Three Last Things *or* The Hounding of Carl Jarrold, Soulless Assassin* *(Coming Soon)*

The Raven & The Yew *(Coming Soon)*

Awarded the Catholic Writers Guild *Seal of Approval

I will lead the blind by a road they do not know,
by paths they have not known I will guide them.

Isaiah 42:16a

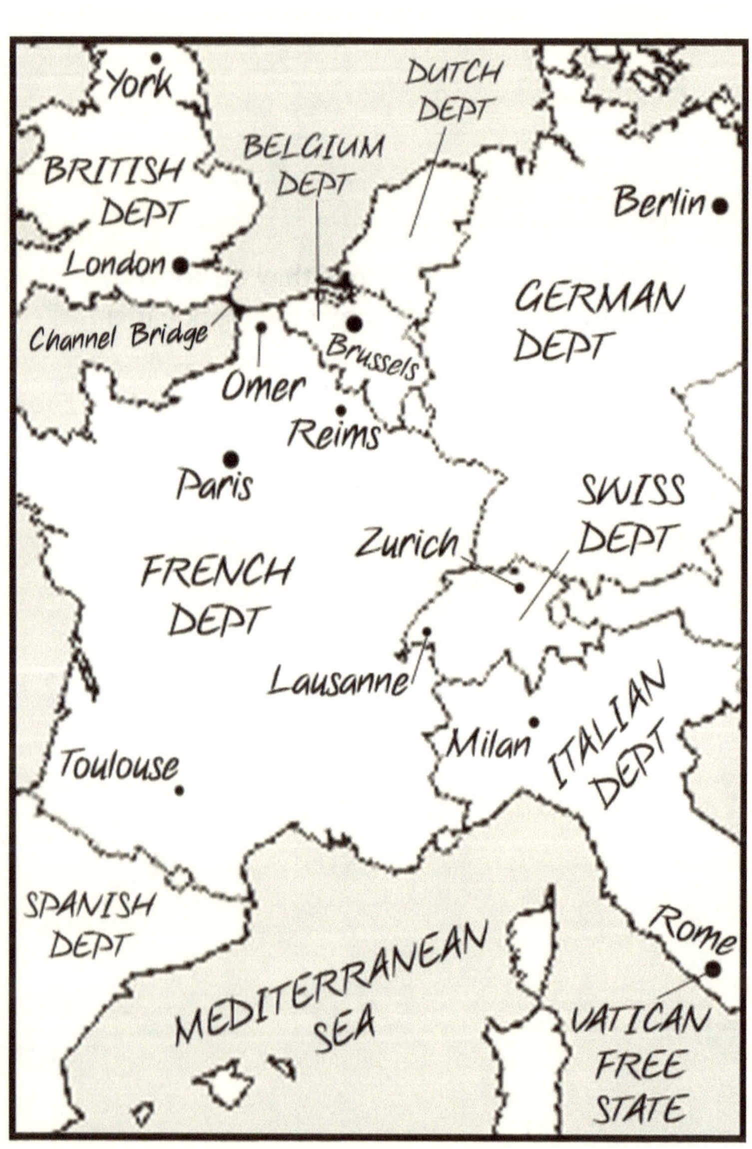

York
BRITISH DEPT
London
Channel Bridge
Omer
Paris
FRENCH DEPT
Toulouse
SPANISH DEPT
BELGIUM DEPT
Brussels
Reims
DUTCH DEPT
Berlin
GERMAN DEPT
SWISS DEPT
Zurich
Lausanne
Milan
ITALIAN DEPT
MEDITERRANEAN SEA
Rome
VATICAN FREE STATE

1

NOT REALLY HERE

Freedom—and comparative safety.

For now.

Mist hung thickly over the trees. No helicopters would be flying today. *Thank you, Lord.* No one searched for us here, anyway—they thought we were off with the Resistance.

"Is the weather going to hold?"

"Forecast's mist for the next week." Bane climbed carefully over a fallen bough. "We had our month's sun the day before yesterday."

The latest painkillers were beginning to work. I hung there contentedly in Bane's arms. *Bane.* Bane, here. Me with Bane. Free. Nothing else really mattered right now.

Swing. Swing. Swing...

...The misty forest just the same. Everything the same, except it was Father Mark carrying me. The pain was getting back up to full strength, but the thought of what he'd risked...*for me.*

"You shouldn't have gone in there, y'know," I mumbled.

"Oh, hush," said the young priest, a smile softening his hatchet-face. "I can go where I like." His eyes raked briefly over me. "Want some more pills?"

"Is it safe?"

His attention returned to the path ahead. "Not ideal. But I wouldn't get too excited."

"Okay, then." I couldn't think straight. "Where's Bane?" Failing to keep panic from my voice...

"At the front. We need someone who knows what they're doing at the front and his arms needed a rest."

"Right. Of course." I clamped my lips together. *I will not scream for Bane. I'm okay here with Father Mark.*

"We're stopping, people, pass it on," called Father Mark. Soon I was swallowing pills. Again. Bane came loping back along the long line of (former!) reAssignees. He brushed hair from my face and kissed me tenderly. "Okay with Father Mark for a bit?"

"'Course," I lied. "Fine."

"I'll just leave you to confess, then." He kissed me once more and hurried back to the front.

"Could I confess?" I murmured, speaking to Father Mark in Latin out of habit.

Father Mark rolled his eyes. "Have you committed a mortal sin since your last confession?" He also used Latin—but spoke quietly. Some of the others had probably guessed by now that Father Mark was a priest and that we were Believers, but no need to be reckless.

"No..."

"Then go to sleep."

I tried to think of a reply...

...My cheek rested on a familiar chest—my insides plummeted sickly—I'd dreamt it all, I was still back at the Facility. But...why was I being carried? I struggled to lift my aching, pounding head...

"Jon...?"

"Hello, Sleeping Beauty. How d'you feel?"

Everything echoed in my ears. The sun was rising above the trees, a brighter patch in the mist. I'd no memory of night. I squinted against the cruel light, focusing on the flat dirt track along which my companions moved. Oh. Not a dream. Bane and Father Mark both exhausted? Or Jon taking advantage of this flat track to do his share? He never let his blindness stop him from pulling his weight if he could help it.

Sarah walked beside Jon, raising a hand and touching his arm when he veered slightly to the left. "Hi, Margy. You feel better?" Proud in her little job as Jon-aimer.

"I'm fine." I tried for a reassuring smile and Sarah stared worriedly at me. But getting words out was like lifting lead to my lips.

"It's too early for more pills, Margo," Jon told me after a

while. Had I mumbled something? He looked worried.

"M'fine," I muttered. Another lie. Major Everington was walking alongside with his empty eye sockets turned towards me, blood trickling down his calm face like tears. He held out a hand, palm cupped as though to receive something. *Eyes?* I shuddered.

"I do think it's very decent of you." I could hear his well-bred voice. "But if you're not going to need them anymore."

"Go away! *You're not really here.*"

"Am I not?" He raised an eyebrow, making one empty socket gape horribly. I shut my eyes tight.

"Sarah *is* here, Margy. I *is.*"

"It's okay, Sarah." Jon's voice. "I don't think she's talking to you."

"Then who Margy talking to?"

"Someone who's not there."

"A *ghost?*"

I whimpered. *Not a ghost, please, Lord?*

"No, no, not a ghost, Sarah. She's running a temperature, that's all. It makes people...see things."

I dragged an eyelid up and risked a peep. The Major was gone. *For now.* I sunk slowly back into a daze of heat and pain...

...Kept hoping my head would clear, but it just seemed to get worse. People were talking, but I could hardly concentrate on what they were saying.

"She needs more pills."

Bane's voice. Anguished. I dragged my eyelids up and tried to focus on his face.

"It's too soon." Father Mark. Very firm.

"But—"

"No. Taking that many pills too often would really be pushing it."

"We've got to do *something* about the fever. Can you put more solution on?"

"No. Every time we unwrap those wounds to add more antiseptic, we also get more bugs in there. Tonight, maybe."

"Well, what can we do?"

"For now, nothing. Give her more pills in an hour."

"Can't you do *anything* else?"

"I'm a priest, not a doctor."

"Much use that is! There's got to be something!"

Father Mark opened his mouth, exasperated—paused. "Well, now that you mention it."

He fished a case from around his neck, taking out a familiar proCamera—or something that *looked* like a pro-Camera. He opened the battery compartment and slid out a little battery-shaped vial full of golden liquid. "I can give her the Sacrament of the Sick. It might make her feel better."

He held out the vial towards me and Bane batted it away.

"Isn't that for dying people?"

"No. It's for *sick* people, as the name might suggest."

"Seriously, Bane, it might make her feel better," put in Jon.

Father Mark turned to me. "Margaret?"

Perhaps it was worth speaking. "Yes, please..." I certainly felt sick enough.

Vaguely aware of Father Mark sliding a second 'battery' out and shaking a few drops of Holy Water over all of us. Jon crossed himself but my hand went all over the place—Bane put his hand around it and moved it for me.

"*Penitential rite,*" Father Mark was trying to catch my eye again. "Do you confess your sin?"

"Umhmm..."

...Father Mark's cool hands rested on my pounding head as he prayed over me...then his thumb ran lightly over my forehead, damp with holy oil, marking a cross beside the bandage-covered one Major Everington had cut into my flesh.

"Through this holy anointing may the Lord in His love and mercy help you with the grace of the Holy Spirit..."

"Amen," Jon said and Bane mouthed. Father Mark took my hands gently, one at a time, to anoint my palms—finished by reaching out to silently anoint my eyelids—I closed them helpfully, giving wordless thanks that they'd rescued me when they had.

...Father Mark was tracing a cross over us and putting the

vial away. The disguised Mass kit disappeared back inside his shirt. "All done."

"I'm sure she feels a lot better," said Bane sarcastically.

But I did. Not any more *with it,* but a whole lot calmer. Like I'd had a spiritual infusion.

"Except I bet you do, knowing you." Bane pressed a gentle kiss onto my cheek and picked me up again.

2

THE STABLE DOOR

I woke with a jolt as the bus went over a pothole.

"Okay?" Bane looked strange in the unfamiliar school uniform.

"Yeah. It's not hurting so much now."

"It's been almost six days. The skin on your legs should be re-attaching."

"Can't be too soon." I eased up to sit on the bus's rear seat instead of lying along it, Bane's hands hovering around me against the assault of another pothole. "Are we on schedule?"

"Yep. Should reach the Channel Bridge in about two hours."

A knot of icy fear twisted in my belly. The Channel Bridge. Far, far more dangerous than going to a private school on the outskirts of York, changing into uniforms and boarding a bus for a supposed school trip. Marian Forbes, a teacher who said she wanted to get into the Vatican State anyway and wasn't this an easy way to do it, had accompanied us.

Bane and Father Mark had filled in all the forms themselves, but the headmistress, Mrs. Clayton, had told them exactly what to write. She'd even donated the cost of the bus rental. In cash. But even if she could prove the travel application had been forged, if the government asked her to make the Divine denial... *Lord, protect that brave woman!*

"How much money have we got left, come to think of it?" I asked.

"The Resistance donated the ration packs and the foil blankets, I just had to pay for the camping stuff, the admin fees and a few other things. I sold your laptop and anything else we had that was worth a bit—we've enough to get us to Rome, especially walking."

I shuddered—looked out the window again. I'd been determined to see all the counties we'd passed through, since who knew if we'd ever be back, but I'd still slept through quite a few. Huh. Another factory farm. A square concrete building all too like the Facility. Happily our meat back home came from the Fellest, stored in the butchers' freezers after each yearly roundup and cull. But the big cities of the south didn't have our huge forests and couldn't waste crop space on animals, or so they said.

"Don't you dare let me miss the Channel Bridge," I told Bane.

"You've only said that a hundred times."

"Okay, sorry, but I've only seen the sea once. And I've never seen the largest bridge in Europe."

"Me neither. But I'll be waking you so you can pretend to be asleep."

Excitement at the thought of the mighty bridge washed away in a wave of terror. I swallowed hard—he saw it in my eyes and gathered me close, cupping my face between his hands. Spoke low and intent.

"I'm going to be sitting in the row ahead, okay? And I here and now swear on...*on my life* I will not let them take you again, okay? I will do whatever it takes to save you from them."

I think I know what you mean by "whatever it takes" and it's not something I can condone. But my cowardly mouth stayed shut.

"Don't *you* go overreacting to anything," said Jon from the other end of the seat.

"I'm not an idiot," retorted Bane.

"No, just hot-headed, which in this case is almost worse."

"Oh, shut up."

They bickered fairly good-naturedly—like the best friends they were—for a while...

...Huh?

"Everyone back here had better get organized." Father Mark stood in the aisle. We were pulled over to the side of the road, but I didn't remember the bus stopping. Must've dozed off.

Bane promptly moved to the row in front and several other girls joined me and Jon on the back row. As—arguably—the two most recognizable faces, Jon and I sat in the two darkest corners of the bus's solid rear wall. During our brief visit to the school Bane and Jon had, with equal reluctance, allowed their hair to be cut very short, to make the distinctive coal black and autumny russet less noticeable. My own brown hair had been dyed blonde.

'It'll start growing out quite quickly,' Bane had said, 'but it'll be so much less noticeable. You'll just have to wear a hat.'

Now Rebecca peeled off the bandages on my forehead, Harriet carefully applied makeup over the cuts and Caroline arranged a bit of hair casually over that, spraying it with hair spray to try to make it stay—then Father Mark was calling for everyone to get in their positions.

Jane sat down beside me and crossed very long bare legs. She'd taken off her school socks and rolled up her skirt until it was little more than a belt. Her school blouse was unbuttoned to a dangerous depth, her dark hair flowing around her shoulders. I'd always assumed she was a non-Believer—and I'd been right. Even in the few days since she'd found out about my faith, she'd made it clear she thought it was dangerous and silly—but she understood what was at stake.

"Don't you worry, Margo," she told me. "They won't be looking at you."

"No, they'll be looking for an excuse to impound the bus for the day," said Bane. "Don't be *too* obvious, right?"

"I'm not going to throw myself on them," sniffed Jane.

"Couldn't imagine that." Jon's dry comment earned him a scowl from Jane. He'd not forgotten how she'd tried to get him into her bed, not realizing he was a Believer like me.

My body was beginning to shake uncontrollably. Surely the bridge guards would take one look and recognize me as the girl who had authored a subversive best-selling book and masterminded the breakout of seventy-odd teenage non-persons from a government facility?

Father Mark bent to look me in the eye. "Hey, Caroline and I are at the front with the two remaining nonLethal pistols, okay? Any trouble and we'll shoot our way out. Just relax and enjoy the view."

Lying through his teeth. Shoot our way across the Channel Bridge in a bus with just two nonLees? The Resistance, who scorned nonLethal weapons, had allocated fast trucks, five bazookas and an arsenal of small arms for this mission, along with a coordinated strike by the French Resistance on the Continental checkpoints.

But I smiled and nodded at Father Mark. He straightened and headed back up the bus, calling, "Places, everyone. If you're supposed to be sleeping, start doing it now."

Bane climbed half over the back of his seat, kissed me hard on the lips and got back down into his sleeping position as the bus moved off, cap pulled low over his face. I did the same, half concealed against the curtain.

Jane adjusted my stiffened hair and laid a jacket over me, further shielding my face. "Now, *don't move.*"

I was still not used to her being so nice to me!

Out of the corner of my eye I saw Emily stop fussing with Jon and drape herself on his shoulder. Also showing a lot of leg. Was I feeling a faint stab of...jealousy? *Oh, for goodness' sake, Margo! It would be nice if he and Emily did get together.*

Okay, keep breathing. Just say a Rosary. Concentrate on that. Hail Mary... My fingers twitched slightly as I tried to keep count. *Hail...hail...what came next?*

The bus slowed and drew gently to a halt. Father Mark wasn't a bad bus driver. I tried to draw deep, steady breaths, keeping my eyes closed.

The door hissed open.

"Hello." Marian Forbes' bright voice. "Are you coming on board?"

"We need to see your travel documents. Are you a school group?"

"That's right. Heading for Venice."

"Group pass, then, please."

"Of course. Here you are."

A little beep as the guard scanned the group pass and the list of names appeared on his hand scanner. All real New Adults, safe in their beds somewhere in Yorkshire. The defection of most of the Facility's boys to the Resistance had called for some last minute amendments—Miss Forbes and Mrs. Clayton had taken care of that whilst I was being carted half-conscious through the Fellest.

"Forty-five students?"

"That's right."

"We must perform a headcount."

"Of course. Come aboard."

The heavy tread of someone mounting the stairs... I tried desperately not to tremble, not to gasp for breath, not to squeeze my eyes too tightly shut. Miss Forbes stayed silent until the footsteps were perhaps halfway up the bus, then began to talk again, presumably to a guard who still stood by the door. Hoping to distract them just that little bit more?

"Must say, I've been on quite a few school trips to the Continent and this is the first time the barriers have been up on the bridge. Looks like you've had some trouble. Is it because of that escape?"

"Just a precaution," was the noncommittal reply.

The footsteps reached the back of the bus, a slight pause—about the length of two pairs of long legs—then they retreated again.

"Forty-five," confirmed the guard.

"Glad to hear it!" laughed Miss Forbes.

"I'm sure you are," said the voice, tolerant but uninterested. "On you go, have a nice trip."

"Thanks. Have a good afternoon."

The door hissed closed. The bus eased forward.

"I don't know about your joining the Sisters of Revelation, you should go to Hollywood," said Father Mark, once we were moving again. Miss Forbes laughed rather hysterically.

Easing my eyes open a crack, I looked out the window as the barrier slid past. Rows of bullet holes scored the concrete walls of the checkpoint booth and over by the side of the bridge a patch of freshly scorched and bubbled pavement suggested something large had been blown up. An armored vehicle?

The Resistance were supposed to have gone through here three or four hours ago, about the time we'd left

York, making very sure to be noticed. They'd done that, all right. Luckily for us. Knowing—or so they thought—exactly where their quarry now weren't, the EuroGov had promptly relaxed the checks on those travelling through and exiting the British Department.

The bus sped sedately on—sitting up and opening my eyes properly, I stared out at the channel. Grey blue, stretching away to the horizon. The mighty supporting arches of the bridge towered above us. Among all the climate crises and unending economic slumps, mankind had still managed a few technological achievements since the dizzy highs of the late twentieth century—and this was one of them.

Bane took Jane's place and slipped his arms around me, feeling me trembling.

"There, we did it! And getting off the island was always going to be the hardest bit, wasn't it?" He put on a confident voice—I rested my head on his shoulder and didn't mention the one and a half thousand kilometers still to go.

"Quite a sight, isn't it?" I said instead.

"Is it just. One sec." Gently detaching me, he moved along the aisle, opening all the roof windows. "Smell the sea, Jon?"

Jon stared into space with an entranced look on his face.

"Thanks, Bane. I've never been to the sea."

"Well, you're *over* it, now."

The Resistance had gone to town on the French check-points. Only one booth left standing, bullet holes and blistered pavement everywhere, and a group of engineers still trying to winch in a tank that had smashed through the thick bridge wall and dangled precariously over the water. No barriers left to put down—the lights were green anyway. The horse was gone, why cause backups by shutting the stable door now?

I peered grimly at it all from behind the curtain.

"I wonder how many guards they killed." The Resistance hated the EuroGov just as much as I did, but they placed no more value on human life than the EuroGov—personally I thought they deserved each another.

Bane said nothing.

"Perhaps they ran for it," said Jon.

"There's nowhere to run," said Bane.

"Did you know about this?" I asked him.

"They said the Frogs would distract the checkpoints when they reached the other side, that's all."

"You knew what they were packing, though."

"Yeah, but if you're going to try and run the Channel Bridge by force, you don't leave the bazookas at home, do you? They weren't going to use more than they had to. Didn't look like they *had*, at the other end. But I didn't speak to the Frenchies."

"S'pose not." He'd a point. From the look of the crumbled remains of the booths, most of the bazookas had come from the landward side.

Bane's face lightened slightly. "I'd love to hear the story behind that tank, though!"

"What tank?" asked Jon.

A massive highway sign hung over the traffic on the main autoroute out of Calais. My breath caught in my throat at the three photos displayed there, six meters high. Me. Bane. Jon. Beneath, it simply said 'Wanted: call 112 immediately'.

"How'd I make the three most wanted?" muttered Jon, after Bane filled him in.

"You're too easy to spot," Bane murmured back. "They figure if they find one of us three, they find us all."

Everyone's eyeballs pretty much rolled up in their heads as the sign went over us.

"Margo," demanded Rebecca, "why *do* they want *you?* They were after *you* back at the Facility, weren't they?"

"What did you do to annoy them so much?" asked Jane, eyes narrowed.

"Look in that bag, Marian..." Father Mark's voice came quietly to us, "that's right. Pass that book back to Jane and Rebecca."

A shiny new copy of *I Am Margaret* arrived in Jane's hands—she stared at it uncomprehendingly.

"You wanted to know where the stories went. There

they are," I told her.

"The winning postSort novel," said Bane. "Ignore the name on the front, that's just some treacherous tart back in Salperton—Margo wrote that book."

"It's all about Sorting," said Jon. "They published it 'cause they thought it was fiction, then Margo told the world she wrote it and it's all true and the EuroGov developed this terrible thirst for her blood."

Jane opened it wonderingly, her brows drawing together as she skimmed lines here and there. She looked up at last with a troubled gaze, as though something had just occurred to her. "Margo...what *exactly* did they do to you in there?"

My insides dissolved as the memories flooded me—the pain, the terror, the helpless hopeless helplessness...

"*Nothing.*" I grabbed Bane, burying my face in his chest— I felt him shaking his head at Jane and no doubt glaring at her.

We drove on until we began to see signs for the town of Omer, by which time I'd stopped shaking and disentangled myself from Bane enough to look out the window again. Father Mark left the main autoroute and drove into the forest. All very flat forest, here, nothing rising on the horizon. All fields, once, I suppose.

Soon we came to a halt in a turnoff.

Bane looked at me. "Are you sure?"

I swallowed and Jane said, "You'd be better off with us, wouldn't you?"

"No," I said quietly. "The Resistance have now done their level best to disappear. They're heading for the Spanish department and the EuroGov will probably be vaguely on their tail. But because they can't be quite sure where they are, there'll be checkpoints at every major town on the continent. And though they're unlikely to demand individual ID cards from a bus with a proper group travel pass"— *please, Lord?*—"they will almost certainly take a look at each and every person on board. You see why we have to get off?"

"Can't we just drive along back roads like this?" suggested Rebecca.

"A bus off the main autoroute will attract attention," said Father Mark quietly. He'd come up the aisle unnoticed. "Especially one supposed to be driving straight to Venice. Until we get to the Italian department we cannot afford to attract any attention *at all.* All it takes is for them to demand our actual ID cards and... Well. Enough said."

The only person on board with a safe ID was Marian Forbes.

I looked at Bane, trying to ignore the pleading in his eyes and the terror writhing inside me. "We'd better get changed."

Wordlessly, he lifted a duffel bag from the luggage rack and began to empty it. My jeans and tunic, Jon's clothes and his own. Time to part company with my plastic sheet.

Fully-dressed for the first time in almost a week, I wobbled and winced my way down the aisle straddle-legged like a cowboy, then Bane scooped me up, carried me down the steps and stood me on my feet again. Jane and Sarah managed to trail us off before Father Mark made everyone else stay in their seats. Sarah clung to me, crying—Jane just hovered.

Pulling three hiking rucksacks from the bus's hold, Bane and Father Mark began to fasten two of them together.

"Bane," I objected, "Jon can't carry both of those!"

"Well, I'm going to be carrying *you,* so you can't carry *yours.*"

True, but... "It's such a lot for Jon to carry."

"Bane'll be carrying a rucksack and *you.* That'll weigh more," said Jon stiffly.

"I know, but no offence, Bane doesn't need to concentrate so hard on where he's going."

"He brought me a stick." Jon held up a long, thin, telescopic hiking stick. He'd left his old garden cane in the hold—too noticeable.

"We've no choice, Margo," said Bane. "The only stuff we could throw out is food and it won't get us far as it is."

A shiver ran down my spine at this reminder of the difficulties ahead. "Well—I s'pose we can always dump some if it's too much."

"I'll be fine." Jon hefted the combined pack up onto his

back and staggered slightly. "Phew. Not that I'll be sorry when you're walking again!"

"Okay, we'd better move." Father Mark slammed the luggage holds. "Back aboard, you two."

"I'll see you soon, Sarah," I assured her, a slight exaggeration even if everything went exactly according to plan for both groups. "You've got to go back on the bus now. Don't be upset, Mark will look after you, and Rebecca and Caroline and Harriet will too."

"And me." Jane gave Sarah a little pat on the shoulder and pushed her towards the bus. "Go on."

Since Jane had originally treated most of our fellow captives as near-subhuman, I was moved to hear genuine affection in her voice. It must have shown on my face, because Jane hovered for a moment more before finally giving me a quick, awkward hug and chasing Sarah up the steps. Father Mark hugged me as well and clasped hands with Jon and Bane—blessed us each in turn.

"Good luck. May the Lord be with you."

"And with *you*," we said pretty much in unison, our eyes flicking to the crowded bus behind him.

He climbed back on board, the doors hissed closed, the engine started and the bus began to move, roaring away down the road. We stood and waved until it disappeared among the trees—then stood together in a long silence.

3

PRIME REAL ESTATE FOR
HAPPY CAMPERS

"I think...I was kind of hoping he wouldn't actually do it." Jon's voice came out subdued.

"Father Mark can count." My throat was tight, though. "He's not going to risk the forty-two for the sake of three."

"Especially not when the three are *so* determined to be noble." Bane gave me a dirty look.

"Oh, don't start. The more I think about it, the more I suspect we'd be barely any safer staying aboard. How many checkpoints could we get through before someone recognized one of us? Then *they'd* all get killed too. Thought about that, Bane?" This probably *was* our best chance, as well as everyone else's. I wanted to believe it, anyway.

Best chance doesn't mean actual chance, though, does it? I pushed the thought away.

"Yeah, yeah," said Bane, hefting the remaining rucksack onto his back and picking up the sling he'd made back in the Fellest. "Let's get you back in this thing, okay?"

"I might be able to walk, you know," I told him. "It's not as though my muscles were cut or my legs injured or anything major like that."

"Right, of course not, those evil dismantlers just peeled the skin off your thighs while you were still conscious— nothing *major* at all! Get real, Margo! Anyway, if you push too hard, you might get feverish again—Father Mark said so—and we're *not* taking that chance, okay?"

I gave in as gracefully as possible—with considerable relief. After a bit of trial and error—and a few yelps from me—we figured out the sling—and me—had to go on before the rucksack. But eventually we were heading away from the road, up a slight slope into the forest. Bane's omniPhone had illegal trig mapping—technology usually reserved for the EuroArmy—so at least we weren't likely to get lost.

Jon tried walking alongside, swinging his hiking stick in front of him, but we weren't following any sort of trail and the fallen branches and mossy hillocks caught feet and stick every other step. Soon he took Bane's shoulder with his free hand, both to guide and steady himself.

"Let's get at least eight kilometers into this forest." Bane pointed to the screen on his phone as they stopped an hour later for a drink. I blinked sleepily and tried to listen. "Then we can pitch camp and wait until Margo's well enough to start walking in short stages."

Jon agreed, but by the time the sun began to drop in the sky they were both breathing in short gasps and their determined stride—or trip, stride, trip in Jon's case—had become a weary trudge.

Shortly after Bane announced monosyllabically that we'd gone six kilometers, Jon cracked.

"Hadn't we better look out for a good place to stop?"

Man speak for: "I'm done in; surely you're done in?"

Bane just grunted but barely fifteen minutes later we came to a stream with shelving grassy ledges running down to it, and he came to a halt. "Y'know, that looks like prime real estate for happy campers."

"Then for pity's sake let's take up residence without delay." Jon couldn't keep the thread of exhaustion from his voice.

They scrambled down onto the grass of the nearest ledge, and Bane sat me down on a rucksack. "Jon, tent? I'll collect some firewood. Well, I'll scout around first."

"Okay."

"Well, as soon as you bring some wood," I said, "I'll cook. I can do that sitting down."

Bane muttered something about me taking it easy but went off without voicing any more audible objection—must be tired.

Jon unfastened the two identical rucksacks from one another and unerringly opened the closer one. How'd he identified it? Oh, a scrap of fabric fluttered on the top of each one. A length of silk ribbon knotted onto mine, a strip of denim on Jon's and some hairy woolen stuff on Bane's. Clearly Bane had never seriously considered leaving Jon behind.

Jon took out the round tent tin, feeling around the grassy area.

"You've got it smack in the middle of a large enough space, if you won't bite my head off for saying so." I'd a feeling he was actually tired enough to do so.

He just said "thanks" and pushed the lever. The tin's quarters shot in four directions on their telescopic poles, the tent fabric unfolded upwards with a sibilant *whump* and with a thud the pegs went into the ground. A *chink* from one corner—one had found a rock.

Jon traced his way straight around to that corner. *Click-click-click* went the ratchet as he pulled the peg up for another try. *Thud.* All sorted. He began to pull out the guy rope reels and trigger the pegs. *Squeak, squeak, squeak, thud.*

Pulling my rucksack towards me, I unfastened it to examine the contents. My own sleeping bag from home nestled in the bottom compartment—an ancient, ex-tourist one, of course, but still a good three-season bag. Several foil survival blankets were tucked in with it—a fourth season, just in case.

Squeak, squeak, squeak, thud.

I raised the sleeping bag to my face and inhaled—then almost wished I hadn't. *The scent of home*—the wave of homesickness was sharper than anything I'd felt in all the four months in the Facility. Because home no longer existed.

Squeak, squeak, squeak, thud.

The secret sanctuary where I'd been baptized and con-firmed was now an innocuous broom cupboard, the priest hole an innocent alcove. Perhaps some of our things still remained, photographed and prodded and poked through by EuroGov agents, but not the people who made it home. *Lord, please keep Mum and Dad safe!*

Squeak, squeak, squeak, thud.

"There. Home sweet home."

Well, if home was mostly made by people, Jon wasn't

wrong. A normal change for a New Adult, even if my adult freedom had been seized by force and wiles and remained as fragile and elusive as a flower's scent on a windy day.

Our physical home couldn't be much smaller and still fit us all inside. It didn't even have a porch; the legally required enclosed forest stove burned in any weather and the cook would just have to get wet.

"We're going to have to remember we're supposed to be rich, if we meet anyone," I remarked, handing the sleeping mats in to Jon.

Everyone *we* knew from our little town would be out hunting for work. Failing that, showing up each day at the place they wanted or thought they were most likely to obtain a job, begging for errands to run, making coffee and generally getting under-foot until the boss cracked and granted them informal apprenticeship, proper employment, or told them to clear off and never come back.

"Yeah, we'd better get our story straight," said Jon.

If all had gone as the EuroGov intended, our job-seeking classmates—now legal New Adults—would never have thought of any of us reAssignees again after we'd been shipped off to the Facility for medical recycling. But that was before the book—and the escape.

By the time Bane returned, announcing the area safe and carrying an armful of firewood, I'd filled the stove pan with water and Jon was tap-tapping his way back up from the stream with the refilled autoFiltration bottles. Stove lit and water boiled, I added some to three of the special hiking food sachets and mixed thoroughly. The smell was nothing whatsoever like chicken stew. Stewed boot leather, perhaps. Handing the sachets out regardless, I closed my eyes for a moment to say grace and raised a cautious forkful to my lips.

"I think we're going to miss those army ration packs." I chewed the tasteless mush once and swallowed. *Wait a moment.* Suddenly the mush stuck in my throat, though the food I was worried about was already eaten. "Where did those ration packs come from?"

Jon's head rose, the rapid movement of his fork ceasing.

"Well, they were stolen, there's not much doubt about

that," said Bane. "But you knew that. They weren't from...
Wearmfell. As far as I'm aware." Wearmfell. The military
ration-pack factory the Resistance had captured—slaught-
ering all the guards in the process, even the ones who
surrendered without a fight.

"What's that supposed to mean?" demanded Jon. "As far
as you're aware?"

"It means exactly that," snapped Bane, clearly reluctant
to divulge his part in that murderous raid quite like this.

Did it matter? Wherever the army ration packs we'd all
been eating during our trek to York had come from, they'd
probably been acquired in much the same way.

"I *hate* dealing with the Resistance." I stabbed the ground
with the end of my fork. "Let's...let's *not* any more, okay?"

"Gets my vote." Jon started on his safe-but-bland legally-
purchased-from-a-hiking-shop-by-Bane meal again.

"Unless we have to," agreed Bane, guardedly.

"Let's try very hard not to have to!"

When we'd finished, Bane put the biodegradable sachets
into a biodegradable scentSeal bag and went off into the
woods to bury it. Didn't want any bears visiting us in the
night.

"Why don't we turn in?" I suggested when he came back,
though it was barely eight-thirty.

"Okay, but we need to keep watch," said Bane.

"*Seriously?*" I asked

"Yeah, if someone does come along at night, they'll expect real hikers to be tucked up inside asleep, won't they?"
said Jon.

"And what could we do, run away? How long would we
last without our stuff?"

"Gah!" Bane dragged his hands through his hair. "Fine! No
watch, then."

"Though, uh, what about...wolves...and things?" said Jon.

"Tent's supposed to be permeated with some stink bears
don't like much."

"What about wolves?"

"It didn't say anything about wolves."

Jon muttered something rude under his breath about
Bane's tent-selecting abilities.

"*Relax.* I don't think the wolves will come calling unless they really want to eat us, in which case a smelly tent isn't going to help much. A bear may just wander up to have a look around—scavengers, remember? Anyway, they didn't *have* a wolf-repellent tent."

"*And* Margo doesn't mind wolves but hates bears!"

"Which part of 'didn't have' can't *you* understand?"

"Oh, come on," I interrupted hastily. "Aren't you two tired?"

"Yes," said Bane shortly,

"Let's just all pray against fire, theft, and wolves and get to sleep, huh?" said Jon, letting his irritation go in that easy way of his.

"I'll do fire, theft, and bears," I said.

"To the devil with wolves and bears!" said Bane. "You can both do fire, theft, and *humans.*"

"So can you."

"I don't talk to things I'm not convinced exist."

Yes, you do, sometimes. But I didn't say it out loud. Bane ignored my silence.

"Well, my sleeping bag's beckoning." He unzipped the tent and threw the flap back.

From the way his shoulders went rigid a scowl had just appeared on his face—I shifted just enough to peep over his shoulder. Ah. Jon had put my sleeping bag in the middle.

Oh. Yeah... I was going to be sharing a tent with two guys for this trip...hadn't really thought it through before. No way could we carry any extra weight—nor would it even be very safe. Not to mention that most New Adults on camping trips wouldn't worry about such things, so separate tents would be very suspicious.

Looking like you might be practicing chastity was grounds for suspicion of being a Believer—you'd be receiving a court summons to make the Divine denial before you could say *"Credo in unum Deum."* And given that "Practice of Superstition," as Faith was termed, was a capital crime...

PreSorting, all copulation was banned, of course. But in the Facility, Jon and I had been forced to pretend to be a couple in order to avert suspicion and protect our Believing families. Unfortunately, I knew how close Jon was to falling in love with me for real.

Awkward, yes.

But we were running for our lives and there was nothing else for it. I was pretty sure in the circumstances that I could put aside my desire for Bane and after sleeping in such close proximity to Jon at the Facility, I knew how chaste he was. But Bane didn't. He'd taken my word about what had happened, but...

Bane's eyes darted from Jon's sleeping bag to mine, and I could see the suspicion sneaking through his mind. *Help, Lord? Don't let this divide us. I'm pretty sure Jon just wants me beside him because it's comfortingly familiar but Bane isn't necessarily thinking coolly enough to realize that.*

"*My* sleeping bag has got hold of the scruff of my neck and is yanking me into the tent," said Jon into the sticky silence, would-be calmly.

How desperate was he to hang onto this one—only?—possible bit of normality? Once we started hiking properly, he'd be following us blindly day after day across an entire continent, never having anything but the most limited idea where he was or what was around him. *Don't freak out, Bane. This is going to be bad enough for him as it is.*

Bane turned to glare at Jon, opening his mouth as though to attempt some verbal decapitation—shut it again. Did he understand? But he still reached out as though to shift my sleeping bag away from Jon's to the outside of the tent. Then a more calculating look passed through his eyes. Ah yes, anything coming through the sides of the tent would eat either Jon or himself before me.

Clearly the deciding factor. He withdrew his hand. I breathed a tiny sigh of thanks. *Thank You, Lord.*

"Come on, Margo." He moved to help me to the tent—Jon took advantage of the empty doorway and slid inside; by the unzipping and rustling sounds, he was getting into his sleeping bag with alacrity.

As soft snores started I let the "Night, Jon" die on my lips and concentrated on maneuvering inside. Bane unfastened my sleeping bag all the way, so I wouldn't have to wriggle.

With me zipped in—comparatively painlessly—Bane gave me a goodnight kiss and slithered into his own bag with considerably more ease. Very distantly, a pack of wolves howled—Jon went on snoring quietly. Silence from the surrounding forest.

Lord... I was fighting to keep my eyes open... *Thank you we're alive and free and please look after Father Mark and the others and our parents and all Believers...*

...A domed tent ceiling above me. Bane and Jon snoring on each side, almost drowning out the morning birdsong. I sat up carefully, but they were deep asleep. Unzipping sleeping bag and door as quietly as I could, I looked around.

The sky arched blue and clear overhead, the sun glittering off the little stream and shining brightly on the grassy slopes and ledges. The forest looked green and mossy and inviting. The eerie nighttime blackness—which I'd glimpsed when nature's call had dragged me painfully from my sleeping bag—had vanished like a dream.

Easing gingerly out of the tent, I sat down on a warm rock to breathe the fresh morning air and enjoy being awake for once—felt like I'd been mostly asleep for a week. After only a few minutes, Bane's subconscious must've noticed my absence...

"Margo!" He sprang from the tent like a wolf from its lair, shirtless and knife in hand.

"*Bane!*" I snorted.

"Don't do that to me, Margo!" He pocketed the knife and sank down on the rock beside me, yawning. His skin glowed warm gold in the morning light and I rested my head on his shoulder, my fingers drifting to explore the new, broad chest he'd grown whilst I was locked away.

"Margo, do you *have* to do that?"

My thoughtless fingers stilled. His face was very close to mine and for the first time since my rescue, a heat in his eyes said I was something to be desired as well as protected with his life. My cheeks burned. "Sorry."

He leant in and kissed me. Not one of the "there, there, I love you, everything's going to be fine" kisses he'd been keeping me well supplied with, not even the "I LOVE YOU!" kiss he'd given me just before the Channel Bridge, but a kiss combining "you're my sun and moon and stars" with "and I want to be one flesh with you right now".

Finally drawing away, he buried his face in my hair and breathed deeply for a while. "Why the heck did we let Father Mark drive off without marrying us?"

A snort of laughter escaped me. "Uh, Bane, priorities?"

He sighed. "Yeah, okay. And *practicalities*. Suppose we wouldn't want to be married and sharing a tent with Jon. Nothing doing."

Nope. But still, alas.

"Why don't you get some more rest, Bane? You must be exhausted."

"Well..." His eyes glowed as he set a quick kiss on my head. "Tempting though it is to stay out here... I think I will get some more sleep."

He slipped back into the tent, but the heat had their snores faltering after only another hour and a half. I lit the stove and by the time they yawned their way out I was performing the complicated culinary process of pouring and mixing. The 'bacon and beans' didn't taste very different from the 'chicken stew.'

"We've got to make the food go absolutely as far as possible," said Bane, when he'd finished his. "Have you got your Reader, Margo?"

"Here." I'd brought my coat out of the tent with me for the sake of all the important things in its pockets. He pulled the tiny data cable from his phone and stuck it in my bookReader for a minute, then handed it back.

"There. I bought books on identifying edible plants and trapping rabbits and that sort of thing. We'd better study hard while we're waiting for you to mend."

Dubiously, I placed my reader in a patch of sun and undid the back flap of its case to expose its solar panel. Edible plants, *maybe*. Trapping rabbits? Amateurs never had much luck at that, did they? Still, if we *could* get food that way... Going into towns with no safe ID cards and our pictures everywhere... I shuddered.

"Audio books?" Jon didn't sound hopeful.

Bane shook his head. "Sorry. They don't do them."

"Oh well. I'll just have to hope you don't serve us all deadly nightshade as blueberries or something."

"We'll be careful," said Bane defensively.

"Oh," I put in, "Jon and I were saying yesterday about getting our story straight. You know, we're rich New Adults from the north of England, obviously, and we'll be going to university where?"

"University of York," said Jon. "Gotta be stinking rich to go far afield, haven't you?"

Bane nodded. "Yeah. What are we called and what are we studying?"

"Something similar to our real name. Or we won't react to it. Margo could be Maria," Jon suggested.

I shrugged. "Okay. You can be Josh, studying Physics."

Jon shrugged as well. "Perfect. Bane?"

Bane screwed up his face. Not many B names.

"Dane," I said. "That should be on the British C list." That stupid list of racially-acceptable names the EuroGov made everyone stick to.

Bane snorted. "Right. Dane it is. Studying History." Yep, Bane would pass muster as a history major. At least if they stuck to battles and tactics.

I thought a bit. "I'll say history too. I'd say English, but... Well, I don't want to give anyone any reason to put writing and me in the same thought."

"Too right."

"Can we really walk all the way to Rome in less than three months? That's when university terms start, right?"

"Yes. Hopefully. If we overrun we'll have to say we're taking a year off. Some people do."

"*Really* filthy rich people, mostly," I said doubtfully.

"Well, fingers crossed we make it before then."

"Deo volente."

"Deo volente," echoed Jon.

God willing.

Good weather persisted, we didn't see hide or hair of any other people and we all gradually relaxed and began to take it easy, even Bane. Bane and I studied the woodland survival books and set snares, without any luck. Bane finally found a handful of small berries we dared eat, but it clearly wasn't going to be a very time effective way of getting food.

After a trip to the little forest room on the third night Jon came scrambling into the tent in a cold sweat because he'd heard something padding around nearby—when Bane and I stuck our heads out and shone flashlights this way and that—nothing to be seen. Just possible Jon had misinterpreted what he heard; more likely, something large had simply passed through.

The fourth day dawned nice and dry, yet again. My thighs were so much better we agreed, reluctantly, that tomorrow we must leave. This in mind, I laid out the contents of my pack again and Jon began to do the same. Bane sat and watched. Considering how much thought he'd given to each and every gram of weight, he'd no need to familiarize himself with the contents.

I'd read the long distance hiking guidebook now and we were definitely somewhat under-supplied, but the less of everything else, the more food we could carry. If we got caught, it'd surely be when trying to get food.

I shook the thoughts away. Bane had done a good job, really. He'd packed thermal underwear for each of us—we'd use this mostly to wear in our sleeping bags any day we got wet and muddy, and perhaps for crossing the Alps. We had the all-important waterproofs—trousers as well as jackets with removable fleece liners. But two changes of socks and underwear were the only other clothes we had, other than what we were wearing.

Jon grinned suddenly as he repacked his own rucksack. "So much for, *Captain, Captain, Jon hasn't got enough clothes.*"

I had to laugh, remembering how we'd taken on the sadistic head of the girls' block to get Jon's clothes back. "Yeah. Wonder what's going on back there. Bet the Menace is in so much trouble."

"We can hope."

Bane shot Jon a look. "*That's* unforgiving, coming from you. What's the score with this captain?"

"She kept punching Margo."

"Only twice," I corrected. "But she made us watch Uncle Peter's execution."

Bane scowled. He'd been very fond of my 'Uncle' Peter, a

priest who'd stayed often with my family for most of our lives. "Let's hope she's up to her neck in trouble, then."

"Well, being found fast asleep on the dorm floor in your underwear with not a single one of your charges to be found has got to be a career stopper, at the very least."

"Yeah," said Jon. "It's not like she can put the blame on anyone else, is it?"

"Surely the commandant will be in pretty hot water with the EGD," put in Bane. "If he's alive. He was in overall charge, wasn't he?"

"Yeah, but if he followed all the regulations I don't see what they could get him for. And I think he had. The escape was obviously orchestrated from the girl's block, anyway. At the end of the day, we just weren't supposed to have something that looked like a nonLee."

"And we only had it because the Menace told the Major she'd seen Finchley's door card safely destroyed with her own eyes. I'd say she's going to be in boiling water, quite frankly."

"Yeah, how did you get that card?" asked Bane. "You said you'd tell me."

"Oh dear, I don't want to spoil your day."

"She stole it off a guard while he was groping her," said Jon, about the mildest one could put it.

"*What?*" Bane looked as though he'd sprint back over the Channel Bridge and introduce Finchley's face to a cinder block all the same.

"Calm down," I told him. "It's not how I'd have chosen to acquire a card, but in the circumstances it all turned out for the best."

Bane glowered at his faceless image of filthy Finchley for a while, then calmed down enough to think again.

"Why did they think it was destroyed?"

I let Jon tell him. But he made me sound so clever and cool-headed I wished I'd told it myself!

4

KITTENS

By noon the next day my thighs and stomach grew so sore we had to stop, but at least we were moving. We shared a single sachet for lunch, but after the morning's walking it left us far hungrier than normal.

"How far have we come?"

"Today? Not far." Bane glanced at his phone and put it away.

"What's not far?"

"Five kilometers."

"That little?" From the ache in my shoulders, let alone in my healing areas, surely further! And they'd both spent most of the previous evening sneaking stuff out of my rucksack and into their own packs.

"You can't exactly go fast at the moment, can you? It'll get easier."

Jon made a face. Though free from the weight of a double pack, he still had to hang onto Bane's shoulder for balance, pretty tiring for Bane too—Jon was taller than him, though a bit more lightly built. Jon had roamed our campsite once the tent was up, learning the locations of the trees—but for him the hiking wouldn't get any easier.

The little French town of Fruges lay in the bottom of the valley—a stunning view. But, hovering just inside the forestline, Bane and I were intent on the town itself, viewed through the binocular setting on his phone.

"Are there any food stalls?" asked Jon.

My skin had toughened up despite the week's walking, but we were already sick of the tasteless sachets. Still, we weren't going down there unless certain we could get food without having to scan our IDs.

"It looks like there's some on the main street," I said,

unfastening my dyed hair and letting it fall on either side of my face, then putting my cap back on. The picture on the highway sign had been a recent school photo—none of those with my hair down.

Bane lowered his phone and called up a map, tracing his finger along a road.

"With a bit of luck we can buy food at a stall and walk straight on out the other side. If we get separated, try and meet *here*." He tapped the screen. "Needless to say one of us has *got* to stick with Jon. You two will be playing the happy couple again, so I s'pose that'll be you, Margo."

He clenched his teeth for a moment, then flicked a hand dismissively. "We shouldn't have to split up, anyway. We're New Adults happy to reach a town and buy fresh food. We've no reason to cower or creep along. Happy, carefree, *got it?*"

"Happy and carefree." Jon offered me his arm.

I took it, trying to echo him—but just ended up drawing a deep breath and gripping his arm too tightly.

He ducked his head to me. "Come on, Margo, just think, French bread, pâté, cheese? Yummm."

"Oh yes, worth being skinned alive for." The words were out before I could stop them.

Jon slipped his arm around my shoulders instead. "No reason why anything should go wrong, Margo. Anyway, Bane's going to be just on the other side of me, dying to engage in his new hobby of rescuing you, so there's really nothing to worry about."

"I don't want anyone else dying to rescue me." I stared down at the town. The current tally stood at one helicopter pilot, one dismantler, one—question mark?—commandant and an indeterminable number of bridge guards.

"I didn't mean it like *that*."

"Come on." Bane resolutely ignored Jon's arm around me—practicing keeping his cool, perhaps. "Let's just go down, shall we? We've *got* to pick up as much food as we can now, while it's safer."

Safer! Our pictures will be everywhere!"

"Yeah, okay, Margo, but the EuroGov may still think we're with the Resistance. And once they realize we're not, they'll think we're with the others...assuming the others made it to the Vatican State..."

He trailed off—chilling realization—if the others hadn't made it by now, they probably weren't going to.

"So," he went on, "we're probably still pretty safe at this moment. But *when* they find out we're not in the Vatican and not with the Resistance, that's when the EuroGov will start looking for three New Adults on their own."

I bit my lip. The thought of the EuroGov did strange things to my spine at the moment. Three of the top officials, including Reginald Hill, the so-called 'Minister for Internal Affairs' with his soft voice and cold eyes, had interrogated me before sentencing me to Full Conscious Dismantlement.

Bane saw my expression.

"They may be looking for three of us then, but with a bit of luck they'll be looking *everywhere*. There's a lot of forest in Europe and a lot of cities. They won't know where to start."

"Bane's right," said Jon. "They won't even know we haven't already managed to leave the EuroBloc, will they?"

Depends how good their spies are. I tried to look happy and reassured—Bane wasn't fooled.

"We've *got* to save as many of those sachets as we can for crossing the Alps," he said gently. "So we need other food now."

He was right, but I stared at the town and couldn't move. Like a horse refusing a jump. I knew far too well what awaited me, if caught. Except I still didn't, I knew only a fraction of the horror and even that... My blood felt ice cold.

Bane drew me from Jon's grasp and into the circle of his arms. "It's okay, Margo." His voice was soft. "But the way to true safety leads through this town. We have to do it."

And do it again. And again. All the way to Rome.

"Nothing's going to happen. And if it does... I promised, didn't I? They're never going to hurt you again. Never." Fiercely, he held me close, so close I felt the hardness of the knife tucked inside his jacket, digging into my ribs. And again I couldn't speak, couldn't scold him for that promise.

I eased out of his grasp after a moment, down to sit on the grass, and buried my face against my knees. *Lord, please give me strength. Mine is quite inadequate, always was.*

Jon crouched beside me and put his hand on my shoulder. Praying too. *Lord, please let Margo get up and move?* Fair enough. My cowardly custard attack wasn't getting us any closer to safety. Bane just stood over us like a Doberman on guard.

Let's have a little more trust, Margo, shall we? If you're meant to get all the way to Rome, you will, but you won't be teleported so you've got to get up and put one foot in front of the other.

I lifted my head from my knees and got up on my feet again, marshalling a wan smile for Bane.

"Kiss?"

He obliged quite thoroughly and I bruised my ribs a bit more on his knife before finally stepping away from him and seizing Jon's arm. "Come on, let's go. Quick. Before I have another litter of kittens."

"Hear, hear." Jon followed me. Bane fell into position on his other side, to stop anyone from walking into him. If anyone wondered why Jon couldn't avoid them...

"Everyone got their sunglasses?" asked Bane.

"Yep." Jon slid them down over his face as Bane and I did the same. The sun wasn't exactly glaring down, but fortunately the sort of rich young things we were imitating wouldn't be seen dead without their shades even in midwinter.

"Right, we're all sorted, then. Fruges, brace yourself for three happy, carefree New Adults."

I concentrated on the buildings as we walked down the slope to the road. Though built of creamy stone much like the village hotel of Little Hazleton, Jon's home, they looked foreign to me. The shape of the roofs was strange, little windows sticking out from them, the subtler differences harder to pinpoint. However similar the forest might seem, you'd never mistake this town for a British one.

"Pretty place," said Bane. "Must get loads of tourists here."

"Probably why it's still occupied." My voice almost didn't wobble. Most of the small towns that used to dot the European countryside had died out over the years, what with the reForestation, lingering economic woes, and the attendant—or rather, contributory, though the EuroGov wouldn't admit it—shrinking population.

As we passed between the first houses locals moved briskly past us, speaking French, whilst families and older couples drifted along with omniPhones in hand, exclaiming over quaint nooks and crannies in a variety of departmental languages.

"Look at that." I drew Jon to a halt, pointing at a particularly scenic cottage straight ahead. "Isn't it pretty?"

"Beautiful," lied Jon.

"Let me get a picture." Bane pulled out his convincingly touristy—i.e. shiny—omniPhone. "Go on, you two."

I positioned Jon and myself in front of the cottage. We wrapped our arms around each other and beamed for the camera, then the three of us sauntered on.

"Look, there's some other backpackers," said Bane in an undertone. "And some more, look."

"Here's the stalls." I couldn't quite keep the relief from my voice and forced myself to speak more brightly as we made a beeline for the nearest food stall. "Ooh, look at the nice food."

"This looks like the stuff," said Bane cheerfully, shrugging out of his rucksack and pulling out the reusable scentSeal food bag. "Let's stock up. What d'you think, shall we get some of that sausage?"

"Whatever." Jon turned slightly as though gazing up the street, food shopping being too boring for words, you understand.

"Let's get some cheese." I pointed things out to Bane, no need to pretend eagerness as delicious smells reached my nose. "Oh, and they've got pâté." I switched to Esperanto and smiled at the stallholder. "Um, let's see, could we have that block of Brie, please? My mouth's watering already!"

"Camping rations?" laughed the woman. "It is no good, that camping food. You have come to the right place."

"We certainly have! Is that a meat pie? Three of those, please."

The stallholder wrapped the cheeses and pies each in a sheet of greaseproof paper and then a page from a heap of old newspaper behind her. I kept ordering and Bane put each packet into the bag, packing it just as efficiently as he could without drawing undue attention to the fact, and when it was full, I handed over several twenty Euron notes and scribbled 'Jill Patts—00647961' on the stallholder's record of sales. Market stalls couldn't afford hand scanners, *laudate Dominum!*

As I passed the clipboard back to the stallholder, my eye fell on what was now the top sheet of newspaper. Only the picture was visible, not the headline.

"Actually, could we have one more sausage, please?"

"Where are we going to put that?" asked Bane in English as I swapped a few coins for the sausage.

"I'll carry it. We can eat a meat pie for lunch and make room for it in the bag."

"Fine, just don't get the smell on your coat."

"Yes, fusspot," I said laughingly, because the stallholder was still listening and would understand the tone even if she didn't understand our words. We all smiled and nodded and thanked her, Bane heaved his pack back on and slung the bag over his shoulder, and we walked the rest of the way through the center of the town and out the other side with only the briefest of stops to admire charming buildings. Slipping into the forest again, we walked several kilometers in a brisk, nervous silence before stopping for lunch.

"What's with the sausage, Margo?" asked Bane, digging into his meat pie. Jon had already started on the bread and cheese. "D'you *want* to smell like food to bears?"

"No, I wanted the newspaper."

I unwrapped the page from the sausage and smoothed it out. A front page. Major Everington stared out expressionlessly, immaculate as ever, save there were no gardening gloves at his belt or pistols in his holsters.

5

SCAPEGOAT

FACILITY MAJOR 'MASTERMINDS' BREAKOUT

Early this morning Major Lucas Everington, Commandant of Greater Salperton EGD Facility, was arrested on suspicion of masterminding the mass breakout from his Facility last week. A spokesperson for EGD Security today confirmed that the escape—the worst in the 80 year history of the EGD—could not have happened without inside help.

'All evidence currently points to the Commandant,' the spokesperson said, 'who is known to have had several secret meetings with re-Assignee Margaret Verrall—currently on the run after being convicted of the twin charges of *Personal Practice of Superstition* and *Inciting and Promoting Superstition in the General Population* and also wanted on a charge of *Unauthorized Departure from an EGD Facility*. The Major has not yet entered a plea, but it is expected that... *Cont.* p.4

"Blast," I said softly.

"What?" asked Jon.

"They're trying to pin it on the Major."

"Huh?"

"The escape. He's been arrested."

"Told you." Bane looked over my shoulder to read.

"I suppose he *was* ultimately in charge, but *this* is just absurd. They're saying he 'masterminded' it. Listen..." I read the article aloud.

"Makes sense." Jon shrugged. "They just want a scapegoat,

don't they? Hardly want everyone to know a few reAssignees and New Adults got around their security with a little
help from the Resistance. Give all sorts of people ideas.
Much less embarrassing to blame it all on one traitor on the
inside. The Menace will be delighted to stab him in the back,
'specially if it gets her off a very sticky hook."

"I know they don't like each other, but getting him
executed for something he didn't do seems a bit extreme.
Surely she won't say more than she has to," I objected.

"Oh, she will. She hates him," said Jon, starting on his
meat pie.

"You sound very sure."

"They've got history. Watkins told me." Jon nodded
knowingly.

Watkins was one of the only Facility guards I genuinely
liked. A kind, older man, he'd almost derailed our escape
with his quick wits, before persuading his fellow guard to go
along with us once it was clear they were outgunned—thus
avoiding needless violence. Hopefully the Menace hadn't
managed to put any of the blame for her mistakes onto him.

"I never did know why the Menace hated the Major so
much," I said.

Jon shrugged. "No, Watkins might've been a bit embarrassed to tell the tale to you girlies. See, the EGD have this
really strict rule about officers not, er, *fraternizing* with the
regular guards. Avoids a load of trouble, no doubt. Anyway,
in the little country Facilities where there's just a Major and
a Captain it's apparently pretty much the norm for them to,
ah, *socialize* in bed whether or not they socialize much out
of it, if you see what I mean."

"I don't think those two were socializing *anywhere.*"

"No, well, I'm getting to that. Apparently when Major—
then Captain—Everington first arrived the previous Captain
had just been promoted when the old Commandant
retired—you know that's normally how they do the
promotions, 'cause they try to send the officers to their local
facilities?"

"Yeah, officers have very little leave, so the idea is their
families can go there to see them. Like they're going to want
to."

"As if. Well, the new Major only needed to put in three years to draw a Major's pension—would've been ten years to draw a Commandant's pension and she wasn't prepared to hang around that long. Rumor said she was off to join the old Commandant anyway, so they weren't going to be short of cash.

"Anyway, especially in light of that, she takes one look at Everington and goes, *they've sent me a child!* He takes one look at her and goes, *old hag, not with a barge pole,* and nothing whatsoever happens. Three years pass, she retires, he's promoted to Major—Commandant before he's even thirty, not bad—and they send him a fresh young Captain to be girl's warden. Watkins swears she was a great deal thinner and quite a bit prettier ten years ago. So Major Everington perks right up, and she obviously thinks she's landed right on her feet with him, only he's a bit gentlemanly and wants to get to know her first, which is where it all goes horribly wrong.

"'Cause he takes such a violent dislike to her he can't be induced to go along with the, er, norm. So she follows him around for about three months like an amorous puppy, really embarrassing for everyone, Watkins said. She was pretty much begging him to go to bed with her. One day, he snaps and turns around to her right there in the mess in front of all the guards and says, 'I'm sure you're right, my very undear Captain, that sex is just physical but unfortunately when I look at you I find myself physically unable to comply with your wishes. So sorry and all that.'"

"Well, that told her," snorted Bane.

"*Ouch,*" I said.

"Yeah. Watkins truly thought she was going to pull out her weapon and try to plug him five or six times right there and then, but fortunately for her she didn't."

"Yeah, I reckon even in EGD Security killing your superior is frowned upon."

"Nah, Watkins didn't think she'd have managed it. Thought the Major would've killed her. He's pretty fast on the draw, apparently. Faster than her."

"Oh. Killing his subordinates wouldn't make him very popular with his superiors, though."

"Well, he got away with it later," said Jon, swallowing another mouthful of pie.

"*What?*"

"Watkins didn't tell you that one either? The Major caught a guard doing something to a boy—Watkins wouldn't say exactly what, so it must've been bad—in the Major's garden, of all places."

I shuddered. Was that why the Major didn't want boys anywhere near his precious garden? He'd positively freaked out when Jon had stepped into his private enclave for a few seconds. And considering what he'd done to Finchley for assaulting me...

"I'm guessing that was the bad idea of all bad ideas on the guard's part."

"Oh yeah. The Major had the guy brought to his office later for punishment. Next thing they know, the guard's dead on the floor with his throat cut. Self-defense, according to the Major. Said the guy got the knife and came at him."

"The Major was trying to cut one of his improvised tattoos onto the guard's face?"

"Expect so. But it ended with the Major using a paper knife on the guard's throat. No question about it, rather messy, Watkins said. He reckoned the Major was telling the truth. He just also reckoned Everington could probably have disarmed the stupid beast without killing him—if he hadn't lost his temper. Anyway, given that the Major was a young officer with a clean record and a lot of years service left in him? There was no trouble about it."

"Lucky for the Menace she didn't try anything, then. I take it they just settled down to hate each other ever since?"

"That's about it. So we can safely assume that now she'll tell the Powers That Be anything and everything she can think of and make up the rest, 'specially with her own neck on the line."

Bane snorted again. "When they take that guy to pieces it's going to be a day of poetic justice all right!"

"I don't know about justice," I couldn't help saying. "If they dismantled him for being a Facility Commandant all these years that might be justice. But for something he hasn't done? That's *in*justice."

"You're overthinking it, Margo. He'd have seen you all dead. Let him rot."

My hand crept to the scars on my forehead, hidden—or mostly hidden—under a carefully applied layer of make-up. I hadn't mentioned to either of them precisely how I'd acquired that particular injury. I looked again at the picture. The Major's hands were cuffed behind his back, the Facility in the background. They'd taken a photographer along just to arrest him. A show trial from the very beginning.

"Shame it wasn't the Menace," said Jon. "Oh well, did I hear you buying cakes?"

"Bane has them." I folded the page and slipped it into my pocket.

Skirting an area of hillier forest, we reached another town four days later, buying more food with a blessed absence of any trouble, then heading on. So many back-packers, and who paid attention to photos of fugitives who were supposed to be in the Spanish department with the Resistance?

Three days later and the sun was dropping below the trees, but we were still walking. All my dressings had been gone for some time now, leaving expanses of red, wrinkly—but thoroughly attached—skin, and Bane called later and later stops.

Jon tripped and went down, almost taking Bane with him. Usually back to his feet in moments, he sat back on his heels, rubbing his knees and panting. "Aren't we stopping yet?"

"We can go a bit further." Bane checked his phone. "Still some daylight left."

"It's dusk! I can hear the wildlife, I'm not *deaf!*"

"Just get up, Jon."

"Or *what?*"

"*Or we'll leave you for the wolves!*"

"Bane, *don't talk nonsense!*" With effort, I stopped myself from saying anything harsher. Jon wasn't the only exhausted one. "Look, don't you think it is time to stop? We've a long way to go. Hadn't we better pace ourselves?"

"Great idea, only we really want to reach the Alps before the more deserted passes are impassable. And we...ah...we're not going quite as fast as I'd hoped." His eyes flicked guiltily to Jon—harsh words already regretted?

"Oh." Hadn't even thought about Alpine passes. "How long have we got?"

"Only Mother Nature knows for sure. If we reach them by the beginning of October, we should be safe. Much later and we'll probably have to take a main road or even a road tunnel."

"No! There'll be checkpoints! We *can't.*"

"Or wait out the winter in the French forest?"

I bit my lip. We were under-equipped, we couldn't get food from stalls—no one camped out in midwinter. We'd never survive.

"We *have* to reach the passes in time!" I tried to steady my voice. "Come on, Jon, we can go a bit further. We've *got to.*"

"Point taken."

Jon dragged himself to his feet and we moved on. But it wasn't long before there was a crack and a yelp as our "fast" pace let another branch or tree stump slip past the swing of his stick. A smack as he kicked the object in frustration.

"Ow! What kind of rock is that?" A tap-tap as he sized it up with his stick. "Like a stalagmite!"

I glanced back, as Jon rubbed his knee. A narrow, square stone post stuck up from the ground to about knee height, coated in lichen and with a bit of creeper up one side. Rough patches marred each side about a third of the way down. Something familiar about the damage...

"Hey, it had crosspieces...it's a cross!" I moved around to the other side and found a name carved into it. "It's a gravestone."

"What on earth is it doing out here?" said Bane.

Jon dropped guiltily to his un-bashed knee and ran gentle hands over the recent target of his frustration. "I'm really sorry. I shouldn't have done that." Speaking to God or the stone's owner, or perhaps both.

I put a hand on his shoulder. "You didn't know."

"*Margo...*" Something in Bane's voice made me look

around at once. "*Look.*"

I followed his gaze and for a moment saw nothing but forest in the dimming light. Then from the jumble of undergrowth shapes sprang to the fore—stone posts, hundreds of them, *thousands*—desecrated crosses running in compact ranks away through the trees, lichen-coated and overgrown.

"Oh my..." My neck and scalp tingled as all my hair tried to stand on end.

"What is it?" Jon lurched back to his feet.

"There's more of them."

"A lot more." Bane still sounded strangled. "*Thousands.*"

"What is this place?"

"It's a cemetery!" said Bane. "From one of the Great Wars of the Twentieth Century. Gravestones weren't exempted from the Religious Symbols Act, were they?"

"Even though the forest had grown over them. *Libera nos*, there's so *many.*"

"They killed off half the young men in Europe," said Bane grimly.

"At least they saved what was left of the Jews in the end."

"Yeah, for the EuroGov to try to finish off! Don't people *learn?* Sacrifice half a generation to overthrow an evil power and then just sit back and let another one in. *Doh!*"

"This one crept in so gradually," I said. "Now people don't know what to do. So it's easier to do nothing. But consciences can't be suppressed forever, so sooner or later... Wouldn't like to say *when*, but I reckon it'll be quite sudden and I just hope to God peaceful."

"You wish."

"It's happened before. If every person in the bloc stands up and demands change there won't need to be a shot fired."

"Yeah, but in reality half of them will hide under their beds, so the other half will have to start shooting to make up for them."

"Hope you're wrong."

"History's on his side. Mostly." Gloomily Jon knelt again to trace his fingers over the chiseled writing. "Huh, this guy was our age. I can't read his name."

Bane stood staring out at the sea of graves with an unquiet brow and Jon went on crouching apologetically by the headstone of the nameless soldier of our age, long dead. *May they all be with you, Lord, especially this guy here.*

"Come on," I said quietly. "Unless we want to camp here."

Jon got to his feet at once and took hold of Bane again—they'd barely started forward when Bane threw an impulsive arm around Jon's shoulders.

"I wouldn't really leave you for the wolves, mate."

"Nice to know."

Jon threw an arm around Bane's shoulders in return and they went along like that for a few steps until Bane said, "Watch out, tree."

Two more days brought us to Peronne, as we made sure to pass well below the more populous regions of Douai and Cambrai. Exiting the town on the other side of the river, we turned towards Guise, our next intended point of resupply, with luck only four days away on this flat terrain.

On the second day it rained. Heavily. Swathing ourselves in our worth-their-weight-in-gold waterproofs, we tried to ignore it, but even the most expensive waterproofs in the world couldn't entirely stop water going up sleeves and down necks.

We spent the next morning drying off, then had to take a little detour around a wolf in a clearing that didn't seem inclined to get up and move—a den site?—so it was afternoon on the fifth day when we finally reached Guise. The next town small enough not to have police was eight days away so we collected all the food we could carry.

We stopped while it was still light for what'd already become our normal post-resupply treat. As Bane set to work with the stove, I put the bulging food bag beside me and unwrapped the first item, scanning the page of newspaper front and back. Nothing of interest. I rewrapped the cheese and put it to one side, picking up the next.

"Labrador saves child?" I offered.

"Go on, then." Jon's head rested on his knees. How many articles could he stay awake for?

"Okay. 'Jeanette Paquin from Nancy, French department, had a narrow escape on Thursday when she fell into the river at the bottom of her garden. The five-year-old, who is unable to swim, was alone except for the family pet, plucky Labrador Remy, who went in after her, towing her to safety.' Well, that's a nice little story for a change." Though it was ironic how the press could lavish praise on a dog for saving a child, yet villainize us for saving seventy human lives.

I read out "More strikes in the German department"—("Good," grunted Bane, "give the EuroGov something to think about other than us"), "Man finds diamond in burger"—("Hope it was worth enough to get his teeth fixed!" Bane sniggered), and 'Fifteen Underground members executed after Madrid raid,' at which Jon stirred enough to murmur, *"Requiescat in Pace."*

The next sheet—a *FrenchDaily* front page—sent my eyebrows heading up towards my hair. A small boxed headline at the top of the page, advertising an opinion piece inside the newspaper, read:

ARE YOU ENJOYING NEW ADULTHOOD, MARGARET V.?

Willem von Leffers on the escaped reAssignees unexpected 'New Adulthood'...p. 22

I read it to the other two.

"Weird," said Jon.

"People must be very interested in you," said Bane shrewdly, "if they're writing silly little pieces like that. I mean, it must be pushing it a bit, with the government censors."

Turning over the page, I scanned the inside. "Can I borrow your phone?"

"Here. Why?" asked Bane.

"This thing's totally untraceable, right?"

"Oh yeah. Or I'm going to have to get my money back from the Salperton cell. Why?" Belatedly suspicious.

Biting my lip, I typed a couple of lines. "I thought I might answer their question."

Holding up the newspaper by my face, I took a picture. Nope, it showed my roots. Tried again. Good, just my face, no hair, no background, and just the little box, not the newspaper title.

Bane watched in alarm. "D'you *want* them to know we're in the French department reading French newspapers?"

"They won't." I showed him the inside page. "The article's written by a *DailyNewsCorp* news service journalist from Germany. It's a wire story—it will have appeared in every Department by now."

Bane looked slightly reassured.

"What are you going to say?" asked Jon.

"We are all enjoying New Adult life very much. Thank you for asking. M.V."

Bane's brows drew together as he analyzed this. "S'pose it doesn't let on we're not with the others."

"Short and sweet," said Jon.

"Well, then." I held up the phone, identity-proving photo now inserted into the text. "Send, don't send?"

"Where does it end?" Bane threw up his hands rather dramatically.

"When there are no innocent people sitting around in Facilities waiting to die."

He scowled, so I added, "You started it all by sending me the flyer about the postSort novel competition," and looked at Jon.

After a moment Jon turned his ears from Bane's frustrated breathing, back to me. Spoke almost inaudibly. "Send."

Bane threw up his hands again. "Fine, keep stirring the pot. Doubt the EuroGov can get much angrier at this point."

I pressed send. No way to know if *DailyNewsCorps* received it. Or dared to print it. Still. Felt like I was doing *something*.

A more cheerful article, now? I rustled through several more bits of paper.

"Oh dear...obituaries...*cheerful*, don't expect there's anyone we—" For a moment I couldn't tear my eyes from the picture. "Nope, boring."

"Who is it?" asked Jon.

"Oh, no one important." I tried to wrap the page back around its sausage but my hands shook so badly I failed to evade Bane's grab. "*No...*"

I lunged after the page—he swung it out of my reach,

laughing. Smoothed it out and looked. The laugh dropped from his face. He handed it back to me, avoiding my eyes. Picked up a fork-spoon and began stirring the warming water.

Jon frowned into the silence. "Who on earth is it?

I took a deep breath. "A dismantler. Um... Doctor Richard, actually."

Jon's brow cleared. "Oh, that's okay. I was worried." The frown came back. "Didn't know he was dead."

"Um...I s'pose I'd better read a bit of it. Er, 'Doctor Richard Werrick, forty-eight, was brutally murdered during the mass breakout from Greater Salperton EGD Facility last week. Newly appointed Com...' Ugh! Um, sorry... 'newly appointed Commandant of Greater Salperton Facility, Major Gladys Wallis, spoke of Doctor Werrick's genuine dedication to saving lives through his work...' and blah, blah, blah. Saving lives, I like that!"

"Yeah," snorted Jon. "By carving up *other lives!* Huh. The Resistance must've got him after you were rescued. Well, what d'you expect from murderous dogs like them?"

Bane's face crumpled, his teeth sinking into his lower lip. He dropped the fork-spoon and his hand clenched around something inside his jacket. His eyes found mine at last— yeah, more bothered by this than he'd been letting on.

Jon's head turned slightly to one side, his unseeing eyes intent and not at all sleepy. "What did I say?"

"What on earth d'you mean?"

"I just said something... *wrong?* Something. What?"

"Nothing—"

"No, it's okay," interrupted Bane. "No secrets. I killed him, Jon."

Jon blinked; his eyes widened. "Oh. Uh...why?"

"He was chopping up Margo."

"Good for you, then. Um, what happened?"

"I went in there and there he was, chopping up Margo, as I said. He raises this razor-thing to stab her and...well, I don't remember deciding to do anything, but one moment I'm by the door and the next moment my knife's going into him and then he's dead. Just like that. S'pose perhaps I could've stopped him without killing him, I don't know. It happened very fast, and I kinda saw red."

I saw red. Is that what Major Everington had said after killing the abusive guard? The uncomfortable thought popped into my mind—I pushed it out again. Could *Bane* have stopped Doctor Richard without killing him? Maybe. *If* he'd been able to sit around beforehand and plan what to do. "I wouldn't start playing 'what if', Bane."

"Wasn't planning to. Just saying." Just being honest with Jon.

"Well, it sounds like an unpleasant job that needed doing," said Jon firmly.

"If I had to do it again I dare say I would, but it doesn't stop it feeling a lot like...like brutal murder, as the paper would have it."

"You think you should've let him kill Margo?"

"*No.* Never."

"Well, then." Jon rested his head back on his knees again. "What's next, Margo?"

"Um..." I skimmed down the page and stopped suddenly. "Wait, there's a bit at the bottom under all that eulogizing. Just says, 'The previous Commandant of Greater Salperton Facility, Major Lucas Everington, remains in custody charged with Category One Sedition. It is believed he will plead Guilty. No trial date has yet been set.' Believed he will plead Guilty, huh? Oh, really. So why no date?"

"Bet he's pleading *Not Guilty* with everything he's got," said Jon. "They can't have enough evidence to convict him; he won't confess unless he wants to die."

"Which he will soon enough," said Bane, "though that appears to be taking them a little longer to achieve than they anticipated."

I folded the sheet and put it in my pocket, feeling slightly sick. One commandant to be added to the tally after all, only far more lingeringly than any of the others. How long would it take them to break him?

Lord... What prayer could I offer for this doomed man? This man I'd said I forgave. *Lord, he hasn't done anything...* My hand crept to my forehead. *Okay, he's done plenty, but he hasn't done what he's accused of. Let his suffering not be unnecessarily prolonged?*

* * *

We stretched the fresh food to five days, then it was sachets the rest of the way to Vouziers, though Jon found mushrooms one evening, his wonderful nose!

"But are they safe?" I asked him.

"Yeah, we don't have a stomach pump," said Bane.

"Relax, you two," he told us. "My parents were always serving the mushrooms I gathered to the guests at home."

Vouziers was much like all the other towns, down in a river valley and most of the surviving buildings old and beautiful. Backpackers thronged the food stalls and we had to wait to be served. High hiking season now.

The stall displayed the usual selection of French basics, bread, cheese, meat, with nice looking sausages. One of the New Adults in the group in front was probably the blackest person I'd ever seen, his skin like ebony.

I looked away so I wouldn't stare—a stall further on had a very large selection of pies, perhaps we should go there, the line wasn't any longer.

My eyes crept back to the guy in front and I glanced away again. There were hardly any British B (black people) left in Salperton—or British A (Asians like Jane), for that matter. The Registration Laws had made it so hard for them to find partners of their own exact genetic category that most had moved out of the Bloc several generations ago, or at least to the big cities. The EGD still claimed it was an unintended consequence.

My heart froze. Two men in uniform, a little further up the street, just before the bridge... They stopped a group of three laughing New Adults, who laughed on as they pulled out their IDs and swiped them through the policemen's hand scanner. The policemen joked with them and let them go by. Pistol butts protruded from their holsters... NonLees. I'd just spent four months looking at exactly that type.

Lethals would've been a hundred times less scary.

6

WEIRD CHATTY BRITS

My heart beat again, thundering in my chest. I placed a casual hand on Bane's arm, managing to merely touch rather than bruise.

"Bane," I spoke softly in English. "There are two policemen further up the street. They just ID'd a group of three backpackers; two guys, one girl."

Jon's arm, looped through mine, went rigid.

Bane swallowed—turned casually as though admiring the town. Turned back just as casually. "We need food. It's five days to Clermont. The lot in front are about to pay, let's wait."

Come on, hurry up. The stallholder's wrapping had been brisk enough before but now she seemed to have gone to half-speed. She finally handed over the last purchase and announced an amount of Eurons in French.

One of the New Adults ahead of us—the black guy—took out a wallet and passed over some notes with a polite mutter, also in French. Then took the clipboard and began to fill in his details. He was the world's slowest writer. Or maybe I was just so aware of those policemen, coming nearer, step by step, group by group. Any group of two guys and one girl. The group at the stall were going to get ID'd too. Or maybe not, with one of them so clearly not British C (Caucasian).

"*Merci.*" The stallholder accepted the clipboard back and said something else. The French New Adults looked surprised and queried her, then shrugged—the black boy took out his ID card and displayed it.

Swallowing down panic, I spoke to Bane in Esperanto, as though continuing a previous conversation. "Oh, go on, *let's* get some of those pies? They look so nice."

"We're at the front of the line here, now... Oh, fine, we'll go to the pie stall." We followed close behind the group in front as they moved on up the street, Bane sliding chummily in between the two boys. "Where are you from, then? Nearby?"

"No, we're from the south of the department," came the tolerant reply from the black one.

"Ah, I don't know if we'll be going there. You've got some really big mountains, haven't you?"

"Oh, *oui*, very big."

We had to get across the river so I understood the plan, but without Jon's pressure on my arm, leading me towards those policemen as he followed Bane's voice, I couldn't have moved. After a few steps I got sufficient hold of myself to edge Jon and me alongside the girl.

"They're not as big as the Alps there, though, are they?" I said, trying for friendly curiosity. "Are you all from the same place?"

"*Oui et oui*, but our mountains are more beautiful than the Alps," said the girl firmly. She'd dark hair and reminded me superficially of Jane, though she was French C not French Asian.

"I'll take your word for it," I said cheerfully. Hmm...I'd better try to find out. "Ah...did I see you showing your ID at a *stall?* Seems odd."

"*EuroGov says*, apparently. They've lost a load of reAssignees, you must've heard."

"Oh, that."

"Good for them, I say," said the girl bluntly. "The reAssignees, that is."

"Nuisance for the stallholders, though."

"It's only temporary, she said. Until they've caught them all."

"Oh, right."

We were almost alongside the policemen. Bane had cleverly steered his conversation—from the heads together and low voices—onto the sort of thing guys prefer girls not to hear them talking about. Should I keep my conversation going, make sure we looked like one group? But the police had only to catch the Esperanto and they'd know better, perhaps I should stay quiet.

Or perhaps not. The girl was looking sideways at Jon and me, a rather intent look on her face. Before I could say anything she made a loud comment in French, flung a comradely arm around me and laughed as though I would've understood. The policemen were meters away... I laughed too and so did Jon.

Then the police were behind us! We walked on over the bridge and out the other side of the town, chatting away in Esperanto until we reached a crossroads. The French girl never explained what she'd said and I didn't dare ask. Had she recognized us?

They were heading in broadly the same direction, apparently, but detouring to see some splendid old castle, so they were going right. We needed to go left—no police in sight, so we parted company.

Glancing back, I caught the girl doing the same, as the black boy threw up his hands and said something—the fair-haired boy shrugged in response. Probably something along the lines of, "What weird chatty Brits! You normally have to pry them out of their shells like snails."

Never mind. We'd made it out. And on the correct side of the river for the next leg.

I took discreet glances over my shoulder but the girl didn't seem to be telling her companions anything interesting and they were still heading off along the road when I lost sight of them. Once clear of the town, we plunged back into the safety of the forest.

"Curse it, the EuroGov's on to us," snarled Bane, pausing momentarily and immediately striding on again, making Jon stumble to catch up. "They know who's missing and they suspect what we're disguised as!"

"Suspect or know?" I said uneasily. "Apparently that stallholder said, 'Until they've caught them all.' Have they got the others?"

"'Until they've caught them all' doesn't mean they've actually caught *any* of us yet," pointed out Jon.

"No...but they seem a little close to the truth and if they had caught them—someone would've talked."

"Exactly." Bane stopped again and this time turned to speak to us properly. "And every town anywhere near our likely route would be crawling with plain clothes agents. Which they clearly aren't or we'd never have got out of there. They've just sent a few police to all the small touristy towns backpackers frequent. So it's at least as likely the others have made it, and their spies have got just close enough to know the other boys went with the Resistance but we three went separately."

"In which case they soon *will* know roughly *where* we are and *exactly* what we're posing as," said Jon glumly.

"*Blast.* We were getting on so well." Bane dismissed his regret with an impatient jerk of his head. "Well, we can't go into towns anymore and that's that."

Our supply of sachets weighed a lot but made a depressingly small heap. And we'd well over a thousand kilometers to go.

"How are we going to get food?" My voice squeaked slightly.

"We *have* to save enough sachets for the Alps," said Bane. "We're almost halfway to Zurich already and we can take one of the quieter passes beyond."

"*Half the way there* butters no parsnips if we've no parsnips to eat to get us the other half."

"We could spend more time hunting and gathering," suggested Jon dubiously.

"We haven't caught *anything* yet and we could spend all day gathering and not have one full meal from it."

"Margo's right," said Bane, "that's not going to work. Worst comes to the worst, one of us will have to go into town alone to buy food."

No prizes for guessing which one.

"No. We can't risk that." What to do? I'd never precisely taken food for granted—the lifelong problem of filling the extra mouths of priests and sisters ensured that—but...how? That group from the French department were no doubt walking along without a care in the world, their biggest decision whether to have cheese or sausage for lunch...

"I know! We stop each passing group on a hiking trail at dusk, all friendly and shame-faced, say we're out of food and can' they spare us something for supper? Bet most of them will give us a baguette or a tin or a sausage and it'll add up to a day's food if we're lucky."

"What if some of them have eyes in their heads and recognize us?" said Bane.

"We've been risking stallholders, haven't we? Anyway, we haven't much choice." Better not mention the way the French girl had been looking at me.

"She's right," said Jon.

"I don't know," said Bane.

"Oh, come on, if you go tearing into towns like the lone ranger it won't be long before you don't come back and then where will Margo and I be?"

Bane stopped biting his lip. "*Fine*. Let's get moving."

"Okay, how do I look?" I asked Bane.

His eyes made the familiar circuit. Forehead—make-up applied; hair—loose; hat—well pulled down; shades—in place. Check, check, check, check.

"Nothing like the bloc's most wanted. Let's go."

Jon followed wordlessly as we slid down a bank and onto the evening's chosen hiking trail. No comment about the easier walking; he stumped along in silence, leaning on the stick rather too convincingly. Both his knees and shins were mottled purple-black-red with bruises and cuts. I shot him an anxious look. His face was thinning, dark circles accenting his eyes. But what could we do?

This daily begging routine slowed us down even more—and exposed us to the close scrutiny of ten times more people than buying from stalls. But after pulling it off three nights in a row I no longer had to count on embarrassment to put some color into my pale cheeks. So far only a group of four girls had refused me—so Bane had charmed their backpacks open with a few delightfully pink-cheeked apologies.

It was ages tonight before a group appeared, overtaking us from behind. We stepped to the side to let them pass. *Oh no*. The French New Adults from Vouziers.

"Well, look who it is," the fair-haired boy greeted us in Esperanto.

"*Bonjour*," said the other two.

"Oh, hi again," we chorused in return.

"How was the castle?" asked Bane casually.

"I thought it was fantastic! I have never seen a chandelier that size, ever, for one thing!" The fair-haired boy paused, a slightly sour expression crossing his face. "Not everyone agreed, huh, Juwan?"

The black boy caught his look and shrugged. "I did find it rather disappointing. The fortifications had been so degraded by all the later work to make it *fashionable*. Wouldn't keep out an army of tin soldiers now, let alone the real thing."

The fair-haired boy snorted. "You're supposed to appreciate the *art* and the *history*, not analyze its defensive attributes."

"It's a *castle*, Louis, it *is* a defensive attribute." The girl spoke at last. "Or should be."

Try and get some food off them? Tempting to let them walk straight on by, but...the further from Vouziers the quieter the hiking trails got. This was the first group we'd seen today. Reluctantly, I started my spiel.

"Um, actually, you know, we looked in our food bag earlier and were horrified to find it empty—very silly of us—um...I don't suppose you could spare something for our supper?"

The girl looked us over yet again—she'd been looking us over ever since she stopped. "You *ran out of food?* That's not too bright, is it?"

Okay, she reminded me more than superficially of Jane. I managed an embarrassed laugh. "Yeah, well, one of those silly misunderstandings. Josh thought Dane had checked, Dane thought I'd said we'd plenty left and I thought Josh was in charge of all that. We've got ourselves organized now."

"You'd better have. This isn't Hyde Park, y'know. Guess you should've bought those extra pies."

Just how sharp was she? She'd heard what we said in Vouziers, before we'd even met—and noticed we hadn't done it.

Louis sniggered, but said, "Course we'll help you out. Dominique always buys loads."

"Good job too, eh, Louis? With hapless babes in the wood like these."

Bane's jaw grew rather rigid, but he just said dryly, "Yeah, that's us. Babes in the wood."

"Well—" Dominique broke off as a curve of the path revealed a green forest meadow with a little rivulet trickling through the most distant corner. "Ooh, campsite!"

"Hey," said Louis. "Let's all make camp together and have a feast!"

"Yeah, why not?" said Juwan.

"And you three can wash up," added Louis.

"Well, looks like you've got yourself your evening meal," Dominique told us. "Let's make camp. Dibs on that flowery spot."

I exchanged a discreet look with Bane. How could we refuse their offer and carry on? Too suspicious for words. But how long could they hang out with us before getting suspicious? Especially of Jon. On the plus side, it was almost dark. We had to risk it.

Bane had reached the same conclusion, because he walked casually down the bank to the meadow as though he'd not had a moment's hesitation. Jon stood straight and stiff, ears no doubt straining.

"Carefully down the slope, Josh." I drew him after Bane. "Don't turn your ankle *again*, will you?"

"Babes in the wood," sniggered Dominique, *almost* inaudibly, watching Jon's careful descent.

I ignored her and got Jon seated with his leg on Bane's backpack. He promptly lay back on the grass and closed his eyes. Less time he spent awake and not reacting to visual things the better.

We pitched camp quickly and soon we all sat in a big circle, heating potato cakes from their solar-powered cool bag on our stove while they fried fresh bacon and cubed steak. My mouth watered like mad.

"So how far are you three planning to go?" asked Juwan.

"Oh, we thought we'd toddle along as far as the Alps," said Bane. "Then head down to the south of the department, perhaps, see your mountains too. Depends how Josh's leg is feeling."

"Why'd he go hiking with a bad leg?" asked Dominique.

"It wasn't bad when we started off." I'd better play the

role of indignant girlfriend. "When it started playing up he thought he might be able to manage with the stick and he has, but it does leave him über-tired."

Dominique shrugged. "Fair enough."

"I think the meat's done," put in Louis.

I smothered a suspiciously over-enthusiastic noise and woke Jon. Dominique, Louis and Juwan had taken off their sunglasses some time ago, and it was now so dark Bane and I followed suit. Playfully, I snagged Jon's and put them away for him, drawing a pretend grumble of, "I'm not a complete invalid."

"'Course not." I placed a laughing kiss on his cheek and slipped an arm around him. Staying draped around each other might help disguise the fact he never focused on anything.

I tried not to eat as though I hadn't tasted anything like this for weeks, but fortunately everyone was hungry and for a while there was nothing but silent chomping.

"When's your term start?" asked Louis eventually.

"Beginning of October," said Bane. "You?"

"Same. What are you guys studying?"

"History."

"And me," I said.

"Physics," said Jon, head still on my shoulder.

"I'm doing Chemistry," said Dominique. "I want to be an explosives engineer. Make things go bang."

"You should see what she can do with a cupboard of household cleaning products." Juwan spoke rather proudly.

"Yeah, she *already* makes things go bang." Louis shuddered. "Downright scary, sometimes."

"What sort of career would you be looking at?" Jon would keep awake for science!

"Oh, you can go into lots of things," said Dominique. "Mine and quarry consultants, manufacturing companies, military, research..."

"...Resistance," sniggered Louis.

Juwan punched him in the arm. "Shut it! That's not funny! 'Course not Resistance." He and Dominique glanced at each other, glanced at us. Afraid we'd be reporting the joke a.s.a.p.? Stupid thing to say in front of three complete strangers—especially if there was any truth in it.

Bane just laughed, and Jon and I laughed too.

"Resistance, that's a good one," said Bane. "I mean, seriously, who'd join the Resistance?"

"*Suicidal!*" Dominique twirled a finger beside her head to indicate insanity.

"Absolutely," I agreed.

We all laughed some more while Louis rubbed his arm and glared at Juwan.

"How about you?" I asked Juwan, as Jon shifted to put his head in my lap and proceeded to go straight back to sleep. I stroked his hair—it'd grown quite a bit since we left the British department. Perhaps I'd better not call attention to it. I stopped stroking.

"I'm going into Law. To be a defense barrister."

"Wow, lot more studying, then."

He shrugged, then said, "Huh, Josh really is bushed, isn't he?"

"Anyone got a pen?" said Louis. "We could give him specs and a moustache."

"Oh, come on, be nice," I objected.

"Okay, okay. Don't you Brits have a sense of humor?"

"Only when it's funny," said Bane.

Louis looked offended—awkward silence.

"Well, if we'd known we'd meet you three again, we wouldn't have drunk the wine yesterday, would we?" said Dominique.

"*I* would," said Juwan. "Shocking to waste a vintage like that on *les rosbifs.*"

"Well, these *roast beefs* will live without it," said Bane.

Thank goodness it *was* gone, we'd have hardly dared either drink or refuse!

We chatted for a bit longer, for politeness's sake, then pleaded sleepiness. Jon got into the tent without any obvious groping around, thanks to Bane talking him to the entrance with inconsequential remarks, and soon all three of us were zipped up inside. Sliding into his sleeping bag like a rabbit into a burrow, Jon fell asleep again almost at once, but Bane drew me to him in the dark and kissed me. Horrible for him watching me and Jon be all cozy-cozy.

I burrowed my nose into his neck and he stroked my hair and rested his lips against my scarred brow. Eventually he drew back enough to murmur, "You and I will have to keep watch tonight. Keep listen, anyway, we can hardly do it outside the tent."

"Okay."

"Sorry."

"No, we've got to. Can't be helped. Though if one of them does go into the forest we're not going to know if it's nature's call or a phone call they've got in mind, are we?"

Getting up the very instant the birds began to sing looked a bit suspicious, so I whiled away the time trimming Jon's hair with the tiny scissors on my pocketknife. He didn't stir as I rolled him over to do the other side. Bane woke at the first snip at his own hair, grabbing my wrist.

"*Bane*."

"Oh. Sorry, Margo. What're you doing?"

"Cutting your hair. Go back to sleep. Don't scowl, it's getting too long."

"Okay, okay. We'd better get moving soon, though."

"Yes, so lie still."

A barber would've had a fit, but they'd both be wearing their hats. Hopefully the overnight trim would go un-remarked.

Unzipping the tent, we began briskly and quietly striking camp. We'd just call a goodbye into the other tent as we headed off... *Or not.* Dominique and Juwan emerged, stretching in a way that made it clear they weren't just nipping into the forest and heading back to their sleeping bags.

"If you get some water heating on your stove, we'll warm the croissants," said Dominique, as Juwan went to fetch their food bag from where it was suspended at the other end of the meadow.

"Are you sure you've got enough?" Blast it all! Why were they up so early?

Dominique waved a hand dismissively. "Oh, we can be in Clermont by tomorrow morning and we've enough food for all of us until then."

Blast, blast and double blast. How to get away? Simply refuse and march off? Could set them thinking. If Dominique wasn't thinking already. Get in an argument with them? But if they did suspect...better if they like us.

"It's very nice of you," Bane was saying. "But we don't want to eat all your food."

"We're just going to buy more in Clermont anyway and the old stuff never gets eaten." Juwan dropped the food bag by Dominique's feet. "Here you go, *petite alchimiste.*"

Trying to look happy about this, I went to wake Jon. Bane had the water boiling by the time we emerged, carefully entwined. I propped Jon's ankle on Bane's pack again and he tried very hard not to fall asleep between every bite.

"Are you two registering?" asked Dominique. The normal question New Adults asked each other.

"Yeah, probably," I replied. Hard to avoid all lies at the moment.

"My dad wants me to register with Louis," Dominique said sourly. "He topped up our funds on condition Louis came along—like having to share a tent with him for three months is going to change my mind!"

We laughed and made appropriately sympathetic noises.

"Louis, we're about to eat your croissants!" Juwan chucked a stick onto their tent—a lot bigger than ours, complete with a porch. He glanced at our tent and lack of clutter. "You three certainly travel light."

"Nice to be unencumbered," said Bane.

"You're taking it to extremes with the *no food* thing," snorted Dominique.

"Yeah, we messed up. We did notice." A slight edge to Bane's voice. Also considering the argument ploy or just tired?

Juwan shot us a look and touched Dominique's arm. "I think they did notice, eh, Doms?"

"Okay, sorry, I'll stop going on about it. It's just really..." She caught Juwan's look and threw up her hands. "Oh, never mind!"

Stupid. Yeah, really stupid. So long as you go on thinking that. If that is what you're really thinking. Perhaps it was paranoia, but it seemed to me that she looked at us rather a lot.

Louis ruined any remaining chance of picking a fight with them by scrambling out of the tent, yawning and half dressed.

"Showing your chest isn't going to make me register with you, y'know," said Dominique.

"Ha ha." Louis kicked some twigs her way. "I'm mad at my dad too, okay?" Grabbing a croissant in each hand, he added under his breath, "Though I've not noticed you explaining why you're *so* set against it."

"Well, apart from anything else, my parents are dead against registering before University. They say I can have a fab registration party—but only after I graduate." Dominique sounded, strangely, ten times more bitter than Louis. Wasn't that sort of promise/restriction pretty much the norm for well-off families? She caught my puzzled look and added quickly—and much more lightly, "S'not like I'd want to start a family before then, of course."

"If ever," muttered Juwan blackly. Dominique shot him a look, then began putting away the stove.

"Stable Population Committee would have something to say about *that*, Ju," said Louis nastily.

Juwan lunged at him—he bolted into the trees. Juwan moved to give chase, then stopped, threw up his hands and shouted something after him in French. I'd a feeling the gist of it was, *you're going to wake up one day and find you've got no friends, and don't come running to me when you do.*

He disappeared into the tent, and Dominique left the stove half packed and followed him. A murmur of French came through the canvas wall.

Bane and I glanced at each other and said nothing. Did he share my growing sense that our French companions weren't quite as happy and carefree as most backpacking New Adults? There was something in their group dynamic I wasn't getting, too, and I'd an odd feeling it ought to be obvious.

Bane got on with packing up the last of our stuff—other than the stove it was only the tent, and that was just a question of taking out the pegs, reeling in the guy ropes and pushing the lever to make it retract back into its neat little tin. Juwan and Dominique soon appeared, sleeping bags and mats packed. Louis came back, and they had their tent down in no time. No one mentioned the argument as we shouldered our packs and headed up the slope to the trail, Jon and I arm in arm again, and Bane walking close to his other side.

We didn't need to talk much. Louis babbled on with a steady stream of witty and not so witty remarks, and Juwan and Dominique seemed happy to just walk along ahead of us—though a couple of times they tried to pass something to Jon. Fortunately I noticed each time and took it from them with an "Oh, yes, please," or a "Wake up, Josh!" but was it just my imagination that they looked at Jon more and more as the day went on?

Lunch was more like what we were used to: baguettes, cheese and sliced sausage, but Dominique and Juwan fixed another deluxe camping meal once we'd pitched camp. My mouth watered as it cooked. Mustn't stare at the pan like a hungry dog, no, no...

Bane was also trying not to look at the food too often, but Jon dozed on my shoulder, only my arm keeping him upright—best not to make a big thing of just how tired he was.

"Poor Josh, out like a light again," said Dominique.

So much for that. "Umm, that bad ankle really tires him out," I agreed.

"Despite the snail's pace," snorted Louis.

"We made it clear we wouldn't be offended if you wanted to go on without us," said Bane sharply.

"Okay, okay, just saying!"

"More firewood, Louis?" interrupted Dominique.

"Fine!" Louis stamped off into the forest.

"He's an old friend but he can be hard work," Dominique confided.

"Yeah, we'd...noticed," I said mildly.

"I don't care how large his father's business is. I couldn't register with him even if... Well, whatever."

"Nice to hear," muttered Juwan, for some reason.

I tried to look sympathetic and said nothing.

"I'm off to the little forest room." Bane got to his feet.

"Me too." I stuck my elbow in Jon's ribs as discreetly as possible.

"Huh?" Jon looked up.

"Off to the little forest room," repeated Bane.

"Oh, yeah, and me." Jon got to his feet and walked confidently up to Bane, who'd made sure there wasn't anything between them before speaking. They went in one direction and I headed off in another.

When I got back they were both just returning. Juwan and Dominique had their heads together, talking rapidly in French. As we approached they bounced to their feet and walked slowly to meet Bane and Jon.

I headed that way as well. What was up?

Juwan raised his hands and shoved Jon, hard.

Jon went down in a heap as Bane lunged at Juwan to stop him, then grabbed at Jon to steady him—and managed to do neither. I raced to them and helped Jon up, my heart pounding against my ribs.

"His ankle seems to be just fine," said Juwan deliberately, "I'd say—what was the name again? Jonathan?—has a little trouble with his *eyesight*."

7

STRANGE AND WONDERFUL

"What *are* you wittering on about?" said Bane scathingly. "I'd think you'd know his name by now!"

"Are you okay, Josh?" I rounded on Juwan as well. "What did you do that for!"

"To prove he can't see anything," said Juwan.

"Took us a while to put our finger on it," Dominique added, "but we eventually figured it out."

"Figured what out?" Louis emerged from the forest with an armful of firewood.

"Louis, re-introductions are needed—meet Margaret, Bane, and Jonathan," said Dominique.

"Huh?" His eyes bulged. *"Who?"*

"Margaret Verrall, Bane Marsden, and Jonathan Revan," said Juwan. "Ring any bells?"

"By the Chairman's underpants, do you three have any idea how much you're worth?" choked Louis, the wood slipping from his arms.

Thoroughly wild-eyed by now, Bane slipped his hand inside his jacket. I caught his arm, staring warily at the three New Adults, so smug and excited. So...oblivious.

"I suggest you tell us just what you're thinking of doing next," I said.

"Well, we won't *tell* on you," snorted Dominique.

"We'll help you!" said Juwan.

"Ooh, I'm not sure that's such a good idea!" said Louis.

"Oh, don't be such an ass," snapped Dominique. "We're in the middle of nowhere. Who's going to know? Anyway, think of Piers."

Louis hung his head.

"What can we do?" asked Juwan.

"Forget you saw us!" Bane's hand remained inside his jacket.

I gave his arm a squeeze. "Let's get our stuff and get out of here."

"Oh, come on," protested Juwan, "We want to help. At least let us get you a whole load of food tomorrow."

"Then you can go off if you want and we'll forget we ever met you," said Dominique. "But you need the food, don't you? You eat like you do."

So much for not acting half-starved. I put my head close to Bane's and Jon's.

"We do need the food," I said softly in English.

"But can we trust them?" snarled Bane.

"If they did get us a full bag of food we could go the best part of a week without risking being recognized again," pointed out Jon. "Get us a quite a lot closer to Zurich, wouldn't it?"

"*If* we can trust them," growled Bane.

A rather circular conversation. I turned to the other three and went back to Esperanto. "Why do you want to help us so much? Don't you know it's dangerous?"

"*I* know it's dangerous," said Louis glumly.

"So do we." Dominique gave him a scornful look. "We'll help all the same."

"We *want* to help," said Juwan.

"But *why?*"

Dominique glanced at Juwan, who looked away.

"We'd a friend—Juwan's best mate, actually—he...rather unexpectedly failed his Sorting. Someone that close gets taken—you can't pretend it's okay anymore." She looked grim, no trace of a laugh on Louis's face now, and Juwan's face was pinched.

"A lie detector would come in handy right now, but I think they're telling the truth," I said to the other two in English.

"She sounds sincere," said Jon.

Bane rubbed a hand through his ragged hair, pushing his now-useless cap off. "I'd say they meant it too, it's just...what's at stake..." He swung around to the others and switched language again.

"Do you three understand what will happen to us if we're caught? Jon and I will just be chopped up while we're asleep—we'll die but it'll be painless. But do you understand what they'll do to Margo? They will kill her piece by piece by piece and she'll feel *everything*. Just stop and think about that before you tell me you *understand!*"

Louis looked sick and Dominique and Juwan remained silent for a moment. My guts had twisted themselves into an icy knot.

"We *do* understand," said Dominique.

"We want to make sure that *doesn't* happen," said Juwan. "Since even we got ID'd in one of the last towns, I think you need our help."

"Um...the dinner's burning," put in Louis.

"Let's talk while we eat." Dominique hurried to the stove. Bane and I exchanged looks.

"Oh, come on! Have one more good meal," said Juwan.

Our stomachs propelled us after him and the conversation was abandoned until our plates were clean.

"Really, we're happy to stick with you. *Think about it*," Juwan insisted, as Bane opened his mouth. "They're not looking for a group of six and you wouldn't even need to come into towns to resupply."

"You realize it's dangerous?" I said.

Dominique made a 'zut' noise. "Not for *us*. If you did get caught, we could act astonished as anything. Three poor gullible New Adults taken in by the wily fugitives."

"I wouldn't underestimate just how annoyed the Euro-Gov are right now."

"I'm not. I read your book. But how could they possibly prove we knew who you were? We might get a black mark by our names but we're prepared to risk *that*, aren't we?"

"Definitely," said Juwan.

"Yeah, I s'pose so," said Louis. "Seeing that...well, Piers and all."

Getting over the shock of our discovery... This might actually be a stroke of luck. Safe in our group of six we could use the hiking trails, making much better time and putting less strain on Jon, and keep well supplied with food—without having to go into towns that were fast becoming death-traps.

I glanced at Bane, who sat frowning.

"You can trust us, seriously," said Dominique. "Look, I'll...tell you a big secret." She glanced at Juwan, who frowned, but after a long moment, jerked a nod. "Juwan and I, after uni...we *are* going to join the Resistance."

Louis's long-suffering mutter of "lunatics" was enough to show he'd no such plans himself. Juwan was still frowning—the need for trust ran both ways now.

"So y'see, you can stick with us," said Dominique firmly.

Bane and I glanced at each other and at Jon.

"Really doesn't sound like such a bad idea," said Jon, in English. Considering those flat trails, his neutrality was impressive.

"Does sound good," I said.

"Yeah," said Bane slowly and looked at the other three again. "Well, probably-maybe, but we're going to sleep on it."

"Fair enough," said Juwan.

"*Fantastique,*" said Dominique.

Louis just shrugged.

Bane and I shared watches again, though we'd already agreed it would be the last time if the foray to Clermont went uneventfully and we stayed with the others. The next morning we were nodding over our coffee and croissants worse than Jon!

Helping Dominique wash dishes woke me up a bit. Louis and Juwan were stuffing their sleeping bags loosely into their three rucksacks to make them look full—backpackers didn't generally leave their tents pitched in the forest.

"Let's have your scentSeal bag," Juwan called to Bane.

Bane chucked it across. Dominique eyed the limp plastiFabric.

"You *were* totally out, then."

"Certainly were," I told her.

"Poor little beggars!"

I flicked suds at her and we both giggled. Well, I voted for staying with them. We could be in Rome before we knew it. Three willing confederates, they must be heaven sent, even if their future career plans were a little...disagreeable.

"Are you *sure?*" I couldn't help saying, when they stood

ready to depart. "I am worried you're underestimating how dangerous helping us could be for you."

"We're sure, Margo," said Dominique.

"Of course," said Juwan, his brow furrowed. "You three...you three make me feel so ashamed."

"*Ashamed?* Of what?"

"Of myself. Especially...especially *you*, Bane. I mean, your friends are sent to the Facility and what do you do? You spring them. *All* of them! Me? My best friend's sent to the Facility and what do *I* do? Carry right on planning my hiking trip. Pah." He spat on the ground.

Bane went red. "Don't put me on a pedestal, Juwan. I always knew Jon would fail Sorting but it was only when they took Margo that it actually occurred to me to get off my rear and do something about it. And I only took them all— only took *Jon*, even—because Margo insisted on it."

"You should've left me behind," said Jon.

"Oh, shut up," said Bane and I in unison.

Juwan just shrugged. "Well, it's a darn sight more than I did for Piers."

"I suppose...it's not too late to...?" I ventured.

Juwan's face tightened even more. "It is. Just before we set off they...he...his parents received...*it.*"

I swallowed. "I'm sorry." What else was there to say? "*Requiescat in Pace.*"

"*Requiescat in Pace,*" murmured Jon.

"Yeah," muttered Juwan. "Well, we'd better go." As an afterthought, he pulled out his phone and handed it to Bane. "Here, catch up on the news while we're away. See you in a bit."

They set off briskly through the forest. We'd set up camp some way from the trail last night, due to the position of a stream in the valley bottom, and what'd seemed a nuisance then was convenient now. No need to move our camp. We could've all packed up our stuff, but the others clearly wanted to leave their tent behind as an indicator of good faith. Not just the tent... Bane whistled as he turned the phone in his hands before placing it very carefully in his pocket.

Jon offered to stay awake, so Bane and I collapsed back

into our sleeping bags and slept for another two oh-so-welcome hours before being chased out of the tent by the heat. At the tent entrance, I paused and reached back to poke Bane, tilting my head towards the outside. He peered over my shoulder for a moment, then grinned.

Jon sat on a fallen bough, his head nodding...nod, nod, nod...jerk, up he sat, just before he would have fallen off entirely. A few seconds later, nod, nod, nod...

"Looks like we got the more comfortable nap."

Jon sat up straight yet again as Bane climbed out of the tent. "I'm awake..." He grinned through a yawn, "...*enough.*"

"I certainly wouldn't be any *more* awake this morning." Bane stretched until his joints cracked.

"Well, I figured the very longest I could sleep in one go would be the time it took me to fall off this log onto the floor, which seemed safe enough."

"Fine, with *your* ears," Bane agreed. A professional hunter would have trouble sneaking up on Jon. Or a poacher, which is what many hunters had become when the Euro-Gov banned all hunting.

I shook out the stove and packed it up, then did the same with the other one. "Hey, there's a leftover croissant. I think it's got your name on it, Jon."

"We can split it in three." But he came over so quickly I shoved the whole thing into his hand.

"Just eat it. Nice fresh food on the way, remember. And they left the last of the old stuff here in case we were hungry."

Jon shrugged and tucked in.

"I'm glad we met those three," I said, as we lounged around like basking lizards. "I like them. Doms and Juwan especially."

"I wasn't starting to fancy our chances," said Jon. "If I'm honest about it."

"I like Juwan and Dominique," said Bane. "I don't care so much for Louis."

"*Well,*" I conceded. "He's prepared to help us, though—for that I can put up with a lot of dumb jokes."

"Yeah, true enough!" Bane took out Juwan's phone. "News, anyone? This thing's got TV."

I sat close beside him so I could see the little screen and Jon came close enough to hear the audio.

There wasn't much happening in the world, though, good or bad. Still, that was a nice change after the last...was it really almost two months? Nothing about us at all, until...

"Prosecutors in the Margaret Verrall escape case announced today..."

"Is that what they're *calling* it?" I interrupted the newscaster. Bane sniggered. Jon was snoring softly: even the novelty hadn't kept him awake for long.

"...that they expect to set a date for the trial of Major Lucas Everington, former Commandant of Greater Salperton EGD Facility, sometime in the next two weeks. The Major is charged with Category One Sedition for his apparent role in masterminding the Greater Salperton Facility escape."

"Rubbish!" I said irritably.

"We all know that," said Bane. "But the man may as well sing their tune and make things easy for himself."

"That's what you'd do, is it?"

"Margo, please don't compare me to an EGD Major!"

"Sorry. But this is plain wrong. And don't say—*he was guarding us*—who cares? They might as well put the whole of society on trial!"

"Well, in the cold light of reason, maybe, but trust me, *no one* is going to care enough to do anything about it. Even good people. *Especially* good people."

I frowned at him. "Say that again?"

"No one's going to help him. He's a dead man and it sounds like he's almost ready to accept it."

I stared at the screen, not hearing the minor news story about a child who'd been lost in the Camargue Swamp-Forest and miraculously—they didn't use that word, of course—found his way home.

"Give me your phone."

"What?"

I stuck my hand in his pocket and pulled it out. Typed rapidly. Took a careful photograph of my face. No roots, no background, check, check. Pressed send. Handed the phone back to him.

"What the heck did you just do?" He scrolled through to

his sent messages. *"DailyNewsCorp* again? 'Major Everington is innocent, of those charges at least. Just so you know. M.V.' What did you send that for?"

"Because it was the right thing to do."

"Oh yes. Ask a stupid question. You don't owe him anything, Margo! The man would've watched you die!"

I rubbed my scarred forehead. How to explain the niggling suspicion that the man had, in his own twisted way, been trying to help me? That he'd been less interested in making me answer his questions than in having an excuse to give me the anesthetic? How to explain my certainty he'd been about to give it to me anyway, until Doctor Richard interfered?

But Bane wouldn't understand. And it didn't matter—it wasn't why I'd sent the text. Bane was right, I didn't owe him anything. But what the EuroGov was doing—convicting a man for a crime he didn't commit—was wrong, plain and simple. "All that is required for evil to triumph is for good people to do nothing."

Bane opened his mouth, looking exasperated—closed it again. "Well, *yeah. But.*"

"But what? But we should only oppose evil when it's done to people we give a fig about?"

"That's not what I meant."

"Yes, it is."

"Fine. It is. I'm an uncharitable pagan. I hope you can live with it."

I smiled. "I've managed so far."

When Jon eventually woke up, Bane took great delight in reading him the sent message and denouncing my insanity. Jon found it all a little less exciting than Bane—but he didn't send a text of his own.

When Bane had exhausted the subject—and us—Jon and I started on one of our joint Rosaries, lying on our stomachs in the sun and tapping our fingertips together to keep count. Bane lay with his head in the small of my back, listening and staring at the blue sky.

"...Sancta Maria, Mater Dei, ora pro nobis peccatoribus, nunc et in hora mortis nostrae. Amen...

"Ave Maria, gratia plena, Dominus tecum..." Jon broke off, listening. "I think they're coming back."

Indecision flitted across Bane's face. Insult them by hiding in the woods until we were sure they were alone or stay where we were, better for our burgeoning friendship but very unhealthy if we'd misjudged them?

"How many?" I asked Jon.

"Only sounds like three."

"Well, at least sit up in case we have to move in a hurry, Jon!" said Bane.

"Fine." Jon pushed himself up, sighing. "But it sounds like them."

It was.

"Piece of cake," said Juwan imperturbably. "Who'd look twice at us?"

"Wonderful," sighed Jon, sinking down on a log when we stopped to make camp that evening. "Flat...straight...lovely."

"I think Jonathan's in *luuuve* with the hiking trail," sniggered Louis.

"I think *I'd* be if I couldn't see," said Doms.

"I've got something to show you, actually," said Juwan, once the food was cooking on the stoves. He fished out his phone, thumbed at it for a moment, then passed it to me.

It was a saved webpage from about ten days ago. The phone had internet too? The *FrenchDaily.*

MARGARET: ENJOYING NEW ADULTHOOD, THANKS.

Following our article last week, 'ARE YOU ENJOYING NEW ADULTHOOD, MARGARET V.?' *Daily News-Corp* received this shock text message from Margaret Verrall herself: 'We are all enjoying New Adult life very much. Thank you for asking. M.V.'

The whereabouts of Margaret Verrall and sixty-seven others who escaped from Greater Salperton EGD Facility at the beginning of July remain unknown. But it seems safe to

say they are not only alive and | top daily!
well, but reading the EuroBloc's |

<u>N.B.</u>
<u>If you have any information pertaining to the</u>
<u>whereabouts of any of the following you must phone 112</u>
<u>immediately:</u>

Margaret Verrall (convicted for *Personal Practice of Superstition* and *Inciting and Promoting Superstition in the General Population* and also wanted on charges of *Sedition: Category 1* and *Unauthorized Departure from an EGD Facility*)

Blake (Bane) Marsden (wanted on charges of *Murder: 1ˢᵗ Degree, Sedition: Category 1* and *Destruction of Public Property*)

Jonathan Revan (wanted on charges of *Personal Practice of Superstition* and *Unauthorized Departure from an EGD Facility*)

Any other reAssignee illegally absent from their Facility. Lists of names with photographs available from all police stations.

AIDING AND ABETTING THE AFOREMENTIONED IN ANY
WAY WILL RESULT IN A CHARGE OF
SEDITION: CATEGORY 1.

Bane looked over my shoulder as I read it aloud. The close-up I'd taken of my face was at the top of the page, the same photos shown on the highway sign beside each of our names at the bottom.

"Didn't know if they'd got it or not," I said. "Did they get in trouble?"

"Not that we heard," said Doms.

"Bet they did," muttered Bane, "the censorship may go in cycles—tightening up to hide stuff, then loosening off when the censorship itself becomes the scandal—and we *are* in a fairly relaxed period, but not *that* relaxed. Not for *this*."

He went back to looking sober-faced.

"You really knifed that dismantler?" asked Juwan.

Bane nodded.

"Good for you."

"I was protecting Margo," said Bane sharply.

Juwan spread his hands. "Fair enough. *Zut!* I'd do it for Doms!"

He broke off suddenly—hesitated—then pulled Doms into his arms. Rather defensively.

She planted a kiss on his lips. "I'd do it for you, too." But she shot us an anxious look as well. Louis rolled his eyes.

So that was it! Oh dear, I was staring. Couldn't help it. Something about their black and white cheeks, pressed together—strange and wonderful all at once. I'd never seen two people from different genetic groups...*together*. They'd felt it was a bigger secret than the Resistance...well, some people could be awful. I was still staring... Quickly I mustered a smile. Doms's face brightened and Juwan relaxed slightly.

"Are you two *really* serious about the Resistance?" Bane asked. Changing the subject to show exactly how much he wasn't bothered?

"*Certainment,*" said Juwan.

"Why go to university, then?" said Jon dryly. From his fading expression of surprise he'd understood what had just been revealed. "What is it, a sixty percent chance you'll be dead before you're thirty?"

"That's what *I* keep telling them," said Louis.

"Like the odds for the Underground are much better?" sniffed Doms.

"A bit better than that, actually," I put in. "Forty percent chance of making it to fifty."

Doms waved a hand dismissively. "You really need to ask why *I'm* going to university first?"

"I can count on one hand how many times I've been out with the Resistance and I can wire up a basic explosive device," said Bane. "You don't need a degree."

"Not if you've *got* explosives," said Doms smugly. "If you haven't—you need me."

"Oh great," muttered Jon. "Unlimited explosives for the

Resistance! What a nice thought."

Doms shot him a hard look, and Juwan jumped in, "Well, *I* plan to keep a clean record for as long as possible—"

"Oh yeah?" said Louis glumly.

Juwan ignored him. "...If the guys who get caught had better legal representation, they'd get away with it more often."

"Sounds good," said Bane, "until I think what you're setting them loose to do more of. Do you seriously want to do that sort of thing yourselves?"

"*On ne fait pas d'omelette sans casser des œufs,*" said Doms. "You can't make an omelet without cracking eggs, can you?"

"Yeah," said Bane, "but even leaving aside whether you really want to kill your fellow Frenchmen just for taking work with the major employer that's the EuroGov. The French Resistance are the most vicious in Europe—no offence, it's just a fact. Some of the French cells are putting land mines around the ruined villages out here in the forest where they hide out, for pity's sake! *Anyone* can step on them. Do you agree with *that?*"

Doms didn't meet his eyes this time. "Not everything's right at the moment, we *do* get that."

"We want to help *change* that," said Juwan. "There's got to be a better balance between fighting the EuroGov and the mindless bloodshed that goes on at the moment."

"But the change has to come from the inside," said Doms. "You've got to *join* and *then* you've got to *earn* respect and only *then* will your opinion be heard."

Bane shook his head. "You're dead wrong. You'll go in with a sense of right and wrong, but they'll make you do things to prove your loyalty. Each a little worse than the last. And by the time you have that 'respect' and could actually do anything, you'll have convinced yourself they were right all along, because it's the only way you'll be able to live with what you've done—all the brains on walls and orphaned children. The only way you'll change them is by *not joining.*"

"How will *that* help!" protested Doms, looking slightly shaken by Bane's too-vivid picture of the Resistance's induction process.

"Because if no one joins, they'll *have* to change to get new recruits. That's your power over them now—but once you join, you're in *their* power."

"I thought you were next thing to Resistance," said Juwan, eyes narrowed. "That's the way the press paint it."

"Yeah, well, I did come pretty close," said Bane levelly. "But I thought better of it, somewhat in the nick of time. You know you can't get far in and still back out. *Especially* here in the French department. Bear that in mind too."

"Well, we've got three years to think about it," said Juwan. "But how else do you fight the EuroGov?"

"They've got a monopoly on active opposition, all right," I conceded.

"That's what they want you to think," said Bane. "What's to stop you doing something on your own?"

"Well, in this Department, *the Resistance,*" said Juwan. "Non-affiliated groups are subsumed or...dissolved. In a very permanent way."

"Have you even been out with the Young Resistance— the, what's it? *Résistance Juvénile?*"

They both shook their heads. "No, we've been keeping our noses clean. Didn't want to incriminate our parents."

"And, to be honest, we've got a *lot* more interested in joining in the last six months," admitted Doms.

Since Piers?

Bane sighed—feeling rather old? "Well, for pity's sake think about it, right?"

"We've got three years," said Juwan again. "We're hardly going to make a rushed decision."

"We're not joining the Underground, that's for sure," said Doms. "No offence. You don't even fight the EuroGov—you just really cheese them off."

I shrugged and spread my hands.

"Actually," said Bane unexpectedly, "I think the Underground fight the EuroGov just by existing."

"Depends how you define *fight,* I suppose," said Juwan wryly.

"So it is you and *Bane,* then, not you and Jon?" asked Doms the following evening, after watching Bane kiss me before heading off with Juwan to collect firewood.

"Oh yes," I tried not to blush. "Definitely me and Bane." Jon was asleep on the grass and Louis had gone off in a huff again, so it was just us two girls...women. "Jon and I just keep having to pretend. Well, you said you read the book."

"Yeah, I knew it was supposed to be you and Bane. That's one thing that was throwing me off when we first met. Because," she glanced at Jon and frowned slightly, "it doesn't seem so like *he's* pretending."

My cheeks burned unstoppably, but I wasn't going into that. "So you did suspect, then? Even in Vouziers?"

"Well, it did *cross* my mind, but I thought I was letting my imagination run away with me. 'Cause your hair was wrong and what I could see of your face under the sunglasses was too thin, to say nothing of you being with the wrong guy."

"So why the French when we were passing the policemen?"

"Oh, I *was très très* certain you didn't want to scan your IDs! I'm not stupid! I just thought, well, *pourquoi pas*, let's get them past. Being the good little EuroCitizen that I am!" She laughed bleakly.

"Well, thank you. We really appreciate...well, everything, y'know."

She waved this away. "What's the saying? The enemy of my enemy is my friend? That's one the Resistance could remember a bit more when it comes to the Underground."

"I think they feel anyone who objects to them killing whoever they feel like is an enemy too."

Doms shrugged. "Well, I'm not Resistance yet. Friends, then?" She stuck out her hand.

I took it. "Friends."

She shook solemnly, then kissed me on both cheeks, French-style. It *was* nice to have her around—I loved Bane and Jon to bits, but they were both guys.

But there was something I needed to say. "Please think about what Bane said. He knows what he's talking about. They tricked him into something he's always going to regret. But he was brave enough to do the right thing and get out, though it means living with that guilt, rather than diving further in and trying to bury it—which was what they wanted." Doms' face had gone rather closed again. "Sorry, not meaning to nag."

"Relax. Bane *has* given us something to think about, I admit. But there's so *few* options. Would staying *out* really help? Feels like it would just achieve *nothing.*"

"Might save you from having to choose between your life and your conscience somewhere down the line."

"Yeah, but...perhaps some people standing up to them on the inside *is* what's needed. Except they've got such a fatal way of dealing with opposition—inside or outside... I don't know. I s'pose I'm glad we've got so long to think about it."

"Yeah, I can see that."

She grinned, brightening. "This feels right, though—helping you guys. We'll get you all the way to Rome, see if we don't!"

I grinned back, then asked, "So how did you and Juwan...you know?"

She lit up even more. "He moved to our town from Paris when we were twelve. I thought he was the most handsome guy I'd ever seen the first time I set eyes on him. Didn't tell *anyone,* of course. For several years I was kind of afraid to get to know him. I s'pose...you see why?"

I nodded. Liking someone you knew you could never have—if you'd even the smallest scrap of self-preservation, you'd try to keep your distance.

"Anyway, he hit it off really well with Piers, and they became best mates. I knew Piers too, so I hung out with Juwan now and then—tried really hard to think of him as a friend, y'know? When I was fifteen it started to get harder, somehow. I even decided I wasn't going to be around him any more *at all*—but I s'pose it was too late. We saw more and more of each other, like neither of us could help it. And then one day when we were seventeen there was just this moment when I couldn't bear it any more. And I kissed him. And he kissed me." Her smile had gone rather dreamy at the memory.

"And then he was like, are you sure, are you sure, for about three months. And even after that he absolutely insisted we keep it secret. He couldn't bear how people would treat me. I wasn't too thrilled at the thought of how they'd treat him either. Piers and Louis know—knew—and my best friend, but that's it in the whole world, other than you and Bane and Jon now."

"Well, I'm happy for you. Though I just wish...the world was different." It was bad enough the way some people treated *Bane*, his parents included, just because his skin was a little too dark for British C.

She nodded silently, but after a few moments, she burst out, "If Juwan and I stay *out* of the Resistance, what sort of life will we have? Well, we know, don't we!"

I knew *of* such matches, even if I'd never actually seen one. Because they were unable to register with one another, when they turned thirty, the Stable Population Committee would match them with another unregistered person from their local area and demand they produce the regulation two children. They could split the kids with their assigned breeding partner, taking one each, so they'd end up with two to raise—neither the child of both of them. Wherever they went as a family, people would stare, mutter, perhaps even spit at them. The children would endure a waking nightmare at school—one black, one white, claiming to be siblings—an irresistible target for bullies. But...

"The Resistance hate the EuroGov, but that doesn't mean they're not just as bigoted as some of the rest of the population. I wouldn't assume you'll have an easier time of it with them."

"But the whole thing about no Genetic Mixes was started by the EGD! It's a major EuroGov policy! Before it started people registered with whoever they wanted, like they still do in Africa, and it did no harm at all. Surely the Resistance wouldn't care!"

"Bullies just want targets, and I think there are a lot of bullies in the Resistance. Why don't you just go to Africa? You've passed Sorting. You're free to travel."

"Because it's not right!" Doms's eyes were fierce, but they filled with tears as she went on, "Don't you understand what we'd have to give up? My family would never speak to me again. And Juwan should inherit the family business one day, but they'd cut him off if they knew about us. And...*it shouldn't be like this!"*

"Won't they do that anyway if you...live together...here? Sooner or later, if you want to raise children...you'll have to go public."

"Juwan doesn't even want children any more. Not after... Piers."

"If he stays here, they won't give him a choice, will they?"

"I don't know." Doms' face went bleak. "I'm rather afraid... I'm afraid he thinks if we join the Resistance...by the time we're thirty we'll be compromised and living in a safe house anyway, so it won't come up. Which...doesn't seem like a terribly good solution to me."

"Heavens, no! Well, it's none of my business, but for what it's worth, I vote for Africa. You can live a long happy life as a normal family, without making a mess of your conscience."

"Not by killing, maybe," said Doms. "But I'm not sure what it will do to my conscience to sally off to Africa and leave *this* wrong unfought."

I didn't have an answer to that.

Another day brought us all to Commercy, where we needed to resupply. The others hadn't dared fill the food bags too full at Clermont in case someone remarked on it.

"Not like we need to eat old food, anyway," said Doms cheerfully as she put her sleeping bag in her pack. "We might as well enjoy fresh as often as we can."

"You always look fresh to me," said Juwan, pulling her to him for a lengthy kiss.

Louis stuffed the last of his sleeping bag into his own pack with unnecessary vigor. Not just their parents who wanted him and Doms together, was it?

With murmurs of *"Je t'aime,"* Juwan and Doms broke apart again.

"Any special requests?" asked Doms.

"Yeah, *don't get caught,"* said Bane.

"Relax, no one is going to suspect us of anything."

"Our IDs are clean, and we won't buy too much. It'll be fine," said Juwan. "See you in a couple of hours. Oh, here, you can borrow this again."

He gave his phone to Bane, they shouldered their packs and headed off.

I relieved Bane of the phone and began to scan through the last few copies of *FrenchDaily*. Nothing.

"Y'know, I *really* don't think they're going to print it," said Bane.

"They probably got their knuckles rapped by the Euro-Gov over the last one," added Jon.

I resisted the temptation to throw down the phone in disgust and simply handed it back to Bane.

"It's not going to help, anyway," said Jon.

"I know," I sighed. "It'd just be nice if *something* undermined their crooked little trial."

Sometime after noon, I stuffed my bookReader back in my pocket and checked my watch. I couldn't concentrate. "So how far is it to Commercy from here, Bane?" I tried to speak casually, but the others had been gone four hours, which was an hour longer than last time.

Bane pulled out his phone and glanced at the screen, though he probably didn't need to. He had the map up already; he was getting worried too. "Less than five kilo-meters."

"Where are they?"

"It was a harder walk to Clermont," Bane admitted.

"So where are they?" Jon echoed me.

"Perhaps they're just more relaxed this time," I suggested. "Taking their time more."

"Perhaps," said Bane. Still frowning. After a moment he double-checked something on his phone—probably the time, because when he pulled out Juwan's phone he went straight to the TV—he chose the local channel.

A newsreader was talking. "And the top story—shocking events unfolded this morning in the town of Commercy in the French Department, resulting in two New Adults arrested..."

"*Oh no,*" I breathed, gripping Bane's arm and moving to get a better view of the screen.

"...and a third held on suspicion of aiding and abetting the fugitive Margaret Verrall and her companions. None of the three have yet been named. The unfolding drama was captured on a shop CCTV camera."

Footage of a street took the newsreader's place, though her voice continued. "We see the three backpackers shopping at street stalls in Commercy a little before ten AM."

Doms, Juwan and Louis, clearly recognizable.

"We see one go to another stall, then when his two companions aren't looking, he approaches a nearby policeman."

Louis. Louis approaching the policeman. Speaking to him rapidly. Juwan and Doms suddenly missing him and turning.

"He speaks to the policeman for only a moment before events take a shocking turn..."

Juwan snatches something solid-looking from beside the stall, crosses the street in practically a single bound and brings it down with devastating force on Louis's head. Louis falls in a heap like a dropped doll, and Juwan spins around and bolts. The policeman jerks a pistol from his holster and fires. Juwan falls....

My fingers bit into Bane's arm. "NonLee?"

"Can't see, shss, listen."

"The policeman drops the attacker with his nonLethal..."

"Thank God!" I managed to relax my grip on Bane a little.

"...and looks for the third New Adult, but she's disappeared. We now fast forward to fifteen minutes later."

The footage sped up, showing two policemen running to and fro, doing first aid on Louis, then standing around the fallen bodies waiting...finally a police van and an ambulance arrived and the footage slowed to real time again as both bodies were lifted onto gurneys, and Louis was wheeled into the ambulance.

BANG!

An explosion rocked the vehicles on their wheels, people screamed and dived for cover, though there was no one near the spot from which the flash and the smoke were drifting. The policemen converged, nonLees in hands and a figure darted out behind them, grabbed Juwan's gurney and started to push it frantically down the nearest alley. The policemen turned, saw her, their guns came up, she fell, the gurney rattled on a few paces and came to a halt. A third gurney was brought, and Doms was slid into the police van along with Juwan.

"Oh, blast," I whispered again, as the bulletin ended. "Oh blast, oh blast, oh blast..."

"That sums it up," said Jon, in a thin voice.

"Is there any way we can help them?"

Bane groaned and stuck his head in his hands. "Margo, no! It's not *possible*. They're *gone!* This happened hours ago—they're already at some Facility: we don't even know which one, and how many months planning did it take to get you lot out? Out of a Standard Facility, not a Detention Facility? With Resistance help. Please, be serious!"

Jon frowned but didn't disagree with Bane's analysis.

"The only thing we can possibly do for them," Bane went on, "is get where we're going and then see if we can arrange help. Professional help."

"You've got the wrong secret organization, Bane," said Jon. "The Underground doesn't keep trained extraction teams."

"Well, perhaps it should!"

"You'll have to start one." Bane gave me such an intent look I added, bemused, "*Joke.*"

"Was it?" he said thoughtfully. "Anyway, we need to leave, *now—*"

Jon froze. Listening. Bane's hand flew to the phone, killing the sound. I fell silent as well, not that I expected to hear something Jon had to listen so intently for.

"Dogs," said Jon. "Coming this way."

"Dogs? Walkers?" I asked.

"Coming very fast if they are."

Bane was on his feet so fast I missed it. "Pack up." He shoved the pile of old food onto the foil blanket on which we sat and bundled it up and into his pack almost before we'd moved off it. We'd put our sleeping bags away already, *laudate Dominum*—I chucked him the stove, shrugged into my precious coat and went to help Jon. Thermals, sachets, check, check.

By the time we were done Bane had his jacket on and was fastening his rucksack. I zipped up the tent; paused as loud barking reached my ears. Several dogs. Approaching fast.

Jon hauled out tent pegs frantically, but Bane sprang to his rucksack and snapped it shut as well. "Leave it, if—" More barking. Coming *very* fast. "We can come back for it, come on, let's go, *move*."

Practically flinging the pack onto Jon's back, he towed him to where I waited by the stream, then dragged us both down the bank. The water almost reached my knees and may have been cold—I didn't notice, splashing after him with all speed.

Jon sloshed along in silence as well, and we all clung to each other for balance as our feet slid and slipped on a stony stream bed slimy as oiled glass. The stream wound swiftly into the forest, and the campsite was soon out of sight—and more importantly, we from it. Before long Bane paused. A rocky outcrop plummeted down to the stream on the right.

"Think we can see the campsite from there?" I said.

"I should think. Let's take a look."

We skidded and lurched our way up to the rock and climbed up onto the lowest ledge. We'd all read—or been read—the survival books, so right now rock made us think— shows no tracks, retains scent less than soil.

"Jon, can you stay here with the packs?"

No time to pretend he could do everything we could do and as quickly.

Bane and I started to climb even as Jon nodded, and soon we peered over the top of the outcrop, panting.

"Perfect," breathed Bane. We could see the tents by the stream, most of the clearing unobscured by trees. He rested his phone on the rock, keeping one hand cupped over the top of it to avoid sun glint, and zoomed in. Still deserted. Had we had time to take the tent? The dogs might not even be coming there. Some people did run with their dogs, didn't they?

You wish, Margo. I do wish, Lord, I really do. But after that news bulletin I don't really hope...

Then my hand closed around Bane's sleeve as three large dogs bounded into the clearing, noses to the ground, each

towing a uniformed soldier behind them.
    We'd not had time for the tent.

8

COLD BUT SATISFIED

"Curse it!" hissed Bane.

"What were you expecting? Chihuahuas?" My voice shook.

"I know." More rifle-carrying soldiers jogged into the clearing behind the nothing-like-Chihuahuas and their handlers. "Come on, let's get away from here. A long way away from here."

I fumbled my way back down to Jon, feeling half-numb with shock and fear.

"What is it?" asked Jon.

"Soldiers."

"Worse, scent hounds," said Bane tersely. "Juwan must've silenced Louis before he could give our location—my God, do we owe him for that! Come on, back into the stream."

Jon's face paled slightly, but showed no surprise, so pausing only long enough to check all the rucksacks were fastened properly, we set off as fast as we could, which wasn't very. The water was getting deeper. At least the packs were waterproof.

"Note to self," Bane muttered savagely after we'd gone some way. "Never trust someone whose first words are about your *value*, whose next are about how dangerous you are to *their* health, who looks like they're about to *throw up* when dismantling is mentioned, who can muster no more enthusiasm than '*I suppose so*' and who doesn't answer when asked if they're *sure.*"

Greedy and scared. Not a good combination.

"I hope Doms and Juwan have...have a chance," I muttered.

Bane was silent for a moment. "We *can't* do anything."

It was almost unbearable to just travel on and leave them to whatever fate awaited them, but Bane was right.

We'd three pocket knives and no backup or local knowledge whatsoever. Right now, we'd be lucky to get away ourselves.

"I hope to goodness Louis realized they'd be in danger and was careful exactly what he said."

"Wouldn't be surprised if he was trying to put it all on Juwan," said Bane. "Like that will wash. Come on, less talking and more splish-sploshing, huh?"

We splish-sploshed on until eventually the stream began to curve.

"Whoa a minute," said Bane, just as my feet slid in different directions for about the tenth time, plunging me up to my neck in icy water. I could feel how cold it was now despite the warm sun—either the adrenalin was wearing off or I was getting chilled. Probably both.

Bane helped Jon haul me back onto my feet and pulled out his omniPhone. After consulting this for a few moments he jerked his head onwards. "Come on."

"But it's turning to the southwest. We need to keep going southeast." I'd looked at the map too.

"No," said Bane, grim again. "Not now."

"They knew we were heading for Zurich, didn't they?" groaned Jon.

"Yeah," said Bane. "We'd be mad not to assume the EuroGov know that's where we're heading—or will do soon."

"So which way?"

"Southwest for fifty kilometers to get us out of their likely search area, then southeast for the passes beyond Lausanne. Not actually too much further, since whichever way we go, we have to make a bit of a dog-leg over the Alps into Italy. Huh, speaking of dogs, come on."

The stream got deeper and deeper still and soon we were half-swimming. The current buffeted us, making it twice as hard to keep our footing, until we were all soaked from head to foot.

"Wait a moment." A fallen bough lay right by the bank. "Let's be smart about this. We'll get a lot further, a lot faster, if we go with the current, won't we?"

Bane saw what I was looking at. "Brilliant!"

We got the log poised to fall, without touching the bank and leaving our scent—then edged Jon back so he wouldn't get hit.

Splash!

Soaked yet again. Ah well. We fitted ourselves between branches, Bane on one side and Jon and I on the other to balance it, then took our feet off the ground, letting ourselves float.

"Ah, that's more like it," sighed Jon, resting his head on his folded arms as the log drifted along, turning sedately in the water.

"Tell me about it," I murmured. Wading was decidedly hard work.

"I hate to mention this," said Jon, after a while, "but what will we eat in the future?"

"Carry on the begging routine?" I said doubtfully.

"You'd dare?" snorted Bane.

"No... The whole area's going to be on red alert. And I really thought we could trust those three. Even Louis. If we couldn't trust *him*...I don't want to go near anyone. But Jon's right, what *are* we going to eat?"

Bane grimaced. "We're heading into a much wilder area. Fewer towns and therefore fewer hiking trails. Not many opportunities to beg food anyway. The isolation's good for evading the EuroGov but as for what we're going to eat...we'll have to go a bit slower and spend more time practicing those hunting and gathering skills."

My heart sank. Slower. What about those Alpine passes? And *what* hunting and gathering skills?

We floated on in a bleak silence. Lunchtime came and went without any of us suggesting we broach our meager food supply. Our stomachs rumbled. The afternoon wore on, and on we drifted. The banks remained forested and non-threatening as we struggled not to doze. Nothing at all happened except, sun or no sun, our teeth began to chatter.

"Is anyone else frozen to an icicle?" asked Jon.

"Just slightly," I shivered. "Perhaps we should get out now. We must've come kilometers; they'll never bring the dogs this far."

"We've come tens of kilometers." Bane sounded cold but satisfied. He cupped his phone carefully in a shaking hand to check our position yet again. "We're going far, far, faster than we could walk, so I vote we stay afloat as long as the river is going the right way."

"Heard of something called hypothermia?" said Jon.

"Oh, stop whining. D'you really want to walk all those extra kilometers?"

"Hmm." Jon said no more.

"WAKE UP, YOU TWO!"

My eyes flew open. After the threat of rapids finally forced us to disembark, Bane had driven us mercilessly to our feet—my legs feeling precisely like jelly, so cold I could barely feel them and wholly unable to support my weight—and got us walking. But despite the need to get our blood moving, we hadn't gone far. Couldn't go far. We'd stopped in the first well-sheltered hollow we found and after putting on my dry thermals to collect wood, I'd slipped into the sleeping bag to try to warm up a bit while Bane got the stove lit. I must've nodded off.

"Calm down, Bane, the way we're shivering, I don't think hypothermia is imminent," I mumbled.

"Neither do I, but the food's ready."

"Huh?"

I rolled over and focused as he placed a steaming pan and the three fork-spoons down by my head and slithered in beside me. On Bane's orders, Jon had zipped all three sleeping bags together to make one giant one, wrapped in foil blankets, so we could share what little heat we had left. Jon and I must've actually warmed up a little, because Bane felt ice-cold.

Jon hadn't stirred. I prodded him with my elbow. "Jon, food." Jon carried on snoring. I shook his shoulder. No reaction.

"Try howling like a wolf." Bane's flash of weary humor drew an equally weary smile from me.

"Heard that," muttered Jon, surfacing at last.

A real wolf howled, somewhere not a million kilometers away. I opened my eyes. Moonlight bathed the hollow; it was deep night. I'd gone and nodded off again! I still felt chilled; inside, in my core. Bane was a lukewarm shape on my right, Jon a shivering weight against my side.

How late was it? Would the rocks I'd put to warm in the stove pan still be hot? Easing free of Jon, I began to slide out to check. Bane woke with a start and produced something that glinted in the moonlight. "Who's there?"

"*Me*. Relax."

"Margo. What're you doing?"

"Checking those rocks. Jon's still freezing and I don't feel too warm myself."

"Oh. Me neither." Something less sharp and deadly appeared in his hand, glowing. "Hmm. We've only been asleep a couple of hours. The stove will have only just gone out."

I felt the pan and drew my hand back quickly. "Yep, still hot."

Plundering the rucksacks for our spare socks, I filled each one with rocks, and Bane arranged them around the edges of the bag, where we were least likely to roll against them. Several more wolves took up the song as I climbed back in and, of course, that's when Jon woke up.

"Gah, *wolves!* I take back my complaints about the smelly tent, Bane. *Any* tent's better than none, even if it is just psychological." But his shudder had nothing to do with the wolves. "Ugh, I'm so cold!"

"Careful, we've got those hot stones in here now, around the edges. Hopefully that'll warm us up." The fantasy of another pan of warm soup materialized in my brain and almost escaped via my tongue—I swallowed it back. Hot rocks were pretty much unlimited: soup wasn't.

Jon eased away from me as though suddenly conscious of the absence of the usual sleeping bags—or even blanket—between us, so I rolled over and snuggled up to Bane. Bane's fingers found my cheeks, traced their way to the nape of my neck and drew my mouth to his. Yep, he was definitely the warmest. Though far from thawed out, and only fortified by a scant few hours sleep, I shared his relief. We'd escaped—as far as we could tell.

We stole a couple more kisses. We were surely far too tired to fall into great temptation, quite apart from...

"Do you two mind?" protested Jon.

"Why is this the *one* time you're *not* asleep?" complained

Bane.

"I'd blame the wolves, but actually I can't sleep for the smacking sounds."

"Well, for your information this is entirely medicinal— just warming her up, y'know?"

"Need any help with that?"

Thud. A gasp of pain from Jon. I caught Bane's arm as he lunged over me again.

"Bane, knock it off."

"I'll knock his *block* off!"

"Enough, you hit him already and, yes, he asked for it." I couldn't keep the anger from my voice, not when Bane had been so, so forbearing about the sleeping arrangements and everything. "If you don't like it, Jon, keep your stupid remarks to yourself!"

Silence.

"Jon? Did he knock you out?"

"No." Jon sounded subdued. "Some sense into me, maybe. I was just...thinking better of my...*stupid remark.* Sorry."

It wasn't clear if the apology was for me or Bane or both, but after a moment Bane said stiffly, "Did I hurt you?"

Jon snorted. "On the list of things likely to kill me at the moment, the bruise is fairly low."

"Good. *Night,* then."

"Night," muttered Jon.

"Night," I said.

Ahh-wooooo, said the wolves. *Good night, helpless little humans.*

9

A DISTINCT LACK OF BUTTERED PARSNIPS

Bane and I woke with sniffles and Jon something more like a full-blown cold. It would be him, he'd been the most tired before. We slept a couple of extra hours out of consideration for our general exhaustion, then breakfasted on some of the perishable food, which was doing just that: perishing. Bane bolted his portion and went back to going through his stuff, over and over.

"It's not there, Bane," I said finally, as he made to take everything out yet again.

"*Gah!*" He snapped his rucksack shut again. "How could I lose something that valuable? To say nothing of useful!"

When we'd tried to check the news first thing, Juwan's phone had been nowhere to be found.

"You probably dropped it when we heard the dogs. S'pect you pocketed *your* phone automatically, but you're not used to having a second one, are you? *Yours* is actually much more valuable to us, anyway, because it's untraceable and has trig mapping."

"I know, I know. It's just...well, it wasn't even mine, was it?" Not that Juwan was likely to be needing it, unfortunately. "Come on." He heaved his backpack on at last. "We've got to get away from that river. The EuroGov aren't totally stupid, y'know. Okay, they probably won't come this far, but we don't want to take the chance."

Jon's "just a cold" lasted for several days, but he trekked stubbornly on, refusing the rest day Bane eventually offered him.

"Unless we can do better than this," Jon said, as yet again we had to supplement our day's gathering with a sachet, "we've simply got to get where we're going as fast as we can."

But the hungrier we got, the slower we went. A single sachet served as soup for breakfast and we had no lunch. We set snares every night, and caught nothing. Nettles were the only supposedly edible thing we could count on seeing—every forest clearing had flourishing patches.

"Told you boiling got rid of the stings," I said, the first time we resorted to eating them—and cooked seconds at their eager request.

Nettles became the mainstay of our morning and evening stew, quite often the only component. They didn't taste bad—a bit like beans—but talk about monotonous! Sometimes we found dandelions, and occasionally wild garlic, which we couldn't eat in any quantity, but the taste made a nice change. Too early for acorns and most nuts, but once or twice we found wild fruit trees with ripe fruit—we filled up the scentSeal food bag, then loaded our packs as well. No choice now. Starvation was a far nearer danger than bears.

"I am never going to look at a nettle in the same way again," I said, as I munched our breakfast stew. Bane had put aside the bare minimum of sachets we'd need for crossing the Alps, but all the others were gone now.

"I'm never going to be *able* to look at a nettle again!" But Bane dipped his spoon into the pan with alacrity and passed it on to me.

"I've never had to look at a nettle," said Jon faintly, "so I don't know what I'm missing."

Bane and I glanced at each other. The light-hearted remark was so welcome. Jon had gone very quiet again. He was pale and thin and had energy for nothing other than walking and sniffing for food. Every time we successfully identified an edible plant, we'd give it to him to smell. He'd found several more patches of edible mushrooms, and a number of times his pausing and making me look more closely around an area had resulted in a find.

Light-hearted remark or not, he lay down on the moss that evening without even taking off his backpack, and went to sleep as though he'd been clubbed over the head. I spread out the sleeping bags myself and wrapped them in the foil blankets, then started shredding nettles into the pan with leaden hands.

"Bane," I said, when he came back with the wood, "where did you put the sachets?"

"We *can't*. We won't have enough..."

"Bane, we've no choice! There's nothing in these nettles—okay, five percent protein or whatever, better than most plants, blah, blah, but it's nothing compared to meat! They fool our brains, but they can't fool our bodies. What's the point worrying about what we'll eat going over the Alps if we're not going to get there? Hand one over!"

Bane pulled a face, but rummaged in the bottom of his main compartment, and came out with one of the little foil packets. My stomach ached dully. I could've ripped the packet open and eaten it raw and dehydrated and to the devil with the other two.

"Found something?" Bane eyed my handful of leaves hopefully.

I scowled at my bookReader. Put my hand over the bottom of the screen and showed it to him. "Is it a match? Take a good look."

Bane took a leaf and held it by the screen, comparing. "Yep."

I drew the Reader away momentarily—held it out again. "Sure? Look closely."

Bane rolled his eyes and checked again. "Yes, it's definitely the same plant."

I groaned.

"What? Can't we eat them?"

"Well, you just confidently identified them as one plant, which is edible, and also as another, which is poisonous, so *no.*"I flung the leaves into the nearest bush.

A pheasant exploded from underneath.

"Grab it!" I yelled.

"Get it!" Bane blocked the bird's path. It swung around and hurled itself into the air, heading for Jon. He lunged for the flapping thing—it swerved and pretty much flew into my chest. My desperate hands closed around it.

"Meat!" said Bane.

"Protein!" I licked my lips. A while since even the cutest

and furriest animal had looked like anything else. All the same...

The pheasant scrabbled frantically, head bobbing from side to side.

"Uh, get your knife, Bane, hurry up."

"Oh...yeah...uh..."

If a dangerous human came into sight, Bane would've had that knife in his hand in about two seconds, but now he just groped around in his jacket, muttering. The pheasant went on struggling, eyeing us with wide, panic-stricken eyes.

"Oh, for pity's sake!" The books were pretty clear. Turning the bird around carefully so as not to lose it—I'd have sat down and wept!—I gripped it round the neck; twisted and yanked as hard as I could. "Ugh!" The bird's head hung by a few folds of skin, its feet jerking spasmodically. "I think I overdid it!"

"Margo! I'd have done that!"

"Yeah, in about half an hour when you found your knife! Poor thing was frightened out of its tiny mind. Better to be quick about it."

Bane bit his lip. "Sorry."

"Don't apologize to *me*. Shall we eat it now or keep it for later?"

"We'd better keep it for later."

"Huh?" Jon started as though he'd been dozing standing up.

"Pheasant," I said.

"Oh... I didn't dream that, then... We never catch anything."

True. We'd scrambled after a number of rabbits and pheasants over the last few weeks—increasingly frantically as hunger began to bite. All the others had shown us a clean pair of heels.

"This is the last sachet," said Bane, how many days later? I was seriously losing track. "Do we have it now, or keep it?"

The last one. We'd been making do with a sachet every other day, but... "Perhaps we'd better save it."

Bane plunged it back into his backpack.

"I keep thinking how one of us might get food in a town,"

I said, starting to shred nettles.

"The question's moot. No towns around here."

"None?"

"None. This region's practically deserted. We'd have to walk so many kilometers out of our way that we'd hardly gain anything even if we got food."

"Oh. Bother. Pass me Jon's bag."

Bane handed me the scentSeal bag. Almost empty. Jon just stumbled along between us like a zombie now.

"Let's see the map, Bane," I said, once the stew was cooked and the last scrap consumed. "That might cheer us all up."

"Doubt it."

"Oh. Never mind."

Cold struck up through the smooth tiles, seeping into bones and flesh. Sometimes heat filled the tiny cell, thick enough to choke on. How much more?

The silence pounded like hammer blows. Hum, scream, anything to break it but no, no, I must not speak.

Why...? Lips clamped together, and together, and together, aching with trying not to speak, to chatter with cold, to sing...why not sing? Maddening, surely...

No. I must not speak. *Why not? Why?*

Body aching, cold and pains mingled... Is it night or day? Are the voices even real?

Speak...

Sign here...

Then you can rest...

The pain will all go away...

The door creaks—they are here...real now...body tensing into cowardly knots...so confused, where, what, why...only know the pain will start now, the real pain...

Only know...teeth chattering, body shaking, hands seizing, heart hammering and lurching, agony in anticipation...and all I know... I must not speak. I must not speak. I must not speak...

"Margo, wake up..."

Someone was shaking me but I kept my lips tight closed, conscious only of an overwhelming need to remain silent and utter terror of what was about to happen...

"Margo? Are you awake? Talk to me." Bane's voice. A glow suddenly illuminated his face—he'd switched his phone screen on. "Are you all right, Margo? It was just a nightmare."

A nightmare...yes. I shuddered. "I'm fine, Bane."

I managed to relax, then peered at Bane's face. His hair was plastered damply over his forehead and he looked a tad wild-eyed himself. Beside me, Jon was whimpering, hands fighting to escape the sleeping bag. We slept like a pile of puppies these days, the way we had when we got out of the river. It was the only way we could stay warm.

"Are you okay, Bane?"

"Fine. I had a nightmare too, though." He reached over me and shook Jon firmly. "Something we ate, I reckon. Jon, it's just a nightmare, wake up..."

Jon woke with a choked cry and jerked his fists clear of the bedding with unusual aggression.

Bane grabbed his wrists. "Jon, nightmare, calm down."

Jon blew out a long breath...let his arms go limp. Bane released him.

"Thanks for waking me," Jon said.

"You're welcome. I suspect those berries. We've never had those before."

"And we're not having them again," I said immediately. "Unless they're the last edible thing in the forest."

"I second that," groaned Jon, turning on his side and closing his eyes again.

"Motion passed, then," said Bane. Not protesting that food was food? His nightmare must've been bad!

I woke in the morning, head fogged from a night of horrible dreams, as Bane ran a hand up my ribs.

"Not thinking of misbehaving?" I mumbled. "I can be relieved you've got the energy, and slap your face at the same time, y'know."

"Alas, no. Margo, you're *so* bony." Very unhappy he sounded about it.

"Speak for yourself, Bane. And Jon—s'like having a skeleton curled up next to me."

Bane sighed—didn't speak. We were, totally *un*metaphorically, starving.

All the same, we made do with nettles for breakfast, though edible leaves were getting harder to find as the season changed and they died back, shriveling into gaunt stalks. Stomachs full if not wholly fooled, we dragged Jon upright and set off. At lunchtime, we shared what little we'd found which didn't need cooking, a bare mouthful each. Bane divided everything exactly in three, and when I redistributed a little of mine as usual, he said, "Give it to Jon," so I did. Jon didn't seem to notice; he ate mechanically and we towed him on again.

Several hours later Jon crumpled and went down like a felled tree. I grabbed for him, couldn't hold his weight and went thudding to my knees beside him. "Jon? Jon?"

Bane dropped down on the other side of Jon. "What's wrong?"

"He just collapsed!"

"Keep your hair on, he's probably just passed out. Can't blame him." Bane wriggled Jon's rucksack off and inserted it under his feet.

Couldn't blame him, either. I was lightheaded all the time, like I was floating around. I'd taken to being rather careful about fast movements and so had Bane.

Bane was balancing his own pack under Jon's feet as well. Too tired to want to hold Jon's feet up himself, for however short a time. "Come on, Jon, wakey-wakey."

Jon's forehead felt cold and clammy. Slipping off my backpack, I pulled out my sleeping bag, unzipped it and tucked it around him.

"Come on, mate, wake up." Bane kept patting Jon's cheeks and after several anxious minutes Jon stirred, muttered drowsily, turned on his side and went sound asleep. Bane sighed and desisted. "I think he's okay."

"Yeah." A snort escaped me. "*Okay*. What a joke."

"Yeah, I know."

"We'd better camp here, hadn't we."

"Not much choice, have we? I couldn't carry *you* right now."

Too true.

As soon as a small lot of water was boiled, I mixed up

the last sachet. The smell of the nutritious meal, full of protein and fat, unadulterated by nettles, filled my mouth with saliva. How'd I ever described it so uncharitably as stewed boots?

Bane sat on the other side of the stove, staring hungrily. Sachet in one hand, I held up a single fork-spoon in the other and gave him an enquiring look. He licked his lips, clenched his fists, bit his lip and finally gave a quick, jerky nod. Towards Jon.

"Wake up, Jon, food. Food, Jon, food…" Finally Jon stirred. "Here, open up…" I started spooning the mush into his mouth. He was barely half-awake, it was like feeding a baby bird. The sight and smell of the food…

"*Margo.*"

I blinked—oh, I crouched, mesmerized by the spoonful I held. Bane looked pretty mesmerized himself—he hadn't come any closer—afraid he'd snatch the sachet from my hand?

"Sorry," I muttered, not sure who to.

When I'd fed it all to Jon, I used my pocket knife to cut the sachet packet open and passed one half to Bane. We fell on the pieces like hyenas; we licked, sucked and chewed until nothing but crumpled metal balls remained. Only then could I turn my attention to cooking.

"Bane, show me the map," I said, when we were gorged on nettle stew and feeling a brief respite from the worst of the hunger pangs.

"Oh, here you are." He tapped the screen of his phone and held it out.

I bullied my sluggish mind into action. A little red dot showed our position. I used my finger as a ruler and made measurements, checked the key. My heart slid down into my boots.

"*Miserere nobis,* there's so far to go! It's still a hundred kilometers to Lausanne and to arrive at the foot of the Alps in the Italian department is two hundred and seventy-five kilometers! What are we going to do?"

"If we can reach Lausanne, we'll get food, by hook or by crook. Break into private houses if necessary, and empty the larders—don't get excited, we can leave some money."

"I'm not getting excited. Are you sure there are no houses around here?"

"Every village and farm I can find is yellow—abandoned or supposed to be."

"How long to Lausanne?"

"At the rate we're going? Ten days, minimum. Probably more. This forest isn't going to get any flatter."

Caught between exhaustion and despair, I stared at Jon's sleeping form. I couldn't walk for another ten days up hill and down dale on our current diet. One square meal wouldn't enable Jon to, either. "We're not going to make it."

Bane bit his lip fiercely as though struggling with himself. "Then start praying! That's what you do, isn't it?"

Hopefully the obvious would've occurred to me in a few moments without Bane having to point it out. Shame heated my cheeks; I felt like a bug.

Go away, demon of despair. We're not dead yet.

"Best thing we can do, anyway."

"It's the only thing we can blasted well do!"

Hang on... *Bug?*

10

NEVER LOOK A GIFT DEER IN THE MOUTH

My feet squished slightly...a tiny damp patch in the bottom of a hollow, a rare survivor of the summer's heat. Since my brainwave a few days ago, that had come to mean only one thing.

I dropped to my knees and so did Bane, letting Jon flop down on the ground between us. Tearing a rotten log from its nest of moss, I turned it over...

"Feast!" Bane's triumph was monosyllabic; his fingers already closing around a fat beige grub.

I grabbed another, too hungry to agree out loud, shoved it in my mouth, chewed and swallowed, groping for more. Forced myself to shove the third one into Jon's mouth. Bane did the same.

The bare soil and underside of the log were picked clean all too quickly. One other little bit of wood lay in the damp patch, but it yielded only two grubs. Bane turned over anything nearby, then gave up with a shake of his head.

"Too dry. Or they've turned into beetles or whatever and skedaddled, I don't know. Don't fancy guessing what other insects are safe."

"No," I sighed.

With immense effort we heaved Jon back to his feet—his skeletal form was apparently made of lead. We lurched on like a six-legged sloth. The forest was blessedly flat here, up atop a range of hills, but toiling under the weight of the packs and Jon, we panted heavily.

"Protein, Lord, protein, Lord, protein, Lord?" I muttered as we walked—until we began slogging up yet another slope. "Bane, *must we walk up every hill in the French department!*"

"I'm trying to avoid the worst ones! Just how many extra kilometers d'you want to walk? And you call this a *hill?*"

A slight incline, nothing more. My anger was already gone. "Sorry, Bane."

"*Love you.*" Not the most logical response, perhaps, but none of us were feeling at our most rational any more.

The sun was dropping in the sky.

"Shall we stop?" suggested Bane.

"Haven't any nettles yet, might as well carry on."

"Oh yeah." He raised his head and began scanning the passing forest again. Oh, and I was supposed to be doing that as well, wasn't I?

Protein, Lord? Protein?

The most horrible scream split the silence. Bane and I stopped dead, hairs rising on the back of our necks, and even Jon's head came up.

"What the...?" he gasped.

A distant crashing in the undergrowth. The scream rose to full pitch again, a sound of agony and death, then trailed off. We stood frozen, straining to hear. Snarls, a few yaps.

"Wolves!" Understanding burst on me. "They've killed a deer."

"Well, they won't want us." Jon's head sank again. Too tired to be afraid?

The distant sounds of lupine feasting continued and my mouth watered.

Fresh meat.

"Bane, help me get Jon up a tree."

"Do *what?*"

I practically dragged them both to the likeliest tree and dumped my rucksack. *"Help me."* I got a shoulder under Jon and shoved. "Jon, climb up."

Bane joined in, and a bewildered Jon grabbed a branch and scrambled onto it.

"Are the wolves coming?" Not quite too tired to wish to avoid death by devourment.

"No, just a precaution. We're leaving the packs here, Jon, we'll be back soon. Don't nod off and fall out, for pity's sake."

"Yes, but—"

"Bane, grab a big stick and follow me."

"*Oh no*, this is not a good idea!"

"We haven't got much choice! Never look a gift deer in the mouth."

"Unless it's guarded by a whole pack of wolves!"

"They'll just have to share. Come on or stay here! Suit yourself." I selected a hefty stick, whacked it into a tree to test its strength and strode off towards the sounds. Cursing, Bane followed suit.

"Don't you dare get eaten!" Jon called thinly.

I winced. Jon's fate if we failed to return wasn't pleasant to contemplate. Well, we'd just have to return, wouldn't we?

Free of our burdens and full of adrenalin, we walked briskly, sticks ready.

"Don't be frightened," I told Bane, as we got closer, "or you'll smell like prey."

"Oh, thank you, Margo. That makes it easier."

"Just act confident." *Lord, be with us. Angel Margaret, help us?*

We rounded some bushes—there was the pack and their kill. A red deer. Large, good. A gust of wind carried the tang of blood to us. The last of the entrails were disappearing and wolves were already tearing through the ribcage. One particularly massive wolf seized a hind leg, pulled and twisted— the leg tore clean off the body with a crack of splintering bone.

"Merciful heaven, Margo, are you sure about this?" whispered Bane, appalled by a show of brute strength he couldn't come close to emulating even in full health.

"I'm guessing you smell rather like chicken just now," I said. Anger would be a better scent than fear. I stepped forward, walking straight towards the pack at a steady pace, Bane following. "Hello, wolves, I apologize for disturbing you at dinner time, but it's an emergency."

The wolves wheeled to face us, snarling and astonished. No wolf now alive had been hunted, not for many generations. They weren't that afraid any more.

"We'd be very grateful if you'd let us have some venison," I went on firmly. "You don't exactly look as though you'll miss it."

The five adult wolves had shiny coats and rippling

muscles; the three younger ones were less heavily built but just as sleek-coated and well cared for.

Most of the wolves dropped back slightly as we approached, forming a hostile group just the other side of the kill. The big wolf stood its ground, showing its teeth, fur bristling. My gaze fell on the detached leg. Blast, right by the alpha wolf, but so easy to carry. Snatch and run would be better than expecting them to just stand there while we carved up their food.

"That will do very nicely, thank you, Father Wolf." I tightened my grip on the stick and walked unhesitatingly forward.

The wolf gave an experimental lunge, growling, so I brought the stick down on the end of his nose hard enough to hurt. He leapt back with a yelp. The other wolves whined anxiously as I bent to seize the leg. It was *heavy.* Needing both hands to pick it up, I let the stick fall to the ground...

Father Wolf exploded out of his uncertain crouch with a ferocious snarl, nothing experimental this time. *How to club him with a deer's leg I could hardly lift?* But Bane hurtled forward with a roar that would've made any mate of any species whatsoever proud and slammed his stick into the end of the wolf's nose—*crack.*

The wolf dropped to the ground with a howl, writhing on his belly and pawing his muzzle—snarled and raised his head again... With another roar, Bane walloped him on the side of the head. Father Wolf sprang up and retreated to the other side of the kill, dropped his haunches to the ground and whined.

"Well, look at that, Bane." I was almost too breathless with fright to speak at all. "Looks like you're dominant. Dominant-ish." Father Wolf wasn't engaging in full submissive behavior... "Er, let's be going, shall we?"

"You think?" panted Bane.

I began backing away nice and steadily, making sure to carry on addressing the pack. "Thank you very much, Father Wolf, for the meat. I hope your nose isn't too sore but it's very bad manners to attack your guests, y'know, even if they are uninvited. I hope you enjoy the rest of your meal. Good hunting."

The wolves snarled after us, seeming bemused. I stopped talking once we were past the bushes but carried on walking backwards. Father Wolf licked his muzzle and another wolf came to nuzzle him—Mother Wolf? Once we were about twenty meters away, the three young wolves gave wolf shrugs and tucked in again, and with the choicest bits disappearing, their adult siblings quickly joined them.

I turned my back at last and we walked away rather more quickly. I took discreet looks over my shoulder regularly, though. Jon was right that wolves were quiet.

"Here, swap." Bane offered me his stick.

"Yeah, take it, before I tuck in here and now."

"Umm, it does smell wonderful, doesn't it?" Bane hefted the leg with much greater ease than I had.

I flung my arms around him from behind to avoid the gory thing. "We did it! Do you know what this means?"

"We can make it to Lausanne." He spoke grudgingly but the beaming smile said he appreciated the change in our circumstances.

"Yes!" I kissed his filthy, stubbly cheek.

Thank you, Lord, for sending us a deer and the means to catch it!

"Margo? *Bane?*"

"We're fine, Jon," I called. "More than fine!"

We both came close to running the rest of the way, though skipping was definitely too much effort.

"Feel, Jon!" Bane hefted the leg.

Jon's hand traced the hoof and his face lit up. "You got a deer's foot! Can we eat it now?"

"We got a deer's *leg!* A haunch, I think they'd call it."

"That's great...um... I don't know how to get down...and... I'm going to fall down any time now."

We took a quick look around for the wolves, put the leg on the ground and hastened to lift Jon down, or at any rate control his fall.

"How did you do it?" he asked.

"Hah," snorted Bane, "you're lucky you weren't there. Margo just strolled in there chatting to those savage beasts as though she was at a tea party, walks right up to the largest wolf there and tries to make off with the meat it's just chosen for its own dinner! Which didn't go down terribly well!"

"Bane had to bash the alpha wolf a couple of times with his stick," I elaborated. "Then the wolf decided the rest of the deer tasted just as good and let us have the leg. Quite a well-mannered wolf, all things considered."

"He tried to rip your throat out!" objected Bane.

"Well, I had just performed robbery with violence."

"Yeah, Margo bashed it first," Bane told Jon.

Jon looked even whiter than usual. "You're right, I'm glad I was up a tree quietly giving birth to kittens. Could we please eat?"

"No," said Bane. "We are walking well away from here before we stop, just in case...well, just in case." Just in case the wolves come after their missing food, but hopefully Jon wasn't processing fast enough right now to fill in the missing bit.

"We need to do something about the blood," I said.

"Yeah."

Bane fished out a scentSeal bag and slipped it over the messy end. Cutting a piece off the thin rope he had in his pack and binding it tightly around the leg to prevent seepage, he wrapped the whole thing in our scruffiest foil blanket. Only then did he shove it into his backpack. Very, very far from scent-proof, but the best we could do. He heaved the pack onto his back, staggered, groaned, but said nothing.

"Give me something else to carry, Bane." Though with the adrenalin wearing off fast it was all I could do to get my own rucksack on.

"No."

Jon's hands rose to search his chest. "Oh no! I...I've lost my pack...and my stick!"

"You've not had them for days, you numpty." But Bane was so pleased at Jon's burst of awareness he didn't sound scathing at all.

"Oh...you'd better give them to me to carry."

"Just start walking."

We took Jon's arms again and off we went. Felt like

singing.

Deo Gratias.

We had to hang our flashlights from the trees when we finally stopped; the sun was almost down. Jon had gone quiet again, but the promise of meat kept him more alert than he'd been for ages.

"How are we going to *cook* it?" I asked.

"We'll have to risk an open fire in the morning. Right now, I'll just skin one little patch and cut some strips to cook in the pan. I'll hang it from a nice bear-proof tree then."

Bane was right. An open fire was the only way, but apart from being totally illegal and very visible, it'd take ages to roast the entire haunch.

I gathered firewood quickly and looked hungrily into the pan when I returned, trying not to drool.

"That's enough, Bane, we'd better not gorge."

"S'pose," sighed Bane, taking out his lighter to light the stove.

Jon's head rose suddenly. "What was that?" His listening pose intensified to quivering alertness. "Bane, there's something very large out there."

My hands crept over my mouth to muffle any squeak of terror. A wild animal could probably smell the blood a mile away. *Angel Margaret, stick with us... Sorry, stupid thing to say, of course you'll stick with us. O Lord, protect us.*

Bane dropped the lighter, snatched up the cut-off length of rope and bound his knife to the end of his stick. Pulling it tight and knotting it well, in only moments he was gripping a makeshift spear.

Crack.

This time we all heard it. I fought back rising panic.

"I think it's a bear," whispered Jon.

Advice heard a thousand times ran through my mind; black bear—harmless unless it has a cub—shout and make a racket and chase it away; brown bear—dangerous at all times—try and sneak away but if it attacks, play dead.

"We can't lose that meat!" My voice squeaked horribly. "We cannot lose it!"

"No, we can't," breathed Bane, staring into the darkness.

For a second we'd gone back in time, cavemen crouched ready to defend our food with our lives...

Something shuffled from the trees and I clutched Bane's shoulder with both hands.

Bear.

"Black or brown?" Bane's eyes were fixed on it. "Black or brown, come on, black or brown?"

The bear stepped into the light.

Brown.

11

STABBING A MELON WITH A NEEDLE

The scream rose inside, but my throat was too constricted to let it out—all that escaped was a strangled "urk".

It was Bane's turn to yell at wild beasts. "*Clear off!*" he bellowed. "If you think we're going to lie on the ground while you take our food you can forget it!" He held his coat wide open, "spear" still clutched in his right hand. "Look, we're almost as big as you and there's three of us, so *clear off!*"

Hastily I unzipped my coat and held it open as well, then grabbed the pile of metal fork-spoons and began clattering them as loudly as I could. "Beat it! Or we'll beat you, you mangy bear!"

The bear paused and peered at us in the gloom. Puzzled by our failure to run away screaming?

Jon hadn't joined our little defensive line—just too weak to stand unaided?—I was too busy shouting at the bear to worry about it. The bear sniffed the air—lumbered forward again.

"*Our* venison!" roared Bane, stamping and waving his coat flaps like a maniac. "Ours!"

"You can't have it!" I rattled the cutlery even harder. "Clear off!"

The bear was very close now. It eyed the noisy obstructions irritably and rose on its hind legs, swiping the air with horrible claws and roaring back.

"Go away!" I shrieked.

"*Go. Away!*" shouted Bane.

The bear roared again. Definitely trying to scare us off, but that didn't mean it wouldn't attack if we didn't run.

"How d'you kill a bear, Margo?" Bane let go of his coat and held his spear ready.

"Heck, Bane, don't poke it with that thing!" I tried to sound fierce rather than terrified. "It'll go nuts and kill us all."

"It's thinking about killing us all anyway! If it tries it, I won't have much choice. In the throat, d'you think?"

It did seem about the only place that would do any good. Except... "Or the eye!"

"Yeah."

The bear bellowed and gave some rather more serious swipes with its claws, though they still fell short of us.

"I wonder if we *could* kill it," shouted Bane rather savagely. "It's edible, y'know."

"We couldn't possibly eat it all..." Then I caught on. Animals weren't easily fooled, so I pictured a heap of fresh, succulent bear meat, fried in its own fat, and a bar of chocolate for good measure. My mouth watered and a primeval surge swept me. "Yeah," I howled, "Let's eat the bear! Kill it and eat it!"

"Kill the bear! Kill the bear!" yelled Bane, making little threatening jabs with his spear.

We spread out just slightly, not enough to invite it to rush between us, but enough to suggest a pincer movement. I pulled my pocket knife out and unfolded it, imitating Bane's little lunges—hunger and the blood pounding of the hunt consumed us.

"Get the bear!"

"Get it!"

"Kill it, kill it, kill it!"

"Eat the bear, eat it!"

The bear's head turned from side to side as we prowled up and down in our little pincer shape. It dropped to all fours and backed up a step. We smelt like humans but we didn't act like them. We were hunting it, we smelt hungry and unafraid, and it was outnumbered.

It backed up again and we followed, barely retaining enough willpower to keep from turning bluff into reality. Halfway to the edge of the clearing... I dragged my mind from the primitive mist—time to stop and let it clear off by itself...

Bane paused as well and the bear rose on its hind legs for one last—decidedly half-hearted—wave of its claws...and caught one paw on Bane's knife.

Bellowing in mild pain and hypochondriacal fury, it shuffled forward on its hind legs and swiped for us, no bluffing now. We leapt back to avoid the deadly claws. What now? We couldn't retreat, still couldn't let it have the meat, but to actually fight it? *Whoa...* The bear came at me again, I dodged sideways, trying to lead it away from the food and give Bane its back.

My foot slipped on a twig and the bear's claws were coming for my face... Bane's spear drove into its thick neck, with all his force behind the blow.

The bear whirled, howling, and Bane leapt back, but the bear's paw caught his shoulder and flung him a frightening distance, spear flying from his hand. Darting between them, I grabbed up the makeshift thing and howling almost as loudly as the bear I lunged for its eyes...couldn't reach... thrust into its neck instead...the bear recoiled and lashed out again...something knocked me out of the way—Bane, on his feet!—he grabbed the spear and stabbed again but the bear was learning, it swiped at him so fast he had to dodge before the knife blade could touch it...we needed a better plan than this...

"Hey, you stupid bear!" Jon's voice, raised in a hoarse yell. "You're messing with *homo sapiens*, remember?"

He came rushing past me as I tried to regain my feet, a ball of fire in his hands. Oh, not a ball of fire—the stove, with flames pouring from the top.

"Jon, stop!" yelled Bane, as Jon got as close to the bear as seemed wise, fire or no fire.

Jon already had: the monster's breathing couldn't be hard to hear. "So clear off or we'll set you on fire!" he wheezed.

Good idea, that'd kill it...all that mattered, now. Killing it before it could kill us. Simple rule of nature.

But we were humans and we didn't belong wholly to nature. Perhaps we could just drive it off. Already it backed away, on all fours again, roaring in fear and confusion as the flickering flames illuminated the shadows.

"Here, Margo," Bane thrust the spear to me and grabbed the stove from Jon.

"Just drive it away," I blurted.

Bane had already sprung forward, shoving the flaming thing so close under the bear's nose it must've singed its fur.

"*Homo sapiens'* venison, *get* it?" he bellowed.

The bear recoiled, whimpering—turned and fled, crashing through the bushes.

Bane dumped the blazing stove on the ground and grabbed Jon's wrist. "Stream, come on."

"Wait, you're bleeding—"

He shrugged off my searching hands. "It's not bad, Margo. Make sure the whole forest doesn't go up."

Uh oh, good point. I hastily rewrapped Jon's jacket around the stove and lifted it, carrying it back to the little area we'd cleared for it. Ah, that's why they both had their hands in the little stream. The jacket didn't make a very effective oven glove.

The interior flameGuard partition lay on the grass, the tip of Jon's pocket knife still shoved through one of the slits—very, very illegal to light a stove without it in, but under the circumstances the EuroGov could take that rule, along with their hunting ban, and stuff it somewhere unmentionable.

I picked up the knife, all the same, and slid the flameGuard back down into the stove, immediately damping down the flames, though they licked up through the slits in an impressive manner. Jon must've used all the dry kindling, followed by several handfuls of fresh wood; it'd be blazing for a while. I adjusted the tube vents running up each side of the casing to maximum so it wouldn't go out from lack of air, and put the pan in place just to ensure no stray flames could escape. Then added water to stop our dinner burning.

"Do you two need the first aid kit?"

"Not urgently."

"Okay. I'm going to turn the flashlights off for a minute."

Flashlights off, I waited a little to let my eyes adjust to the darkness, then scoured everywhere in the vicinity. No telltale glow betrayed a smoldering twig—I put them on again and took the medical kit over to the stream.

"Are you two okay? Jon, that was brilliant!"

Jon shrugged modestly. "Recalled wild animals are s'posed to be afraid of fire."

"I'm a complete idiot!" fumed Bane. "Messing around with string and an itsy-bitsy knife; I should've lit the stove and set the stick alight."

"Oh, come off it," I said. "By then the bear would've had its pick of human or venison for supper."

"Hmm, I s'pose. Might not've come at all if the stove was lit, though."

"D'you know how badly you hurt it? I hope it doesn't meet anyone else."

"If it runs smack into a search party of EuroGov troops, I'll consider it a job well done. Not sure I hurt it that much, anyway. About as much use as stabbing a melon with a needle. Margo, could you shine the flashlight...good, no blisters. Jon, show me your hands."

Jon spread his hands for inspection. A rather bright red, but...

"No sign of blisters." Bane sounded satisfied.

"*Laudate Dominum,*" said Jon. "We've enough to worry about without injuries."

"How's your shoulder, Bane?"

"What's wrong with his shoulder?" Jon's head turned.

"Bear knocked him clean across the clearing," I said.

"Actually that was mostly me, diving away from the force of the blow. But I do seem to be bleeding, which is a right blinking nuisance," Bane conceded.

"You'll have to sleep in a scentSeal bag," I giggled rather hysterically.

"I may put one over the dressing," said Bane seriously. "Much good it's likely to do."

"Has to be better than nothing," said Jon.

"Come on, let me see," I urged.

While Bane peeled off his jacket, shirt, and thermal top I hung the second flashlight from a branch above us, direct-ing the other at the wound. Three bloody gashes ran across the very top of his arm where it joined the shoulder, three gashes and one raw red scrape—one claw had missed him entirely.

"I think I need to stitch it," I told him. "We want to stop all bleeding as fast as possible—to say nothing of keeping infection out."

"If there's any hope of that," snorted Bane. "I doubt the bear washed its claws before attacking us. Stitch away, then, I put in needle and thread. Let's be quick, I want to get that venison up a tree before we have another visitor. Though how much point there is worrying about it now I smell like dinner too...huh."

I washed the cuts with filtered water from the bottles, packed in as much antiseptic cream as would stay with them pinched together and set to work with the needle. Bane sat rigidly and endured, albeit muttering a monotone of oaths and distractions under his breath.

"It may hurt less if you relax," I told him.

"Oh, come on, Margo, I'm sitting still: what more do you want? Blast, blast, blast, venison dinner, nobody eaten by bear and a nice venison dinner, curse it, ouch, ow, venison dinner, Margo wedding night..."

"Excuse me?" I demanded, hiding a smile. "What was the last one again?"

"Nothing, venison, venison, lots and lots of venison... Ow, ow, Margo in a lace nightie...ouch, Margo *not* in a lace nightie..."

I cuffed the side of his head gently and cut off the thread. "All done, Bane. I see the mere promise of a venison dinner seems to have a remarkably invigorating effect on you."

He smirked tiredly at me. "Takes something a little out of the ordinary to take your mind off being stabbed repeatedly with a needle, y'know."

"Yeah, yeah, any excuse. Now hold still so I can get this covered up." I dressed the wound carefully and taped a scentSeal bag over the top, then picked up his bloodied clothes. "I'll get these washed ASAP."

"I'll get the venison hung up."

"Wait...you're not going into the forest by yourself?"

"With a bit of luck, Margo, we're in that bear's territory and there isn't another one. But yes, I'm going into the forest, 'cause I'm certainly not hanging it anywhere near camp."

I bit my lip and realized my hands were gripping his arm. He'd be alone out there, smelling so tempting. What if the wolves came this way?

Jon's head turned from one to the other of us, as though what wasn't said told him as much as what was. "I'll go with Bane. Two of us will be less enticing."

"Yes," I said quickly, before Bane could speak. "You go with Bane. I'll be safe here with homo sapiens' secret weapon."

"So secret only one of them thought of it," muttered Bane, still irritated with himself.

"Oh, go hang the venison, then we can eat."

"Yes, please. Come on, Bane." Jon attempted to drag Bane off and almost fell in the stream.

"Wait," snorted Bane in amusement. "I haven't got the grub."

"I don't think we need to eat any more grubs."

"Oh, you did realize what we were feeding you, did you?"

"That many legs are a little hard to miss."

Clothes washed and sleeping bags arranged—nothing to do but wait. When had I last been this alone? Every rustle made my muscles tense. Shadows crept between the light of the flashlights. I began to shake. No longer proud *homo sapiens* safe by my magic fire, I was just a girl—a sort of New Adult—alone in the dark in the wilderness. To my shame and fury, I started crying.

I heard them coming back, but couldn't seem to stop.

"*Margo*... Margo, are you hurt?" Bane's steps approached quickly and his arm wrapped around me.

"Not hurt, I'm not hurt," I sniffed. "Just being silly."

"Oh, Margo." His other arm wrapped around me as well, enfolding me in warm, safe *Bane*. "Not being silly. You hate bears. Of course you were scared. You were so brave."

"Poor Margo." Jon's hand stroked my hair. "You didn't get to stay up a tree, did you?"

With my pack around me again, I began to get hold of myself. "You sweetie-pie, Jon. I know you really want to say for pity's sake, Margo, stop sniveling so we can eat."

"That too," he grinned.

Eat we did. We speared the pieces of venison on the fork-spoons and gnawed at them like the wolves we'd stolen them from.

"If I live to be a hundred and fifty," sighed Jon, three venison strips later, "I will never eat a more delicious meal."

"S'gorgeous," I managed around a mouthful.

"Divine," said Bane, barely pausing his chewing.

We washed it down with weak nettle tea as the clouds drifted slowly away across the night sky. Bane propped his back against a tree and slipped his un-clawed arm around me as we sat gazing at the now moon-drenched clearing. Jon put his head in my lap and lay staring up as though he could sense the brilliant stars above us. Bane was so used to me doing double-duty as a pillow he didn't even twitch.

"We're going to make it," he said softly. "Am I allowed to say it?"

"Fire away," said Jon sleepily.

"Of course you are," I said. "Seems pretty likely, at least to Lausanne. Vatican State...*maybe*..." *Please, Lord?*

"Wonder if Anne's still there?" said Jon.

I blinked. "Who's Anne?"

Bane shot me a look as if to say, you shared a bunk with this guy for four months and you have to ask *that?*

Jon just said, "My sister."

I blinked again. "Isn't she...dead?"

"Isn't your brother Kyle *dead?*"

"No, surely you know that...*oh*. She went to follow her vocation too?"

"Yes. Years ago. So she's probably *not* there now, even if she made it."

Nice to learn that his sister wasn't—necessarily—dead, but my mind drifted quickly back to Lausanne. Then the Alps. Italy. Vatican State. I moistened lips dry with excitement. Could we really do it?

Lausanne. Food. Danger. If the theft—well, one could not precisely say *theft* if we left money—if the *break in* was reported, we might find the EuroGov waiting for us at the passes.

"We must pick the house, or houses, very carefully," I said, listening to Jon's soft snores. "Check the living rooms—

if only we could find one with oak wreaths."

"Brilliant, Margo," said Bane. "We'll look until we find one."

Some parents dealt with their child failing Sorting by removing all photographs, by never mentioning them again. Others did pretty much the opposite, keeping—*adding*—photos, each crowned with a little wreath of oak leaves and acorns. A small defiance of the system.

We could've slept where we sat, bellies full and hearts light, but before long habit and prudence—and the nip in the air—drove us into our sleeping bag.

"Thank you for the venison, Lord," I murmured, "and for not letting us be eaten by the bear."

"Or the wolves," muttered Bane dryly. "Ta for the grub, I s'pose. Night, Margo."

"Night, Bane."

...Blackness all around...a bear snuffling in my ear! I screamed...

"*Margo*," said the bear, sounding startled.

"Bane? *Bane*, what the heck are you doing? I thought that blasted bear was back!"

"Uh, nothing. Nothing." He sounded embarrassed. Stroking my hair or sneaking me a kiss after stoking the stove? We'd decided to try and keep it alight tonight. Probably it wouldn't normally have alarmed me.

"What's going on?" yawned Jon.

"Nothing," I groaned. "Just Bane doing a fine imitation of *ursus major*. Back to sleep, back to sleep."

I settled my head on the mat and closed my eyes...

...Warm sun struck through my eyelids. Day. I opened my eyes and looked around. Everything untouched. Bane, a hot shape on one side; Jon, a warm form on the other—good, nothing had snuck up and eaten either of them. Okay, feeling a little paranoid.

Bane's forehead was rather *too* hot, his bad arm burning. Infected, surely. He didn't stir as I slid out. I fetched a water bottle and the first aid kit, read the back of a packet of antibiotics, then shook his shoulder.

"Another half hour..." He tried to roll over.

"You can have as long as you like. The meat will take ages to cook. But you've got to take one of these now, okay?"

He pushed himself up on his good arm, looking blearily at what I held. Grimaced. Okay, we all knew how important it was not to take antibiotics unnecessarily but...

"You need them, Bane. Come on, open up."

He took the pill from me instead, popped it in and washed it down with a quick swig of water, then flopped back. "I'll help you with the meat in a minute..."

He started snoring again.

"You do that," I murmured, "...in your dreams. I dare say I can cope."

I managed to construct a safe open fire according to the instructions given in the books, then two little tripods out of sticks to hold a spit. Following Bane's marks on the trees to retrieve the meat, I skinned it rather ineptly, then fastened it to a spit and balanced it over the fire.

Midmorning by the time all was arranged and I could turn my attention to breakfast. I followed the first few of Bane's marks back to a reasonable patch of nettles and put a pan of those to cook over the fire, with a couple of slices of venison for each of us in with it. The smell now arising made my stomach gurgle and woke Jon.

He'd rolled into the space I'd vacated and now sighed sleepy contentment. "Bane's nice and warm."

"Nice has nothing to do with it."

Jon blinked and came somewhat more awake. His hand found its way to Bane's injured arm. "Oh dear. See what you mean. Antibiotics?"

"I've given him the first one already."

"'Course you have. Any of those gorgeous smells breakfast?"

"Yeah. Venison and nettle stew. It's ready, let's tuck in. Don't wake Bane, he can have some later."

Jon and I polished off the entire panful, so I made another trip to the nettles and put a new stew on for Bane, who slept on, oblivious.

"We may as well eat as much as we want," I said. "We can more easily do the last few days to Lausanne on nettles only than on rotten meat."

Sitting back against a tree, I took out my bookReader, which'd survived its earlier soaking in the stream—clearly not too old to be waterproof—and re-read the sections on bears to Jon.

It was just as irrelevant to people whose lives depended on their food as I remembered, and he snorted when I'd finished.

"And not one of them mentions chasing them with fire."

"In light of the dry summers of recent decades, funny, that."

He winced. "Yeah, I s'pose it was chancing it a bit. I'm quite sure the average hiker would be well advised to let the bear have what it liked."

"Huh, you've done everything..." a drowsy voice broke in. Bane, propped on his elbow, peering around the clearing. "Sorry..."

"Don't be silly." I checked my watch and picked up the antibiotics. "It's time for your next one of these, anyway."

"Okay." Bane slid slowly up into a sitting position as though his head ached. "Is there something to eat?"

"There's a pan of stew for you. How do you feel?"

"Fine."

"Honestly, Bane?"

He shrugged. "Okay, a bit off. But better than this morning."

"Good. Perhaps that pill's working already."

We stepped out as briskly as we could the next day, racing against the changing season, racing against our finite food supply, and racing against the search potentially fanning out from our original route to Zurich. We still collected any edible vegetation that caught our eye for the sake of the extra nutrients, but we needed speed, now, not food. But every time we heard wolves in the night we murmured thanks—even Jon.

Bane remained feverish; his step heavy, his head clearly foggy, he avoided using his arm as much as possible. I took over both the map and the task of driving us on. Frightening to find myself the fittest.

"Here's your pill, here's your water." I passed them to Bane as we made camp well after dark three nights later. "Come on, get in the sleeping bag, don't get cold."

"Margo, I'm feeling heaps better." He gulped the pill down. "Stop babying me."

"Shall I apologize for loving you?"

"No," he pulled me into his lap, "but you can swap the entire evening's fussing for one big kiss right now."

"I *could,*" I agreed, rubbing noses with him. "I might not manage to stick to a promise not to fuss, though."

"I'll take the chance." He kissed me thoroughly.

He practically had a beard now, scratchy but I didn't care. I kissed him right back. He was warm and alive and who in their right mind would care about more than that in the one they loved?

Drawing apart, I nestled my cheek under his grubby, bristly neck. "I love you, Bane."

"I love you too." He kissed the scar on my forehead as though he could make it all better. As he almost could. On those mercifully few occasions I'd dreamed of my dismantling and woken, drowning in sweat and terror, I'd cuddled to him until it all drifted away again.

We remained snuggled together for the amount of time it took Jon's stomach to overrule his manners, so probably longer than we realized.

"Sorry to interrupt, but is one of you going to cut this meat or shall I do it?" Jon was still kind of shaky and we weren't letting him wield the knife—one sliced-up person was enough.

"Coming," I said. "We'd better get the stove lit as well, so we don't have any furry visitors. Bane, are you going to get in... Uh. Okay, never mind. Can I have the knife?"

I hefted the foil-wrapped haunch onto my lap and un-wrapped it enough to reach the meat. Our prudent restraint on the first night had saved us from anything worse than stomach ache, and we'd been stuffing ourselves ever since. But still plenty left. The taste getting stronger, but not gone off yet.

"How many slices, you two?"

"Three again," said Bane.

"And for—" Jon broke off, his head snapped round and he called in Esperanto, "*Who's there?*"

Bane lunged forward, reaching for the knife—

Click.

Light blazed, swallowing the puny glow of the flashlights and fixing us like rabbits in car headlights.

12

RABBITS IN THE HEADLIGHTS

I flung up a hand to shield my eyes, heart hammering in my throat. The shadowy form of a person behind the light—just one, but...the long slender silhouette of a gun barrel pointed in our direction.

"Don't move," said Bane softly, in Esperanto, "it's a shotgun. A Lethal."

"Very good, young man." The voice came from behind that blinding light. Some sort of high-powered hand light. "It is a shotgun. Now why don't you tell me what you're doing here?"

I blinked. *What are you doing here* implied he hadn't recognized us. My bare forehead felt horribly conspicuous. How long had the man been there and how much had he heard? "Is this private land?" No need to pretend surprise. It wasn't marked as such on the map. "We had no intention to trespass, sir. Our map must be wrong."

The man didn't tell me whether it was or was not private land. Instead he demanded, "*What* is that in your lap?"

I gulped. The deer's hoof stuck out of the wrappings. "We didn't kill it, sir, we found it dead."

"You found it dead." His voice was heavy with disbelief.

Fair enough. Most New Adults would recoil from a dead deer in horror—or try to give it a decent burial—not whip out a knife and carve it up for tea.

"Where is your tent?"

"Trust me, sir, it's a long story," said Bane lightly. "We're very sorry if we've trespassed. We can leave right away if you want, or first thing in the morning."

I didn't dare look at Jon. Staring straight into that blinding light, oblivious?

The light was lowered slightly, allowing us to see a middle-aged, bearded man in rough country clothes. A dog stood quiet and obedient at his side.

"I can believe it's a long story." His weathered face broke into a smile. "You are without doubt the sorriest lot of New Adults I've seen in a long time. You'd better pick up what little you have left and come along to my cottage for the night. I'm sure I can find you something better for dinner than carrion and..." the light flicked over the heap beside the stove, "half-dead nettles. And soft beds afterwards. Come on, come on with you." An absent-minded jerk of the shotgun invited us to follow.

I looked at Bane. For all the grin and the genial tone, the gun hadn't been lowered. Invitation or order? We didn't want any of us getting shot; the reward was doubtless for our bodies in any condition whatsoever, provided they were identifiable.

Food. A soft bed... If he lived out here in the middle of nowhere, perhaps he didn't even have a television. No. More likely he just hadn't figured it out...*yet.*

"Very kind of you, sir." Bane began unzipping the sleeping bags to put them away again. Not prepared to risk the shotgun. Well, when we reached his cottage the man would have to either put the gun down or make his intentions plain.

Casually, I put my hat back on and went to help Bane, slipping the knife to him. He slid it inside his jacket while his back was turned to our insistent host.

"What's your name, sir?" asked Jon, perhaps to conceal the fact he didn't help us. "I'm Jeff, that's May, and that's Brad."

"I'm François. François Bernier. You're in my old game park."

That explained that. Deeds to old hunting estates might still be held by the owners, but the EuroGov marked them as common forest on maps. Hard to tell in the darkness, but the man must be at least sixty if he'd run this place as a game park for any length of time before the ban. Also explained how he'd come up to us without Jon hearing him, even allowing for our talking and me rustling the foil wrappings.

"Oh. I see," said Jon, in a suitably commiserating tone.

"I doubt you do, really, at your age." But François's tone was still friendly. "Well, chop-chop. I've got a stew at home, real stew with rabbit, potatoes, and veggies. Plenty to go round."

"Sounds nice," said Jon, as Bane stuffed the deer's leg back into his pack as surreptitiously as possible.

I fished out Jon's stick and handed it to him. "Here you go, Jeff, you'll need it again tonight after all."

I helped him up to support the impression of a bad leg—hopefully it'd explain why he carried no pack. He managed the full day's walking more easily now, but he was still so weak that we'd fended off his attempts to reclaim his share of the load.

"This way." François turned and headed into the forest.

I led Jon after him, and Bane fell in on the other side.

"Should we make a run for it?" I stared at the Frenchman's shadowy back.

"He's still got that gun ready to fire," Bane murmured back. "When you're not using a shotgun like that you break it and carry it open over your arm, but he hasn't, and the trees aren't close enough together to provide much cover."

"And speaking for myself," put in Jon under his breath, "None of us are in top form for sprinting."

Jon would surely trip and fall and get shot. We'd better go quietly. For now.

It wasn't too long a walk. François soon dropped back to join us and with his handheld spotlight lighting up the path ahead we made almost as good time as in daylight. Eventually a high mass of tumbled stones rose before us— the gaunt skeleton of some ancient hunting lodge, half demolished and ivy-twined.

The light gleamed off the dew-dampened terracotta roof of the little cottage which leant against the ruin, perhaps once part of one wing. It looked in reasonable order, and no lights showed in the windows—hopefully we'd only the old hunter to worry about.

Unlocking the back door, he ushered us inside, pausing in the porch to remove his footwear. We stood in an awkward silence, pretending not to notice. I'd no wish to be parted from my walking boots. What if we had to make a run for it?

Without any comment about our rudeness, he joined us inside the house, pulled the door shut, and locked it. Turning, he caught me and Bane with our eyes on the key, and very deliberately hung it from a hook beside the back door. A fraction of tension eased from my shoulders.

Still without saying anything, François opened a long thin metal case beside the back door, and put the gun inside—ah, it was a gun cabinet!—fished a handful of cartridges from his pocket and deposited them on the top shelf, closed and locked it. This key he returned to his own pocket. Bane relaxed even more than I did. What'd he picked up on? Ah, François hadn't unloaded the gun, so had it even been loaded in the first place?

Unless he just thought he might want it in a hurry.

We stood in a kitchen, its floor paved with stone slabs worn smooth by countless feet. The cupboards were as old as in most houses of my acquaintance, but from the solid wood they'd been expensive thirty years ago. A scrumptious savory aroma came from the old cooking range.

"Go through to the hall," François urged. "I must make up the beds. There are only two in the spare room: will that be all right, or would one of you like the sofa?"

"Two will be ample," said Bane quickly. He was no keener than I to sleep scattered around the house. *If* we slept here.

We stepped into the hallway—long, narrow and tiled, with a flight of stairs at the far end and the front door half-way along. After a few steps, Jon stumbled into us as Bane and I stopped dead, staring at the photo hanging immediately opposite the main door, the first thing anyone entering the house would see. A photo crowned with an oak wreath.

We both bent to peer at it in the dim light.

The same young man twice? The background gave the lie to that. Twins. Identical. My gaze lifted to the wreath. Wreaths. Two, nestled together. *Oh.*

We turned back to François, who'd followed and stood watching, his face closed.

"Your...sons?" I wouldn't normally raise the subject uninvited, but...

François nodded. "Yes. Very unexpected. A heart defect. They both had it."

I swallowed. Poor man. But much as I hated to prod old wounds, we had to know what we were dealing with. "That must've been a terrible shock for you and...their mother?"

François swallowed, closed his eyes for a moment, spoke with a certain amount of resignation. "It was. Too great. My wife put a noose around her neck not three weeks later. Now, I must make up the beds. The living room is on the right, please make yourselves comfortable."

He waved a hand towards a doorway opposite the stairs and paused only to glance at and pocket a little portable unit from a charging base on the hall table—the alarm unit of a movement sensor, probably attached to the gates at the end of his long, long drive. An expensive but common security measure for those who lived in the middle of nowhere. Nice to know no one could sneak up on the cottage; not in a vehicle.

Once François made his escape up the stairs, Jon's hands rose and travelled delicately across the wall until they touched the portrait. They brushed over the oak leaves and acorns and dropped again. "Ah."

The dog followed us into the living room and when we settled ourselves on the battered old sofa—Bane and I exchanging a look and a glance at the television in the corner—it put its head between Jon and Bane. Jon stroked its soft fur a couple of times before letting his hand rest tiredly on his knees. Bane didn't seem to notice the dog's appealing gaze, so I reached across to pet it. Quite a mean-looking dog, actually, but pretty tame after the wolves.

The dog moved its head to Bane's lap—still got no response. Bane was...drooping. Taking one hand from petting his new friend, I put it to his forehead. That persistent heat still gnawed away at him.

"Are you okay, B... Brad?" I asked cautiously.

"M'fine. Thought you weren't going to baby me tonight?"

No, but he seemed worse. Not that I'd entirely believed his protestations of being so much better, not when he was still letting me handle the map reading. No doubt back in our—as we'd thought—safe little camp in the middle of nowhere, we'd have been fed and abed by now.

"Perhaps François has something better for that shoulder."

The dog abandoned us and ran to the door as François came back through it. "Shoulder?" His eyes settled on Bane's torn jacket, rather more visible in this well illuminated room. "What's up with that, lad?"

"Bear clawed it."

"Did it, now. That what happened to you all, eh?" His broad wave encompassed our missing tent and general condition of starved desperation, also laid bare under the electric lights.

"Yes," said Bane, just as uninformatively.

Well, we needed to change the subject anyway. I said, "Brad's got a bit of an infection in those cuts. He's been taking Naromil but it's not quite healing it."

"Dirty bear claws. Might need something stronger," grunted François. "Come on, Jeff, shift over, and let me take a look at your friend."

Jon's head rose in suppressed panic and I jumped up hastily. "Oh, don't get on that leg, Jeff. Sit here, sir."

Bane shifted along so the older man could sit on his injured side, and reluctantly pulled off his layers. Oh...perhaps this hadn't been such a good idea. His gaunt ribs stuck out with inescapable horribleness in this civilized setting.

François whistled. "You three *have* been through it, haven't you? Well, let's take a look."

He unwrapped the dressing, which due to our limited supplies was well overdue changing, and peered at the inexpertly stitched cuts, red and inflamed and oozing pus.

"Well, it's infected, all right. Time for the big guns—I've some Cortimil which should mend it fast enough. You must finish the other course as well, though."

"Of course," said Bane politely, *I'm not stupid* barely kept from his tone.

"Well, you can take the first one with dinner, which is ready when you are, which is now, from the look of you." He left the room briefly and returned with a clean dressing and a box of antibiotics.

"Bear got your food, eh?" he said as he finished applying the dressing. "Better to let it have it, you know, even if you are in the middle of nowhere."

"Isn't hindsight a wonderful thing?" Bane's tone was edged this time.

François just laughed and got to his feet, slipping the box of antibiotics into his pocket. The dog jumped up, following close at his heels. "Well, you're not dead, so you lived to learn. Let's eat. Oh, this is Hugo, by the way."

He led us through a door into a small dining room and disappeared through another door which opened into the hall, opposite the kitchen. Reappearing almost at once with a stack of four plates, he glanced at Jon's arm in mine. "If...er...Jeff...wishes to use his stick inside, I've no objection. I'll try not to leave anything lying around."

Jon's arm stiffened in mine. François *did* know who we were. Of course he did! If he'd found three genuine hikers in our condition—certainly once he'd seen the state of Bane—skeleton thin, oozing wounds—he'd put all three of us in the old truck parked outside and drive us straight to the hospital, even if it were many kilometers away. But with us? Not a word of it. Just pills and dinner.

Of course, he'd probably guessed the moment Jon failed to react to the light. Perhaps deliberately caught us in the beam for that very reason.

"Thanks," said Jon stiffly. "It does help with my leg."

"Yes. With your leg." The old man smiled knowingly. "I'm sure it does." He went back through to the kitchen, leaving us exchanging meaningful looks or hand squeezes.

"He knows," murmured Jon. "What shall we do? Can we stay?"

"Surely we can trust him?" I whispered...but that's what we'd thought about Louis.

"We can't trust anyone," muttered Bane. "But I'm not sure I want to leave without that box of antibiotics."

It was official, he felt worse than he'd been letting on.

"Then we don't leave," I said firmly.

"What if we did stay a bit?" Jon put in. "That venison's been a lifesaver, don't get me wrong, but a few proper meals...do us a world of good."

"No," said Bane, "I vote we sneak off with the box in the night and put as much distance between us and this place as we can by morning."

Tears of dismay started in the corners of Jon's unseeing eyes. The thought of a desperate night march—though the night only affected him indirectly through Bane's and my tripping and stumbling—clearly brought him near despair.

"Let's stay, Bane," I said softly. "At least a day or so…unless we've any reason to suspect it's not safe. We need to rest." Bane scowled. He'd seen Jon's face too. "We'd have trouble sneaking past Hugo, anyway."

"Ugh, blasted dog, didn't think of that."

The blasted dog licked Bane's hand and pushed at him again until he stroked it absently. Unlikely to be so friendly if we started sneaking around at the dead of night.

François shouldered back through the door carrying a steaming pan. "Come on, sit down, you three." Depositing the pan in the middle of the table, he started to ladle its contents onto the plates. "Big helpings, I assume?"

"Yes, please." We moved towards the table like bees to pollen.

"I won't try and get you to chat tonight." Our host pushed a heaped plate in front of each of us. "S'pect you're exhausted. I didn't make the beds up either, I confess. Took one look in the airing cupboard and thought better of it. If you don't mind using your sleeping bags tonight, you can get cleaned up tomorrow, and have clean sheets after."

"That's fine, thank you," I said, in between mouthfuls of something so gorgeous it came a close second after our first venison meal for the position of *most wonderful thing ever tasted*. "We wouldn't want to put you to any extra trouble."

François waved this away with his fork. "S'no trouble. Living out here in the middle of nowhere, s'quite a treat to have some hapless hikers fetch up on my doorstep."

Actually, *you* fetched us to your doorstep at gunpoint… I just smiled politely.

He *did* know who we were. Why the gun, if he wanted to help us? Hmm. Perhaps because he *did* want to help us. Tough love. He'd never actually threatened us: the gun had simply been there and we'd assumed the threat.

We just about managed to gobble seconds and thirds before beginning to nod at the table.

"All right, bed time," smiled François.

"Oh, let us help you clear," I muttered.

"Leave them, leave them. Upstairs with you. Oh, here's your pill, Brad, better take it."

Bane washed the pill down with his last swig of tea, but stopped at the hall door. "I don't suppose we could have a glass of water each to take up with us?"

I smiled hopefully in support of his request, secretly mystified. *Glass of water?* When our heads hit the pillows we weren't going to know a thing until sometime tomorrow. Keeping watch had definitely passed from difficult to impossible.

Trudging up the stairs behind the old man, a worm of unease turned in my belly. Were we making a huge mistake? We needed to rest, yes, but did we need it badly enough to trust a stranger to this degree? He'd a phone, he could have the EuroArmy here in less than an hour.

"There you go." François waved me through a doorway.

A nice little room with bright blue curtains over the window and two unmade, coverleted beds. Shelves on the wall held a few books and a clutter of boyish treasures—birds' nests, glittery rocks, a—bat?—skeleton. Of course. His sons' bedroom. Surely if we could rest safely under anyone's roof it was his?

"Thank you." I took the tray of glasses from him and went all the way in.

"Drink the water now if you want it," directed Bane, as soon as François had gone.

I obeyed, too sleepy to stop and ask questions. As soon as we'd each popped out to the bathroom Bane placed a chair behind the closed door and balanced two of the emptied glasses right on the edge. The slightest movement of the door would make them fall. For good measure, he placed the metal tray underneath for them to land on. The third glass he balanced on the windowsill. Burglar alarms set.

Spreading out my sleeping bag, I climbed in, any lingering doubts fast swept away by approaching sleep. Jon was already asleep on the other bed; he'd almost made it all the way into his bag.

Bane flopped his sleeping bag onto my bed, top to tail, and climbed in. I raised a leaden eyebrow at him as he settled his feet beside my head.

"Doesn't make sense for the two *largest* people to share, does it?" he retorted.

And you don't want to be on the other side of the room if the EuroGov burst the door down. Selfish coward that I am, I'm not sure I want you to be, either.

My head touched the pillow...

13

THE MAJOR'S CONFESSION

Smash-Crash-Clatter!

I jerked upright. What? Where? My eyes came to rest on a metal tray on which a single glass still spun amid a litter of broken shards.

Burglar alarm.

François peered around the door, lips pursed ruefully as he looked at the damage. "Easy to see how you three have come so far," he remarked, almost under his breath, albeit politely in Esperanto.

Daylight poured around the curtains. Just François peeping in at us. No soldiers piling past him. *Gratias Domine.*

"You can put the pig-sticker away, Brad, I've just brought your next pill."

No need to look at Bane to know what he held. It'd gone back wherever he'd had it by the time the old hunter had crossed the room. Bane accepted both pill and glass of water, downing both.

"Thank you," he said with exquisite politeness, perhaps conscious of both broken glass and rudely brandished knife. "Ah...I have a phone—if you just give me the box I can set an alarm to make sure I don't forget. Less trouble for you."

"S'no trouble," said François, with a smile I interpreted as "nice try." "More sleep...or food?"

"Ooh, that's a hard one," murmured Jon.

My stomach grumbled.

"Food?" I ventured.

"Food," agreed Bane.

"Oh, good," said Jon.

"Come on down when you're ready, then. You can have baths afterwards," said François over his shoulder as he picked up the tray of broken glass and ducked back through the low doorway. "S'more stew. Just needs to go on a plate. *Hugo*, back downstairs, bad dog." A disappointed whine and a patter of paws as the dog preceded him.

Bane beat me out of bed. Much livelier than yesterday, good. Huh. Could've sworn Bane and I were top to tail last night. *Oh.* My cheeks heated slightly—it was *me* who'd somehow got myself turned around, sleeping bag and all. Ah well. Our sleeping bags kept us nicely separate.

We weren't far behind François. Most of the meat in this stew was surely venison, not rabbit—the former hunter-gamekeepers had to live on something. Not a meal to serve to a government inspector.

François still didn't try to make us chat, and afterwards Bane and Jon went up to make a start on the rather daunting undertaking of "getting clean."

I followed them out into the hall to hiss, "Don't you dare shave off the beards. Either of you! Best disguise any of us could hope for!"

Jon groaned and Bane rolled his eyes, but neither contradicted me, so I went back into the kitchen to help François wash up.

"Take it you lot haven't seen a bath for a while, eh?" he said when we'd finished.

Quite embarrassing just how smelly we'd let ourselves get. "We were so short of food. You get so cold washing in streams. We didn't have the time or energy."

"Oh, you did the sensible thing. No good catching your death when you're starving." Opening the fire box of the wood-fired boiler, he packed it full of wood; clapped it shut again. "I'll just keep the hot water coming, eh?"

Bane was shaking my shoulder gently. Oh. I'd fallen asleep on the sofa. I sat up and stared at him. Shockingly clean and wearing unfamiliar garments. François's sons' clothes, no doubt. He'd tidied up the thing growing on his face, but not cut it off, and he looked about ten years older than when I'd last looked at him. Last *really* looked at him.

"You look wonderful."

"So do you." He leaned in to kiss me and I fended him off with a grimy hand.

"Careful! You just got clean!" I processed what he'd said. "Liar. I look like something the cat dragged in during a famine."

"A very wonderful something." He made another attempt at my lips—I continued to hold him at arm's length.

"Back off, I reek, and I know it."

"Hurry up and have your bath, then."

"Has Jo...Jeff finished?"

"Yeah. I made him go first in case he fell asleep and drowned or something. He's now safely asleep on his bed again."

"Not back in that filthy sleeping bag?"

"No chance. François's carried them off for a date with destiny. With his washing machine, anyway."

"That is nice of him. Right, I'm for a soak. I've completely forgotten what color my skin is."

"I haven't," smirked Bane. I threw a cushion at him as I left. I wasn't the only one feeling better.

Lovely to be clean. Less lovely to be dressed in what must be some of our host's dead wife's clothes, but beggars couldn't be choosers. When I went back into the bedroom to tie a scarf around my head, bandanna style, to hide my roots and scar, Jon woke up, and came downstairs with me. François, wonderful man, immediately produced coffee and biscuits, on which we gorged shamelessly.

"So," I said, when the biscuit plate was empty, "we've...er...been away from civilization for a bit. What's been going on in the world?"

François shrugged. "Not much. The EuroGov are still turning the bloc upside down looking for...certain persons, mostly."

"Have any of these...persons...reached their destination?"

"There were rumors soon after the escape that the majority had reached the Vatican Free State. The EuroGov denied it completely and nothing more's been heard, so who knows?"

"Hmm."

"Something you might find interesting, though. As of Tuesday last week, the postSort prize novel was placed on the list of banned books. Category one."

Owning a copy of *I Am Margaret* in any shape or form was now considered on par with owning a copy of the Scriptures, the Koran, or one of a whole host of other books the EuroGov judged unsuitable for general readership. It must've been selling extremely well.

Jon groaned. "That's a shame."

"Category one?" A grin spread over Bane's face. "Brilliant!"

Jon looked startled. "Brilliant? What's brilliant about it? Now people can't read it!"

"Silly." I patted his knee. "How many banned books have you read?"

Jon looked taken aback. "Well, I've *heard* a fair few."

"And so have most people. Ba...Brad's right, this is the best thing that could've happened. I mean, how many copies have they sold by now? And the electronic copies? It's too late!"

"Practically everyone will read it now," said Bane smugly. "It's really incredibly stupid of them."

"Hasn't stopped them banning goodness knows whatever else, has it?" said François. "They don't seem to learn. I thought that might be of interest, anyway."

A slightly awkward silence. Insane to out and tell him who we were—just on the minute off chance he *hadn't* realized.

"Now, let's see...where's that newspaper I had a few weeks ago?" François flipped through a pile lying beside his armchair. "Ah, here's the one." He handed it to me.

Uh oh. The paper version of the *FrenchDaily* article. A front page. Bane glanced over my shoulder; we both eyed François warily.

"You do look more like your photos now you're clean, I must say," he said. "Did you really text the *DailyNewsCorp*?"

I moistened my lips slightly. The pretending was over. "Um, yeah. Didn't know if they'd really print it when I sent it."

"Oh, they were delighted enough with its exclusivity that they dared. They were very careful not to say they wanted you to *go on* being alive and well, you'll notice."

"Yeah," snorted Bane.

"Has there been anything on the news," I asked, "about

the New Adults who helped us? In the last...um...month?"
Exactly how long had we been trekking through that wilderness?

The smile left François's face. "Yeah," he said grimly. "Brave kids. Shame."

"Have they set a trial date?" asked Jon quietly.

"No. I imagine what they most want to get them for is aiding and abetting you three, but they can't prove either of the charges concerning that until the other boy is fit to testify. If he ever is."

"If he ever is?" I echoed.

"The Louis boy woke up a week ago but clearly isn't making much sense as yet."

"Certainly didn't look like Juwan held back with the treacherous rat." From Bane's tone, he wouldn't have held back much either.

"The EuroGov are dragging their heels setting up any trial, because they'll only be able to do Juwan for hitting the other boy, though they've got the girl stone cold for making and setting off that little squib."

"Didn't think they worried about *evidence*," I muttered uneasily.

"Depends," said François. "Two New Adults—well, they've got to be seen to have a hundred percent fair trial, haven't they? Public sympathy's on their side. Not like an EGD Security Major, say. No one cares about one of those."

"Any news about Major Everington, then?"

"Dead man walking, he is. Still...took them almost three months to make him plead guilty." Grudging respect in François's voice. "Stubborn fellow. That is, I've been assuming he's *not?*"

I shrugged. "Oh, not guilty. He's a scapegoat, all right."

"Well, he's singing their tune now." No trace of sympathy in François's voice. Yet really the whole of society was just as guilty as the EGD staff... Bane caught my eye and glared. François's dead sons... I kept my mouth shut.

"Wonder how it went," François muttered, and switched on the TV, navigating to a saved program. A large courtroom came on screen, expensively furnished, every curtain and bit of upholstery either yellow or blue.

"They've tried him already?" I said, startled. Three months...he could've only given in in the last week or two.

"This morning. Be over by now, I expect. Since he confessed."

Or maybe not. Timer numbers showed in the corner of the screen. Still recording. "Where is that? Doesn't look like London."

"Looks fancy, doesn't it?" said Bane, and gave a quick description of the opulence for Jon's benefit.

The voice of the newscaster answered our question. "For anyone just joining us, I'm here at the High Courtroom in Brussels for the trial of Major Lucas Everington, former Commandant in EGD security."

"Brussels!" I murmured.

"Oh boy, that guy's had it." Very pleased Bane sounded too.

"As you can see, the jury are entering..." Twelve decidedly uncomfortable looking people filed into the jury stand. "And now they will bring in the defendant. This will be the first time Major Everington has been seen in public since his arrest at the beginning of July. Reports suggest he has been an uncooperative prisoner, suffering considerable ill-health during his detention due to repeated hunger strikes."

"Hunger strikes!" snorted Jon. "One way to put it."

"Plenty of hunger and much striking, I imagine," I said darkly.

"If he got away with as little as that, he's lucky," said Bane, more soberly.

The door behind the dock opened, and two guards hustled out a figure even more slender than I remembered. They stood him in the middle of the dock and took up positions on either side of the closed door, nonLethal truncheons in hand. NonLethal, but most definitely not painless. The ReAssignees Welfare Board had got them banned from Facilities, thank you Lord for small mercies.

The figure remained motionless, head down, like a dog expecting to be kicked if it so much as twitches. The camera zoomed in, but couldn't see much. The fair hair was clean and neatly trimmed, mostly hidden by the officer's cap, the rest of the uniform similarly neat, but the lack of some degree of exacting crispness suggested—at least to me—that the Major hadn't been responsible for his appearance.

As the guards behind him remained still, the Major finally began stealing looks around court, wary as a snared bird. A glint of green as his gaze darted over the camera without registering it—then his eyes came back, narrowed in an apparent struggle for comprehension—stared right into it.

Ah yes, those green eyes. So like mine. It gave me a weird feeling of kinship with him. Bit creepy, really.

"All rise, all rise," came from the TV—jury, lawyers and viewing gallery all got to their feet as the judge swept in.

The Major's head rose all the way and the camera zoomed eagerly back to his face as he stared at the judge. One hand crept to his chest, touching the uniform. Sudden anger blazed in his eyes—he snatched the cap from his head and hurled it with scant strength but good aim at the judge, who had to duck to avoid it.

The two guards raised their truncheons, but the officer of the guard standing beside the dock gave his head a small, angry shake. The Major had gone motionless again, and I suppose everyone was aware they were on live TV. The guards stepped back again hastily and the hat was returned to the dock, but placed to one side. Afraid of a repeat performance?

Various formal court proceedings took place, then the prosecution read out the charges in a bizarre mixture of emotive language and legalese—show trial, what did one expect? Apparently the Major had betrayed his uniform, betrayed his department, betrayed his subordinates, betrayed the young expectant mothers who might lose their unborn child or their own life as a result of his despicable actions...blah, blah, blah. The prosecutor repeated himself freely, gesticulating and talking himself into a frenzy.

The camera quickly got bored of him and went back to the Major, who now clawed at his uniform with bony fingers. "I hate this uniform," he was muttering. "I hate this vile uniform." Several buttons came to grief before his hands dropped again, tiredly, but he didn't shut up. "Haven't made me wear this vile uniform for months, why now? Why now?"

The officer of the guard shushed him, but he took his head in his hands, messing up his hair, shaking his head like a man trying to come fully awake. Had they given him something to make him more cooperative or was he just struggling to throw off the mind-destroying effects of almost three months of torture? In fact...there would have been no point torturing him after he'd signed the confession, so maybe he'd already had a week or so to recover.

"Why?" he said, apparently to himself. "Ask a stupid question, you know why." His attention shifted to the prosecutor, still in full flow. "What the blooming heck are you going on about?" he demanded. "The EGD kill unborn children every day. Born children too. Grown-up children. Everyone knows that. Are you a raving idiot?"

The judge banged on his desk with his hammer thing. *Order.* The defendant will remain silent unless spoken to."

The two guards twitched their truncheons slightly and the Major's shoulders hunched; he said nothing more. His hands clenched into fists—frightened? Angry? Both?

The prosecutor wound up his ravingly idiotic speech and proceeded to a quick summary of the evidence. Mostly completely made up, as far as Jon and I could tell. My two barely-five-minute meetings with the Major in his garden were expanded into lengthy half-hour conferences. No mention of Finchley—apparently the Major had provided the card used in the actual escape and made most of the arrangements himself.

"What a load of utter nonsense!" I reached for what was left of my own coffee. Stone cold. They'd been at it that long already?

The prosecutor announced the clincher: the defendant had signed a full confession. Then fell smugly silent.

"And how does the defendant plead?" asked the judge.

The defense lawyer stood, appropriately grave-faced, though no doubt being paid to fail. "I believe my client has something to say."

Silence from the dock.

"Major Everington, do you have something to say?"

demanded the judge.

"Doesn't the lawyer just enter a guilty plea?" I asked.

"Not at *this* sort of trial," grunted François.

"They want everyone to hear it from his own lips," said Bane.

"I expect they think it sounds more convincing," agreed Jon.

The Major stood, head down, his hands twisting together. A desperate look on his face, like a man wrestling with a momentous decision. It was hard to identify this pale, jumpy individual with the man I'd feared for four months. The man who'd come far, far closer than the EuroGov to breaking me, in the end.

"Major Everington," repeated the judge, more harshly. "Do you have something to say?"

The Major raised his head again. Sweat beaded his brow—with his torn shirt and messed-up hair, he looked half-mad. His eyes flicked fearfully in the direction of the guards behind him, then he drew a long, long breath and spoke very quietly. "Yes, I have something to say."

The cameras cut back to the judge's smile of satisfaction.

The Major drew another breath and stepped forward to the very front of the dock—moving away from the truncheons? His thin fingers hooked over the wooden barrier like talons. "I have something to say." His voice strengthened. "I retract my confession. I signed it under extreme duress and it is all lies. I met Margaret Verrall in private twice and that is the only truth in the entire thing."

His voice rose still further over the babble of noise from the gallery.

"We spoke for *five minutes*—there's my confession, you lying rats!"

<h1 style="text-align:center">14</h1>

<h2 style="text-align:center">NOT GUILTY</h2>

"Oh my word." Jon sounded stunned.

François whistled, long and low.

"Wow," said Bane. "He's either insane or some sort of masochist."

An angry movement from the guards sent the Major skittering into the corner of the dock, but his eyes blazed with defiance.

"Now they have to lay it all out," I crowed. "Every flimsy stitch of evidence!"

"*No*," said Bane, "only until he can be persuaded to retract his retraction. So no doubt the trial will be over tomorrow morning, latest."

Better not to think about what sort of night the accused would have.

"Still. You tell me you're not enjoying the looks on their faces!"

The judge's flabbergasted expression gave way to fury; he glowered at both the prosecution and the defense. The lawyers quailed, jaws sagging in dismay, and glared in turn at the detention officer. He was the only one who remembered they were on live television, because he remained expressionless, except for a tiny shake of his head to quell the guards.

"Am I to understand," snarled the judge at last, "that the defense is entering a plea of *not guilty?*"

The defense lawyer stared at the man in the dock, looking appalled. "Major Everington, you must reconsider..."

"You heard me, you aphid!" The Major leant over the edge of the dock as though he'd like to spring at the man. "*Not guilty*. Tell them!"

Wilting under the combined glowers of Major, judge and prosecution, the lawyer spread his hands to demonstrate his helplessness. "The defense enters a plea of *not guilty.*"

So the scowling prosecutor, after a hasty whispered conference with his colleagues, began to lay out the evidence, which clearly hadn't been intended to see the light of day in anything other than summarized form. He spent as long as possible on each item, and the defense lawyer dragged things out for all he was worth as well.

The judge sat and tried to smile—occasionally he forgot himself and started scowling again.

"Bet they're wishing they'd chosen the Menace as a scapegoat," I remarked, as they prepared to wrap things up for lunch. A very late lunch was probably what François had slipped out to attend to, actually.

"Yeah," snorted Jon. "The trial would be done and dusted months ago. Don't think *stubborn* was one of her qualities."

"Why's this guy bothering?" asked Bane. "He must know he's had it."

"I know you bit my head off before for comparing you with him, Bane," I said, "but seriously, you'd make it drawn-out and messy and embarrassing for them too, I know you would. I mean, he worked for them for fifteen years, and they turned around and stabbed him in the back. Of course he knows he's had it, and he's pretty miffed about it."

Bane shrugged. "Still, there's a limit to how much pain I'd be prepared to take, just for revenge."

"True. Well, I don't know, perhaps he has a fondness for the truth."

"In EGD Security? You've gotta be particularly good at lying to yourself to do that job."

I shrugged as well, attention drawn back to the screen as the judge invited Major Everington to speak before they adjourned for half an hour.

The Major had been prowling up and down the front of the dock like a caged tiger, paying no attention to anything, but now he stopped and gripped the wood again.

"What do you want me to say?" His voice was low but fierce. "Oh, yes, you want me to tell a pack of convenient lies. Well, I'm so sorry, but you never ordered me to *write* the security protocol, only to *stick* to it. Which I did. And it wasn't *me* who decided a young lady capable of winning an internationally-recognized prize whilst simultaneously writing a bestselling novel and organizing a mass breakout wasn't fit to live. So I don't even think your useless security procedures are the real issue, do you?"

A bark of laughter from the doorway—François was back. "You tell them, dead man." That grudging respect in his voice again.

The judge turned purple and in a few choked words adjourned the court for the lunch break. The camera went back to the Major as judge and jury filed out. The Major's hands trembled as the guards unlocked the door behind him. No food or rest would await him after this morning's performance.

"The lunch is ready," François informed us.

"Come on, let's eat quickly," said Bane. "This is proving even more entertaining than I expected."

"Don't be so ghoulish, Bane," I objected. "A man's life *is* at stake, y'know."

François snorted, muttered something that sounded rather like 'good riddance,' and headed back towards the kitchen.

"It's not at stake!" said Bane. "He's been a dead man since the day they arrested him. It's just taking them a long time to work out the funeral arrangements."

His levity might bug me, but he was right. There'd be no funeral for Lucas Everington, though. He'd be dismantled, his brain burned, the ashes placed in a storage facility for a few years, after which time, no relative having stepped forward to claim them, they'd be scattered on the fields as fertilizer. A bleak end.

But then, I barely knew the man, let alone his family. The only living things I'd seen him care for were his precious plants. The press had tracked down only a sister—who apparently hated him so much she wouldn't even say his name, let alone why. So my gut feeling was probably right: that all the man's nearest and dearest had chlorophyll running in their veins instead of blood.

We helped François wash up in double-quick time after

we'd eaten, then sat down and switched to the live broadcast. They hadn't adjourned for the day yet. The Major stood there in the middle of the dock, shaking. He looked exhausted. Had he been stood there, shaking, since lunch? Before long, he sat down on the floor, scooting into the front corner where only the two guards—and the cameras mounted on rails all around the ceiling—could see him, sitting there with his forehead on his knees. The judge ignored his disappearance from view: nothing was going to affect the outcome of the trial, so he clearly couldn't care less.

The phony evidence hadn't improved. Jon and I booed and hissed at the worst bits, and eventually I snapped and threw a biscuit at the prosecutor's head, which was apparently the funniest thing that'd happened all day, in Bane's opinion. But soon it was almost five o'clock and the judge was again asking—demanding—that the Major speak.

The guards pulled him up and stood him on his feet, but to start with he just went on staring at the hideously geometric blue and yellow carpet.

"Major Everington," persisted the judge, "this is your opportunity to speak, I *most strongly* advise that you do not waste it." Translation: last chance to spare yourself a night at the tender mercies of Reginald Hill and the Department for Internal Affairs.

The Major shuddered and raised his head at last. "What can I say?" His voice was very low, now. "Why don't you just have them take me out the front, put me up against a convenient wall and shoot me? Save the taxpayers *so* much money. How about that, *your honor?*"

His tone was mocking, but something deadly serious shone in his face, as though riddled with bullets was a highly attractive way to end the day. Of course, considering his alternative...

"Very well," said the judge coldly. "Get a good night's sleep, Major. We'll see what you have to say for yourself tomorrow."

After a rather quiet evening meal that followed closely on the heels of our late lunch, we went back to the sitting room with coffees. Were Juwan and Doms in a place rather like where the Major had been taken? No, François was right: they wouldn't want any suspicion of torture. Not with New Adults.

Hugo thrust his head onto François's lap, whining. The old man stroked him without looking down, gazing at a framed photo on the table by the sofa just beside me. It showed the twins, François standing behind them, his face less lined, less tired, hair less grey, his arms around a much younger woman, made beautiful by her shining smile.

"Is this your wife?" I asked.

François nodded. Added calmly, "*Yes*, she was younger than me," as though to spare us from coming up with any polite comment to this effect.

"Doesn't matter. If you were happy." Bane peered around me at the photograph. "Y'look happy."

"She had a beautiful smile." I had to say something.

François nodded wordlessly; his nostrils quivered.

"Could you...describe her?" asked Jon softly.

François swallowed hard and it was a moment before he could speak. "I'm sorry. I don't think I can. It...it has not been long enough." After a moment he leant across, touching a finger to each figure as he spoke their names like a caress. "Marie... Philippe... Jean..."

"There was nothing you could do," I said, remembering Juwan's guilt. Repeated in how many homes and hearts across the EuroBloc?

At least one. François sighed and glanced at Bane. "How to even know where to begin? No Resistance contacts, me. Always sought to keep my hands clean. So much for that. I'd take...I'd've taken help from the devil himself."

"Never a good idea, that," remarked Jon, in a tone of theological certainty.

Bane rolled his eyes and kicked him in the ankle. "We entirely understand, I assure you. I do, anyway. I *did*, so Margo would have it."

"Not quite the devil," I said, "some of his lesser minions, certainly."

"Are you complaining?"

"No. I'm not a *saint*, I'm afraid."

François looked sunk in bleak thoughts, so I added, "I wish there'd been a way, François."

"Hmm? Oh, yes. Me too. Me too."

We went to sleep in crisp clean beds for the first time in...well, in a long time. I still hadn't got around to asking Bane the date. François remained so quiet and strained... shame the conversation had to end up on his lost ones, but...probably inevitable.

I felt safer, but not quite safe enough to ask for a separate bed for myself, and Francois hadn't offered. I arranged an extra sheet between me and Bane, not bothering trying to sleep top to tail again, but it took me ages to settle down, even after Bane was snoring. I must've caught up on my sleep better than I thought. Eventually I said a rosary—the Sorrowful Mysteries—for all those suffering under torture that night. Especially stubborn green-eyed stick insects. And slept at last.

Broad daylight filtered around the curtains. We'd slept late again. Bane's forehead was normal temperature, good; his arm—still hot but less so.

"Am I on the mend?" he murmured.

"Doctor Margo would say so."

He slipped a hand behind my head and tried to draw me down for a kiss but I squirmed free and sat on the edge of the bed, yawning. Sharing a bed for protection was one thing, but I couldn't just lie around praying, "Lead me not into temptation, Lord": I had to keep myself out of it as well! He smirked at me, correctly feeling flattered rather than rejected by my hasty withdrawal.

"Had your pill yet?"

Bane screwed up his face. "No. I'd better go down and get it."

"When are we going to carry on to Rome?"

Bane frowned and pulled out his phone. "First of October tomorrow."

I glanced at Jon, still sound asleep. We both knew how weak he still was. "Set off again tomorrow, then, d'you think?"

"We have to."

"Yeah."

Bane took his clothes into the bathroom. I'd just finished dressing when there was a patter of paws up the stairs. Hugo nosed the door open, bounded into the bedroom and started licking Jon's face. Jon stirred sleepily, fending him off.

I caught the dog's collar. "Come on, Hugo, let him sleep. Good dog, let's go and find François, shall we?"

Hugo simply slipped from my grasp and raced out of the room.

Jon sat up in bed and stretched. "Morning, Margo."

"Morning, Jon. I'm just off, if you want to get up." I shut the door behind me.

Hugo's tail disappeared around François's bedroom door...a crash from within.

"Hugo!" Hurrying in, I grabbed for his collar again. He breezed past, saw I'd closed the other door and pattered off downstairs.

"And you wonder why you're not allowed upstairs!" Standing a small bedside table back up, I replaced clock, coaster, flashlight, and pile of letters. Turned to leave... Wait...

There was something terribly familiar about those letters. I picked up the top one.

Hand addressed, to François's post office box in the nearest town, with a big red stamp across the front:

CLEARED

– EGD CENSOR –

Oh. His sons' letters. I placed it back on the table—snatched it up again, peering at the frank. *September.* My eyes checked the year...the letter had been sent *this month*. Were his sons taken but not yet dead?

I put it down and headed downstairs. No wonder he found it all so painful to talk about! His wife might've been dead barely six months—a year and a half, maximum. How horrible. So much easier for him to let us assume them long dead and gone, but...well, I knew now. I'd rather get it out in the open.

Bane was in the sitting room, just turning on the TV to sneak a look at the trial.

"What's happening?" I asked.

"They haven't started yet. Can't expect a judge to be up at this time, can you?"

I snorted. We were hardly early.

"Look at the dock," Bane said. "The judge must be afraid of another hat attack."

They'd put up Perspex screens around it.

"Seems a bit excessive. He could hardly stand up. Oh look, here he comes."

The guards entered, the Major stumbling between them, looking lucid in an exhausted sort of way. He staggered when they let go of him and almost fell. His eyes narrowed on the Perspex, and he raised a hand to touch the cap, which was back on his head.

"No chance," sniggered one of the guards.

Without changing his expression, the Major snatched the cap and hurled it at the Perspex. It bounced off and struck the guard square in the face. Clutching his nose, swearing, the guard lashed out furiously with his truncheon. His partner grabbed for his arm—

Too late. The prisoner was down on hands and knees, back arched in pain, a thin sound of agony coming from his throat, and the gallery was erupting, delighted reporters scribbling about "brutality in the courtroom," no doubt. The officer of the guard looked as though he wanted to personally lay the truncheon across his subordinate's backside.

The Major remained as he was for several long moments, shuddering, then his arms buckled and he slumped the rest of the way to the ground. But as the minutes drew on, those long spasms of pain died down, his body gradually relaxed, and his breathing grew slow and deep—he'd fallen asleep.

The guards seemed afraid to lay a hand on him—the one was busy plugging his bleeding nose with tissue. They just left him lying there on the carpet, sleeping peacefully in front of the watching world. Clearly he'd *not* had a good night's sleep.

"Oh, typical, here's the judge." I muttered, making room for Jon on the sofa as he came in.

"All rise, all rise..."

The guards shook the Major's shoulder—he curled straight into a protective ball. Hissing and muttering at him to get up, they finally pried his arms loose and simply lifted him onto his feet.

The judge settled himself behind the bench, as calm and self-possessed as he'd been the previous morning.

"Obviously expects things to go right today," said Bane.

"Surely you don't think that would be a good thing, do you?" I said scathingly. "Not like you to side with the EuroGov!"

"I'm not siding with the EuroGov! The more embarrassed they are the better. Just don't expect me to shed any tears over their victim. The man would've watched you die. You and Jon both. And all the others."

"Actually he didn't used to watch. That was the Menace."

"Speaking *metaphorically*...wait, she actually *did?* All of them, not just...?" Not just Uncle Peter.

"Oh yeah. Twisted witch."

"Yeugh. Perhaps I understand a bit better why you and Jon wish it was her in that dock."

"I don't think I'd wish anyone in that dock." I hoped that was true. "But her before him."

"Yeah," said Jon. "He gave me a cane once. And there *was* Finchley's face." He tamed an involuntary grin. "Of course, I'm just glad Finchley was *punished*. Not that it was...y'know. Like that."

"No, I don't know," said Bane. "What did happen to foul Finchley's face? Hope it hurt."

"Major Everington happened," I said.

"Yeah, he cut...um," Jon's head turned slightly in my direction, his cheeks heating. "Uh, he cut a...*phallic symbol*...into Finchley's cheek. For what he did to Margo, y'know."

"A phallic...oooh." Bane nodded in sudden understanding, then his eyes widened. "He *did?* Sweet!" He glanced at the dock. "Y'know, the man's suddenly grown on me a bit."

Jon laughed, and I concentrated on the screen. So long

as neither of them made the connection with the equally, er...imaginative...design on my forehead. I certainly wasn't ready to try and explain my suspicion that in his own twisted way, the man might've been trying to do me a favor.

"Major Everington, do you have something to say?" said the judge, having opened the session.

The guards were still holding the Major upright, because he refused to put his weight on his feet. Chin on chest, he stared down at his limp toes and said nothing.

"Major Everington!" The judge's confident tone disappeared. "*Am I under the impression you wish to speak?*"

The Major wouldn't even look up. Showed every sign of imitating a silent sack of potatoes all day, in fact, so I dragged myself from the sofa. François was probably hard at work getting our breakfast and anyway, I wanted to speak to him.

Hugo slipped passed me as I went into the kitchen. Yes, François was there. Oh dear, his face was still grey and strained.

"Good morning, François."

"Oh, Margaret, *bonjour*. Is your young man far behind you? I haven't given him his pill, have I?"

"Don't worry about it," I reassured him. "He'll be through in a moment."

"Oh...good. Good." His hand flew suddenly to his chest and he drew a sharp breath. His face whitened even more.

"Are you okay?"

"Fine, fine. Just a touch of heart trouble, it's always like this. Nothing to worry about. Ah, glad you're here, though, would you do me a favor?"

"Of course." Was he really okay? He seemed so agitated.

"Could you get me an armful of wood from the woodshed? Just follow the garden path to the bottom, by the forest."

"Oh. Yes, no problem."

"I'll...I'll lay the table." He grabbed a pile of plates and disappeared.

I took the key from the peg and unlocked the back door, heaved it open. I could mention the letters when I got back.

"Where are you off to?" Bane had managed to drag

himself away as well.

"Just getting some wood for François."

"I'll do that. You go and rescue Jon from that blinking dog. He's being licked to death."

"Oh..." Well, I'd get a few minutes alone with François. "If it won't hurt your arm. Woodshed's right at the bottom of the garden path, apparently."

"I'm sure I'll find it." Bane breezed out, slamming the doors behind him. He still hadn't taken his pill. Oh well. A few more minutes wouldn't hurt.

François came back in, still holding the plates, and looked shocked to see me. "Margaret? Aren't you fetching the wood?"

"It's okay, Bane's getting it. He doesn't really take no for an answer, y'know." How to bring up the letters? He looked so...anguished already. Perhaps I should just let it lie. If he'd *rather* pretend they were dead and...dismantled...

The door smashed open... *Bane, gently!* I spun around.

Not Bane. A soldier stepped across the threshold, rifle in hand.

15

A DEAL WITH THE DEVIL

No time to think, I snatched in a desperate breath and screamed at the top of my lungs, "Soldiers, François!" I wanted to warn the others, while not letting the soldiers know they were definitely here...

The soldier cannoned into me, slamming me back into the fridge. By the time his huge hand clapped over my mouth, I was silent already, breath knocked from me.

François stood as though paralyzed, still clutching the plates. How could he not have dropped them in the shock?

Soldiers pushed past into the rest of the house, knocking the plates from the old man's hands. They rung and shattered deafeningly on the floor. One spun on its edge, round and round.

Crack-Crack. Crack. Crack-Crack.

A volley of shots from outside. My chest constricted around my heart, crushing it. Bane? *Bane?* I couldn't breathe.

A black-uniformed Captain stopped in front of me—uh oh, specialCorps: they only did secret stuff. Big-shouldered and heavy-browed but with a shrewd glint in his eyes and a greedy look that scared me far more. He held a nonLee in his hand, a Lethal pistol holstered at his right hip. A more junior officer—lieutenant?—hovered at his side.

"Here's the big prize." Smiling, the Captain used the point of the nonLee to push my hair aside, baring my forehead.

Had François's gate sensor failed? Been circumvented? Did he not have the alarm on him?

A soldier rushed in from outside.

"Well?" demanded the Captain.

"We found a boy answering the description of Blake Marsden at the bottom of the garden, sir. My men are pursuing him."

"He got away?"

"Took off into the forest like a startled deer," said the soldier defensively. "We fired at him, but missed."

The Captain hissed angrily through his teeth. "They'd better not let him escape!"

The crushing pressure in my chest eased slightly. Once in the forest, Bane was unlikely to be caught, not with any kind of head start. *Thank you, Lord, that he used his head! Thank you he didn't come rushing back to the house to try and help me...would've been useless.*

Jon...had they got Jon? How could he have escaped? My scream would've given him mere moments.

And François...they had him. He'd die for helping us, just like Doms and Juwan.

Another soldier shouldered back through from the hall. Hugo followed, snarling, and ran to François.

"No one else in the building, sir. We found this in the living room, against the sofa. The dog was in the room and the TV's warm." He displayed Jon's long, thin, hiking stick.

I struggled to keep my face smooth. A stick, abandoned against a sofa...let's hope the Captain was stupid, after all.

He swung around to face me. "Where's Jonathan Revan?"

Not that stupid, apparently. I kept my mouth shut. He wouldn't expect me to tell him immediately.

"Where is he?"

I said nothing. His big hand flew out and caught me across the face. I staggered back, just taming a yelp to a mere indrawn breath. Jon had managed to hide, but if he heard me...

"Where?"

I said nothing. He hit me again. My head thudded into the fridge door. François flinched and clung to Hugo's collar as the dog's growl grew ear-shattering.

"Where is he? I can keep this up until your face is pulp."

Would, too; the creep was enjoying it.

He raised his hand again.

"Don't!" I cried. "What does it matter! He's dead! The bear killed him!"

Bother, hated lying. Wasn't good at it, either. Tell lots of truth, Margo...

"Bear?" He raised his eyebrows and casually flicked his

hand across my face again.

"I *told* you! Bear! It attacked us. We were starving, we'd found a dead deer, the blood brought the bear. We didn't dare leave the meat so it attacked. Clawed Bane's shoulder and killed Jon."

"Show me this living room," the Captain told the soldier. "Bring the reAssignee."

Marching me along the hall, they pushed me through the doorway.

"Where was the stick?"

"Against the sofa."

"The boy was here, then." The Captain ran his eyes around the room. "Can't have gone far." He turned back to me. "ReAssignee, Jonathan Revan is alive and here in this house. Tell me where he is before I get nasty."

Nastier.

I said nothing. He didn't believe the bear story. And I'd no more idea than he did where Jon had hidden.

"I suppose you don't know either," he muttered. "Well, let's give him a reason to come out."

He grabbed my blouse and ripped. Buttons bounced and flew around the room. I tried to get my arms free of the soldier holding me to pull my blouse together, but he squeezed until I gasped in pain.

"Put her on the sofa," said the Captain with a horrible smile. I couldn't see the soldier's face, but without hesitation he yanked me backwards and flipped me onto the cushions, holding my shoulders down effortlessly.

Oh, come back Major Everington, all is forgiven.

The Captain climbed on top of me—hot, heavy, terrifying weight—*No!* His cold hand touched my bare skin...a scream rose in my throat...no, I mustn't, Jon's *life.* I panted with the effort of choking it back. *A knee, could I get a knee up?*

"Don't plan to make any noise, huh? Well, Jonathan Revan, I'd better fill you in. Your girlfriend and I are about to have some fun. If you hear her moaning, don't worry, she's not in pain. Not much, anyway."

His hand slid to my waistband. I twisted, tears spilling down my cheeks, my breath catching more and more noisily, but I couldn't help it, I had to get away from him I had to, *please, please, get off me, just get off me, get off me, get off me, GET OFF ME!*

Just when the words must've escaped from my throat, a sooty shape dropped from the chimney, hurtled across the room and tore the Captain away. The sofa went over backwards with the force of the rush, Jon and the man rolling into the wall in a heap.

Thunk, smack! Jon's fists found their target. I'd been yanked from the soldier's grasp as the sofa tipped, and I grabbed for my blouse... But two soldiers were pulling Jon off the Captain already. They flung him down on the floor and raised their booted feet, drove them into him.

I dived forward, trying to shield him. "Leave him *alone!*"

They desisted. So they'd stand back and watch their Captain treat me like that, but they weren't prepared to kick me themselves! Bastards!

"Jon, are you okay? Jon, I'm so sorry! Why did you come out? Why did you come out!" I tried to hug him, thought I was comforting him until he managed to sit up, wheezing and clutching his chest with one arm, and got the other around me. Suddenly I was clinging to him like a vice, crying.

"Shss, Margo, I've got you, I've got you." He eased his other hand from his chest and started rubbing my back, his breathing labored.

The Captain climbed to his feet, a small trickle of blood coming from one nostril, otherwise depressingly unaffected by Jon's blows.

"I suppose you meant to say he was *channeling* the bear," he sneered, wiping his nose on his sleeve. "Well, that's two of them." He looked up, over us, and there was François, between a pair of soldiers, clutching Hugo's collar and staring at my torn blouse in sick dismay.

His eyes rose to the Captain. "Please, where are they? Where are my boys?"

Oh Lord, no! François had turned us in. Yet...he'd been a hundred percent committed to helping us, hadn't he? Right up until the moment last night, when he thought of doing a deal with the devil...

"You've got two of them!" François went on, when the

Captain said nothing. He couldn't meet my eyes. "Two for two, where are they? You were supposed to bring them!"

It all made sense. Heart trouble, no, he'd felt his movement alarm go off. And asked me to fetch wood. Supposed to be me running through the forest, free, and Bane back here with Jon. Two boys, two painless deaths, an even trade. But Bane's gallantry upset his plan and now...

I blocked off the conclusion to that sentence. Shoved it to the back of my mind and locked it away before I could do something stupid like faint or throw up or cry even harder.

"Please...my boys?" François sounded frantic.

The Captain regarded him contemptuously.

"The EuroGov does not do deals with traitors... Don't try to deny it!" he spat, as François's mouth opened in desperate protest. "By your own admission you sheltered them for thirty-six hours before doing what you should've done straight away—and then you tried to attach *conditions!* Well, the EuroGov *did* agree you would have your sons—and here they are."

He waved his hand and a soldier stepped forward and set two objects on the coffee table. Two small, square boxes. The kind that held ashes. François's face drained to a horrible grayish white and he thudded down on his knees; reached out a trembling hand to touch one...

Hugo's collar slipped from his other hand and the dog leapt for the Captain, snarling. I made a hasty grab and dragged him back—Jon rubbed his fur and wheezed, "Shhh, shhh," rather frantically.

"Bit of a rushed job," smirked the Captain, ignoring the angry dog. "Rather wasteful, I imagine."

The foul, evil...trying to wring every scrap of pain from the old man. Mercifully François hardly seemed to hear. He held the boxes to his chest now, one in each hand, silent tears running down his cheeks. I had to look away from the desolation on his face.

"But," went on the Captain, "since the EuroGov does not do deals with criminals, naturally no one must know."

I glanced at him, saw the gleam of anticipation in his cruel eyes.

"François," I said quickly. "François, I forgive you."

Jon's head rose. "I forgive you too, François, do you hear me?"

François's head turned, his eyes focusing slightly. "*Je suis désolé.*"His voice caught so badly it was hard to make the words out. "I'm sorry... I just wanted... I just wanted to save them..."

"We know," said Jon. "It's okay."

"Okay," snorted the Captain. "How very touching. I didn't know any definition of *okay* applied to Full Conscious Dismantlement."

My stomach lurched, my throat closed—I clutched Jon's shoulder, squeezing my eyes shut. *Breathe, Margo, just breathe.*

When I opened my eyes again François's face had crumpled in on itself, crushed by grief and guilt.

"I forgive you," I whispered, meeting his eyes. *Please believe me.*

"Well, the EuroGov doesn't." The Captain drew his Lethal. "François Bernier, you have been found guilty by your own admission of Sedition, Category One, for which the penalty is death. Your organs being so old and useless, justice to be rendered a little more directly."

He raised the pistol and fired point blank into the old man's face. I shut my eyes a second too late—when I opened them again François lay on his back, a box resting beside each out-flung hand. Hugo strained against Jon's grip, barking furiously.

I took a step towards the Captain—Jon's arm tightened around me, holding me back much as his other hand held the dog. He couldn't hold my tongue, though. "You *filthy, lowlife slave* of a *corrupt satanic kakistocracy—*"

The Captain's fist flew out and caught me in the face, sending me hurtling back into the wall. Everything went vague and confused, like looking through cotton wool. Spinning cotton wool. As if in a dream—nightmare—I saw Hugo pull free of Jon as he reeled from trying to stop my fall. The dog went straight for the Captain's throat—with shocking speed the pistol appeared in the man's hand again—a crack and a horrible whine and Hugo went down in a thrashing heap.

"Get them outside," ordered the Captain.

"For pity's sake!" shouted Jon, pointing towards the whimpering dog, now kicking its life out on the carpet. "But I s'pose you don't know what pity is, do you!"

The Captain drove his boot into the dog, drawing an agonized yelp, and Jon leapt at him. A vicious shove from the Captain and he landed on me, hard. Even the muzzy nightmare lost clarity...

...A strong smell of petrol... I lay on the garden path, my head in Jon's lap. Blood ran down Jon's face from his nose. Several soldiers were unscrewing the lids of petrol cans and chucking them into the cottage. A whining and scrabbling came faintly from within.

"Monster!" I gasped, struggling into a sitting position.

The Captain ignored me, focused now on his work. Why *was* this secret, anyway? No one would consider this a bargain made with a criminal...not *kept*, anyway. *Ah*, the secrecy wasn't for the general population but for all those who might yet be tempted into trying such a bargain. Wouldn't want to scare them off.

"Get them in," the Captain ordered the soldiers standing over us.

A small secure transport van had been backed up to the garden gate. The soldiers hauled us both to our feet and marched us to it; shoved us up into the back. Two of them climbed in and sat opposite, rifles trained on us.

The Captain leant in to speak to them. "This door does not open until we reach the Detention Facility, understood? Be aware, they may try to provoke you. Shoot them in the leg if necessary, but don't kill them—the bosses would prefer them alive."

"Sir."

"Sir."

The Captain slammed the doors shut. Through the bulletproof rear window, we could see him issuing final orders to the other soldiers, clearly remaining behind to carry on the hunt for Bane, then he got into the passenger seat and nodded to the driver. Bumping forward, the van maneuvered around the troop transport truck and onto the drive. The cottage was barely out of sight when a pillar of black smoke began rising above the treetops.

Lord, let that poor dog die quickly. And receive François, Jean, and Philippe to yourself.

Then...nothing to think about but...where we were going. The word *Facility* had started strange cold shudders all down my spine.

Would it happen quickly, when we got there? Would they just give me the injection straight away? Or try again to break me? The final instruction to the dismantlers had already been signed, hadn't it? The final instruction...the final instruction...the *dismantlers*...

"It's okay," Jon whispered into my hair—I fought free of my mental maelstrom enough to realize I was sobbing into his gaunt chest. "It's okay."

Unfortunately the evil Captain was right: there was nothing "okay" about what awaited me. An icy ball of panic had taken the place of my stomach, and my heart juddered in terror.

Why had we even tried this crazy trek? Now all was lost...

The thought of the dismantlement itself drove all reason from my mind; the thought they might try to break me plunged me into a dark place of mindless dread I'd never had the misfortune to visit before.

'Cause I'd barely held out last time.

No, no, no, no, no, no, no, no, no, no, no, no, no, no, no...

...There was sound, a gentle humming. Familiar. Soothing. It floated into the darkness of my fear and drew me up and out, towards the light. A tune. A tune that summoned words into my mind, words which acted as a blowtorch on the icy blackness.

Ipse tantum est petra mea et salus mea,
Praesidium meum: non movebor.

> The Lord is my stronghold and my deliverer,
> my protector: I will stand unmoved.

I clung to the tune and the remembered words, allowed them to tow me to the surface, where I found...Jon. Of course. Jon rocking me gently, his hands rubbing my hair and back as he hummed that lifeline.

Breathing shallowly, I clung to the psalmody, let it fill my mind and drive the terror away.

Lord, please don't let them try to break me. Please don't let them try. The prayer came at last. *Let them just give me the injection. I might be able to hold out that long.*

"What if they break me, Jon?" I whispered in Latin, regaining the use of my voice.

He hummed a few more bars, still rocking me slowly, slowly.

"All you have to do is your best," he murmured. "Just do your best, and the Lord's mercy will take care of the rest. But they probably won't try again and if they do, I don't think they *will.*"

"How d'you know!"

"Think it through, Margo." His lips brushed the top of my head and he must've felt my breathing speed up, because he started humming again.

I grabbed the sound once more, clung to it. *Think it through?* How would that help? Because I could see it, all too clearly, back on that gurney, with those swine tempting and threatening, could hear those awful words squeaking from my cowardly throat. I shuddered and burrowed against Jon.

They'd still dismantle me in the normal way for the Sedition charge, of course. But not before they'd paraded me in front of the press, had me say it again and again... I choked, my head flying up. "I will not say it in front of the press! I *will not.*"

Jon *was* right. I wouldn't say it to the press. So how many times could I get myself on and off the gurney, like that? I must hold silent: simply no point doing anything else.

I rested my head against Jon's shoulder, breathing as though I'd just run a race, and looked through the cab and out the windscreen. Forest. From the way we bounced and jounced, we were still on the drive.

"I wish you hadn't come out, Jon."

"What, you'd rather I was still in the house! I beg to differ."

"You know what I mean. I wish you were free like Bane."

"Never mind *me*. I wish *you* were free like Bane. Or *instead* of. And I can say that as his friend because I'm absolutely certain he'd agree."

"It was meant to be me who was free," I whispered. "François asked me to go out to the woodshed. But Bane went instead." Jon should know, however briefly, that François hadn't meant me to die like this.

"Oh. Poor Bane. François's dead, isn't he. And his sons." It wasn't a question. He'd followed what was going on just fine.

"Yes," I murmured anyway. *"Requiescant in pace."*

"Requiescant in pace," sighed Jon. "Stupid thing to do, though."

Never a good idea. He'd been right, of course. You never got more from the devil than he took, but it could be hard to remember that when he had something you wanted *so much*. François's sons. Probably the only thing for which he'd have betrayed us.

Wearing only François's wife's ripped blouse over her ill-fitting bra, I was shivering. My jacket, complete with my bookReader and photos and everything, was back in the cottage, being devoured by the flames. One lonely button remained on the blouse—I fastened it and huddled closer to Jon's warmth, my arms wrapping around his back. Easy to be resolute and calm—comparatively—with him beside me.

Which of us would they take first? I swallowed down resurging panic and closed my eyes, breathing in his oh-so-familiar Jon scent.

"If...you're first, I'll be praying for you," he murmured in my ear. "Don't forget it."

Mind reader.

"And vice versa."

He gave a faint snort. "Yeah, well, I'll just be snoozing my way into the next life, don't worry yourself about me." A moment's silence. "Margo, anything I've ever done to you, I'm really sorry."

My turn to snort. "You've never done anything to me, Jon, nothing bad, anyway. Anything *I've* ever done to *you*, I'm sorry...I'm *so* sorry for." *Letting you fall in love with me, for example.*

"Margo, you have nothing to apologize for. Nothing."

We were silent for a while, then the van went over a particularly vicious pothole and one of the guards cursed.

"Longest flipping driveway ever," he grumbled in Esperanto. French accent.

"You know these country places." His companion sounded German. SpecialCorps was multi-departmental, wasn't it? "Anyway, only twenty kilometers to the Facility once we hit the main road. Could be worse, eh?"

My blood chilled again. Twenty kilometers. A fairly short trip, even on curving mountain roads like the ones around here. I tucked my nose under Jon's chin again, clasping my hands behind his back.

"Jon, you're my best friend and I love you, you know that, right?" I pressed a kiss onto his neck since his face was half covered in beard and rested my cheek on his shoulder again, swallowing back a sudden wave of tears as I turned my engagement ring on my finger. Oh, *Bane*—former best friend, current fiancé...never to be husband...

"I know, Margo. Love you too." His lips caressed the scar on my forehead. No best friend qualification from him.

His nose slid into my hair, putting his lips by my ear. "Now we've dealt with all these very important matters, tell me, is there any possible way of getting out of here?"

In other words, *now that you've stopped being catatonic, Margo, look around for me, will you?*

Under cover of looking out the front, I stole a glance at the guards. Eyes fixed unwaveringly on us and their grips on their rifles firm.

"The guards are very alert," I said just as quietly, despite the fact we were both speaking Latin. "If we try and jump them they'll probably just shoot us somewhere non-fatal: you heard the Captain. And getting out..." I turned as though to see out the back windscreen. "It's a code lock. We can't get out without shaking the code out of the guards or getting someone to open it from outside." I sorted through my confused recollections of being loaded into the vehicle. "No, it's code locked from outside as well. Blast, I *hate* code locks."

If every lock in the Facility had been a code lock with a covered keypad, we'd all still be there. Hellishly difficult to get around—unless you'd a lot of cash handy.

Jon gave just the tiniest wince. "Doesn't sound too encouraging."

"'Fraid not."

"By the time we get there it'll be too late. Let's see. We can't reach the driver. What's the back like? Bulletproof?"

"Looks like it."

"Well, if we can't think of anything else by the time we're a bit closer, perhaps we should just throw ourselves on the guards and give it our best shot."

Translation: if it works, wow, brilliant; if not, well, we might just get some nice lethal ricochets flying around back here.

"Up for it?" he asked.

Nothing wrong with an escape attempt. "Yeah, count me in."

"Right."

I settled closer to him and he snugged his arms more firmly around me, starting on a rosary. I joined him, the better to avoid spiraling back into that black place of fear. The van bounced on up the drive and other than the soldiers' occasional curses and our soft murmur all was silent in the back.

My mind was jolted from its only marginally successful attempt to meditate on Our Lord's Agony in the Garden as the van bumped to a halt. In the cab, the Captain threw up his hands in a frustrated gesture; the driver spread his in the universal disclamation of responsibility.

"Which idiot shut that?" echoed one of our guards.

"Don't look at me," said the other. "I never got out of the truck."

Oh, there was the cause of all the irritation. The gate at the end of François's endless driveway had been closed by whichever over-zealous soldier opened it. Of course, if by some miracle we'd got hold of François's pickup and made a run for it, the overzealous idiot would be getting accolades for foresight and *using his initiative*.

The Captain flung his door open, slid out, slammed it shut, and strode up to the gates, opening them and dropping the gatestops to hold them open. Good strong gates—in that other reality, they probably would've stopped the old vehicle.

The Captain freed the last gatestop—and a dark shape darted from the forest and yanked open the driver's door.

16

FRIENDS IN HIGH PLACES

"Bane!" I gasped. Jon froze; I could practically see his ears straining.

A glint of silver and the driver went rigid. Bane's lips moved, some fierce command—but the driver cut the engine. The Captain turned, his hand went to his right hip, drawing the Lethal, but Bane was behind the door.

The driver still didn't move. Bane snapped something else, and from the man's flinch and the rapidity with which he suddenly vacated the vehicle, Bane's words weren't the only thing that had pierced his skin.

The Captain fired twice as Bane dived into the driver's seat—the shots ricocheted off door and hood, missing the gap between—he began to sprint towards the van and he was *fast*. Bane slammed the door and scanned the control panel...quick, quick, *quick!*

Snick.

The doors locked just as the Captain lunged for the handle. Our guards watched, wide-eyed, paralyzed with in-decision. *Don't open the door until you reach the Facility.*

The Captain stepped back and began firing methodically into the lock. Fumbling with the controls, Bane ignored him. The engine roared back into life: Bane slammed the van into gear, the wheels spun and we were off, tearing through the gates and onto the marginally-smoother road beyond. The Captain fired several more shots after us—at our tires, from the slant of his pistol.

Of course, this not being a movie, he missed, pistols being decidedly inaccurate things over any distance what-soever, or so our new driver had told me often enough.

"I'm guessing Bane's now driving," gasped Jon, feet against the opposite seat and one arm withdrawn from around me to brace us against the front of the van. I'd adopted a similar position, my free arm against the rear window.

"Yep," I gasped back.

Bane kept up the insane speed, throwing us around the bends as the road left the valley floor and climbed quickly up towards the next pass, growing steep and flanked by precipices. It wasn't me and Jon he was trying to shake around, of course. Gasping as they were flung to and fro, the two guards held a muffled conversation involving a lot of "Buts...?" and "Whats...?" and not many conclusions.

We reached an unusually straight stretch of road with the usual mountainside on the right and precipice on the left, the entire forested valley stretched out below us—enough to give anyone vertigo, no matter how serious the situation.

Bane brought the van to a screeching halt and all four of us flew forward and smacked into the window—the guards recovered quickly and trained their rifles on us again.

"Sit back," one of them snapped. "You sit there and don't make any sudden moves."

We were quite happy to sit and get our breath back whilst Bane took the vehicle out of gear, put the parking brake on and hunted for the intercom button.

"Are you two okay?" His voice filled the small gloomy compartment as he peered through the window.

"We're fine." No point babbling just at the moment. How did he plan to get us out?

His attention shifted to the soldiers and his face hardened. "Open the door and let them out."

The French soldier snorted. "Oh, *oui*, and would you like a glass of wine, while I'm at it?"

"Let them out." Bane's voice thrummed with menace. "I'm warning you."

"Look, you filthy jackal pup," said the German soldier. "We may not be able to catch *you*—though by all means stick around until someone does it for us—but we're certainly not letting *these* two out. You can't make us, out there with that pitiful little knife. End of story."

"Oh, I wasn't planning to use the knife," said Bane softly. "Margo and Jon have a friend in a very high place and He's provided a much, much more impressive weapon, which I may just borrow. So *let them out.*"

"Perhaps we'll put a bullet in each of their legs," said the French soldier. "Think that'll shut you up?"

Bane's face went very bleak indeed. "You don't want to leave me with only the one option, trust me. Just. Let. Them. Out."

"No," said the soldiers, in unison.

"Fine." Bane's face was as grim as I'd ever seen it. "If you're going to change your minds, you'd better do it awfully quickly." His eyes shifted to mine, softened. He mouthed, "I love you."

I mouthed it back to him. Slowly, deliberately, he put on the seatbelt. What was he going to...?

He slammed the van back into gear, slipped off the parking brake and put his foot on the floor. We accelerated rapidly, tearing headlong towards the unfenced drop on the corner a half kilometer away...oh. Of course.

My heart sort of went *thunk* up into my throat and I clutched Jon, despite my brain's instant comparison of dismantling and precipices coming out highly in favor of the latter.

"What's happening?" Jon sensed my body's alarm. Internally I felt rather calm. Compared to what'd awaited me...this was like getting an unexpected treat. Except for the horrible fact that Bane and Jon were in the vehicle too.

We sped on. The point of no return was coming up awfully soon—Jon still waiting for me to respond...

I managed: "Act of perfect contrition, if needed, *now.*"

Translation: *we are about to die.* His grip on me tightened, and I heard him murmuring—praying. I couldn't take my eyes off the approaching drop, watching it racing towards us with fascination as my body tried to panic and my mind floated on a cloud of relief. *I'm spared. Thank you, Lord. I'm sorry it's been so long since I got to Confession or...or anything. You know Bane means well; I hope you'll take us all just as we are.*

As the cliff edge got closer, it occurred to the soldiers Bane wasn't bluffing. They wasted another second looking at me and Jon—our expressions must've provided the final confirmation.

They lunged for the microphone.

"Stop!"

"Stop-we'll-let-them-out!"

Bane's foot slammed down on the brake.

Smack.

The four of us hit the window twice as hard, and watched, faces pressed to the glass, as the edge approached. Rapidly. *Too late. We've had it.*

We'd slowed to a crawl... The edge of the precipice disappeared under the hood of the van. *Uh-oh...* And...wait for it...

...Stopped?

The front wheels must be *touching* the edge. No one moved. The soldiers panted, shallow breaths, not daring to twitch.

I tightened my grip on Jon. "Hold still," I breathed.

"Oh."

He didn't understand but I didn't explain, too busy watching Bane. Bane was also doing the not-daring-to-breathe thing, but now he reached out, slowly, carefully, and put the van into reverse. From the gentle, gentle vibrations of the engine, he pressed the accelerator as though it were a butterfly's wing about to crumble to dust.

The van eased backwards several inches and stopped again. Bane didn't take it out of gear or put the parking brake back on, nor did he turn to speak to us again. He looked in the rear view mirror instead. His first words explained why.

"First of all, the accelerator is flat on the floor. So is the clutch. If you give me the slightest reason to suspect you're not following my instructions to the letter, I'll simply lift the clutch. So unless you actually think you can jump clear in time, you'd better do as I say, understood?"

Sweat trickling down their faces, the soldiers nodded.

"Okay. Listen carefully. One of you is going to swap with Jon so you're both pressed against this window. If I see any part of your side leave the window after that, I will raise the clutch. Then you're going to pass your rifles to Margo and tell her the door code. They're going to get out and close the doors again. Providing you behave, we'll leave you here safe and sound. Though, if I were you, I wouldn't get out in a rush once we're gone, because I won't be putting the parking brake on. Understood?"

They nodded again. *Quick, let's get this done before they recover.* Not much they could *do,* when any attempt to recapture us would make Bane drive off the cliff...still, better not let them think too hard about how angry their superiors were going to be.

Seating reorganized, I accepted each rifle, checking the safety catch and making sure there wasn't a round in the chamber, then passed them to Jon to hang onto. Who knew my years of tolerance for Bane's passion with weaponry were going to prove this useful?

"Code?" I asked.

The French soldier licked his lips and glanced at his companion. Fear of the EuroGov beginning to kick in? "We don't know the code. Only the Captain knew it."

Ninety-nine percent sure it was a clever lie or what would've been a clever lie in different circumstances.

A worm of ice twisted in my stomach nonetheless. "Inconvenient," I said.

"Very," said Bane over the intercom. "Too bad, I did warn you about leaving me with only one choice."

He raised the clutch...slowly.

Biting point...the van quivered...

"Five six four nine," said the German quickly.

The Frenchman spoiled the glare he gave his companion by simultaneously sagging in relief.

I typed quickly.

5 6 4 9...

Click.

Deo gratias!

I scrambled out, turning to take the rifles from Jon and help him quickly down.

"Not one twitch..." Bane was threatening.

I slammed the doors shut. How to stop them getting out? The lock! No way was it as bulletproof as the rest of the van.

"Just...stand here for a moment..." I moved Jon around the side of the van for safety and cocked one of the heavy guns. "Oh, I'm about to shoot the lock. Don't be alarmed. You might want to cover your ears."

Taking careful aim at the keypad—there'd be ricochets if I missed—I glanced in the wing mirror. Bane gave me a thumbs up—he'd got his foot on the brake.

CRACK! CRACK! CRACK!

Ears ringing, but keypad trashed, I made the rifle safe again and hurried to the driver's side. Bane was just closing the door gently, white-faced. We each grabbed one of Jon's arms, and we bolted.

We'd made it about a hundred yards up the road, looking all the time for a way up the mountainside, when Bane seemed to notice my appearance. He jerked me to a stop, his eyes travelling from my swollen, bloody face to my gaping blouse. His face darkened. *"WHAT DID THEY DO?"*

"It's okay." I flung myself into his arms. Pressed my face into his shoulder, inhaling. Dirt, sap, sweat, Bane. I held him like he was the most precious thing on earth.

"It's okay," I told him again, as his arms closed around me. "The Captain was rough with me, but he didn't do anything." But my stomach fluttered at the thought of the Captain.

Jon's hand came to rest on my shoulder and very comforting it was too. It'd been a rough half hour. "He did do *something*," he panted, "just not *that.*"

"I should've run the piece of filth over!" snarled Bane.

"It's...okay." My conviction rather lacking. A few more words spilled out, "I just...just..." I trailed off with a gulp.

Bane hugged me so protectively he seemed to be trying to merge us into one and Jon went on rubbing my shoulder until Bane released me—in a surprisingly short time.

"Look, sorry, we have to move." He shrugged off the loose shirt he wore over the borrowed t-shirt. "Here, put this on. Seeing you like that makes me want to kill some...thing." His eyes strayed back to the van. Probably better not to mention that one of those soldiers had been holding me down on the sofa. Did Jon know? I'd learnt not to underestimate what Jon picked up on. If so, he kept quiet.

"Did you really leave the parking brake off?" I eyed the precipice uneasily as I slipped into the shirt and buttoned it up. Much less draughty.

"Yeah. But I slipped it back into reverse while they were staring like they'd never seen a girl with a gun before. Doubt they'll be able to tell from in the back. Now let's move before I go back there, take it out of gear and give it a good shove."

He was joking. Just. Sort of.

"Oh, first things first..." He grabbed the rifle from me, examined it, swore in a rather unsurprised sort of way—then *chucked it over the side of the cliff!*

"What did you do that for?" I demanded.

"What?" asked Jon.

Bane reached for the other rifle, but I grabbed it from Jon and held it tight. "Have you gone *mad,* Bane? We've got the SpecialCorps coming after us—to say nothing of all the starving, the wolves, the *bears!*—and when we finally get a rifle you *throw it* off a *cliff?"*

"Margo," he said calmly, still holding out his hand for the gun. "These are EB-14 rifles. Complete with embedded trackers. They were developed specifically to reduce theft by the Resistance. If we keep them, the EuroGov will know exactly where we are. And disabling the trackers will take hours. We haven't time."

"Oh." I let him take the rifle from my unresisting hand and hurl it into space.

Then we ran. We found a way up the slope, but it was rough going. Even after our thirty-six hours of sleep and meals, we were still gaunt and low on energy. But stumbling and tripping, we ran, each of us holding Jon by one hand. Once out of sight of the van, we ran west.

"They'll expect us to go southeast," panted Bane, as we went. "Or possibly south or east if we're trying to confuse them. But they'll assume we won't entirely stop heading for the Alps. I hope. So we'll go west until we lose them, and only then cut down for the Alps again. By the way...François turned us in, right, the snake?"

"Yes. But Bane...he tried to swap us for his boys," I puffed.

"Huh?" Bane's head swiveled to look at me and he stumbled over a fallen branch.

"They weren't dismantled yet; he was trying to save them."

"*Tried* to swap us? Looked like he succeeded!"

"You do have a high opinion of the EuroGov. They killed his boys and brought him their brains' ashes. Or said they had. Evil rats. Then shot him, left Hugo in the cottage and burnt it down."

Bane was silent for several paces. "Oh. Okay, it was stupid, and he shouldn't have done it, but...well, I'll take the 'snake' back, at least."

The afternoon wore on. We gasped for breath, our run turning to a stumble. All these mountains and hills to slog up...we just couldn't *run* up them and it took so long. We hadn't gone very far, not as the crow flies. Our ears strained endlessly for the sound of rotor blades. A helicopter would be the end.

Perhaps the helicopters were searching to the southeast, as Bane predicted? On we went. We didn't talk much. We'd no breath to spare and anyway, we all knew how grave our situation was. No venison, no thermals, no sleeping bags, no stove, no waterproofs, no water bottles.

We'd just the clothes we'd put on for a day relaxing in a warm cottage and the contents of our trouser pockets: Bane's omniphone and knife, the penknives we'd been using to mark trees whenever we left our camp, two flashlights, and one remaining lighter. And we'd thought ourselves under-equipped before.

From the patch of open ground we were crossing, the twilight still illuminated a breathtaking view—a freestanding peak towering inside the horseshoe ridge on which we walked. Occasional lights down in the curving valley showed a main road, a rare—and unwelcome—glimpse of civilization.

We'd dropped down from the ridge line when the trees thinned, to avoid being silhouetted, and now hurried over the rocky ground as fast as we could. The forest picked up again only meters ahead; even the reForestation machines had been unable to tackle this rocky stretch trailing down the mountainside...

A strange *smack*...

...a gasp from Jon.

I looked round just in time to see him fall, clutching his thigh, crimson blood gleaming wetly around his hand in the twilight...

17

HIGH VOLTAGE

"Jon…"

Bane practically picked me up and hurled me forwards into the shelter of the forest—I managed to roll as I hit the ground and sat up unharmed. Bane was already pulling Jon's arm over his shoulder. I lurched forward—froze. Run out there and Bane would probably stop to shove me back. "Bane!"

What'd happened? Had Jon been *shot?* There probably were other explanations, but I couldn't think of any right now.

Crack, shriiing…

Okay, someone *was* shooting at us. Bane went into overdrive and drag-carried Jon into the trees in a frantic burst of energy.

"Where the heck are they?" I asked.

Bane glanced out through the trees and pointed at the big mountain. "There. They've got a blasted sniper stuck up there with a high-powered rifle—good position, must be able to cover an enormous amount of ground. We're lucky it's so dark."

Crouching beside Jon, he didn't elaborate further. Didn't need to, I could figure it out. Must've taken the sniper most of the time we were in the open to identify us and by then it'd been too dark for good shooting. Or knowing the Euro-Gov, perhaps he'd deliberately shot to wound.

I crouched on Jon's other side, taking his hand as Bane cut a square from his bloody trousers to get a look at the wound.

"S'okay, Jon." I stroked his hair back from his face—it was growing out again. "S'okay, Bane's going to fix up your leg." He was cold and clammy and shaking—going into medical shock. Needed warmth and a hot sugary drink. Curse it! We had *nothing.*

Bane stripped off his t-shirt in one quick movement, rolled it into a strip and bound it tightly around Jon's leg. "I think it's a flesh wound. Think the bullet's still in there. But I'm not a doctor and we have to go, *now.*"

Troop trucks would be racing up the valley road, stopping to disgorge their loads onto the mountainside. Blast, blast, blast. What's that saying about it can always get worse? Admittedly we were still better off than when we'd been trapped in a secure transport van on our way to a Facility…but not much better.

"What?" mumbled Jon, as though only just realizing Bane had spoken.

"I said it's not serious," lied Bane, "and we've got to move."

"Move?"

If only we had a blanket to ward off shock… I unbuttoned the shirt Bane had given me and slipped it off; Bane helped me sit Jon up and ease him into it. Buttoned up, it was better than nothing. It was absolutely all we could do for him, anyway. Night was only just falling and I could feel the chill. The blouse I still wore had been thick enough for daytime, but now… Bane was worse off, though: goose pimples dotted his bony chest—Jon's t-shirt bandage was already red with blood.

"Come on," said Bane ruthlessly, but he waited until I'd got Jon's arm over my shoulder before beginning to lift him to his feet.

Jon moaned and went so white it looked like he'd pass out. "Wait…" He stood for a moment, head down, swallowing hard. "Okay."

We started forward into the darkening forest, no doubt leaving a trail of blood a man could follow, let alone a dog. But any watercourse would be in the bottom of the valley; no question of going down there.

No running, now. Jon's emaciated condition was no benefit; we were almost as weak as he was. I was actually glad we didn't have the packs to worry about any more. Jon was more important than sleeping bags and a stove.

Slowly, painfully slowly, we reached the end of the horseshoe ridge and descended. A pitch black night, no moon, clouded sky—a cracking summer storm gathering above us? *Good.* Rain would wash away our scent, it couldn't come too soon.

Bane led us slightly north; towards an area of wilderness where troop trucks couldn't follow and safe streams might be found. All was silent; no sound of pursuit reached our straining ears. How long would it take them to bring dogs?

The lights of the distant road receded and were gone. Finally the curve of a stream crossed our path. We splashed down the bank into it as though to follow the left hand curve, then turned immediately and headed right instead. Northwest. All this effort to get *further* from our goal. It all seemed to be becoming more and more pointless. *Angel Margaret, stick close, we're in a fix.*

We stayed in the stream for less than a kilometer before climbing out again. The cold water was doing nothing to help Jon's condition. Oven-ready chickens had warmer skin. Blundering into tree after tree, scratched and poked by every branch in the forest, we soon fell into another stream. Followed that for a kilometer and left it, and so it went on.

My legs moved like lead. Jon could no longer put any weight on his bad leg. He hopped lurchingly along, bad leg dragging—he wouldn't keep that up for long. I didn't feel hungry, the only silver lining of extreme exhaustion, apparently. Because there wasn't going to be anything to eat any time soon. Even if we found nettles, they had to be carefully folded to be eaten raw. No time for that.

Jon's good leg buckled, throwing all his weight on us, and off balance, the three of us crashed to the ground. A long, pained gasp from Jon...

"Sorry," panted Bane—landed on Jon's bad leg? "Jon?"

No reply. He'd passed out.

"Oh, rats."

I just sat there, literally shaking with exhaustion.

At last I said, "Perhaps we should stop for a bit."

"No." Bane's voice was a weary rasp. "They can't be far behind us. We *cannot* stop. Soon as Jon comes round, we're moving."

I flopped down on the ground—but Bane had Jon awake again before I'd even got unconscious myself. Staggering upright, we hauled him to his feet by sheer brute force. He managed a few hops and his good leg crumpled. We managed not to fall this time, putting our heads down and plowing on, carry-dragging him between us.

Jon told you to leave him behind at the beginning, an evil little voice said in my mind. *He was right. You should have left him. Now you and Bane are going to die too, because you were so sure you could make it with Jon along. Stupid, Margo.*

But we weren't sure we could make it with Jon, I told that little voice. *We just knew we couldn't leave him behind to be dismantled.*

Bane *thought you could make it*, whispered that little voice. *Or he'd have left him.* Bane *got it wrong.*

Oh shut up, I retorted.

We didn't speak. Soon we scarcely thought. We just walked. And walked. And walked.

Step, step, step, heave Jon's arm further over my shoulders, step, step, step...

The wind was getting up; its icy slap against my face drew my attention from the mindlessness. But Bane's arm, lying under mine across Jon's back, was oddly warm. His left arm. Oh no. He'd had no antibiotics at all, today. I didn't bother trying to look at him. Too dark. Nothing to be done.

Step. Step. Step. Jon slipping...heave. Step. Step. Step.

The rising wind made it hard to hear, but still no sounds came from behind us. Surely we hadn't stayed in any of the streams long enough to throw them off the scent?

Finally a trip from Bane or myself—two seconds later when we all hit the ground I'd already forgotten which—had us lying flat out, gasping. When Bane didn't drive us straight back to our feet, I shifted to feel his forehead and arm. That insidious rising heat was definitely back.

"Any suggestions, Doctor Margo?" His voice would've been dry if he hadn't been panting so hard.

"I'll just have to kiss it better," I panted back, and leant over to press my lips to his brow.

"Best medicine in the world. Come on, let's get up."

I made it to my feet, but my arms shook like jelly and try as we might we couldn't get Jon up between us.

"We'll have to rest, Bane," I gasped, as we lowered Jon back down as gently as we could.

Jon's level of consciousness had been debatable for some time. But now his voice came thinly out of the blackness between us. "Bane?"

"I'm here."

"Take Margo and go. You've done everything you can. Just leave me here, I'll be fine."

"No, you won't."

"Fine. I won't. Doesn't make any difference now. *Go.*"

"No," I snapped, biting back the evil voice in my head saying, *Told you so.* "We're not leaving you. We just need to rest for a bit, then we'll carry on."

"Bane." Jon ignored me. "Do you want them to catch Margo? For pity's sake—for *her* sake—*leave me.*"

A long silence from Bane. Jon clearly wasn't wasting his arguments.

"Sorry, Jon," said Bane eventually. "I'm under the thumb of a very determined young woman, and I don't think she'll hear of it. Anyway, Margo's right. We just need a bit of rest."

I let out a relieved breath. Under my thumb, yeah right, Bane would leave Jon if he had to, to save me, but the threat of capture would need to be rather more imminent and the alternative considerably more impossible.

"Lie down, Margo, I'll keep watch first," said Bane, ignoring Jon's eloquent silence.

"Seriously?"

"Well, I'll try. I'll put an alarm on a ten-minute snooze. Have a good listen each time. After a bit, I'll give you the phone and you can do the same."

"Okay."

Bane moved to lie on my other side. I snuggled to his too-hot body, Jon shivering against my back...inspiration struck. Stiffly, I got up and climbed over Bane.

"Huh?"

"Go in the middle, Bane. You make a lovely radiator."

"Oh." Bane rolled over into the space I'd left and I snuggled up to him again. On his other side Jon made a happy little noise...

...Bane was shaking me awake—he pressed the phone

into my hand.

"Put it under your ear, I think I missed a few."

"Okay." I struggled into a sitting position. Didn't want to fall asleep before I'd even checked the alarm. Then I lay down and used the phone for a pillow. Wasn't awake long enough to notice if it was uncomfortable.

BEEP-BEEP-BEEP...

I jumped almost out of my skin. Swallowed a groan and my racing heart. Sat up. Listened hard. Checked I'd hit the snooze button. Lay down again.

Did it again and again and again.

Listening... My bleary eyes were closing even sat up. Check alarm...

Wait.

A shout? A *bark?* Impossible to tell over the wind.

"Bane!" I shook his shoulder. Lunging over him to shake Jon, my hand found thin air and I fell on Bane—he started awake.

"*What?*"

"Jon? *Jon?*" I climbed over Bane, feeling around frantically. Nothing. The ground where Jon had lain was cold.

"What's wrong?"

"Jon's gone! And I heard something."

"He's *what?* Oh, I'm going to wring his neck!" With this expression of fraternal concern, Bane started to crawl around as well. But we both knew what Jon had done. We wouldn't leave him, so he'd left us. Maybe that evil voice had been speaking to him, too.

"He thinks this is going to *help?*" growled Bane.

"Doubt he was thinking much in his condition, just desperate not to get us caught. He couldn't walk, he can't have got far." Stupid, *stupid,* Jon, you know we won't leave you.

A dim shaft of light pierced the blackness. Bane's flashlight, his hand shielding the end.

"There..." A trail of blood-smeared grass and disturbed loam led from Jon's place into the forest. Back the way we'd come. The direction the noise had come from. I didn't mention that. No need to test the bonds of friendship too far.

We hurried just as fast as we could go without losing the trail. Jon was crawling, he couldn't go far, he couldn't...

Another noise. A bark, definitely a bark. Bane froze, quivering. Every instinct telling him to turn and run the other way. Knew how he felt.

"If we don't find him very soon," he muttered, "we may as well give it up 'cause we'll never outdistance them even if we do."

We hurried on, trying to go twice as fast and twice as silently, all at once.

Another bark. Closer. Bottom of this slope? Hard to tell over the wind. Bane stopped dead again. "Okay. We've got to go, Margo."

It wasn't okay, but...Bane was right, if we found Jon, we wouldn't be able to get him away.

"Just a little further?"

"It's your dismantling!"

I swallowed. Took his flashlight arm and drew him onwards.

An agonized cry from somewhere ahead.

"Jon!" We both hissed it and started forward. Quiet, quiet, quiet...

There...a light. A handheld spotlight. Not as good as François's. In a clearing? Bane switched off his flashlight and we groped our way forward to the edge of the trees. There were two figures with the light, looking down at something on the ground.

"Should've kept a gun, tracker or no," Bane muttered.

"Come on, sing, my little blind songbird," came a harsh voice from one of the silhouettes. "Sing a pretty tune..."

A muffled groan.

"That's not a tune, try again..."

Jon cried out—Bane raced through the darkness like a ghost and slammed into the nearest soldier, carrying him to the ground. I tore after him and arrived just in time to grab the barrel of the second soldier's rifle as it swung towards the struggling pair. One-handed, the soldier yanked the weapon out of my feeble grip—I kicked the spotlight from his grasp instead. It tumbled across the grass and he spun round in shadowy confusion.

"Don't move or I swear I'll put your eye out... Ah, *thank you.*" Bane lurched to his feet, heavy rifle in his hands, and snapped, "Hold it, you."

The second soldier held it. Even let me take his rifle from his unprotesting hands. I rolled the spotlight over with my foot so it illuminated the clearing properly and pointed the rifle in the right general direction, leaving the safety off to make it look a bit more serious.

"Perhaps you two should've kept watch instead of torturing a blind boy?" Bane was shaking with rage. "Now lie on the ground, face down. Keep your hands where I can see them."

The soldiers exchanged an uneasy look. Obeyed. Bane promptly rammed the muzzle of the rifle into the base of the first soldier's skull.

"*Bane...*"

For another second he remained, quivering, his knuckles white, then he reversed his grip on the rifle and brought the butt smashing down on the soldier's head. Without a sound, the man went limp. The other soldier began to roll over; swiftly Bane struck him, too. Two unconscious soldiers.

Bane flung the rifle away from him as though he didn't dare have it in his possession for another second. I made the one I held safe, and slung it over my shoulder, picked up the other and did the same. Deposited them both beside Jon.

Bane was already there. "Hey, mate, you awake? Jon?"

I took Jon's head and cradled it in the bend of my arm. "Check his leg..." I stretched out to grab the spotlight and draw it closer, pointing at Jon's thigh. Uh oh. Blood glistened everywhere.

"Where's the t-shirt gone?" Bane started looking around.

"Margo?" whispered Jon.

"You are awake! Are you okay? What did they do?"

"Oh, nothing, mostly just kicked my leg and stuff. Don't worry about me."

Knowing Jon, not nice to think what "mostly" and "stuff" consisted of—at least he was conscious and making sense.

"Well, Bane's going to sort your leg, then we'll move. Come on, Bane," I added urgently. "These two weren't just out for a nighttime stroll."

"Gah!" Abandoning his search for the missing "bandage," Bane went to the nearest soldier, rolled him over, and began to search him. He transferred a few things to his own pockets before finally holding something up with a triumphant, "hah". When he ripped the wrapper off and began to unravel it, I realized it was a proper bandage, complete with a cotton pad.

I sighed in relief and stroked Jon's hair. "Can I borrow the light for a moment?"

"Yes. Why?"

Picking up the spotlight, I shone it around, careful not to raise it too far from the ground—it would show up a lot more if I pointed it into the distance.

"Just trying to figure out what these two *were* doing out here. If it was a net to catch us, we'd be in sight of the others, but there's no one there or they'd have shown up by now. So *what*... Oh."

I raised the light a little further, for confirmation. The treeless area ran away from us into the distance in both directions. "It's a fire break, not a clearing. These soldiers were supposed to spot us crossing it as we fled from the others. We must've been further ahead than they realized."

Putting the light down, I took a magazine from one of the rifles. Ah, quick load, how convenient. I popped the catch to release the rounds, caught them as they dropped out and hurled them into the distant grass. Didn't want the soldiers shooting us in the back if they came round before we were out of sight.

"Yeah, we must *have been.*" Bane tied off the bandage and punched Jon in the arm. A dog barked. Closer. "Come on, let's *go.*"

"For pity's sake, Bane," whispered Jon, "you're not seriously going to take me along, even now?"

"Shut up!" snapped Bane. "Or I'll clout you on the head too. Won't make any difference when it comes to carting you around! Come *on*, Margo."

I flung the magazines in the opposite direction to the bullets, switched off the light and chucked it into the forest, then dumped the rifles beside the soldiers. Until someone showed up with a flashlight, our sleeping friends were going to be pretty ineffective. But they might need more than a light, and the trackers in the rifles would ensure they got a medic a.s.a.p. They were definitely alive—one was snoring—but how healthy, I wouldn't like to say.

Getting Jon's arm over my shoulder, I bent my knees and groaning, Bane and I hoisted him up. *We could lift him again.* An irrational wave of optimism swept the demon of despair from my mind.

"You're mad," gasped Jon.

"Shut it!" we told him so fiercely that the demon seemed to let go of him too. He shut it, anyway.

Running when we could—downhill—we staggered on. Time seemed suspended. We'd not had anything like enough rest to carry Jon again and twice as fast. Every time we began to feel sure he'd fall to the ground, a bark sounded, closer, always closer, and a fresh surge of adrenalin drove us on...

...I'd lost a chunk of time and forest somewhere. Now we stumbled, shuffled, no more running, even the nearing barking couldn't speed our steps. *Any ideas, Lord? Angel Margaret?*

On. On. On.

"*Stop!*" Jon's voice, hoarse and totally unexpected.

He was conscious?

"What?" whispered Bane thickly.

"Do *not* move!"

We'd already stopped, our bodies more than happy to obey even if our brains didn't understand.

"Why?" I managed.

"Train tracks. High voltage..." Jon's voice was labored, his head barely raised from his chest. "Just ahead..."

"How on earth...?" started Bane, but dismissed the question. "You smell or hear it, who cares? Margo, can you get your flashlight out if I try and take Jon's weight?"

"Okay."

I took my hand from Jon's back and wriggled it into my pocket, eased the flashlight out. Got my hand cupped around the front and switched it on.

"Oh..."

"...rats," finished Bane.

There in the shaded light of the flashlight was an electric rail. Bane had already stepped over one of the outer tracks unawares and his foot was just a couple of inches from the live metal. For a few moments we just stared at the insignificant looking obstacle. The tracks ran along a ridge rising from left to right; on the other side of them, the forest fell away again.

"Let's just step back while we think about this." I switched off the flashlight and very, very carefully, we did so.

"Never thought I'd see the day when we'd be stumped by a tiny thing like that." Bane spoke almost under his breath. "But there's no way we can lift Jon over."

"Could we go along them?"

Bane turned and looked back down the slope. Lights twinkled in the trees behind us, in a long line. From the closest point came yet another excited bark.

"We'd be caught in minutes, now. We have to get over."

"Then get over, you stubborn idiots!" wheezed Jon.

I ignored him; more surprisingly, so did Bane.

"Let's put him down, I need to get something."

"We'll never get him up again—"

But Bane had already lowered Jon to the ground and from the rustling, was groping in his pocket.

"Here." Bane produced a little strip of blister pack, three pills long...from a compartment in his pocket knife?

"What on earth is that?"

He popped one out and fed it to Jon, placing a precautionary hand over Jon's mouth until he swallowed. "Stimulant. Very powerful. If Jon can support even a bit of his weight, we'll get over okay. I was thinking of breaking these out anyway, but they last less than fifteen minutes so let's keep the other two just a little longer."

"Why only three?"

"Had to sell your printer to get these."

"Oh."

"Wow." Jon's voice sounded stronger. He pushed himself up into a sitting position, shaking his head in bewilderment. "Am I dead? I feel heaps better."

"So you should, but it'll wear off fast enough, so let's go."

said Bane.

Prudently, I switched the flashlight on and shone it on the rail, hooded once again with my hand, before we all staggered to our feet. Jon only needed help to rise. We got a good grip on him and cautiously shuffled forward towards the rail.

Bark-bark.

Our heads all came up at once.

"Where did that come from?" said Bane uneasily.

I waited, ears straining. Thunder rumbled overhead. Please, please let it be a trick of the wind...

Bark. Bark.

Quickly I clicked off the flashlight. "It's coming from the other side of the rail."

18

SURROUNDED

For a moment we just stood, staring down the slope beyond the rails, hoping Jon would contradict me.

Bark bark.

That was from further along. There...a light gleamed. And another. And another. If we could turn and sprint alongside the tracks we wouldn't be fast enough. It probably wasn't two lines, it was probably a circle.

Trapped.

With unspoken agreement, we stepped back again and eased Jon to the ground. Dropping to my knees, I spread my hands to the inky blackness of the sky.

Shouts from behind. Barks from ahead. I didn't open my eyes.

Lord. Lord. Lord. Lord. An almost wordless appeal. I fought free of despair enough to put words together. *Is it time for acceptance? Was the van just a trial run? But we've come so far! Lord? Has it all been for nothing? Did we ever really have a chance?*

"We're totally surrounded," said Jon.

"Thank you for that incredibly perceptive observation," snarled Bane.

I said before that we'd get to Rome if You willed it. Well, it's never been as true as it is at this moment. If You want us to get out of this, You'll have to save us even more than normal. Save us, Lord. Save us, Lord... If it is Your will. Save us!

"Come off it," said Jon, "biting my head off is really the last thing you want to say to me?"

"Oh, shut up, Margo's doing some serious praying."

"Think I'll join her."

I breathed slowly, in and out, reminding myself of trust. *Lord, if You've got us halfway across the continent just to fail*

*now, I trust Your better judgment, I really do. But it seems
more likely to my feeble mind that You want us to make it.
So send me an answer, quick!*

The wind howled—was that the crack of branches under
distant booted feet? They were closing in. Acceptance, then.

*Domine, jam nunc quodcumque
mortis genus prout Tibi placuerit,
cum omnibus suis poenis
ac doloribus suscipio.*

> O Lord, I now, at this moment,
> willingly accept whatever kind of death
> it may please You to send me,
> with all its pains and sorrows.

Amen. But just for the record, Lord, this does really suck.

"Margo..."

Bane. He drew me to my feet and into his arms. His skin
burned and a fine tremor of exhaustion racked his body. "I
love you. I love you..." He kissed me frantically, tenderly, his
arms gathering me closer as though to protect me from the
night. From what was in the night.

Shouts from across the tracks, now. Soldiers calling to
one another. Dogs barking. And from behind. Even the wind
couldn't drown them out. How far away? As little as a few
hundred meters? They couldn't see us yet, for the trees, but
we could see their lights.

"I love you."

"I love you too." I kissed him, my arms wrapping around
his hot, bare back, and tasted salt on my lips. He was crying.

"Love you, Margo. Love you forever..." He clutched me to
him with only his left arm, now, his right hand slipping into
his pocket...

I kissed him, just kissed him, didn't want to think,
couldn't think about anything else. *I love you, Bane...*

My eyes opened in the vain hope of seeing his face, but
the darkness was too great. Save those winking lights,
coming closer.

"Love you..." His voice shook.

And *that* light...that great, great light, approaching...

approaching so *fast*...so...

My hand flew down Bane's right arm and closed around his wrist. "Stop!"

Too dark to see what he held—alas, I was a selfish cowardly wretch and I *did* know really, just pretending I didn't. Pretending to myself. Committing a bad action for a good reason didn't make it okay—yet I would really let Bane take this on himself?

"Margo! This isn't the time for high-minded—"

"No. *Look*. Behind you..."

Bane turned. "Where?"

"The light."

"A train! Are you actually thinking..." His head turned—immediately calculating the gradient of the slope, its length. Steep and long. "In our condition? We'll fall under the wheels trying."

I nearly laughed. "Well, that'll be nice and quick, won't it? Come on, we haven't got any choice! We're getting on. We're *supposed* to."

"Supposed...? Oh, I'm not even going there. No choice, I'll give you that." His head turned back and forth again, still calculating. We'd done this loads of times in our early teens, with the slow cargo trains that passed through Salperton, but *Jon*...

"Okay," he said, "I'll start a little way down the slope, get on first. You help Jon run alongside, I'll haul him on, you climb straight up after. Think you can do it? You'll be running alongside the longest."

"I'm *going* to do it. We're *all* going to do it."

In that moment I was quite, quite certain. I had asked Him to send us an answer, and here it was. Unusual for a prayer to be answered quite so literally, but I wasn't looking a gift train in the mouth.

Bane swapped what he held for something crackly—the remaining two pills. Hesitated for a moment.

"Jon, here, take another." He pressed one out. "The three of us are about to jump a train."

I didn't miss the note of unease in his voice as he stuffed it into Jon's mouth. "Is it safe?"

"Safer than dismantling."

"Yeah. S'pose."

Jon swallowed it uncomplainingly.

"I'll cut this one in half," said Bane.

"No, you won't! You take it! I can't lift Jon onto the train and if you can't get Jon on, we're done for. You take it."

"I'm not having you left behind." Bane's tone was steely. "You're having a nibble." He pressed the pill to my teeth. "Open."

I sighed and obeyed.

He inched it in a little. "Bite."

I obeyed again. "Yuk."

But I swallowed the tiny fragment. Felt rather than saw him slip the remainder into his mouth, then... Wow. Strength flooded into my shaking legs, the lead bled from my arms...amazing!

"Quick, it's coming up fast," said Bane. "Get behind a tree until the locomotive passes, we don't want the driver to see us."

Let's hope it wasn't a passenger train.

Jon scrambled to his feet unaided. "Bring on the train, I could tackle Mount Everest!"

He sounded almost drunk, but he followed as I led him behind the nearest of the trees crowding close to the tracks. Bane headed down slope a little way—paused first to hurl something across the tracks as far as he could. A flashlight or a lighter, at a guess. To make them think we'd gone straight over.

I spoke as loud as I dared over the noise of the train. "Jon, do you understand what we're doing? Bane will get on the train first, we'll run alongside, when he grabs you and starts pulling you up, jump on and climb up as best you can, okay? The ladder will probably have wide-spaced rungs, a good foot apart. I'll climb up behind you." I lowered my voice. "And if something goes wrong, try not to let Bane jump off again, okay?"

"Huh." Not exactly agreement, but he'd definitely heard me. 'Cause if anyone didn't make it on, it would be me, but there was no other order in which to do it.

"Okay, be ready. I'll try to give you a count down, then we run. And *don't* fall."

Jon grimaced. "I'll pick my feet up. I can't even feel that hole in my leg now."

"Good."

The train was approaching rapidly now. In fact...it was closer than I thought.

"It's going too fast!" called Bane softly, from behind his tree, and immediately added, "We've no choice! We have to try. I'll need to be further away."

His silhouette flitted away as he moved to hide behind another, more distant tree. The train was so close the light dazzled us. Flip, it *was* going fast. The long climb up the mountain had hardly slowed it down at all!

I stopped looking for Bane after the locomotive passed him—no light, not a passenger train. Flatcars loaded with containers.

"Get ready, Jon. Sprint like you've never sprinted before. Three, two, one..."

Whine. The engine passed us.

"Run!"

We ran. Awkwardly, with his arm around my shoulders, because whatever he said, his body still knew he had a bad leg, and he needed the support, but we ran, fueled by adrenaline and Bane's drug. Ran *fast.* I could feel my feet tearing up the gravel—*Lord, don't let my foot slip now!*—I steered Jon closer to the cars.

Flatcar...flatcar...flatcar...

Bane's face was suddenly alongside, a white blur against the blackness of the cars... It-was-going-*so*-fast! I shoved Jon over to him; felt his arms flail as he searched for the ladder. Bane must've got hold of his arm because suddenly Jon was on the side of the car, pulling rapidly ahead of me. Far too rapidly. Couldn't reach the car now, let alone once Jon was out of the way.

"Next car...don't panic..." I gasped, hoping Bane might hear me over the noise of the wheels and wind.

The next car...already coming alongside. Legs burning. Chest burning. Legs going wobbly again... One chance... There was the ladder...

I lunged as blindly as Jon had...a moment of heart stopping panic as my hands travelled unimpeded through the air—I'd missed! Then—*slap!* My hands closed on a rung, and my arms were almost yanked from their sockets. I just managed to drive my legs in one more tremendous step, pushing me forward...leap!

My flailing legs found the bottom step of the ladder, and for a few moments I just hung there, gasping, the rush blowing my hair back from my face.

Made it. *Laudate Dominum. Deo gratias.*

The top of the hill was coming up... I didn't want Bane to jump off to look for me before we reached it...driving my shaking body into action, I climbed the last few rungs to the narrow platform at the end of the flatcar, then ran my hands over the container. No ladder. Blast! I groped around a bit more, frantic to reach Bane. Right, hinges and door latches for footholds, those long straight locking rods for hand holds, and I must do it all in one rush, if I'd a hope of grabbing the top of the container.

I imagined Bane jumping off again, back into that net of soldiers...and launched myself up the steel side, feet scrabbling for the sticking-out bits, fingers clinging to those narrow metal rods. Without Bane's stimulant, I wouldn't have made it. As it was, I dragged myself up onto the roof, allowed myself a couple of breaths to rest, then slithered along on my stomach for safety. Heard Bane before I saw him.

"Margo! Margo!"

"Bane, shut up! I'm coming." I reached the front of the container and looked down at two dark shapes huddled on the platform at the back of the flatcar in front. Phew. I wouldn't have to climb the next container after all. Not sure I could!

"Oh thank God!" said Bane, as he saw my silhouette.

"That's unusually polite of you." Lowering myself from the top of the container until my arms gave way, I dropped, grabbing the locking rods again to stop myself going over the edge. Then, quickly but carefully, I crossed the shifting joint between the two cars. Feeling around when I reached the other side, I realized why Bane hadn't come to look for me. Jon was unconscious, and Bane didn't dare leave him on the swaying, rattling platform in case he was flung off. "Is

Jon okay?"

"Just passed out. Not surprisingly."

I felt Jon over quickly to make sure he hadn't lost any body parts to the wheels. His left leg was totally soaked in blood despite the bandage but his foot was still there. "Well, that's that."

"*That's that?* I'll say!"

"Why're you so cross? We've escaped, haven't we?"

"Hasn't occurred to you yet, has it? How the heck are we going to get *off?*"

Oh. Yes, problematic. A lot more dangerous than getting on, at this speed. How to get Jon off...no more pills, we'd have to pretty much pick him up and throw him, which we probably couldn't do and which he probably wouldn't survive.

"Well, if we get inside a container we can sneak out while it's stopped somewhere quiet."

He took a couple of deep breaths. "True. Okay, can you sit here and stop Jon rolling off and I'll go and see about getting a container open? This one's got a flipping code-lock on it."

"Okay."

As I shifted position, another crack of thunder boomed overhead and rain began to fall. Slow big drops, rapidly increasing to a downpour. Good. It'd wash away both tracks and scent, and this train was surely going so fast it wouldn't occur to them we could've got on. Why so fast, though?

"I'll be as quick as I can." Bane leapt across the gap to the flatcar I'd just come from, but a muttered curse told me that the door there was also locked. He crossed back and scaled the container I was sitting against as easily as climbing a ladder. I stifled a twinge of envy.

He was a long time, not that it mattered. I was just glad to sit still and hold Jon. How would we get Jon into one of the other containers, anyway, come to think?

The clackety-clack and the motion of the train brought back those summer holidays when Bane and I jumped trains every day...riding through the Fellest and up to the passes, feeling like anything was possible. Happy times.

The lash of the rain on my face soon brought me back to

the present—but the knowledge that every passing minute put more miles between us and the searching soldiers made this an even happier time.

It was clear as soon as he plunked down beside me that Bane didn't share my high spirits: he was hopping mad again. "If your almighty Friend really did send this train, Margo," he hissed, "I don't think much of His forward planning!"

"What's *wrong?*"I spoke as calmly as I could after the last twenty-four hours.

"It's a weapons' train, Margo! Code-locked containers, every one. Guards on the front and back of the train—they didn't see us get on, small mercies! There's an extra engine at the rear so it doesn't slow to a dangerous speed up inclines!"

Yes, the Resistance would love to get their hands on a train like this. Two engines. I stared at the shadowy ground rushing past. No way we should've been able to get on at all, let alone in our condition.

"And there's no way," he went on—very quiet now, "there's no way it's going to stop anywhere where it'll be safe to get off. We can't get into a container so as soon as the sun comes up we'll be seen. And we'll be caught. Say thanks from me to your Friend, will you!"

The train would speed through green lights all the way until it drew to a halt inside a military compound.

But still... "Calm down, Bane! We're not caught yet, are we? So stop whining! Where's it going, anyway?"

"Manifests on the container doors say Rome."

"Rome!"

"Caught at daybreak, *remember?*"

"Yes, but..." Tantalizing that the train was going exactly where we wanted. "Sure there isn't anywhere we can hide?"

"Why d'you think I've been so long? I've been from one end of this train to the other, just as close to the guards as I dared—we're almost at the back, here. The containers are all locked. We're too weak to cling underneath, nor have we anything to tie ourselves on with—we'd probably get electrocuted, anyway."

"The container roofs?"

"In full sight of the guards, when there's light to see by. Just face it, we're done for."

"We're less done for than we were half an hour ago! Since when have you been so negative!" Oh... I reached out to touch his forehead. Burning. Of course. He shrugged me away, but my anger died. "Come on, it's still some time before morning, isn't it? Why don't you try and get some rest?"

"I'm not tired."

"Fibber."

Shivering violently now in my poorly-fastened blouse, I turned to Jon again. His skin was cold under my hands, his clothes as wet as mine. He was totally and frighteningly un-responsive. I shifted until I could lie between him and the cold metal of the container as human insulation.

"Come on, Bane, please lie down and try to keep Jon warm. He's not in a good way."

Bane didn't speak, as though becoming aware he was playing the bear with the cut paw. He shifted until he could lie down and, reaching over Jon and I, hold onto a bar to keep us all aboard.

For all Bane's fears and worries, my eyes wouldn't stay open. We were safer than we'd been half an hour ago and that was that. This train was bound for Rome. Who knew how many towns it'd actually go through? Who knew who'd actually look closely at yet another train?

I wrapped my arms around Jon's chilled body in a hope-less attempt to give heat, as the cold rain hammered down...

...Sunlight blazed through my eyelids. Turning away and opening my eyes, I found myself looking into Bane's deep sunken, dark circled, fever-bright eyes. My mouth was parched—I attempted to moisten it before speaking. "What time is it?"

"Ten o'clock."

"When's this thing supposed to reach Rome?"

"Some hours yet, Margo." He took one hand away from the bar, flexing it and wincing, took out his phone and consulted the map. "We're close to Milan." He put the phone away and returned to his job as safety rail.

Milan. It penetrated slowly. "We're over the Alps!"

He smiled crookedly. "Yes, we are over the Alps."

His tone was dry, but his mood had improved. It must've been light for some hours, and we'd not been caught yet. We couldn't be very conspicuous, lying down like this. We probably looked like old sacks, or something. I licked my lips again. Would we reach Rome before we were spotted? We'd travelled a long way south as I slept.

I turned my attention to Jon. Unconscious. His face a pasty gray color. His skin, despite his sun-dried clothes, still clammy. "He needs a doctor."

Bane grimaced. What was there to say? Jon needed a doctor. He couldn't have one. He'd probably die.

I stroked his autumny hair gently back from his face. "Come on, Jon. Stick with us. We're on the express to Rome, lots of doctors in Rome. Just hang in there."

He couldn't hear me. *Lord, watch over him, please, please, please?*

I touched Bane's forehead instead. Could've fried an egg on it. If I had one. Shouldn't have thought about eggs. My stomach was gnawing my backbone in half. From the look of Bane's face, he needed a doctor too. Perhaps wouldn't die without one—not quite yet, anyway.

"Truthfully, Bane, how are you fee—"

A flash of light reflected off the container above—the next second the sound slammed into us, like the fireworks all over again. The entire train jerked and hurtled sideways. In a strange slow motion the locomotive tumbled past us as though through midair, flying end over end...everything dissolved into a maelstrom of tilting, rolling flatcars and spinning ground...

Blackness.

19

DEAD MEN TELL NO TALES

Shouts from across the tracks. Soldiers calling to one another. Dogs barking. And from behind. Even the wind couldn't drown them out. How far away? As little as a few hundred meters? They couldn't see us yet, for the trees, but we could see their lights. They were coming.

"I love you..."

"I love you too." I kissed Bane, my arms wrapping around his hot, bare back, and tasted salt on my lips. He was crying.

"Love you, Margo. Love you forever..." He clutched me to him with only his left arm, now.

I kissed him, just kissed him, didn't want to think, couldn't think about anything else. I love you, Bane...

My eyes opened in the vain hope I might see his face, but the darkness was too great. Save those winking lights, so close. Almost here.

"Love you..." His voice shook...broke...he drew such a deep breath his body shuddered with it—his right arm moved unseen beside me, hard and fast.

A sharp pain pierced my side; a coldness touched my heart. Bane's arms were both around me again, holding me, what'd happened to my legs? I couldn't even feel them. Bane lowered me to the ground, cradling me to him, kissed me again and again. "Love you, Margo, love you, love you..."

The blackness was getting blacker. Even my lips were going numb.

"Love you, Bane," I whispered, 'cause it seemed very important I say it, one more time.

His tears filling my mouth and his lips on mine were the last thing I felt as darkness swallowed me...

...Light, beyond my eyelids. I dragged them open, crackling with sleepy dust. A plaster ceiling, sort of amber stucco.

Bane's face suddenly blocked it from view. "Margo?"

"Umm..."

"Your Friend is an idiot! No, y'know..." He sprang off the bed and paced the small, sparsely furnished room. "I don't even believe in Him! It was all coincidence, all of it. I mean, why the heck put us on a weapons train about to be blown up by the Resistance? Why?"

I struggled to kick my floundering mind into gear. Bane's face was flushed more with anger than fever, so he'd found some more antibiotics. His right arm rested in a sling and he kept moving it to gesticulate then wincing—apart from that he looked remarkably well.

"I assume since you're yelling at me I'm quite all right?" I managed at last.

He sat on the bed again; bent to kiss me. "Don't wave your left arm around." I looked down to find it too, lay in a sling. "It's sprained or slightly fractured: the doctor didn't have access to x-ray."

"Are you okay?"

"Yes, this is just sprained." He jerked his head down towards the sling. Of course, he must've held us all on the car just long enough that we didn't fall to the ground in its path and get crushed...or something.

"*Jon?*" I struggled up into a sitting position.

"Fine." Bane flipped his left hand. "Well, I say *fine*. He got off more lightly than any of us in the derailment but of course he was so much worse beforehand. But he should pull through, says *il dottore*."

I let out the breath I was holding. Jon okay. *Deo gratias.* "So, where are we? The Resistance blew up the train, you said?"

"Yes, this is one of their safe houses near Milan."

"Have you asked them yet if they'll help us get to Rome?"

"I thought you didn't want to accept any more help from them?"

"Well, if a big enough, fast enough moving hint clackety-clacks up to me and dumps me in their lap, I'm capable of taking it. So will they help us?"

Bane rolled his eyes. "Yes. Luciano says he'll take us all the way to Rome, easy-peasy, then we can use one of the

Rome Resistance's tunnels into Vatican State."

Many of the secret tunnels dated from the Great Wars or earlier and remained in the possession of families with ancestors in the Resistance movements of those earlier times. One of the few things for which the Underground actually had dealings with the Resistance. Difficult and dangerous enough to gain access to the blockaded Free State—no one was turned away just because they came through a Resistance tunnel instead of an Underground one.

Father Mark had given Bane the most up-to-date procedure he had for contacting the Rome Underground when we left, but we'd always known it'd probably be out of date by the time we got there. To be put straight in contact with the Rome Resistance would be—probably was—a God send.

"So, Bane." I smiled at him. "Why *do* you think we were put on a train about to be blown up by the Resistance?"

He sprang off the bed as though he'd received a slap, not a smile. "Oh, shut up!" He strode to the door. "Why don't you get some more sleep?"

But he didn't leave. Just stood, staring at me, nostrils quivering. Upset about something much more than the fact that the—previous?—night's string of life-saving "coincidences" was dancing a jig on his determined irresolution about certain matters.

Turning his face away, he drew in several deep breaths, then with a gulp, rushed across the room and flung himself on me. He managed to miss my possibly-fractured limb and I rubbed his back with my uninjured arm as his shoulders began to shake.

"Bane, it's okay, shss, it's okay. What's wrong, Bane? Come on, everything's okay now, isn't it?"

"Okay?" he gulped, his head buried against my chest. I could feel his hot tears soaking through whatever I was wearing. "*Okay?* I almost... I almost had to... Back then...by the tracks... I almost... *Okay?*" He went back to crying harder than I'd seen him do for years and years and years.

I hugged him as tightly as I could with one arm and gave up talking. He'd been having similar dreams to me. Nightmares.

"Hush, hush," I murmured at last. "I'd probably have stopped you, anyway. I hope I would've."

"Well, I don't hope you would've, you lunatic!" he managed a watery snarl. "Not if the train hadn't come."

"Oh, you *like* the train now, do you?"

He was silent for a moment, sniffing slightly. "It had its good points." He nestled his head against my chest.

I let him nestle for a while, until his sniffs petered out and his expression began to suggest he was getting more enjoyment than comfort from his pillow—then prodded him.

"Off—come on, don't just smirk at me."

He made do with shifting his head to my shoulder and kissing my neck. "My beautiful Margo. I'm really starting to look forward to getting to Rome."

"How long have we been asleep?"

"Well over twenty-four hours. Jon's still out."

"I'm not surprised."

"No. He looks like death warmed up."

"Did we have to go in separate rooms? I don't like us being split up."

Bane grimaced. "Nor do I, but I made a few tentative probings on that subject and it immediately became clear they'd be offended if I tried to change it. Think we didn't trust them."

"I *don't* trust them."

He gave a slight laugh. "Neither do I. All the more reason not to offend them, huh?"

"I s'pose." But I didn't like it. Felt very unsafe for the three of us to be separated. The pack mentality talking? Or perhaps common sense.

Footsteps outside. Bane sat up and swiped a sleeve across his face, removing salt from his cheeks and breaking up clumped eyelashes. His eyes were pretty much normal color again.

A tap on the door and in came a tall young man about Father Mark's age; dark hair, swarthy skin, looked very Italian. A—brother and sister, surely?—followed him; they shared his Italian looks and were a similar age, perhaps a little younger. Two even younger men, one no older than us, peered in behind them.

"Thought I'd find you here." The first man spoke to Bane in Esperanto. "And Margaret Verrall, you've joined us in the land of the waking."

"Yes, I have. Thank you for taking care of us."

"We did *cause* some of your injuries when we deprived you of your transport in such a surprising fashion."

"Not half as surprising as our little find," said the young woman dryly.

"Uh, that's Carla," said Bane. "Her brother, Francesco, and Luciano, leader of the Milan cell. I've not met the other two..."

"Hello," I said.

They all nodded in return, and the younger of the other two piped up, "I'm Lanzo, that's Ruggiero." He looked like he might say more but Luciano silenced him with a wave of his hand.

"So you want to go to Rome?"

"Yes. If you could help us, that'd be great."

"*Si*, it is a very simple matter. We travel to Rome without passing through road blocks all the time. The Rome cell will have you under those ancient walls in less time than it takes to say *Viva l'Italia*. We are happy to help you."

"Really?" I couldn't help it, it popped out. Generally the Resistance viewed the Underground with scorn if not outright hostility. The disgust was reciprocated; we did tend to preach at them rather.

Luciano smiled at my frank disbelief as Lanzo and Ruggiero sniggered. "You have caused a great deal of trouble for the EuroGov, Margaret Verrall. I'll wager if you live, you'll cause a whole lot more. On this we are allies."

Carla sniffed pointedly.

Luciano grinned. "Carla is a little less happy with you."

"Oh? Why?"

Carla glared at me. "Our mission is to restore sovereignty to our glorious nation but since your book came out all anyone anywhere wants to talk about is Sorting and Religious Suppression. Which are pretty low on our list of grievances. Or *were*."

I snorted. "*Your* glorious nation wasn't a nation at all

until the beginning of the twentieth century."

Bane elbowed me. *"Margo."*

Luciano ignored my less than tactful remark. "Trouble for the EuroGov aids our cause, Carla. Any trouble of any kind. You don't have to like them, but you must be able to see their actions are benefiting us."

Carla's mouth twisted, but she nodded.

"I'll take you up to Rome myself as soon as Jonathan is fit to travel," said Luciano. "In the meantime, please do not leave this building for any reason. It won't be a safe house for long if Margaret Verrall and Bane Marsden are seen sauntering around outside." He strode to the door, graceful as a lanky cat—glanced back. "Oh, if you are well enough to get up, do join us for dinner."

"Thank you, I'm fine."

"Good. Until then, *Signora*." He departed, Carla and Francesco at his heels and the other two trailing behind.

"Was he flirting with me?"

Bane looked surprisingly unmoved. "He's Italian. I think they flirt in their sleep. I wouldn't take it personally."

"Wasn't planning to. Can we go and see Jon? Do I have clothes?" I looked around the room. There, on a chair…

"I'll let you get dressed." He stole a kiss and off he went.

I eased slowly out of bed, wincing. Twenty-four hours was apparently long enough for every muscle in my body to stiffen up to an agonizing degree, but not to recover. It hurt to use my left arm—but not a fracture, surely? A patchwork of bruises covered me, most from the crash, no doubt. Some—especially on my battered and swollen face—from the charming specialCorps Captain. Shuddering, I slipped into the skirt and simple top as quickly as I could.

Getting the fiddly sandals done up, I shuffled out into the passage to join Bane, who was moving stiffly too. He grinned sympathetically at my geriatric progress, slipped his left arm around me and walked me two doors further on.

The room was almost identical to mine. Jon lay in the bed, pale and unmoving, but his face was no longer that terrifying grey color. A peep under the blankets revealed his thigh neatly and professionally bandaged with clean white dressings. I sat on the bed and stroked his hair for a minute—but he was well out of it.

"The faster you get better, Jon, the faster we get to Rome," I told him encouragingly, then stood up, hissing under my breath as my muscles stretched. "When is dinner, anyway?"

"He said six, when we spoke earlier." Bane fished out his phone, which'd apparently survived the crash. "About two and a half hours."

"Oh." Disappointing. I was unspeakably ravenous.

Bane laughed. "Don't look like that. We can help ourselves in the kitchen. I had a big bowl of pasta soon as I got up, but I could eat some more. Come on."

I let Bane sit my aching bones at the kitchen table and watched him cooking. Where did he get his energy from? Sickening. Not that it was complicated—fortunately. He put pasta in boiling water and put sauce from the fridge into a pan to heat. Slopped the result onto two plates and handed me a fork.

After an unconventionally short grace—*thanks, Lord*—I tucked in like a runner leaving the starting blocks. Bane ate more slowly, chewing his food and grinning as though watching me eating was the most enjoyable thing he'd done in ages.

"D'you have to sit there watching me make a pig of myself?" I managed eventually.

His grin remained unrepentant. "S'just nice seeing you safe and well with food in front of you. Not exactly a common occurrence recently, is it? S'been driving me mad."

"You really are overprotective, you know that?"

"You may have mentioned it. Once or twice. Don't see you complaining, though."

Not when he cooked for me when my body felt like this. "Thanks for the pasta, Bane, it's lovely."

He snorted into his own meal. "You haven't tasted a bite!"

"It's lovely anyway." I went back to shoveling my lovely pasta without tasting it. Food, glorious food.

We'd just finished washing up as well as we could one-handed when Carla and Francesco came in. From the way they began moving around the kitchen, they were beginning preparations for dinner.

"You two going to want to eat?" asked Carla.

"Oh, we'll fit something in." Hollow cheeks lurked under Bane's short beard.

"Can we help?" I asked.

"Go and rest," said Francesco. "You're rather, how do you say it?" He spoke the next word in English, "'Armless?" Grinning, he went back to Esperanto, giving Bane a comradely wink, "Though I don't expect that dismantler would agree with me."

Bane replied with something more like a grimace. "Is there a television here?"

"Upstairs, room above this one."

We went up and switched on the TV to see if the news was on. A familiar courtroom appeared on the screen.

"Oh my! They're not *still* at it!"

"What's this, day four of the 'over-by-lunchtime' trial?" Bane sniggered. "The EuroGov must be going mental."

But my heart sank as the camera went to the man in the dock. They'd given up on the hat entirely—point to the prisoner—but that was the only positive. His face had been smeared with make-up in a futile attempt to make him look a little less like a walking corpse and he kept making funny batting movements with his hands, eyes darting and lips moving soundlessly.

"If you ask me," said Bane, "that guy is hanging on to his reason by the tips of his fingernails."

The camera went to the witness box...wait, that was one of the Facility guards!

Looking anywhere but at the man in the dock, the guard proceeded to swear I'd been in the Major's garden for over half an hour. From what the Prosecution were saying, he was the last of the four guards to tell the lie. He needn't have worried, though—the Major didn't look at him once.

No doubt the guards couldn't see any point martyring themselves for a man who was doomed anyway. Still, it was the one thing about which there were actual witnesses, and it was used by the prosecution to support their falsehoods!

"I do believe steam is about to come from your ears, Margo," said Bane gravely. "Would you like me to get you a cup of cold water?"

I almost thumped him—checked myself in the nick of

time. "Don't start, Bane."

"Keep your hair on." He'd seen my fist clench.

"Oh, shut up, would you."

"Someone's grumpy."

"Watching a travesty of justice makes me grumpy—funny, that!"

Bane kindly shut up.

The judge had just paused proceedings. "Major Everington. Do you have anything to say?"

"Yes..." The Major looked up at last, not sounding the slightest bit collected any more. Just rambling. "I don't understand how anyone could think *I* did this? Never done anything in my entire life I could be proud of, me. Never. So it's impossible, you see..."

"Are you saying you are proud of your heinous act?"

"Not my act. Not heinous. *I* would be proud. I might as well say it. Why not?"

"Because you speak sedition with your own lips."

"Sedition? I'm terrified. There are other things I could say. I could say that one of my guards—name of Finchley, nice fellow—tried to rape Margaret Verrall—ah, yes, I thought the gallery would find that exciting. He was punished, of course, but yes, hate to break it to you, it does happen, I know you like everyone to think it doesn't..."

"I suggest you consider your words *very carefully*, Major Everington," interrupted the judge, as Bane burst out, "I thought Jon said he tried to *grope* you!"

"Well, it's a preliminary, isn't it?" I muttered.

"Because," the judge was snarling, "You are digging your own grave!"

"Am I going to get a grave, then?" the Major maundered on. "That's nice, I always wanted a grave but recently I *had* assumed I wasn't going to get one. Why should I be careful, anyway? You know what they say about dead men—"

"Yes!" The judge was clearly goaded beyond endurance. *"They tell no tales!"*

The Major paused for a moment, blinking, then he turned his head, his eyes glinting so wickedly that for a moment he actually looked like the man I remembered.

"Oh," he said softly, "I think you'll find they sometimes

do."

"*Major Everington! Do you* have anything to say pertinent to the case at hand?"

The Major just blinked dazedly and plunged back into his interrupted ramble. "I was thinking of dead men have nothing to lose, actually, so I can think of lots of things to say if you want me to carry on talking. How much ink do the gallery have in their pens? There was that rumor about the Head of the EGD and your honor's..."

"THAT WILL DO, Major Everington!" The judge had turned purple. "Henceforth, unless you have something relevant to say, you will be *silent!*"

"But you keep telling me to talk..."

"SILENCE!"

The judge looked so absolutely livid Bane started choking and a snort of laughter escaped me as well.

"The prisoner is overwrought," the judge continued, poison poorly-concealed in his tone. "The prisoner must have a few minutes to rest. The court is adjourned for thirty minutes. Take him out."

The guards stepped forward but, last vestiges of calm suddenly disappearing, the Major hurled himself from the chair, screaming incoherently and leaping up at the Perspex like a wild animal. He fought them every step of the way as they dragged him out—I had to look away.

An impromptu news bulletin—a special "Margaret Verrall escape case" update—came on to fill the gap. They showed truckloads of soldiers combing the forest around and beyond the railway lines back in the French department. If it'd occurred to anyone to rethink the assumption that we couldn't have boarded an unboardable train, they weren't telling the world.

The two soldiers from the van were fine, the other two under observation in hospital with severe concussion. It sounded like the EuroGov playing it up as much as they could, though, because there were a couple of shots of the brave soldiers sitting up in bed and they looked pretty healthy to me.

"Bastards," said Bane.

But he snugged me closer, a whole coil of tension

draining out of him. So he hadn't smashed their skulls, *Deo gratias*. Good thing his arms weren't as strong right now as they used to be.

"And now, back to the trial of Major Lucas Everington..."

They shuffled the Major back to his seat, staring vacantly into space.

I winced. "Doesn't look like he knows what's going on any more."

Then, horror of horrors, they began dealing with my rescue from the lab and soon I was curled up almost in Bane's lap, shuddering more than the Major.

"Major Everington, do you have anything to say?" demanded the judge before long. I glanced at my watch. Almost five o'clock.

The Major didn't seem to hear.

"Fine, I will have to adjourn the session. Take him away." The judge raised his gavel and the guards reached for the Major's arms. The Major shot out of the chair and slammed into the Perspex.

"*No!* I did it! *I did it!*"

20

KAKISTOCRACY

"Whatever it is you say I did, I did it!" the Major screamed. "All of it! I rescued...rescued whoever. I killed the snails, I'm sorry, I did! They were eating my plants so I killed them all... I smuggled elephants, I bought chocolate—it was very good, but I put it in mousetraps. Anything, please... I did it...please...please...please..." He started whacking his head on the screen in time with his words. "It was my fault, it was my fault, it was my fault..."

I looked away, stomach churning.

"Smuggled elephants?" snorted Bane. "He's going to keep kicking them in the teeth until he hits the very bottom of the rope, isn't he?"

"Oh, thank you for that graphic description!"

"Sit down, Major Everington." A frustrated look covered the judge's face despite his satisfied tone. "The court has heard your confession."

"If you can call that a confession," muttered Bane.

"Am I therefore to understand, Major Everington, that you wish to change your plea to Guilty?" continued the judge.

No reaction. The guards pried the Major from the Perspex and dumped him back in his chair, but he just went on whispering, "It was my fault," over and over, rocking to and fro. Was he even talking about the escape?

"Major Everington, are you trying to convey that you wish to change your plea to *Guilty?* The *escape* was your fault, *yes?*"

The Major's attention seemed caught for a moment by these words. He stared at the judge and shook his head earnestly, giving a rather surprised, "*No,* not *that.*"

The judge actually turned a faint green color, said quickly, "The jury will go out to consider their verdict," and whacked his gavel down hard, as though daring anyone to object. Terrified the Major would retract his confession a second time?

The jury filed out and despite that flash of semi-lucidity from the prisoner, it quickly became clear the judge was worrying for nothing. But he might have waited a long time to extract a clear "Guilty" from the man who now stared into space, hands moving systematically and drool running unnoticed down his chin. In his own way, the Major really had beaten them. Forced them to break his mind before breaking *him*, thus ensuring they never got the proper confession they wanted. Stubborn, stubborn man.

Filing back in after a token couple of minutes, the jury sat looking anywhere but at the madman drooling and potting his imaginary plants in the dock. They'd found him guilty. What a tremendous surprise for all present.

The judge made a lengthy speech about the importance of a fair sentence and the need to review all the facts to achieve the aforementioned, finally announcing that the date for sentencing would be determined within the week.

"Huh," I snorted. "Trying to be all unhurried and fair with the final legal steps. Like we don't know what the sentence will be!"

"Well, they'll be desperate to salvage some face from this farce," smirked Bane.

When the guards tried to take Major Everington out, he clung to the chair so tightly they picked it up and took it too. He obviously didn't weigh a lot. The judge left, the jury hurried shamefaced from the room, and it was over. The station went back to news.

"That has got to be their worst show trial *ever*," said Bane.

"Perhaps it'll stop them from being quite so keen on them in future."

"I don't know, they'll probably just choose their victim a bit more carefully."

"Well, maybe—" I broke off as the newsreader's words registered.

"...the main headlines. Six soldiers have been killed in the derailment of a munitions' train in the north of the department. The Italian Resistance have claimed resp—"

Bane switched off the TV with a quick flick of the remote. I looked at him. He looked at me. "Well, hearing about it isn't going to change anything, is it?"

True. But all six soldiers probably hadn't died in the crash.

"I really don't like the Resistance," I muttered.

"Keep your voice down! D'you *want* to attempt another few hundred kilometers on foot?"

"Calm down! I've had my orders." I put my head on his shoulder for a moment or two, but kept shifting restlessly. "Shall we go and sit with Jon?"

Bane sighed, as though he'd not been able to settle either. "Nap with Jon, maybe. We've an hour before dinner."

When we'd hobbled to Jon's room Bane stretched out on the narrow stretch of bed to Jon's left, I climbed up on Jon's right and rested my head on his shoulder, careful not to knock his leg. He looked no different than earlier, white and still.

"The doc was here when I woke up." Bane sensed my anxious thoughts. "Had him on a drip—salts and liquids—he'd given him a blood transfusion too. He'd lost so much. But he said he'd pull through. Probably quite quickly. I was right about the leg. Flesh wound. He took the bullet out. Jon can keep it as a souvenir."

He pointed to the bedside table. Sure enough, a little scrap of innocuous looking metal lay there.

"I'm sure he'll be delighted."

Bane just laughed, and after a few moments began to snore. I shifted my head on Jon's shoulder and let my eyes close. He didn't smell right: strange sheets and strange clothes, but he was still Jon. Surely a bad idea to leave him lying here alone...

"Ah, *here* you are." A musical Italian voice jerked me awake. Luciano stood in the doorway, Carla looking over his shoulder.

"We've enough beds for you all," she said pointedly.

"We just thought it might be better for Jon to have us with him. Subconsciously, y'know," I said.

"You know, you might be right," said Luciano. "He's

certainly not in good shape. We'll bring the other beds in here."

Carla rolled her eyes and walked out.

"Time to eat," said Luciano and followed her.

"See, that wasn't so hard," I muttered to Bane, then clenched my teeth to keep from gasping in pain as I eased off the bed.

"You get away with it 'cause you're a girl," snorted Bane, wincing as he straightened. "From me? Rampant paranoid suspicion. Wasn't going there."

"Fair enough. Let's go and eat. I'm not sure what happened to that plate of pasta, but I'm starving."

I managed to make it back downstairs without whimpering. The meal was—surprise!—pasta, with a more complicated sauce than the one we'd had from the fridge. Guest or not, I could concentrate on nothing but the heaped plate in front of me. Bane, having made more headway with his food deficit, found time to talk to our hosts in between bites, but for a long time the murmur of voices barely penetrated my happy munching.

Our hosts: Luciano was in charge, Carla and Francesco his lieutenants. I'd not heard Lanzo's and Ruggiero's voices for some hours. No doubt they lived in their own homes, like the rest of the cell; the other three must be too compromised. No wonder they knew how to travel without passing through road blocks.

"You're just content to leave your country under the oppressor's boot?" Carla's raised voice drew my mind from the food. "Have you no honor?"

"*Honor?*" retorted Bane, "*My* honor is more concerned with making sure my fiancée isn't cut up to fix those who've already lived their span of years! *My* honor is more concerned that people cannot say *I believe in a God* without dying for it! My *honor* thinks the woman who conceives a third child without purchasing the necessary permit shouldn't have that child slaughtered inside her!

"My *honor* objects to the EGD saying those of different races cannot love one another! My *honor* objects to the Stable Population Committee requiring every adult to enter into a registered breeding partnership before the age of thirty regardless of their personal feelings or situation! My *honor* despises the stranglehold that kakistocracy has on business, keeping their supporters rich and everyone else poor—"

"That...what did you call them?"

"Haven't heard that word before, huh? Kakistocracy. It's Old Greek for 'worst possible government.' But in short, my 'honor', if you want to put it like that, finds all that—and more!—*far* more important than simply being able to say *Britain* or *Italy* again."

"*We* say Italy *now!*"

"Please yourself! They're *departments* at the moment, so that's what I'm calling them. I'm not getting in trouble calling a spade a hoe when it is actually a *spade!*"

"How horticultural," sneered Carla.

Bane slammed his fork back down on his plate. "*How* can you think changing what the departments are *called* is more important than ending the murder and misery of millions?"

"If we were a sovereign nation again we could make our own laws! Do away with the bad ones!"

"Well, yay for you! When's that going to be? You lot have been at it for almost a century. A *century*. It's not working, so let's try it some more? Very clever."

"And what would you suggest? Here I thought you were almost one of us!"

"I was," said Bane, quiet but firm. "Almost. Happily I thought better of it."

"Why?" Luciano spoke equally quietly, cutting off Carla's scornful snort.

"I went on a raid on a factory with my local cell. They shot all four guards."

"Good for them!" said Carla.

"They killed four ordinary, decent men, doing ordinary, decent, socially acceptable jobs. Working hard to support their families. Four sons, four brothers, four husbands, four fathers, *gone*. And yes, one of them *was* a father: his daughters are called Lily and Rosy, his wife, Katie."

"Well, if he would work for—"

"No! That is not an argument. Do you work? Do you pay

taxes? Why don't you shoot yourself, huh? You pay them with one hand and kill them with the other!"

"I don't pay taxes," snarled Carla.

"Then I'm guessing you haven't got a family. It's awfully simple when you've only your own life to throw away, isn't it?"

"And what do *you* propose?" scoffed Carla, waving towards me with a piece of bread. "You going to *pray* the EuroGov to its knees?"

"It'd do a darn sight more good than what *you're* doing!"

"What *would* you propose?" asked Luciano softly. "Cut off the head of the snake? Kill the High Committee itself?"

"A, it's been tried and it's a quick way to die. B, it wouldn't solve anything. They've a large enough party that their places would be filled quickly enough and nothing would change."

"Kill them all." No smile on Luciano's face now.

"Logistically unfeasible and in my opinion, a very bad idea."

"A bad idea?"

"Yes, a bad idea. What'd happen if you suddenly removed the entire power structure? The whole of the continent would dissolve into multiple bloody civil wars. And much as I hate to say it, compared to *that*, we're better off as we are."

"So exactly what *would* you suggest, then, *Signor*-not-Resistance, not-Underground?"

"Work from the inside. Get the really important things changed, get power shifting back to the sovereign nations."

"How?"

"Leverage. The population itself. They're the only force which can hope to influence the EuroGov. The government can't kill them all—they'd have nothing left to rule."

"The population will not rise up. We've had ample proof of that."

"It won't rise for *you*. Whilst you're murdering their relatives, you're as much the enemy as the EuroGov."

"It won't rise for anyone. It's too cowed."

I swallowed my last bite. "They'll rise. Sooner or later."

"Ah." Carla threw up her hands in mockery. "*Signorina*

Silver-tongue speaks!"

I ignored her and so did Luciano. "Why do you think that?" he asked me.

"Because history says so. The people *always* rise in the end. The problem with the EuroGov is they're clever. They never touch the innocent—not unless they fail Sorting. They make absolutely certain a person who behaves themselves has no *need* to go around afraid—a person *anyone else* is going to care about, anyway.

"But they work very hard indeed to maintain the fiction of being a democratically elected government. 'Cause people are afraid, but it's *action* they're afraid of. So people play along with that fiction. You must've heard them. 'Oh, they're a bit corrupt, but they *are democratically elected.'* Or, 'I don't agree with everything they do, *but the other parties are even worse.'*"

"They run *all* the parties!" spat Carla.

"*I* know that. *You* know that. Any reasonably well educated person who's prepared to face up to the truth knows that. But there're a lot of people who'd rather *not* face up to the truth. Because if they face up to it, they feel they ought to stand up to the government, and it's only *that* which gets you in trouble. So the people will rise, but who knows when. Because they won't be rising for self-preservation, as they do against a dictator: they'll be rising for their consciences.

"But Bane's right, they won't rise for you. Your mindless slaughter makes people side with the EuroGov. And you may not like it, but that's the truth."

Carla looked like she'd spring across the table and stab me with her fork. So much for not offending anyone.

"Interesting," said Luciano calmly. "I don't agree. I cannot accept the way things are. To me, to not fight against it would be unthinkable. But at least you both have an opinion, which is more than most people."

"A quailing, cowardly opinion fit for old women," snorted Carla.

"Carla," said Luciano rather patiently. "Margaret Verrall may not be prepared to pick up a gun and fight with us, but if we can get her into the Vatican, she will sit there and stab people's consciences with the sharpest quill she can find. Can you really not see how useful that is? She will whip up opposition and some of it will join *us*, not her."

I looked down at the table, embarrassed. "You have a rather high opinion of my quill."

"We've read the book. So's half the world, by now. It's making people think, and there's nothing the EuroGov hate more. Would you like to know how many new recruits we've had since it was published?"

I swallowed. The law of unintended consequences... "Actually, I'd rather not."

"Fine. But take it from me, your quill is sharper than you think."

I shrugged.

Carla threw up her hands. "You went and *won* the *PostSort Competition*, you stupid *Pregatore!*" Italian for "Pray-er"? Clearly a derogatory name for one of the Underground. Diplomacy obviously not being Carla's strong point.

Perhaps fortunately, the conversation turned to less controversial topics and by the time Bane and I made it back upstairs after the meal, Luciano and Francesco were carrying the second extra bed into Jon's room. Save us falling off and bashing our bad arms in the night.

The warm plasterwork glowed in the sun. Jon's chest moved steadily against my cheek and I lay quietly, enjoying the warmth and the morning silence. Luciano's acceptance of our difference of opinion had actually been quite re-assuring.

Shame Jon hadn't been there. Or perhaps a good thing! He'd some pretty well-developed opinions on the subject as well: we'd have been there all evening! No wonder Bane knew every argument in the book. Though Bane's own views had shifted and hardened noticeably since that ill-fated night at Wearmfell Factory. In a reassuring direction.

Hang on. Jon's breathing had sped up, his body tensed.

"Jon? It's okay. You don't need to pretend to be asleep."

"Margo..." His voice was a thin whisper. "It *is* you. Didn't know where we were..."

"We're safe. Bane's asleep just the other side of you. Do

you remember getting on the train?"

"Yes. Could've climbed a mountain...then nothing."

"You passed out. I think that stimulant of Bane's was pretty evil stuff. The train took us over the Alps almost to Milan, then the Resistance derailed it, found us when they came to get their loot and carried us off with them. We're in a safe house and as soon as you're well, they'll take us to Rome."

"Milan?" He sounded shocked. *"Rome?* Really?"

"Really. You just rest and get well. How d'you feel?"

"My leg hurts a bit. Otherwise fine."

"I can hear some understatement screaming for mercy."

"Fine, my leg hurts *a lot* and I feel awful."

I forced my abused muscles into just enough action to place a kiss on his forehead.

He smiled. "Feeling better already. Rome. Right. I'll give getting well my fullest attention."

For the next day or so, Jon remained desperately weak and spent most of the time asleep. "You don't have to stay with me all the time, you know," he whispered, waking to find me and Bane again chilling out beside him.

"Don't be silly," I said lightly. "There's not much to do in a safe house, y'know."

Actually we did pop and watch the news sometimes, but whenever we'd been gone for a bit longer—for dinner, say— he seemed worse. The stress of being alone and helpless in a totally unfamiliar place always sapped his strength like nothing else.

So we stuck around, even though he slept soundly most of the time. Under the regular assaults of a powerful anti-biotic, Bane's arm stopped oozing pus and began to heal, finally. My swollen face and aching muscles subsided and pretty soon Jon started to rally.

The doctor had ordered he stay off the leg until the wound closed up, but despite his emaciated condition, being so close to our goal revitalized him a little too much.

"I *will* sit on you," said Bane, as Jon made as if to put back the covers.

Jon desisted. "Don't you want to get there?"

"Yes, I do. So I don't want to be stuck here for days extra because you tore that hole open again with your impatience. I thought you were the most patient one of us!"

Jon flushed slightly. "Yes, but...well, Resistance safe houses get raided all the time, don't they? Let's not get too complacent about our safety here."

"Please don't say that to Luciano," I appealed. He was very proud of his cell's security.

"'Course not. But the sooner we get there the better. From the news, they're still looking all over the place. What if their spies learn the Vatican is definitely our destination? Then it'll be a hundred times harder to get in."

True. I wanted to be moving and so did Bane. But Jon had to be able to walk—and preferably run, though Luciano swore it wouldn't be necessary.

"Ah, good." Luciano looked up from the table a few days later as Jon appeared in the kitchen doorway leaning on his new hiking stick. "I go down to Rome every few months to liaise with the Rome cell and I'll be going tonight. The meeting's all prearranged, so if you three are ready to move, it will be a very uncomplicated way to get you to them. What do you think?"

Bane and I both glanced at Jon. A few more days would make the world of difference—yet surely it was far safer to go by tried and tested routes to a routine meeting than to depart from normal procedures.

"I'll be okay, really." Jon scratched his unaccustomed moustache. The soldiers had seen his beard, so he'd got rid of most of it. "I managed the stairs fine, now that you finally let me try." He had limped downstairs without any noticeable difficulty.

"Okay..." Bane's eyes questioned me. They'd not got a good look at him so he'd kept his beard.

"If you get back upstairs okay," I qualified.

"Yeah," said Bane. "So a provisional yes, Luciano, if that doesn't give you trouble."

"Doesn't make any difference. You either get in the car with me after dinner or you don't."

* * *

We got in the car with him. Not so much a car as a four-by-four jeep thing kept out of sight in a little courtyard. Jon winced as he maneuvered up and in, then pretended he hadn't. Carla and Francesco came out to see us off. Well, Francesco had come to see us off, anyway. "Good luck. Get stabbing with that quill, eh, *Signora* Silver-tongue?"

I grimaced at the nickname, but smiled and bid him goodbye.

"Here." Carla suddenly acknowledged our existence, shoving a scrap of fabric into my hand.

I unfolded it and found one of those bandanna hair-bands. "Thanks."

"Luciano said to find you something." Stiffly, she added, "Good luck."

"And you."

Luciano strode out into the courtyard, clipping a magazine into a Lethal. Pausing to tuck the pistol in the back of his waistband and shake his jacket over it, he swung into the driver's seat and made to slam the door—Carla caught his hand.

"Be careful." Sweet on him, definitely.

He kissed the back of her hand. Did he like her too? Avoiding the perils of romance within the cell's command structure, perhaps. They were both rather wedded to their cause. Of course, they weren't Believers, so for all I knew they could be at it like bunnies and just pretending to their subordinates.

"I'm always careful." Luciano slammed the door as soon as Carla's hand was clear. He lowered the window a few inches to say, "Expect me before dawn day after tomorrow."

Carla nodded and stepped back. Francesco was opening the gates; Luciano started the engine. In the flood light's glare Carla looked more anxious than hostile now. How safe was this run really? Probably safer than walking by our-selves. Probably a lot safer than that.

Luciano drove out of the courtyard and cruised through what appeared to be a mostly deserted country village. Not quite abandoned, but close to it. From Bane's map there were a lot of settlements like this in the Italian department. The houses had bright plaster walls, which was about all we could see in the headlights.

As soon as we'd left the village he turned off the bumpy but nominally-maintained road and onto a quite definitely abandoned road. Decades of locals and Resistance had kept it clear of encroaching trees but that was about it. The jeep tore through bushes, bouncing from rut to pothole like a manic kangaroo. Bane and Jon clung to the roof handles and I clung to them.

"You all right back there?" Luciano asked after a while. "I perhaps should've said—it's a bumpy ride."

"Fine," said Jon, unclenching his teeth momentarily.

"We'll live," I said.

Luciano chuckled. "Yeah, well, you can imagine the EuroGov don't like to send their expensive vehicles onto these roads. Anyway, I've got to keep my foot down a bit or it'll take forever to get there."

"We're fine," said Bane, just as the roof smacked him on the head again. "Though I think I preferred the train..."

"It gets better," said Luciano.

This humorous warning—as I thought—turned out to be a factual statement. The road bump-bumped its way to a genuinely desolate area and the surface took a sudden turn for the better. Luciano put his foot down even more and we made better time at the cost of fewer bruises. Color returned to Jon's face, and soon he nodded off.

The moon came out, and I watched the Italian forest passing, subtly different from the French forest much as the French forest was from our native Fellest. We passed picturesque ruins, these villages fully abandoned. Terracotta roof tiles still much in evidence, but the walls were white-washed—once whitewashed—stucco and the windows had heavy—sometimes ornate—grills fixed over them...

...The jeep jerked to a halt. I lifted my head from Bane's shoulder, confused. The grey light of dawn filled the air.

"Here we are," said Luciano. "Rome."

Rome? I'd just slept through several hundred kilometers of the Italian department.

I peered out the windscreen. Forest, still. "Doesn't look exactly how I imagined it."

"Well, we're not *quite* there," grinned Luciano. "But we

change vehicles here. Out you get."

Bane and I slid out and hurried around to winch Jon from the vehicle; his leg had stiffened up. White-faced, he gripped his stick and limped along determinedly as we followed Luciano along a forest track, breathing in the fresh morning air. Coming to another clearing, the three of us stopped dead in shock. Or Bane and I stopped dead and Jon stopped with us.

A city taxi sat there in the middle of the forest. Luciano laughed at our expressions and went up to the driver's window. The middle-aged fellow was glaring at him.

"Sorry we're late," Luciano grinned. "I had some delicate passengers."

What? He had actually slowed down on those early tracks?

The taxi driver grunted something in Italian.

"He says it's going to be a tight fit," Luciano told us. "He's right. But it's not far. Come on."

He opened the back door, and by the time we joined him he'd lifted the seat cushions to reveal a hidden compartment running under the back seats and right to the rear of the trunk.

"Okay, I see what he means." Bane eyed up the space available.

"Well, thanks to a certain Free State smack in the middle of Rome, they scan IDs at the city gates. I'm not up for that, and unless you are, we'll just have to squeeze in. Ladies first."

"What if someone rear ends us?" objected Bane. "I'll go first."

I rolled my eyes. Pretty unlikely, though admittedly, with the reputation of Italian drivers... I climbed in next, then Luciano helped Jon in and called, "Move up."

"Ha ha," retorted Bane.

"*Seriously.*"

Jon, Bane and I did our best to imitate sardines, and Luciano finally managed to wriggle into the remaining space. The taxi driver guffawed and slammed the seat's cushions back down.

"Glad someone's enjoying themselves," said Jon faintly.

"You okay?"

"Fine."

"Okay with small dark spaces?"

"I'm fine with small spaces, Margo, but my leg is all bent up so please let's do this as fast as we can."

Luciano shouted something in Italian which sounded rather like the Latin for, "Make it quick, jackass!" The driver guffawed again. But mercifully he started the engine and off we went.

The road was every bit as bumpy as the early one. It was much like being shut in a sardine tin—or a coffin—and rolled down a hill. Jon suffered especially; he began muttering a rosary under his breath, his body rigid with pain. Luciano ignored him until we heard other traffic around us—a lot of horns beeping. Italian drivers.

"Hush," he said then, "we're coming to the city gates. No one make a sound."

Jon fell silent—I took his hand and pressed it and he seemed to be trying not to crush it in return.

The taxi only stopped, lurched forward and stopped a few times before speeding up again.

"Get here early and you don't have to wait in line, y'see," murmured Luciano.

We were through the gates! My heart began pounding quite uncomfortably. So close. *So* close. Of course, we still had to meet the Rome cell and be taken to the tunnel. But by the end of the day? Maybe?

I swallowed my heart back down. *Your will, Lord.*

We passed quickly through the city; we'd definitely beaten the morning traffic. Eventually the taxi drew to a halt and this time it wasn't a red light, because we heard the back doors open, the seat cushions were lifted and a pistol barrel or two were stuffed into the opening.

"Relax, all's well," said Luciano. I think that's what he said, anyway, it was in Italian. Whatever it was, the pistols were withdrawn and a hand inserted to help him. He immediately reached back in to get Jon, pretty much dragging him out, with me pushing. By the time I emerged Jon sat on the short flight of steps which connected the garage to the house, head in one hand, the other massaging his leg.

"Just breathe," Luciano was telling him.

"I'm *breathing*. I'm fine..."

Bane scrambled out behind me like a rabbit from a burrow and we went to sit beside Jon.

"Who on earth are *they?*" The three strangers began speaking in Italian and my brain offered a possible translation to some of it and took a guess at the rest.

"*Diamine!* I know who they are!"

"Those three reAssignees."

"Not the three most wanted?"

"It's them, isn't it, Luciano?"

"Yes, it's them. They just need safe passage into the Vatican and the EuroGov will be cursing fit to burst."

"Okay. They don't speak Italian, I take it?"

"Of course not" replied Luciano.

Blearily, Jon opened his mouth to say, actually, he was getting the gist of a lot of it, but I stuck my elbow in his side. His mouth snapped closed again and he went slightly pink. No point giving away any advantage. Especially not to people who seemed so thrilled to see us. Not.

"Come on," said Luciano cheerfully, in Esperanto. "Let's go inside. You good to move, Jon?"

"Fine."

But Jon allowed me and Bane to hoist him to his feet, leaning heavily on the stick as we followed Luciano. Carla's antagonism to us was hardly unexpected—it was Luciano's attitude that was more unusual—but I was a little surprised this lot weren't more welcoming. Surely here in Rome the Resistance should be more used to getting on with the Underground?

When we reached his office and were introduced to him, Gino, the leader of the Rome cell, warmed up a bit. "You look tired. Just sit down in here and have some refreshments while I take care of my business with Luciano."

We smiled and thanked him—we could hardly demand to be taken to a tunnel at once!—and going into the ante-room indicated, settled ourselves on a battered sofa. After a surprisingly short time, a woman came in with a tray of hard boiled eggs, a sort of pasta soup and a loaf of bread. As she left, I could see Luciano sitting with Gino at his desk, talking.

Hungrily, we demolished the brunch. The last egg eaten, I looked around the little room. We seemed to be un-observed. Slipping up to the door, I put my ear to the hinge. The Italian was fast and quiet and hard to catch.

"What about the three of... ...get them in before I go back?"

"Haven't you heard? ...didn't come back from the raid. All taken."

"What has that to do with...?"

Gino said something I couldn't catch, but I caught Luciano's response quite distinctly, his voice raised in shock and incredulity.

"You want to do *what?*"

21

CROSSING THE WHITE LINE

Bane was suddenly by my shoulder. "What're you doing, Margo?"

"Eavesdropping."

"You don't speak Italian."

"No, it'd help. *Hush.*"

Gino was talking: "...the only way to save..."

Luciano cut in: "Won't save anything... ...no sense at all!"

"They're the perfect..."

"They *don't bargain!* ...told us what happened to some old hunter... ...the same as you're..."

"We'll be careful. Make safeguards..."

"Can't believe you're even considering... ...The EuroGov are the *enemy.* ...may be *Pregatori* but... ...more our allies than..."

"...have my brother! ...know what will happen...?"

"What will happen to us all..." Luciano's voice was grim. "Doesn't mean we can *ever*..."

"No! ...preaching like one of them! I'll not let Paulo die, not when thanks to you..."

"I won't let you do this."

"You think you can stop me? My city..."

I drew away from the door, my heart pounding now with fear and unease, and said softly to Jon and Bane, "I can't hear it all and what I can hear I'm not sure I'm understanding correctly. But I'm almost certain—I am certain—Gino wants to sell us to the EuroGov. To save his brother? Something. Luciano's opposing him, but..."

Bane went pale. "This is Gino's patch, Luciano hasn't a hope..." He bolted across the room to the window—looked out and eased it slowly, cautiously, open.

I put my ear to the door again.

"This is wrong. They..."

"Now you really sound like..."

"If you touch that phone, I swear, I'll..."

"Just try it, Milan rat!"

Hurrying to Jon, I led him to the window. "Come on, quickly."

Bane shot me a look. "You sure Luciano won't talk him round?"

"Sounds like they're about to come to blows."

"Let's go, then." He paused to tug the bandanna further down over my forehead, then flung a leg over the sill. "It's first floor, just hang and drop. Jon, I'll break your fall."

With a grunt of pain as his weight fell on his bad arm, he was gone.

"Over you go, Jon," I said.

"You first."

"Get through that window!"

Glad I'd insisted—he needed help lifting his injured leg over the sill. He hissed for a moment in pain, then twisted onto his stomach and let himself down with me hanging onto his collar to take some of the weight off his arms.

He and Bane both went sprawling on the ground as he landed, but Bane got straight up so, waiting only to see Jon sit up too, I scrambled out and dropped. Rather sooner than I'd intended—my one arm wouldn't hold my weight at all, but I didn't quite flatten Bane and he took the weight off my ankles as I landed.

Grabbing a nearby broom, Bane poked the window closed so it wasn't quite so obvious where we'd gone, then we dragged Jon to his feet and headed off down the quiet back street. Bane ventured briefly onto the main street ahead of us to buy football caps for Jon and himself. Why hadn't I trimmed their hair before we left Milan? Still, the caps hid most of it. It would've been good to reapply the makeup on my still conspicuously-bruised face but I didn't dare spend the time.

"Where're we heading?" I asked Bane, as we sauntered along as though we hadn't a care in the world. We must be quite near the historic center of the city; no acting ability required to stare at the magnificent buildings. "I think Gino was going to phone them. We may not have long at all."

"We probably don't. He may call them before he even realizes we've flown the coop and even if he finds out first— if he's stupid enough to think he can do a deal with them he'll likely try to salvage what he can by letting them know we're in Rome and headed for the Vatican. We have to get in. Somehow, we have to get in right away."

We rounded a corner and there, on the skyline, towered a familiar dome.

My heart constricted. "There it is. Saint Peter's..."

Jon's head rose. "You can see it?"

"Yes. We're so close."

We picked up our pace, still making sure to gawk around a lot, and soon we reached the Vatican wall, an immense, ancient thing, the top festooned in tens of kilometers of very modern razor wire and dotted with CCTV cameras. Several meters away from the base ran a painted white line overlooked by regular guard towers, all sheltering machine guns and EuroArmy soldiers.

"Absolutely no way in here," muttered Bane. Not that we'd expected one.

"What about the contact procedure Father Mark gave us?" I asked.

"Be at the statue at three o'clock and do the thing with a newspaper. But it'll be out of date and by three o'clock I've a hunch every street in this city will have checkpoints."

We carried on walking as we talked, mingling with the crowd and keeping well back from that white line. It was common knowledge in the Underground that in Rome, "crossing the white line" was the local euphemism for suicide; it was the favored method in this city.

Sweat trickled down my backbone, though the sun wasn't high yet. A clock ticked deafeningly in my head. Had Gino and Luciano come to blows? Was Luciano on his way back to Milan with a flea in his ear? Had Gino picked up the phone yet? *Lord, what do we do? We're stumped!*

We reached St. Peter's Square, invisible behind the high concrete wall built and manned by the EuroGov, broken only by two sets of massive steel double gates. They stood open—it was late enough that the tour buses had started running. A sign stood beside the embarkation point.

The Forbidden Square: The Official Tour

Enter the Vatican Free State itself!

View the Forbidden Square from the safety and comfort
of a EuroGov-approved tour bus.

100% SAFE—100% SECURE
The one and only official tour!

Ê300 per person

The *only* tour, period, hence the jaw-dropping price.

Bane stared at the sign, his foot tapping as though he too, heard that clock ticking in his head. Was Gino even now speaking to the EuroGov? Trying to hammer out a deal before revealing what he knew?

A tour bus waited by the embarkation point, partly full. Bane crossed to the signboard and picked up a leaflet, returning to where Jon and I stood, apparently admiring what little we could see of the square through the gates.

"They go every half hour until ten, then every ten minutes," he told me in English, holding it so I could read it too. A whole lot of stuff about how secure the bus was—yeah, because people really thought the Vatican State would open fire on them! Anyone with even one brain cell knew the buses sported triple-locked doors and bulletproof glass to keep people from getting *off.*

"How would we get out of the bus, Bane?"

"I think we can do it."

He pulled out his wallet and counted the money inside. Seven hundred Eurons. Oh no. If none of the SpecialCorps were the richer for it, what money Jon and I had been carrying was ash.

"We're two hundred short," I muttered.

Jon took a breath.

"If you say 'leave me,' I'm going to hit you." I didn't look up from the cash.

"So am I," said Bane.

Jon let the breath out again and said nothing. Bane's foot tapped even harder. My heart raced. Time was running out.

In cold reason I couldn't be sure, but I *was*. Bane could feel it too.

Bane pulled out his phone. Checking for other ways in? There were no other ways. Only tunnels we couldn't get to. Oh...he was polishing the screen on his sleeve and blowing dust from the keyboard. He saw me watching him. "This is worth fifteen hundred Eurons. Perhaps we can get, say, seven hundred for it, in cash..."

"Where, Bane? We don't dare go in a pawn shop."

He bit his lip. We couldn't just go up to people and offer to sell them an expensive omniPhone for half its value in cash. How d'you spell "suspicious," again? But every other stitch and scrap we possessed wasn't worth more than fifty Eurons put together.

A rather stealthy movement to one side...

A young Italian in a leather jacket was approaching along the side of the buildings. Eyes on us.

"Hi," he said in Esperanto, seeing he was observed. "Nice phone, *Signore.*"

Bane shrugged casually. "Thinking of getting a new one, actually. Like to buy this one?"

"How much?"

"One thousand."

The Italian guy scoffed in the time-honored manner of bargainers the world over.

"Too much, *Signore*. It is not a new model now. Nice phone, still, but not new. I'll give you five hundred. Then you go on the Vatican tour, *si?*"

My heart climbed to my throat, juddering there as that sense of imminent dread increased by the second, as did my conviction this guy suspected more than he let on. But what was he? Resistance? Underground? Sharp-eyed local sympathizer? Genuinely pursuing a bargain? EuroGov informer?

"Thinking about it, yeah," drawled Bane. "Don't want to trek off to a cash machine and seeing I was going to get rid of this anyway... Can't take less than eight hundred, though."

Well below the phone's value. Unlikely this guy would buy Bane's pretence of being stinking rich and ridiculously lazy.

"I have only five hundred in my wallet, *Signore*. You will have to take it or leave it."

Bane was trying not to scowl. To give up our sole remaining asset for so little...yet if we didn't have two hundred Eurons very soon, it'd all be moot. "That's really not very much."

The Italian reached into his pocket and Bane's body tensed—he simply took out a wallet and opened it to display a one hundred Euron note and a pair of two hundred Euron notes. He was telling the truth.

He removed a handful of cards and held out the wallet enticingly. "Five hundred. I give you this..."

He'd left one card in place. Blue and yellow. His ID card. Bane and I were both staring, we couldn't help it. He suspected...a lot. No one would offer an ID card to a normal tourist. I looked down at the leaflet in my hand; searched for the small print. There, in black and white.

TOUR EXEMPT FROM *SMALL TRADERS EXCEPTION* TO *IDENTIFICATION ACT.*
ID MUST BE SCANNED WITH PAYMENT.

Of course. You had to scan your ID, same as in a shop.

Bane read over my shoulder—his eyes flicked to the Italian's face. For once Bane's black hair and slightly dark skin did him a favor. The young Italian was clean-shaven. With the beard... Bane'd pass for him on a cursory inspection. They never looked at the picture in shops, anyway.

Bane drew in a deep breath, his jaw tightening. In my head a voice shouted, *hurry, hurry, hurry...*

"Why not?" Bane shrugged. He flipped open the back of the phone and removed his omniSIM, tucking it securely in a pocket, then held the phone out and exchanged it for the wallet.

"*Grazie.*" The Italian pocketed it. "Enjoy your tour." Off he walked.

Bane transferred the money and the card to his own wallet, dropped the other in a nearby bin and swallowed hard. "Come on, let's do this before I have time to think about it."

Before he had time to wonder if the young man's ID might be compromised—was he Resistance or criminal, and the ID useless to him? No, surely he was Underground or concerned citizen—or greedy citizen—or even a more decent member of the Resistance—who'd recognized us and realized our dilemma? He'd got a good phone out of it and if he meant us well he'd proceed at a very leisurely pace to the police station to report his wallet—and ID—stolen.

If he didn't mean us well—we'd be caught when we used the card. Bane was right, better not to think about it.

He went on, "Okay, what we'll do is— no, they're about to go, come on."

We hurried across the street, for the bus had just started up, and climbed on.

"Hi." Bane deliberately dulled his English accent but didn't attempt an Italian one—an Italian wouldn't speak in Esperanto. "Three for the tour, please."

"Nine hundred." The driver didn't take his eyes from his newspaper.

Bane took out the money. The driver probably would look up when he put it through the slot in the bulletproof glass... I wound myself around Jon and hid both our faces in a passionate kiss. Could see the driver out of the corner of my eye and he didn't glance at Bane at all, thoroughly distracted by me and Jon. Bane calmly inserted the ID card into the reader without being asked, as though buying his groceries, and for a second I forgot to move my lips against Jon's.

Peep.

One happy cardReader. *Oh, Lord shower blessings on that Italian guy!* Bane took the card out and I went back to kissing Jon.

"Bit of a waste of money taking those two in there, isn't it?" smirked the driver.

I think Bane rolled his eyes.

"Tell me about it." He took the tickets from the machine. "Thanks. Come on, you two."

Catching Jon's arm he towed him down the aisle. Still quite a few free seats this early in the day—he pushed me and Jon into one and sat opposite. Jon and I detached casually and leant forward as though to look at the leaflet. Other people were chattering and the engine would cover any seditious talk.

"Okay, here's the plan..." Bane broke off and scowled at Jon. "Quit looking so happy, Jon! My temper's not that good!"

"It's not good at all." But Jon considerately assumed an expression suitable for a morgue and Bane managed to bring his mind back to the matter at hand.

"Right. According to the leaflet, the bus cruises halfway round, stops at the base of the basilica steps for five minutes, then cruises back out. While it's stopped, Jon and I will start arguing. I'll pull the knife and the driver will come out of that locked cab to break it up. Margo, you'll be right by the cab admiring the columns and you'll catch the cab door and stop it closing. I'll persuade the driver to leave us alone, and we'll climb out the driver's door. Okay?"

"What if the driver just leaves us to it?" asked Jon.

"Next question," said Bane grimly.

"Are you sure we'll be able to get out the driver's door?" I asked.

"If he can get out, we can. If he's actually locked in here with us...next question."

"What do we do once we're off the bus?" asked Jon.

"We run as though all the hounds of hell are behind us."

"Run? You'll have to leave me—"

Bane and I smacked him on the head pretty much simultaneously.

"Ouch. Okay. Run like heck. Got it."

The bus doors closed. The locks engaged. *Clunk-click. Clunk-click. Clunk-click.* All safe and secure from the evil Underground. The bus moved forward, travelling across the white line and through the gates.

The colonnades of St. Peter's Square—actually a circle, of course—appeared around us, curving and graceful. My eyes followed the ancient Roman obelisk towering in the centre, up, up, up...then went to the front windshield as the basilica drew nearer and nearer.

I was looking at a church. The hair stood up on the back of my neck. Not a church building. A real church. Our Lord was in there, safe in the tabernacle, and people went in there and openly worshipped...

The bus drew to a halt—further away from the steps than ideal. A line of immense steel bollards set into the ground prevented any tour bus—or EuroGov tank or troop carrier—approaching too close. Up the center of the steps ran a ramp.

"Aim for the ramp," I murmured to Bane. "It'll be easier for Jon."

"Yeah, and the bus will provide a bit of cover in the center, at least for a few moments."

I moistened my lips, managing not to turn and look at the machine guns over the gates. But everyone turned as a deafening noise penetrated the bulletproof glass.

Screech...

The 'in' gate was closing, slowly and most definitely not silently.

"Well, folks," said the driver on the intercom, "No more tours today if they're closing the gates—some sort of security alert, I imagine—you just made it. Five minutes—take your pictures."

I let out a long breath. Sweat was soaking through my t-shirt. Had Gino told them? No going back now.

"Margo," said Bane softly. "Go." *I love you*, said his eyes, *but I might attract a bit of attention if I kissed you after that little show with Jon.*

"Love you," I mouthed. Getting up, I drifted to the front windshield. Hopefully no one would notice not one of the three of us had a camera of any kind. I gawked around, trying for ditzy rather than terrified.

"It's none of your business!" roared Bane, springing from his seat.

Jon leapt up as well. "None of my business?" he bellowed back. "You had your hand on her...I *saw* you!"

Typical. Boys. Well, they'd probably manage to be pretty realistic about it.

"I didn't see her objecting!"

"That's not the point!" Feeling his way along the seats with his stick, Jon backed carefully down the aisle as though afraid of Bane. "You're supposed to be my mate!"

"You don't own her!"

Jon groped momentarily for some response rather more inflammatory than agreement.

"Knock it off, you two," said the driver over the intercom.

"She's mine, you just keep your hands *away from her!*" Jon managed at last.

"Are you telling me what to do?" The knife appeared in Bane's hand. People gasped and screamed, fleeing to the rear of the bus.

"Hey," yelled the driver, "put that down!"

"Well, are you?" Bane advanced on Jon with what certainly appeared to be lethal intent.

I hovered in position, ready to grab Jon and pull him back if he seemed likely to stumble onto the blade. From Bane's watchful eyes, he was conscious of the danger.

"She's mine!" said Jon with apparent recklessness. "Mine, get it?"

"Shut up, you stupid boy!" came from the intercom.

"I'm going to gut you, you arrogant—" Bane made a noisy lunge, Jon knocked his arm aside with his stick and the driver came scrambling out of his cab.

"Drop it, lad, or you'll be in for it, I mean it! There're cameras on here, y'know. Hey, what are you—"

He turned as I grabbed the door to the cab. Then he sucked in a sudden breath and held it, eyes bulging, as Bane's knife tickled his throat.

"Please don't move, I've absolutely no wish to hurt you," said Bane, with rather cold sincerity.

"Fools! You'll be shot..."

"We'll take our chances."

Door wedged open with someone's bag, I drew Jon after me into the cab, my blood racing. It *was* possible to get out, the driver had as good as said so! I found the handle and turned it. The door opened. I eased it back just far enough to slip out, then talked Jon out.

"...Step down, big step..." I hung onto him as he half fell out. "You're down. Come on, Bane."

Hearing the name, the driver's face went white. He spun around and stared at my forehead. "*Bane*... Oh no, no, no..."

"Oh, uh... Yeah, this is for your own good." Bane's arm went back, his grip on the knife shifted and he struck the driver hard on the jaw with the haft.

The man crumpled to the ground—dazed or unconscious, either way the bruise would prove him an unwitting victim of our wiles. Bane sprang over him, scrambled past the driver's seat, jumped down beside us, and pulled Jon's other arm over his shoulders. "Drop the stick, Jon, okay? Let's *go!*"

We ran. We ran as I'd only once run before, racing across a sandy exercise yard towards a small wall gate in the Facility. My chest heaved and my lungs burned. My legs were like lead—I drove them on. It was all Jon could do to keep his legs moving and not be dragged between us.

Uphill. *Oh Lord, why does it have to be uphill?* The basilica towered above us, higher and higher as we tore up the slope. Silence from behind: the guards hadn't seen us, perhaps intent on closing their gates; my back prickled with horrible anticipation...

Gasping for air, my limbs shaking with exhaustion, the strength was going out of my legs, leaving them jelly-like. A bit further, a bit further—there was the top of the steps, just ahead; the portico beyond, nice strong, wide, *bulletproof* pillars. Closer, closer...

Tat-tat-tat-tat-tat-tat-tat-tat!

A hail of bullets sprayed across the ramp beside us; flying stone struck my face. Closer, closer, *closer...*

We flung ourselves behind the columns, gasping. The machine guns fell silent

After a few moments, a small door in the center of the enormous ones moved, just slightly. A shockingly cheerful voice called, "Ready when you are."

Bane didn't hesitate. "Go!" he wheezed, dragging us forwards.

We stumbled out into the open, carried halfway in that first mad rush. It was dark in the portico's shadow and we were almost there, almost...

Tat-tat-tat-tat-tat!

The door swung open ahead of us and we tumbled through. *Thud.* It closed behind us, and for a moment there was a *thwang-crack* of bullets hitting ancient bronze.

"*Vandals,*" said the voice. "Right. Through you go."

We were in a dim internal porch. We picked ourselves up and stepped over a wooden lintel into... An impression of vastness, then my eyes focused on the muzzles of a large number of pistols pointed straight at me. At all three of us. NonLees...the most terrifying weapons of all...but...my stomach twisted. Had the Vatican fallen, all unknown to us?

"Please don't be frightened." A small smiling man in a dark gown...a cassock?...stepped through behind us. "We've just got to get you ID'd and all that."

I let out a shuddering breath. Of course. They weren't going to let people just wander in. I managed to look past the muzzles to the men behind them. Half wore smart orange, red, and blue uniform—Swiss Guards?—the other half something equally smart in a much plainer navy. Vatican police? Both figures from many a childhood tale, they hardly seemed real.

My eyes moved beyond, to the building. The largest building I'd been inside in my entire life. Beautiful towering walls...and at the far end, underneath a towering metal canopy, a glimmer of red light...

Running footsteps echoed around...a man was racing down the side aisle, tall, slim, black cassock flapping.

"Ah, Father Mark! Is it them?" asked the cheery door-keeper.

Father Mark just flung his arms around me, hugged me tightly, hugged Bane, hugged Jon.

"Ah, I'll take that as a yes. Go on, stand down, you fellows."

The pistols disappeared into holsters—I hardly noticed. Father Mark let go of Jon, and I hugged him again, demanding, "You made it? You all made it?"

"Us? Oh yes...but you three, oh, I really was afraid we'd seen the last of you! Yet they hadn't *caught* you yet." He hugged us all a second time. "My goodness, that is not the advised method of entry into this State, you know!"

My eyes had already strayed back to that red dot, wondering. Was it? Could it be...? Father Mark smiled, turned, and genuflected to what must be the distant tabernacle at the other end of the mighty building, presence declared by that little winking light.

"Yes, Margo, He's here. 'He who guards this city neither slumbers nor sleeps.' Pope Cornelius the second had a beautiful Holy Spirit hanging pyx made so that He could hover over the main altar, to welcome all who enter."

I dropped to one knee, then both knees, my throat closing. Like entering another world...a wonderful, wonderful world of freedom.

"You mean He...?" Jon interpreting silence as easily as words. Or perhaps just sensing the Divine presence.

"Yes." My voice shook.

Jon sank down on his knees. Bane frowned faintly and did his usual I'm-respecting-Margo's-feelings-but-don't-think-it-means-I-believe-any-of-it head bob.

After a moment I pried myself from the little red light and what it meant and got back to my feet. Jon struggled up as well, only to gasp and clutch his side as he straightened.

"Oh no, thought I'd just pulled a muscle." Something in his voice caught my attention. He drew his hand away...

Red with blood.

22

INDEFINITE LEAVE TO REMAIN

Jon's legs buckled...

"Catch him!" I cracked foreheads with the doorkeeper as I lunged. Bane collided with Father Mark, but they managed to stop Jon's head hitting the marble floor.

One of the Swiss Guards already had a wristCell to his mouth, talking rapidly in Latin. I heard *doctor* and *stretcher* and managed not to scream for just those things. Father Mark ripped Jon's clothes aside to bare the wound, using Bane's proffered t-shirt to stem the bleeding.

"Keep calm," he said, as I flung myself down next to him. "I don't think it's serious."

"Anything's serious in his condition!"

"Granted he doesn't look a picture of health. But Lord willing, we'll patch him up."

Some very competent guards were already edging me out. So competent that even Father Mark withdrew and left them to it. Soon more Swiss Guards came jogging up with a stretcher, followed by a layman bent under the weight of a large paramedic's kit—we clearly weren't going to get anywhere near Jon for the foreseeable future.

Screeeeeeech...

The deafening sound penetrated the basilica's thick walls.

"The bus driver's recovered," muttered Bane in English, shrugging into the light jacket one of the guards had produced from somewhere.

"I reckon he's going to be very grateful for the bruise," I said absently, most of my attention still on Jon.

"Definitely a case of shutting the gate after the fugitives have gone through it, though!"

Four of the Swiss Guards marched smartly up to the internal porch and disappeared inside. Daylight streamed in as the little sally port opened and out they went...

No shots. Gradually I relaxed.

"What are they doing?" Bane marshaled his Latin as his own tension gave way to puzzlement.

A series of clangs from outside.

"Shutting the portico gates," said the little robed doorkeeper. "We only close them when the EuroGov's gates are closed, for reasons you will appreciate."

Portico gates...yes, there'd been huge iron barred gates, standing open between each pillar. If they'd been closed... I shuddered.

"Keeping them open is just a bit of a security risk." Father Mark had been listening. "But just very occasionally it pays off." He gestured to us. "So one can't call it a *pointless* security risk."

"Don't they shoot the Swiss Guards?"

"Not usually," said the doorkeeper dryly.

"The square *is* the territory of a Free State," pointed out Father Mark, "and they do try to look legal, after all. They're quite happy to make an exception for people pulling a stunt like yours, though."

"We're taking him to surgery." The doctor zipped up his bag as the stretcher was trotted away at the same speed at which it'd been brought. "But he'll be fine and there's really no point in you hovering." He galloped off after his patient, still clutching the bag.

"There, what did I tell you?" Father Mark looked me and Bane up and down. "My goodness, look at the state of you. Canteen, first stop?"

"We ate with the Resistance..." My stomach caught up with my tongue as Bane shot me an incredulous look. "What am I saying? I could eat a three-course meal!"

"Follow me, then."

A pained noise came from a man in grey civilian attire of uniform-level smartness, who'd either been there the whole time or arrived unnoticed.

Father Mark hesitated. "Ah, there is that. If I take you to the canteen first of all, Eduardo may have a nervous breakdown and it's probably better if the Head of Vatican Security isn't reduced to tears. Do you mind if he gets you registered and everything first?"

I eyed the man's impassive face—had he ever been reduced to tears in his *life?*

Bane snorted. "Go ahead. Until recently we've been waiting *all day* for food, another hour won't make any difference!"

"Oh, not an hour," said Eduardo. "Half an hour, at most. This way."

My legs ached and shook as we trudged after his brisk steps, and I was glad of the arm Bane slipped around me. Eduardo led part way down the side aisle, genuflected and went through a doorway. Father Mark and I genuflected as well; Bane did his head bob, saw me trying to muster the energy to rise, and hauled me back to my feet, angel.

A slight bleep accompanied our passage through the doorway. We all stopped as Eduardo pulled out a handheld networkAccessor and consulted it. His eyes went to the spot where Bane's knife was hidden, but he pocketed the Accessor again and carried on without comment. A hidden weapon scannerArch? Knives must be allowed, then. Or he appreciated that Bane might not want to give it up just yet.

"So who is this guy again?" Bane asked Father Mark in a low voice, sounding relieved as we headed along a stone passageway.

"Head of the VSS."

"The Vatican has a Secret Service?" said Bane, while I was still making guesses at the acronym.

"Oh yes. But before your imagination runs away with you, it's almost entirely *counter*-espionage. Though at the moment, Eduardo deals with anything at all relating to the State's security. He's not at all a scary fellow, unless you find being pathologically fearless scary, which admittedly some people do."

Several echoing passageways and a very fine flight of stairs later, Eduardo ushered us into a small office. Taking his place behind the desk, he gestured for us to sit in the collection of comfortable old chairs ranked in front of it.

"You'll stand sponsor?" he asked Father Mark, laying out three passport-like wallets on the desk in front of him and drawing out his computer keyboard.

"Of course."

"Then this should be quick enough." He turned his attention back to me and Bane. "I need to check your identities and take your details, then I can issue you with visas. If you've got your ID cards, we can begin."

"Uh," I raised a finger. "I haven't got mine."

"Where is it?"

"Either burned up or in the EuroGov's possession. Or just possibly a SpecialCorps soldier's souvenir, though I doubt they'd dare. Jon's is with it."

Eduardo sighed, but didn't look desperately concerned. Not that he looked like he was ever desperately anything. He flicked an eye at my scar. "Well, I don't think there's any doubt about *your* identity." He held out a hand for Bane's card. "Thank you."

He looked at the photo, at Bane, back at the photo again. "Well, it won't be possible to prove this is you until you've had a shave and several weeks' meals, but it could be and Father Mark says it is." He twiddled the card at Bane. "I keep this, you understand? Goes in the card vault. You want to leave, you get it back. Okay?"

Clearly people weren't encouraged to flit to and fro from Free State to EuroBloc—probably a recipe for espionage. Most people who came here weren't going to miss their IDs, anyway.

Bane nodded, and placed the Italian guy's card on the desk as well. "Just in case you want this too, some Italian sold us this not half an hour ago. We probably owe him our lives."

Eduardo ran it through the scanner on the desk. "Miguel Appiani; twenty; residence—Rome; languages—Italian and Esperanto; clean record. Can't tell you any more than that."

"You've got access to the EuroGov system?"

"They're not very good at keeping me out." Eduardo calmly scanned Bane's real card. "Blake Marsden, known as Bane...okay, I have to investigate any matters on your record, you understand. Item one, *first degree homicide*, says you knifed a government employee, is this correct?"

Bane glanced sidelong at Father Mark who just smiled encouragingly. "Yes," said Bane.

"Could you tell me the circumstances in which this occurred?"

"Okay. Man was a dismantler. Man was dismantling Margo. Man raised scalpel to kill Margo. I killed man. D'you need more details?"

"Witnesses?"

"Father Mark and Margo." Bane nodded to us.

"Was that description accurate in all important or relevant particulars?"

"Yes," I said. True from Bane's point of view anyway—I wasn't sure if Doctor Richard had his sights on me or on Bane, but it didn't really change anything.

"Yes, from what I witnessed," said Father Mark scrupulously.

Eduardo typed rapidly for a few moments. "Okay, next item...s. Five charges of *Assault on a EuroGov Employee*, three *causing Actual Grievous Bodily Harm*."

"None of them were *grievous*," I objected. "We *know* two of them were just concussions. And what was the *third* one?"

"Well, concussion *is* more serious than people think, but as it happens, I saw the two victims on TV the other night and they looked very well to me. The third charge concerns a knife wound. So, tell me?"

"Two SpecialCorps soldiers were driving Jon and Margo to a Facility to dismantle them," said Bane. "I persuaded the driver out of the van with a knife to his throat—I've done more damage to *myself* shaving, so 'grievous' is just nonsense. I shook the soldiers in the back of the van around quite a bit and left them parked on the edge of a cliff but perfectly safe.

"The other two were normal soldiers who were torturing Jon so I made them lie on their faces and bashed them on the nut with a rifle butt. That or blow their heads off, so it seemed a good idea at the time." Bane shot another look at Father Mark, as though afraid some comment about his temper might be forthcoming—Father Mark just gave a faint, sad smile. "Margo and Jon are witnesses."

Eduardo raised his eyebrows at me.

"All correct. Bane was feverish at the time," I added. "And

we had to shut them up somehow."

"Please don't *imply* things," said Eduardo. "If you want to make a point, make it: it saves misunderstandings."

"Oh. Sorry. I just think he actually showed quite good self-control. In the circumstances."

"Duly noted. This is not a trial, however." Eduardo looked at Bane again. "Next charge, *Sedition: Category One*—you sprung a Facility full of reAssignees, correct?"

"Yes."

"Lovely, not illegal here, very much the opposite. Next, *Destruction of Public Property*. What was the property?"

Bane scratched his beard. "Um, y'know, I'm not too sure. 'Cause the Resistance blew up a helicopter but I tried to stop them. *Idiots.*" Heat leaked into his voice, even after so long. "Margo and the girls were just underneath, you see," he explained, at Eduardo's look of inquiry. "They might be trying to pin that on me but it wasn't. Lots of bullet holes in their Facility, but that wasn't my finger on the trigger either.

"Oh, Father Mark and I did nick a whole load of bottles of antiseptic fluid, a roll of clingfilm stuff and um...a plastic sheet and a couple of bags. And poured the original contents of the bottles down the sink. That's all I can think of."

Eduardo looked at Father Mark who smiled unapologetically and nodded. Eduardo typed quickly again.

"Right, that's you. Next, Margaret Verrall," he typed a manual search, "they don't like you much, do they? There's a list of charges as long as my arm."

"Really?" I said. "It was only four the last time I saw it."

"Well, they've come up with a few more, but...not illegal, not illegal, not illegal, Blake's covered that one... Not illegal... Okay, you're clear. Jonathan Revan, isn't it? Ah yes. He's quite a good boy, it seems. *Personal Practice, Unauthorized Departure* and *Escaping from EuroBloc Custody*. Not illegal here. Clear."

He filled something in on each of the wallet things, then stamped them, signed them and handed two over. "These are your visas, keep them safe."

Taking out three blank pass cards, he slid them one at a time into a card programmer-printer, typing a few commands on the computer each time.

I opened my visa wallet. *Vatican Free State*, I read, *Indefinite Leave to Remain*. I smiled and muttered the English to Bane, who was spelling out the Latin words. Underneath *Issued by* it was signed Ἐδμαρδο... I couldn't read his surname. HEAD OF THE VATICAN SECRET SERVICE, it said afterwards, then *on behalf of* and another signature:

Cornelius PP. III

A moment of surrealism. Was it actually possible I was sitting in a Free State holding an indefinite visa signed by the Pope himself? I pointed out the last signature to Bane, and he grinned.

"Here." Eduardo passed a card to me and another to Bane, placing the last one with the third visa. "These don't strictly speaking need to be visible, but you'd be advised to display them until the guards recognize you by sight. After that, keep them on you—you'll need them in the canteen, supermarket, department store—anywhere like that—and please don't *lose them*."

I peered at mine. He'd used the photo from my EuroBloc record, and the individual card number in the corner, along with the card programmer—making it non-transferable—showed the Vatican weren't making EGD Security's mistake.

Using the card's little clip to fasten it to my collar, I stowed the visa in the pocket of my—Carla's!—jeans. Must visit that department store and get a few clothes. Though we'd only three hundred Eurons between the three of us. Which was, strictly speaking, Bane's money. Thinking about his missing phone reminded me...

"Is it time for your pill?"

Bane put his hand to his pocket, stopped and pulled a face. "Have to buy a watch now, won't I? Is it time, Margo?"

"It's quarter to nine."

"Yes, then. Is there some water anywhere?"

"I just need your religious details and you can go," said Eduardo. "I've got everything else here already. Margaret and Jonathan, Believers, adult, yes?"

"Yep." Adult meant Confirmed in this context.

"Blake?"

"*Bane*," growled Bane.

"Bane, then?"

"NonBeliever, me."

"Any religious opinion whatsoever?"

"Huh?"

"He means, how would you answer the question, 'do you believe in God'?" supplied Father Mark.

"I'd say I don't know."

"Agnostic, good-good." Eduardo typed briefly. "This is just for the records. Anyone else wants to know, they can ask you. Right. I've finished with you. There'll be a summary of the State's laws in your accommodation, if there isn't, ask for one—all extremely basic stuff, goes along the lines of do not kill, do not steal, do not commit adultery... Waste of paper printing it out. Anyway, go and get fed. If there's any problem with your friend, someone will find you."

"Thanks, Eduardo." Father Mark stood up, but I stayed in my seat.

"Do you...know anything about Dominique and Juwan? Are they okay?"

There'd been nothing on the news about them while we were at the safe house. Bane dropped back into his seat, eyes on Eduardo.

Eduardo's lips turned up in a tiny, sad smile. "They are well at present."

"Can you...help them?"

Bane's gaze grew intent.

Eduardo grimaced slightly. "Doubtful, but it's something I'm following with great attention. They are in no immediate danger; the other boy's condition is still too serious to allow him to testify against them."

"And when Louis is better?"

Eduardo held up a deflecting hand. "Miss Verrall, go and get something to eat. Settle in. There will be a better time for this discussion."

That wasn't a no, but...*doubtful* didn't sound good. Had I really expected anything else? I got to my feet and so did Bane. We'd almost reached the door when Bane stopped dead.

"You're in charge of anything to do with State Security,

Father Mark said?"

Eduardo raised an eyebrow. "Correct."

"The Rome cell of the Resistance turned us in to the EuroGov. You can't trust them."

Eduardo's brows snapped together. "You're certain?"

"Well, we didn't wait to have it confirmed absolutely, but we were pretty sure they were planning to try and trade us for the leader's brother and some others who'd been captured. From the way the EuroGov just shut the gates, I'd say they went through with it. The Milan cell had nothing to do with it."

"Milan cell?"

"They brought us the last stretch to Rome. The leader was trying to talk the Roman guy out of his vile plan. Without notable success, according to Margo."

Eduardo looked at me. "Your records only say you speak Esperanto and English."

"Yes—and Latin."

Eduardo nodded. "Ah, I see. Two of the most closely-connected languages in the world—but they do go and forget. Thank you for telling me this." He waved us towards the door, other hand reaching for a phone, mind already far away down some train of—urgent—thought.

"That's not good," muttered Father Mark, as we moved through a sort of hall cum anteroom.

"From his expression it's more not good than I'd guessed," said Bane.

"Yes. The Resistance control the majority of the tunnels out of this place and know the location of most of the others."

Silence for a moment.

"Oh. *Of course.*"

Father Mark opened the door to the corridor and we stepped through.

What the...? Priests, all in cassocks; sisters and friars, in real habits; lay people in normal clothes; and more guards, all crowded around the door.

"It's her! Margaret Verrall."

"It's true, they made it!"

"They're here!"

"Margaret, are you all right?"

"We've been praying for you, all three of you..."

Father Mark shepherded us through the crowd, "Come on, hungry fugitives on their way to the canteen, make way."

Half the people followed along behind us. Embarrassing. Soon we were in a large dining hall, tucking into heaped plates as everyone sat around, watching with the benevolent enjoyment of people feeding lost puppies.

"And I thought having *you* watch me eat was embarrassing," I muttered to Bane, digging into a third helping of lasagna. We'd made some headway with our food deficit in the safe house, but we were still hungry *all the time*.

"Please don't eat all that just to please your fan club," said Father Mark.

"Trust me, I'm still hungry! Is there any way to find out how Jon is?"

"I promise you, Margo, anything wrong and they'd let you know. This state is only a hundred and eight acres; it's not hard to find people."

"Speaking of health—Bane, pill," I reminded him.

"Oh, yeah." He fished the box out and took the next one.

Father Mark picked up the box and examined it. "Antibiotics? Should you be taking these with food? Oh, they're the new type. Well, I was going to say rooms next, but perhaps hospital wing. What are they for?"

"Bear clawed my shoulder." Bane tucked into more lasagna. "It's healing up now, though."

"You'd better both be checked over." Father Mark eyed my battered face. "What happened to you?"

"A vile SpecialCorps Captain and a train crash, consecutively."

He shook his head. "We need one mammoth catching up session."

"Yes. So *you're* here. Where're the others?"

"Oh, we sent the last of them on to safe towns a couple of months ago. A few very much wanted to wait here for you—Jane, Sarah, Harriet, Rebecca and Caroline in particular. But I persuaded them to go and help the others settle in."

"Didn't really expect to see us again, huh?" Dear Father Mark. He'd kept on waiting for his lost sheep, even though his head told him we'd never come.

"Well, I hoped and prayed otherwise, but it did cross my mind the girls might be happier already settled in a new home if or when bad news arrived. Rather than waiting here in limbo. Not much to do here, these days."

"Did you make it here okay?"

"No major problems. A checkpoint just beyond Florence realized we were off course for Venice, and asked for our individual IDs, so—we shot all the guards with the nonLees, scrambled their computer, then I disabled the bus's speed limiter and put my foot on the floor. We didn't stop again until we got to the outskirts of Rome."

I let out a breath. Definitely those few simple words concealed long hours of tortuous suspense as the bus tore along, racing to reach Rome before the EuroGov worked out what'd happened.

"How did you get into Rome?"

"Easy, we walked everyone in along the Appian Way as though we'd gone out on a walking tour. School groups don't need much of a pass to enter or leave on foot—ours was a fake. We had it prepared before we left the British department. I thought it best not to mention it. Sorry and all that."

"No, you were right. No point putting all your eggs in one basket." Since we three couldn't have posed as a school group, we'd still have needed IDs to walk in ourselves.

Giving up on the lasagna at last, I put down my fork, at which two sisters, a priest and an elderly gentleman rushed to offer me what appeared to be the entire contents of the desserts' cabinet.

I eyed the puddings regretfully. "I'm sorry, I'm out of practice with sweet food. Another day, maybe." I tried not to stare at the sisters' beautiful habits. One wore brown with a brown and white veil, the other, blue with a white veil. I'd only ever seen pictures.

"Why are you three half-starved anyway?" asked Father Mark, as Bane also declined the sweet stuff.

"We spent about a month wandering around in the middle of nowhere eating nettles," growled Bane, still munching the last of his lasagna.

"Don't forget the bugs," I said.

"Yeah and bugs. Though there could've stood to be a few more of those around. Okay, I'm actually full."

"All right, hospital wing, then accommodation," said Father Mark.

"Can we see Jon?"

"I expect so, unless they're still operating."

Shedding some more of our well-wishers at the hospital wing door, we located Jon almost at once, tucked up in a room not far along the corridor, sound asleep. Another bullet for his collection—the last, please Lord!—lay in a little dish on the bedside table. He was connected up to some sort of drip, but compared to how he'd been at the safe house, he looked a picture of health. A monitor beeped steadily and reassuringly beside the bed.

Doctor Frederick—who'd tended Jon—dragged me off almost at once for the full check-up Father Mark had threatened. He wanted to know the cause of every last bruise and when he pointed to two particularly nasty ones on my thighs and I said, "that evil Captain, I expect," he promptly offered me the services of a counselor. Which I politely declined. I'd no intention of going over and over the Almost Nothing that'd happened until it morphed into Something, and I told him so.

"Well, that's a healthy enough attitude," he said. "However, if you find despite your best efforts it *is* turning into Something, as you put it, we have people who can help. Now where did you get this one?"

"Look, most of them are caused by trees, the ground or a train, and I really can't tell you which is which. They're fading, anyway. I'm fine."

He eyed my patchwork of yellow, purple, and black skin and conceded defeat, going to his computer. I got my outer clothes back on as he typed.

"Well," he said, "I prescribe plenty of food and rest and a precautionary course of vermicide since you've been eating raw and poorly cooked meat. Oh, do you want your implant out?"

"You can do that right now?" My heart swelled with delight.

He picked up a cylindrical gadget and pressed a button—

the end opened to reveal a circle of needles and some sort
of long flexi-pincer snaking out from the middle.

"Oh yes. This is precisely the same device the EuroGov
use to put them in and out."

"Yes, then." Somehow I'd not imagined getting rid of the
hated thing could be quite so simple. *Silly, Margo. The EGD
take them in and out all the time.*

"Be aware you'll be a bit up and down emotionally for a
few weeks as your hormones get themselves back to the
state nature intended. If you're thinking now's a good time,
roll up your sleeve."

I rolled my sleeve up at once. We were here, we were
safe, and I wanted the thing out of me.

Doctor Frederick moved the cylinder end around on my
arm until it beeped happily. The end opened up again and I
braced myself—a prick and the next moment he drew the
cylinder away, pressing a little square of surgical gauze over
a surprisingly small hole.

"That's the blighter." He took a tiny bloody object the size
of a pill from the gadget's pincer, put it in my hand and
taped the gauze in place. "Souvenir for you."

I looked at the innocuous thing on my palm. Symbol of
so much I hated. I'd carried it inside me ever since the
inescapable defilement shortly after my eleventh birthday.

"I've a better idea." Placing it on the floor, I brought my
heel down on it, hard. Ground it from side to side.

"I wouldn't look too closely and spoil your cathartic
moment," said Doctor Frederick dryly, when I took my foot
away. "They're very hard to destroy. Chuck it in that inciner-
ator chute there, if you like."

Picking the itsy-bitsy thing up, I did so, a happy warmth
in my chest. I'd just removed and destroyed my contra-
ceptive implant without the EGD's permission. Not in the
EuroBloc any more, oh no!

"Okay, you can send the boy in."

"Bane's status as a New Adult isn't in any doubt, y'know," I
pointed out—with a smile—as I rolled my sleeve down.

Doctor Frederick smiled slightly as well. "All right. Send
the *young man* in."

"Take a proper look at his shoulder, won't you?" I urged

him. "It was oozing pus for days, he'd a fever on and off—on and off 'cause his courses of antibiotics kept getting interrupted. I think it is okay now, but..."

"...I'll take a good look."

Bane was a bit longer than me, but not by much. He stumped back out and slammed the door behind him.

"Wanted to know where every last bruise came from. I told him, how should I know? I was too busy running to stop and take notes! Then he offered me a counselor, would you believe? I said what on earth for and he said 'anger management, perhaps?'"

"Not the worst idea I've ever heard," murmured Father Mark. Bane glared at him.

"I think Bane's idea of anger management is punching the nearest wall," I said ruefully.

"Well, he might consider going a little deeper into something besides the skin of his knuckles. But let's find you some accommodation."

After making everyone promise to let us know as soon as Jon woke up, we left the hospital wing by a different door and arrived at a little office in a nearby block with only three off-duty Swiss Guards trailing us, grinning and giving us a thumbs up or V for Victory every time we looked their way.

A middle-aged sister dressed in a green habit and veil let us in and closed the door firmly on the young guardsmen. "What can I do for you?"

"Surely you can guess, Sister Eunice?" smiled Father Mark.

"Rooms for our new arrivals. Three of them, you said?" She looked from Bane to me.

"It will be as soon as Jonathan is out of hospital."

"Well, that's easy enough at the moment," she sighed, sitting in front of a computer and calling up a floor plan. "They could take their pick, but...in hospital? Ground floor, then—yes, St. Athanasius's suite will do nicely."

She tapped at the keyboard for a moment, turned, plucked a set of keys from a wall of key-laden hooks and went to open the door. "If you'll follow me. Go on, you three," she shooed the guards away. "It's rude to stare, you know."

The guards, who didn't look much older than us, stopped following, though they didn't stop grinning.

A smile spread over Sister Eunice's face as we rounded the corner and went down a flight of stairs to the ground level. "Everyone's so happy you're here, you understand," she told me and Bane. "I'm sure all the attention must be a little disconcerting, but people are just showing their support. What you've achieved is amazing, just amazing, especially you, Miss Verrall."

Oh great, yet another Margaret fan.

I quickly gave up trying to keep track of where we were. One building followed another, all interconnected and broken up with courtyards and gardens and covered walkways. Finally we entered a block through a door guarded by a very much on-duty Swiss Guard.

"This is a high security block," Sister Eunice told us. "Persons of especial interest to the EuroGov are quartered here."

"You shouldn't need to worry about assassins, in other words," said Father Mark lightly.

"Nice to know." I hadn't even thought of that! From Bane's souring expression, neither had he.

Reaching a passage broken at regular intervals by doors, each bearing a saint's name, Sister Eunice unlocked "St. Athanasius" and ushered us in. "I know you three aren't actually related," she said, "but Father Mark said we should consider giving you a family suite for now. We know new arrivals often have some trauma to deal with, and it can be a bit tough to transition abruptly to completely separate apartments."

Right. Naturally, in the Vatican State, single men and women didn't shack up or share houses the way they did everywhere else—but right now the thought of being separated from Bane and Jon sent stabs of ice-cold panic through my insides. I shot Father Mark a look of wholehearted gratitude. He was right that the three of us did need an exception, just for a while.

The sitting room we entered was furnished with old furniture of a wide assortment of styles, but looked very comfortable compared to the safe house or even François's cottage, let alone the forest.

Sister Eunice pointed to two doors on the right. "Two bedrooms there." She pointed to the doors along the left hand wall in turn. "Third bedroom, kitchenette, bathroom. The phone there is internal to the State; you can't dial out into the EuroBloc. If it rings, it will be for you, so pick it up. This is basically your home for as long as you are here, so treat it as such..." She paused and sighed heavily, for some reason. "Well, I'll leave you to settle in."

"Yes, um, what about...rent?" It'd never really occurred to me to wonder what we'd live off. I'd been so focused on *getting here.*

Sister Eunice just smiled. "You'll be found work according to your skills. We don't use money much, here. No 'rent' as such; no 'pay' as such. You can eat in the canteen or get supplies in the supermarket, just swipe your card. A cart comes around this block with milk and basics every day, as well. You can get clothes and other items in the store, as you require them. If you make excessive use of your card, it will stop working, simple as that."

"Fair enough." Bane looked more cheerful. No doubt he'd been worrying about how to *provide.*

"Father Mark will look after you," Sister Eunice added, and left us to it.

"I wonder if we could get the EuroGov to cough up your royalties," speculated Bane, going to look into the bedrooms.

Father Mark snorted. "I wish you luck!"

"Well, they must owe Margo a lot of money."

"They owe the Vatican huge sums of money too, particularly for the tour bus profits, which they're supposed to split with us, but there's a limit to how far they're prepared to take the whole legal fiction."

"Or illegal nonfiction in Margo's case."

"Ha ha. Well, I'll leave you to get cleaned up and everything. And yes, someone will phone you if Jon wakes up. Oh, my number..." He crossed to the phone and scribbled on a pad beside it. "I'll come and get you at lunchtime."

* * *

Bane and I took turns luxuriating in the bath and choosing clothes from a wheeled cabinet that looked like it would be trundled off to await the next destitute refugees as soon as we'd finished with it. I selected a couple of nice skirts to supplement Carla's jeans and a few tops and a sweater as well, since winter was approaching. I hung what I wasn't wearing in the wardrobe of the bedroom by the kitchen, leaving the two rooms opposite for Bane and Jon.

Sitting on my bed, looking at my clothes, in my wardrobe, in my room, in my apartment, in this oasis of safety in which I could legally remain and work and live for as long as I liked, stupidly, I burst into tears. I lay on the bed and cried until I felt like a wrung-out dishcloth. Silly. So silly.

Wiping my eyes and sitting up again, the empty bedside table caught my eye. If only I still had my photographs! My parents were safe with the Underground—*please, Lord?* But who knew when, if ever, I'd see them again? They might still have photos of Kyle, Uncle Peter, my grandparents and great-grandparents, but my photos were gone.

Bane knocked on my door. "Margo? How're you getting on? I feel like I've been hit by a truck, all of a sudden."

Wiping my eyes again, I went out to join him. He was clean and tidy and he'd got rid of the beard. He looked a little odd without it. Not quite like his old self, even allowing for the hollow cheeks now on stark display. Older, his gaze steadier. I could tell he noticed my red eyes.

"The truck got me too," I said, smiling. "I think it's a nice sort of truck, really, called total and overwhelming relief."

We cuddled up on the sofa and watched the news. Our escape from EuroBloc territory featured already. Major Everington's sentencing was set for the twenty-eighth of November, the best part of two months' time. A Spanish schoolgirl had fallen into the Tiber and had to be rescued...

...My head lay in Bane's lap. I turned to look up at him. He was playing absently with my hair and gazing out the window into the courtyard. He'd switched the TV off.

"Not asleep? Are you made of the same stuff as the rest of us?"

He flashed me a smile. "Just thinking. I've an idea niggling at me. Wonder what the powers-that-be here would think."

"Yes?"

"All that talk back in Milan about pricking consciences. You're right. That's what's needed. Then I was thinking about Juwan. He felt so guilty. So did François. How many people are feeling guilty right now across the EuroGov, because we proved it was possible to save a reAssignee, if you really wanted it enough?"

"Probably rather a lot. But they'll be soothing their consciences with the not unfair observation that you had a Resistance cell to call on for help."

"*Exactly*. So we should do it *again*. On our own."

23

THREE CHOICES

"Again?" I echoed.

"*Several* more times. Empty more Facilities. Prove it's not a one-off. Prove it's possible."

"Without the Resistance?"

"With the right weapons—nonLethals—we wouldn't need them."

"If we do it, we may inspire a whole load of people to do the same. Not all of them non-violently."

Bane shrugged. "We just have to set an example and not worry about other people's decisions."

I sat up and rested elbows on knees, chin on hands, trying to think, a ball of ice in my gut. We'd just got here. Finally we were safe. And Bane was talking about going into danger again. "Thought you wanted to run off to Africa and have a quiet life?"

He grimaced and didn't meet my eyes.

Pushing away the selfish fear, I tried to consider his idea more objectively. Not just *consciences*, it'd also give hope. I couldn't forget François's desperation. He'd made a deal with the devil because he had no hope. Parents who'd lost a child in the past might feel guilt, but every parent with a child in a Facility or likely to end up there would feel a tiny, insuppressible glimmer of *hope*.

And just like that, Sorting would no longer be silently accepted. A parent secretly hoping their child might live wasn't a parent silently acquiescing to the system. More a person primed, as time ran out—since we couldn't possibly get everywhere—to take matters into their own hands.

With parents seizing—or even attempting to seize—their children back from the EGD, it'd be very hard for society to turn a blind eye to the murder that had been going on silently for so long. Of course, the EuroGov would clamp down on the parental attempts. But that would spread additional pain and loss to the parents, grandparents, great-grandparents and siblings of those executed, and to their other child.

"I don't know, Bane. Even if we managed not to get caught ourselves—people would copy us, and a lot of them *would.*"

"You really think it's worse for a bunch of parents to get executed for doing the right thing than for them to sit back and let their children die, then spend the rest of their life trying to forget what they did?"

"Well..." I stared at the crucifix on the wall opposite—*just hung up there, openly.* Bane was right, of course. And...could this idea turn a *doubtful* into a *maybe?*

"Anyway," added Bane, "Adults have far, far more close relationships than the average preKnown or Borderline. The more they punish the parents, the more other people are unhappy, then *they* have to be punished, then *their* loved ones are unhappy. It's exactly the vicious circle the EuroGov try so hard to avoid. Ripples on a pond—they get *bigger.* Might not be an entirely bad thing."

Orphaned children—real conscience-pluckers. Horrible thought. Yet it was no choice at all, really. Do the right thing, regardless of the cost. Or sit back and let evil continue. In the long term, only the first would do any good.

"Well, perhaps you should think about it a bit more and find out who to speak to."

"Umm." Bane slipped his arms around me and I cuddled close. Soon my eyes closed again.

We were woken by the phone. Jon was awake. Clutching a map, we ventured out and found our way back to the hospital without attracting too large a crowd.

"I thought there'd be more people here in Vatican State," said Bane, as we headed along the hospital corridor. "Several thousands, literally as many as could fit in. But there doesn't look to me more than a few hundred."

"I always heard the population was almost three thousand. They must be around somewhere. How many more people d'you want following us around, anyway?"

"Hah, that's true. Ah, Jon, mate, are you okay?"

Jon's head turned on the pillows. "I'm fine. Are you two all right?"

"Fine, Jon," I said.

Bane grinned. "Yep, the EuroArmy are such bad shots they can only hit the slowest-moving target, y'know."

"Thanks," muttered Jon, then spoiled it by smiling too. "Can't believe we made it."

I sat on the edge of the bed. "I think it's still sinking in. Wait till you see our new place: they let us have a family suite for now. We have a bedroom each, a little kitchen, a bathroom and a sitting room."

"Yeah, it's nice." Bane sat on the other side of the bed. "And we don't worry about rent or bills or anything, they just find us something we're good at to do and it's all sorted."

"Great," yawned Jon. "Though I'm only going to be good at sleeping for a while."

Bane moved the bedside phone so Jon could reach it and wrote our number on the pad, reciting it to him. "Call us when you wake up again, okay? I've written it here in case you forget—get a nurse to read it to you."

"Okay," murmured Jon, and started snoring softly.

We met Father Mark in the passage. "How's Jon?"

"Asleep again. But he seems okay," I said.

"Yeah, stronger than I expected," said Bane. "Last time he got shot he hung around at death's door for ages and scared us half to death."

"You make it sound like it's a regular occurrence."

"*He's* threatening to make it one."

"Well, that's done with, I hope, and it's time for lunch. Then there's a meeting, at which your presence is requested, if you're up to it."

"We're fine," said Bane, as we followed Father Mark. "What's it about?"

"Well, practically everyone who holds a job of any importance whatsoever wants to know everything you have to tell them about pretty much your entire exploit, from start to finish."

"Ah, a debriefing." Bane nodded knowingly.

"That's the idea. It will probably take all afternoon, so don't be too quick to say you're fine."

"Are you fine, Margo?" asked Bane.

"Me? Fine. We just slept for half the morning, Father Mark." Okay, so we'd been bouncing around in a jeep all night, but still. If anything we had to say would be useful to anyone, the sooner the better.

"It was on the news already that we got here," I remarked, after a moment. "I imagine the EuroGov are pretty mad."

"Yes." But Father Mark immediately changed the subject. "Do you like your apartment?"

There it was again. Everyone so pleased to see us, so genuinely delighted at our arrival and yet...an undercurrent of edginess. Why?

"Yes, we were telling Jon about it!" Bane gave a slight, self-deprecating smile. "Um...if you'd seen how we've been living since we last saw you, you'd know why it's such a thrilling topic of conversation."

Father Mark just laughed, cassock swinging as he strode ahead to open the canteen door.

"Y'know," commented Bane as he passed, "I don't usually think men and dresses should mix, but that thing suits you."

"That's because it's not a dress," said Father Mark imperturbably.

"You should've worn it back home."

"No, Bane, that's called suicide, or the next thing to it. Cassocks are not allowed in EuroGov territory."

"You're not completely stupid, then."

"Ah, I've missed that well-mannered charm of yours."

"And I've missed your sermonizing. Oh, wait, I had Margo and Jon along."

"Thank *you*," I said.

We managed to slip into the queue and get our food from the serving window ourselves this time. The canteen was quite full, but Bane was right, still only a few hundred people.

"So who is everyone?" I asked Father Mark.

"Oh, these are all people who do fairly important jobs, though the Papal Council and some others have been in meetings ever since you arrived—the Papal Council are having a working lunch prior to the, ah, debriefing, in fact.

Eduardo will be with them and Sister Eunice as well. There's Father Simeon, though..."

"The doorkeeper!"

Father Mark grinned. "No, the Sacristan, he just happened to be in the right place at the right time!"

"I can't wait to go to Mass in Saint Peter's."

"Daily Mass is at eight in the morning, I'll come by your place, shall I?"

"I'll have Bane ready and waiting."

"Good luck with that." Bane gave me a mock scowl. Then it became slightly more genuine. "There's Doctor Frederick over there."

It'd certainly take more tact than the good doctor possessed to get Bane to an anger management counselor. Wasn't sure what would, actually.

We ate in silence for a while. Some people still came up to our table to greet us and wish us well, but with the first flush of excitement over, it'd clearly occurred to most people that we might not want an adoring crowd following our every move.

Habit-spotting in the canteen was great fun. There was every variation of brown, white, black, blue, and even green like Sister Eunice. A lot of the priests' cassocks had purple or red piping and sashes. The lay people dressed as plainly as most non-city dwellers—fashion was for the rich, after all—but with a peculiar mix of national variations. No guards were present: they probably had a mess hall of their own.

"Okay?" Father Mark glanced at his watch as a clock struck two o'clock.

"Time to go?" I asked.

"If you've had enough."

"We'll live. Hmm, Bane?"

"Coming."

Everyone watched us go, of course.

We traversed another maze of passages and staircases, and finally came to a door guarded by two more Swiss Guards. Their uniform, now I looked more closely, was of a more modern cut than in the old pictures I'd seen, but still in those bright distinctive colors. They checked our pass cards before letting us in.

The room was set up with seating facing a stage, on which stood just a few seats. Uh oh, were Bane and I going to be occupying those? A cluster of people milled around, but not enough to fill all the chairs—the Papal Council still at their working lunch? As I turned towards the wonderful painted scenes on the walls, a voice sang out, "Oh, Margo?"

I spun around, my eyes skidding over the people and fixing on a tall, broad shouldered, cassocked young man, a few years older than me.

"*Kyle?*" Sending chairs spinning out of my path, I tore across the room and flung myself into his arms. "*Kyle, you're alive!*"

"*You* say that to *me* in such a tone of surprise?" he laughed, picking me up and spinning me around in a full circle. "Look at you, little sis, all grown up and saving the world!"

"Hardly saving the world," I mumbled, laughing and crying into his shoulder.

"Well, making a start." He rested his head against mine and rocked me from side to side, half joy, half comfort. "How's Mum and Dad?"

"Fine when I last saw them. By now? I don't know."

"Umm. Oh, hello you, still getting my sister into trouble, I see?"

"Actually, she got me into this," said Bane from behind me.

"*You* sent me the leaflet," I pointed out.

"*You* failed Sorting."

"Fair enough. It's all my fault."

"Well, I'm glad you were there to help her," said Kyle, in a more serious tone than he used to use with Bane.

"So do I call you Father, now?" I stepped back and looked him up and down. It'd been over three years since I'd seen him.

His cheeks went slightly red. "Well, I'm just a deacon, as yet. Through some mischance I got elected Deaconal Representative so I had to stay to come along to things like this. Though this one I don't mind hearing. Save you telling it twice!"

"Do you know if Jon's sister made it here? Anne Revan,

felt the call to the Anchoresses?"

Kyle spread his hands. "D'you know how many people pass through here in a year? You need to ask an official record keeper."

I should've asked Eduardo. Later, then.

Kyle's gaze rose over my head and he bowed. So did everyone else.

I turned...an elderly man dressed all in white was approaching me, his red shoes tapping over the stone floor. I knelt hastily. The man—perhaps seventy?—came right up to me and took my hand. I just managed to place a kiss on his ring before he drew me to my feet with surprising strength.

"Please, please, stand, these stone floors are not good for the knees." His eyes twinkled at me. "So you are the girl who has set the entire EuroBloc on its ear, eh?"

My cheeks burned. "I just wrote a book, your Holiness."

"I've read it. It's very good. I have rarely been so relieved as earlier this morning when they told me you had arrived at last. I have been praying for your safety daily."

My cheeks were surely going to catch *fire!* "Thank you, your Holiness. I think we needed it."

"Well, we shall hear all about it. Forgive me for not greeting you earlier. I wished to give you a chance to settle in."

"That's very kind of you, your Holiness."

He smiled, then turned to Bane and offered him his hand. Bane gave a slight bow and shook it.

"Bane," said the Pope in English, "would you prefer English? I do not get to speak my earthly native tongue much."

"Actually, sir, I think I'd better practice my Latin," said Bane, in that language.

"Ah. True. Well, we are very glad you brought yourself and your friend and your beautiful wordsmith to this roost. And at least forty-four others owe you their lives."

Bane bit his lip and went faintly pink himself. "I just did it for Margo, sir. And it was entirely a joint effort."

"Well, it was well done, both of you," said Pope Cornelius III. "Shall we begin?"

Someone stepped forward and began directing people to seats. His Holiness sat in the front row. Bane, Father Mark and myself, as I'd feared, were on the little stage with a touch-typist and a sister who was apparently going to help keep the narration on track. Beside the stage sat a laywoman at a bank of recording equipment. Clearly no one wanted us to have to repeat the whole thing over and over. Jon could tell his version when he was better.

Everyone else had taken their places. A brief silence. Bane and I exchanged looks. Were we just supposed to start? *Where?*

"Introductions? Then shall we start right at the beginning?" suggested the sister. "Margaret failing her Sorting?"

I glanced at Bane again. "Yes, that'd probably be the beginning..."

The door opened and Eduardo slid into the room like a shadow. He put a piece of paper in the Holy Father's hand; whispered in his ear. The old man let out a long sigh and bowed his head for a moment.

His expression, when he stood and mounted the steps, was sober. "I fear we will have to postpone this meeting. The Vatican Free State has just received an ultimatum from the EuroGov. If by six o'clock this evening we do not hand over the three fugitives who early this morning crossed our borders, the EuroArmy will immediately occupy this State and make it part of the EuroBloc."

My ears rang. I struggled to comprehend what I'd just heard. Ultimatum. EuroGov. Three fugitives. *Occupy...*

"Can they do that?" My voice sounded strange, high and thin.

Eduardo raised his eyebrows. "Legally or practically? Legally, no. Practically? If we send every able-bodied adult to the walls with every nonLee, pike and halberd we possess, we might keep them out for an hour, no more."

"But...why haven't they done this before!"

"Dear me, girl," said a very elderly cardinal, who'd been seated on the Pope's right—Cardinal Hans, had they said? "Governments can't go around seizing other states without the international community tut-tutting at them and the EuroGov do so *love* being all legal. So they've simply block-aded us and made our existence as difficult as they possibly can. But we've always known if ever we had something they wanted enough, they'd take us over in a heartbeat and to heck with the tut-tutting. Well, we have something they want now." He raised a hand and pointed at me.

Any remaining blood left my cheeks.

"We have only three choices," said Pope Cornelius. "Hand over the three most wanted, evacuate or be occupied—and dismantled."

Bane's arm was suddenly around me; his other hand disappeared inside his jacket.

"The first," went on the Holy Father, "is quite out of the question. The third is unattractive in the extreme, which only leaves the second."

I felt cold and sick; my head swam. The most ancient Free State in the world was about to fall, because of...*me?*

"I'm sorry... I'm *so sorry*... I was trying to help..." Was I about to faint? Both Bane's arms were around me, now.

Pope Cornelius's hand came to rest on my bowed head. "Calm yourself, child. The fault is not yours. Things have reached such a pass, it wanted only a straw to break the camel's back. All non-essential personnel have been evacuated now for several months. We will let the EuroGov bear the expense of looking after our beautiful buildings for a while and some day, if the Lord wills it, we will come back, re-consecrate and enjoy them again. But for now, our lives are more important—so we evacuate."

"If we can," muttered Eduardo.

Deo Volente—Cardinal Hans mouthed the words.

God willing.

24

GIFT WRAPPING

A buzz of conversation threatened to consume the room and the Holy Father held up his hands for silence.

"Everybody, please put the evacuation plan into motion. Pack up what you can and await more detailed instructions. A few of you, please, stay here... Eduardo?"

Eduardo reeled off a string of names—everyone else got up and trooped from the room, leaving a small group of less than twenty people, including Father Mark and Kyle. Nobody told me and Bane to leave, so we hovered uncertainly until everyone began dragging chairs into a circle around a table and the Holy Father beckoned us to join them.

Eduardo was spreading out a map of the state.

"Evacuation plan, *marvelous*," snorted Cardinal Hans. "How *are* we actually going to *leave?*"

Kyle looked puzzled.

"Anyone who wasn't in the second half of the meeting at lunchtime should know," said Eduardo briskly, "the Rome Resistance are working with the EuroGov and cannot be trusted."

Kyle paled. "Since when?"

"Since they tried to trade in your sister this morning."

The word that rolled off Kyle's tongue in response to that made him shoot a guilty look at the Holy Father.

"That's just what *he* said." Cardinal Hans smiled like a fox.

"I don't believe it!" said someone else. "Resistance and EuroGov?"

"Nonetheless, it's been confirmed. The tunnels are compromised."

"So how?" said the Pope quietly.

"Only two options. The railway, or the helicopter."

"Both of which are sitting targets," said Cardinal Hans helpfully.

"Both of which are sitting targets," affirmed Eduardo. "Nonetheless, they are the only options."

"Helicopter's out of the question," said Pope Cornelius. "Carries too few people in one go. It must be very old, anyway. It was bought when the EuroGov stopped the Holy See chartering planes from them, which was what, forty years ago?"

"And it hasn't been off the ground for almost twenty years, more to the point," said Eduardo. "Has to be the train."

"So the only thing remaining to decide," said Cardinal Hans, "is what sort of gift wrap to package ourselves in?"

"We're short of time, Hans," said the Holy Father, with a hint of sternness. "Serious suggestions only, please."

Cardinal Hans snorted once more and let his forehead rest on the table.

"Smokescreen?" suggested someone.

"What, *all the way* to a port?" said someone else. "Trains aren't hard to track, you know! Because of the tracks!"

"All they've got to do is break the tracks somewhere ahead and we'd derail. Or block the tracks and force us to stop. Or blow us off the tracks with a fighter plane. It's not going to work."

"We need some way to make them stay their hand," said Father Mark.

"What on earth would make them stay their hand? Now they've finally decided to remove us from the map?"

Father Mark shot a look at me. "Something worth more to them than Margaret, I suppose."

"Nothing's worth more than Margo," declared Bane.

Several people smiled.

"I won't argue with you, but the EuroGov might," said Father Mark. "There's an awful lot of things they value more than human life."

"How much cash have you got handy, then?" asked Bane.

"Not very much, I'm afraid," said Pope Cornelius. "It's mostly tied up in the form of assets which may be worth a mint, but cost a fortune in daily upkeep. Once upon a time we covered the costs by charging admission for some things but it's been over forty years since the last visitor set foot in the Vatican Museums. And they're going to get most of those assets at six this evening, so I can't even imagine how much it would take to buy them off."

"And the instant they had the money, they'd annex us anyway," said Eduardo.

"What about a decoy?" someone suggested. "Set the train running empty while we get out through the tunnels? Or vice versa?"

"Rome'll be sealed tighter than a bung in a beer barrel. I don't think many of us would get through."

"And if vice versa, we're back to being trapped on tracks again..."

Everyone carried on talking but Cardinal Hans raised his forehead from the table and sat very still. After a moment he creaked up from his seat and, lowering himself stiffly to his knees on the hard stone floor, spread his hands heavenwards in fervent prayer. No one seemed to find this an inappropriate response—crazier and crazier ideas were being batted back and forth.

I certainly felt like joining the old man on the floor. Except I'd a strange feeling he wasn't praying for ideas. He'd already had one, and it wasn't one he liked very much. He looked like a man praying for strength. I knew *that* feeling. *I* ought to be down on the floor praying for the strength to hand myself over and save the state, but no doubt no one would let me do that. Bane's grip on me tightened almost as though he could sense my thoughts.

Or perhaps he was just getting frustrated by the increasingly heated—and useless—discussion. Someone had just suggested floating down the Tiber on a raft, for pity's sake.

Cardinal Hans lowered his arms at last and turned his attention back to us. "One of you young whippersnappers help me up, would you?"

Kyle and one of the younger priests hauled him to his feet and he tottered back up to the table and fell into a chair.

"Your Holiness, with all due respect, you'd do us the most good just now on your knees in front of the high altar in St. Peter's. You may as well leave us to hammer out the details of our gift wrapping."

Pope Cornelius threw up his hands. He'd not been saying

much. "Oh, you're probably right. I have no ideas at all. I'll go and pray."

He headed briskly from the room and as soon as the door closed the old cardinal sat up straight in his chair, his lined face intent. "Right, those *schwein* are going to blinking well let us go, or they might get Margaret, but that's all they'll get. Here's what we've got to do..."

He told us.

"But do we *have* any explosives?" asked Sister Eunice.

Eduardo tapped some commands into his network-Accessor, then read out a long list of—presumably—explosive materials and devices—I'd never heard of half of them.

"...And about five kilograms of Semtex."

"How on earth did we get all that stuff!"

Eduardo shrugged. "People bring it with them. I confiscate it. It stacks up."

"Is there enough?" asked Cardinal Hans.

"If we place it carefully. Right. No time to lose. Who here can handle explosives?"

A long silence.

"I can," said Father Mark tonelessly, as a couple of other people sheepishly lifted their hands.

Eduardo waved a finger in an "already counted you lot, anyone else?" gesture.

"Well...I won't blow my hand off," said Bane.

Eduardo nodded. "Good. You go with Father Mark, then. Sister Krayj, Brother Wiesbeck, Claudia, you come with me. Father Mark—Sistine Chapel—select what you think you need, I'll take the rest and see to St. Peter's. The rest of you, get everyone onto that train, with everything that will fit. Sister Eunice, you're in charge. Do a complete roll call, everyone accounted for. Jack, get a team ready to load the Anti-Aircraft Lattices. It'll have to be left until the last minute, but if they get left behind, you *will* see me weep."

"Make sure you tell him they've been left behind," said Cardinal Hans out of the corner of his mouth. "Have a camera ready."

A young man dressed like Eduardo in neat civilian clothes grinned as everyone chuckled—except Sister Eunice, whose pen was already racing over a clipboard, planning. "Pets?" she asked.

Eduardo hesitated. "Try your best. See how the space is going."

"Don't forget Jon," said Bane.

Sister Eunice rolled her eyes. "Emptying the hospital? Of course I wasn't going to bother with *that.*"

She strode out of the room, tutting to herself.

Bane looked embarrassed. "Just saying."

"Come on, Bane," said Father Mark lightly. "Let's go play with fireworks."

"Right. Margo's coming too." Bane hadn't let go of me since Eduardo dropped the EuroGov's bombshell.

"Fine, fine, come on, let's look over what we need." They both bent their heads over Eduardo's handheld.

Everyone else scattered as well. Cardinal Hans retreated to a far corner of the large room for a brief but emphatic conversation with Eduardo, after which Eduardo strode off, grim-faced, and the old cardinal sat at the table, head in his hands, praying again. Why *had* he wanted the Holy Father out of the room? Even my brief half-hour acquaintance with the pontiff left me certain he wouldn't oppose the plan—not the part we'd all heard.

"Come on." Bane was pulling me after him.

We followed Father Mark along more passages and courtyards, coming at last to a comparatively isolated, free-standing shed. The double doors stood open and some Swiss Guards were already stacking boxes outside.

"We need this little lot." Father Mark handed the senior guard a handwritten list.

After getting Father Mark's signature, the guards loaded us up with a large box each. We soon reached very old passages and staircases, and found ourselves in a familiar high-roofed chapel. Familiar from photos, anyway. Even the EuroGov didn't try to deny this was quite possibly *the* supreme achievement of European art. They'd be longing to get their hands on it.

There was no red light burning over the altar, so Father Mark started unpacking the boxes at once, giving Bane a lot of instructions I didn't really understand. In light of what they were handling—well, I'd just leave it to them. The Swiss Guards arrived with a pair of immensely long fire ladders and an equally tall free-standing scaffolding tower—which the guardsmen erected in minutes—and soon I was passing things up to them—or more accurately, climbing up to them with things.

"Don't stint with the glue," called Father Mark from way up atop the tower. "It's water based: it'll come off without damaging anything and we don't want the charges dropping off. They'll have experts examining the CCTV footage about ten minutes after they get it; we've got to get it right."

"Oh, I'm not stinting." Bane pressed another block of something deceptively innocent-looking to the center of the priceless panel portraying the Last Judgment. He poked something into it and dropped a long wire down to ground level.

Temporarily unoccupied, I gazed at the marvelous paintings, trying not to see the spiders' web of blocks and wires creeping slowly across them. Tilting my head back, I stared at the roof. I couldn't tell the actually recessed bits from the painted bits—it was that extraordinarily well done.

Bane finished first, gathering all the wires into the center of the room and placing them carefully in a heap. He watched Father Mark stretching up to position the last charge in the space just below the outstretched hands of God and Adam.

"Y'know, I hope we don't have to push that button. It really is a rather good painting."

I couldn't contain a snort of laughter. "You think?"

"Okay, okay, stating the obvious."

Father Mark climbed all the way back down and frowned at his handiwork. Feeling the guilt of one who appreciates art or just calculating yet again whether it'd all be destroyed?

"Right, out you two go while I connect this all up." He tapped some sort of electronic unit, clearly a remote controlled detonator or something like that.

"Watch what you're doing," said Bane.

"It's not switched on." Father Mark waved us in the direction of the door nonetheless.

Bane towed me out as I tried to admire the frescos one last time and we almost collided with a very elderly priest in the passage outside. He had a dove cradled in each hand.

"We're supposed to be boarding the train!" he told us.

"It's okay, we're coming," said Bane.

"Um, hadn't you better put those in a cage, Father?" We weren't in quite that much of a rush, surely!

"I haven't got a cage!" The old man looked quite upset. "I feed them at my window. I can't leave them! I keep imagining some beastly EuroGov official in my room and the poor things coming to the window ledge, so innocently. What if...?" He broke off, clutching the doves tighter.

How long had he lived here, poor man? His world was turning upside down.

"Well, we've got some cardboard boxes, haven't we, Bane? I'll get one."

Bane beat me to it, darting back into the Sistine Chapel and re-emerging with one of the smaller boxes. He held it open while the old priest settled the doves inside. They bobbed their heads, cooing inquiringly but watching him with trusting black eyes. Thank goodness! I didn't want to chase them around these high-ceilinged corridors.

Box safely closed, the old man hurried on his way, urging us to follow quickly.

"We're coming, we're coming." Once he'd gone Bane added, "Thought I saw something in the rules about no pets?"

"Long-term residents are allowed them, I think."

"Oh." Father Mark came out of the chapel and Bane turned to him. "When's this train supposed to be leaving?"

"When we've persuaded the EuroGov to let it. Come on, let's go and see how they're getting on in St. Peter's. What did you want that box for?"

"Old guy's birds," said Bane.

"An old priest with some pet doves," I expanded.

"Oh, Father Mario. Good, he loves those birds. Come on."

We followed him a relatively short distance this time, and soon came out in that beautiful vastness again. Father Mark paused to stare towards the high altar then went on without genuflecting—the red light was gone. Already, every supporting pillar was garlanded with little cubes and sticks and wires.

"Don't touch *anything*," said Father Mark.

"I'm sorry, I left my brain in the British department." But Bane drew me closer, as though wishing he could help Father Mark and have me a long way from the explosives all at the same time.

"What's to be done, Eduardo?" asked Father Mark, as we found him bent over another electronic detonation device.

"The *Pietà*," said Eduardo shortly. "None of this lot can bear to do it."

Father Mark grimaced.

"Someone's got to," snapped Eduardo with unusual animation.

"Oh, it's your favorite, isn't it?" muttered Father Mark.

"*I'll* do it," said Bane, "just tell me what to do."

"Good idea. This the stuff, Eduardo?" Father Mark pointed to a little heap. Eduardo nodded, still concentrating on his electronic box.

"We could just leave it," said Father Mark.

"No," said Eduardo sharply. "I've been in their system, they've been *counting* on owning this place *some day* for years. They're going to milk it for every penny they can get. They've planned everything out, what's going to be exempt from the Religious Symbols Act on grounds of artistic merit—that's most of it, you'll be relieved to hear—all the info boards written, ready to display beside the 'superstitious' art to minimize the *harm to the general population*, ticket prices, the works. They can rake in two billion Eurons a year just from displaying the *Pietà*: we cannot risk them choosing to make do with that."

Bane whistled. "If they can make two billion from one statue, there's no *way* they're going to risk losing the rest."

"I do hope not." Eduardo smiled grimly. "We're betting all our lives on their greed."

Bane frowned, gathered up the remaining armload of stuff and followed Father Mark, only looking back once or twice—or three times—to check I was following. We went through into a glassed-off side chapel, and there stood the most exquisite statue, pure and beautiful white in the sunlight streaming through the window. No wonder no one wanted this job.

Even Bane scowled for a moment, before stepping forward determinedly. "So?"

"Just lay them all around the figures, especially the faces and any detailed bits."

Bane snorted. "The collapsing building would most likely do for it even without worrying exactly where I put this little lot, surely?"

"Psychological effect, Bane," said Father Mark in a rather patient voice. "Their experts will *tell* them the damage will be irreparable, but you should place the charges so they'll be able to *see* that with their own eyes."

"Okay, okay."

Deliberately not looking at the ancient statue as a whole any more, Bane began arranging the deadly web around it. It didn't take him long. Father Mark connected up some sort of small wireless device and we trooped back to Eduardo.

"Done," Father Mark told him.

"Good. Send your priceless helpers to the station and start familiarizing yourself with this little lot." A wave of his hand encompassed the whole building. "I want you to go over all this." He tapped the electronic thing and the mess of wires and little wireless receivers that lay around it. "Check it from start to finish. Sister Krayj and Brother Wiesbeck will do the same. We don't want a single one of their experts giving them even one grain of hope this hodgepodge might not detonate correctly."

Hodgepodge was certainly the word. Different blocks or sticks or detonation systems wreathed every pillar and painting and statue, all—presumably—connected somehow to this thing Eduardo was working on. Father Mark frowned as though he'd developed a headache just glancing at it all.

"Claudia, are you off to the station now?"

A tall woman had just come up and given Eduardo a wordless nod. "Am I?" she asked Eduardo.

"Yes. Take Margaret and Bane with you, would you? They don't know the way. Keep undercover as much as possible to avoid anyone getting photos of her—no point waving a red rag at a bull."

Hopefully they'd have a hard time picking me out from a distance, but my stomach contracted uncomfortably. I'd almost forgotten, distracted by the charge-laying—this was all my fault.

Oh Lord, please don't let us have to push that button! Never mind that, *please don't let all these people die because of me.* I fought back a horrible urge to start howling with guilt and grief and fear as we followed Claudia quickly across the basilica.

The little state was eerily silent—deserted—as we hurried along. The station stood pretty close to the basilica, the actual station building housing the department store we'd heard about, from the sign. An antiquated electric/cleanFuel hybrid locomotive stood waiting, its six rickety coaches taking up almost all the short rusty track. The great arch-shaped portal in the wall was shut tight.

Here were the missing people, some milling disconsolately, others working hard loading the back few carriages with supplies, equipment and the sort of irreplaceable items the EuroGov would simply destroy—saints' relics, for example.

A young man with a goat on a tether argued fiercely with Sister Eunice as we approached, waving his free hand towards a stack of crates full of fat hens. Oh dear. Hopefully she'd allow Father Mario's doves on board.

"Keep under there." Claudia edged me under the station roof. "I'll go and see where Sister Eunice wants you."

She headed away, glancing warily at the wall. Beyond it were the rooftops of Rome; no telling who was up there looking our way. Bane steered me into the middle of the throng, keeping his face turned away. I did the same.

As we waited some people smiled at me and said kind things about how it wasn't my fault, others hardly seemed to register our presence. Good thing—be a bit of a giveaway if everyone turned and looked at us. A few people were crying and I tried not to listen—made me want to do the same. My stomach was fluttering as though full of flies.

Happily, Claudia was soon back. "Sister Eunice says they're not loading people until our ultimatum's been given to the EuroGov. Just in case they get clever ideas about a pre-emptive attack on the train. I imagine we *could* make them bring us another one, but it's a lot of trouble and it won't be much comfort to anyone who was on board. Anyway, she wants you two inside the store until it's time to board. You'll be in good company."

She led us to the old station doors and a Swiss Guard let us in. Ah—that's what she meant about good company.

"Nobody kneels to me on a day-to-day basis," said the Holy Father hastily, as I began to dip at the sight of him. "They'd all have bad knees! Come and sit down."

He'd taken up residence in the "furniture department" (or corner) with some of his most elderly cardinals, bishops, and advisors.

"Coffee?" he asked me. "Everything is better with coffee. Especially Italian coffee."

"Um..." I felt sick. I felt...dazed.

Bane shot a long look at me, then walked me firmly to a sofa and sat me beside an old laywoman, slipped off his jacket and wrapped it around my shoulders, then went to fetch coffee from the flask. He perched on the sofa arm to put it into my shaking hands and rub my back with his free hand.

"I'm an awful fiancé," he muttered, kissing the top of my head. "You're all shocky and I don't even notice."

"I'm fine," I muttered back. But the sight of the train and the people and the empty corridors hadn't done me any good. Made it real, perhaps. I could do the decent thing and give myself up for Conscious Dismantlement—and no one would have to leave—or I could go on that train, back into EuroBloc territory—and risk Conscious Dismantlement. I swallowed hard and Bane's hand tightened around mine, steadying the cup.

"I'm fine." My voice shook. I swallowed again. "Where's Jon?"

"With the other patients, I imagine. That *was* a stupid thing I said. They're not going to leave him behind."

I sipped my coffee and looked around to distract myself. Everyone sat calmly, drinking coffee and talking softly, or holding real rosaries in their hands as they prayed. All older people, too old to be lifting boxes or doing anything active.

Cardinal Hans wasn't among them, though.

"Wonder where Kyle is."

"Making himself useful, unless he's changed a lot. Don't worry about him."

"I wasn't." The coffee was warming me from the inside and my hands were steadying. Father Mario sat on a garden chair opposite, the cardboard box cooing gently in his lap. He beamed at me in a mixture of relief and gratitude—I smiled back.

"Anyone got any idea of the schedule for this?" asked an old sister in a blue habit.

The Holy Father shrugged. "I imagine sooner or later Eduardo will want me to speak to the EuroGov. Then it's just a question of how long they squirm before agreeing to let us go. Lord willing just a matter of *how* long."

Not *if.*

"You, er, know the plan?" asked Bane cautiously, as though afraid he might have his visa revoked on the spot if the Holy Father knew what he'd just been doing.

Pope Cornelius nodded. "Yes, Eduardo filled me in when he evicted me and Our Lord from St. Peter's with such inflexible politeness." He nodded to the other end of the store—a little strongbox sat there with a red lamp burning beside it.

I managed to get up, genuflect and sit again without spilling the last of my coffee. *Didn't see you, Lord.*

"Did you deconsecrate, your Holiness?" I asked.

"Yes, I made him wait that long."

"What about the Sistine Chapel?"

"Should have been done before your little demolition squad got there. All the chapels have been done."

Ah, yes. Bane and Father Mark had taken quite a while with their list. Probably longer than I realized. I hadn't been feeling a hundred percent since the bombshell.

We waited. And waited. And waited. Sister Eunice came in and reported the train loaded with everything except human—and Divine—cargo and ready to leave within fifteen minutes—and we waited some more. What could be taking so long? If Eduardo had the thing mostly connected up by the time we'd arrived, how could it take Father Mark, Sister

Krayj, and Brother Wiesbeck—all, presumably, also experts—so much longer to simply *check* it?

Bane, sitting on the floor beside the sofa, took my wrist to check my watch. Scowled. I looked as well. Quarter past five. Forty-five minutes before the EuroGov came over the walls. The Holy Father pulled out his phone and called Eduardo again.

"Almost ready," he told us, pocketing it once more.

"That's what he said half an hour ago," pointed out the blue-habited sister.

Pope Cornelius shrugged. The doves cooed a little less gently, so Father Mario slipped a handful of birdseed from his pocket into the box.

Ten minutes later Eduardo strode in, taking in all the store's inhabitants in one glance, genuflecting and turning to the Holy Father.

"It's time to board, your Holiness. We're cleared to leave."

Pope Cornelius's eyes widened. "You've contacted them already?"

"Better to keep you out of the limelight, your Holiness. Not quite such a red rag to a bull as Margaret, here, but trust me, they'd *love* to get their hands on you. And they don't know what you look like—after all the trouble we've gone to keeping you out of sight of the walls over the years, we might as well keep it that way."

"Oh." The Pope conceded the truth of this with another shrug. "The negotiations went all right?"

"No problems to speak of. They're absolutely livid and absolutely *not* prepared to lose the Vatican's treasures. We've safe passage through to Ostia and onto a ship flying a non-EuroBloc flag—all arranged—and out of EuroBloc waters. So let's go."

"Okay, then. Have you seen Hans anywhere?"

"Yes, just now." Eduardo held out a long coat. "Please put this on, your Holiness. We don't want the thought of pictures on the front of tomorrow's papers of you or Margaret boarding a train to freedom to make them do something stupid."

"Ah." The Holy Father slipped the coat on and sat again to change his shiny red shoes for the plain black ones Eduardo set in front of him.

Slipping the red shoes into a bag, Eduardo shepherded the whole lot of us out and across the platform to a carriage near the middle of the train—which was much longer than the platform. A Vatican policeman stood at the door, checking off names as we got on.

Inside were the gutted remains of what'd once been a luxury car, the interior clearly ripped out a long time ago to make room for supplies. When the EuroGov allowed the use of their tracks—an increasingly rare occurrence—there was no space to be wasted.

Crates had been arranged as seats, made soft with priceless tapestries, carefully folded. Eduardo followed us on to say, "Seats for the elderly. Standing room only for everyone else."

He put the bag down beside the Holy Father and out he went again. The coach quickly filled up with most of the people from the aborted debriefing, including, to my relief, Kyle and Father Mark. A stretcher was maneuvered in whilst there was still space, and laid along some more boxes.

"Jon!"

"Oh, Margo, there you are. Somehow I didn't think they'd leave you behind."

"They should just shove me through the gates—problem solved."

"Don't be stupid!" said Jon, unusually harshly. "Stupidest thing I've ever heard!"

"You don't feel the teeniest bit bad we've just brought down the Vatican State?"

"It's not *brought down*, it's relocating."

"This has been expected for years, Margaret," said Father Mark.

"Yeah, ever since I got here it's certainly just been considered a matter of time." Kyle had worked his way over to us. "So you three were the catalyst—so what? Something was going to be."

"Hmm," I said.

Swiss Guards climbed aboard now, packing into what little space remained around the doors.

"How far to Ostia?" I clung to Bane for balance as everyone shuffled up again.

Bane put his hand to his pocket, stopped, shrugged. "Not far, I think."

"I wonder what's happening out there." The Holy Father was sitting nearby.

"I've got a portable TV here, your Holiness," said a layman. "Shall I turn it on?"

"Yes, please do."

The man perched the little set on someone's shoulder and fiddled with it until it was persuaded to ignore all the people and pick up a signal. Doors slammed along the train and the floor started vibrating. Ready to go. A *grinding-squeaking* sound—the wall portal opening?

"...And we can see the rail portal into the Vatican opening for the first time in almost two years," confirmed the news-caster on the TV. "The last time the EuroBloc allowed the Vatican train the use of their tracks was in December the year before last. Relations since then have only deteriorated.

"To bring anyone joining us up to date, in response to the Vatican State granting asylum to the EuroBloc's three most wanted fugitives—Margaret Verrall and her two com-panions—the EuroGov have issued an ultimatum that if by six this evening the fugitives have not been handed over to EuroBloc justice, the Vatican State will be occupied."

"Justice, hah!" said someone. Snorts of derision from around the carriage.

"Half an hour remains before the deadline and events are taking an unexpected turn. The Vatican's rail portal has just opened and it appears the Vatican train intends to come out onto EuroBloc track. Bafflingly, the EuroGov seem to be making no response to this. One moment..."

Silent footage of the open track portal, then the news-caster was back.

"We've just heard that EuroTrac control have received orders to clear the tracks and change the points to allow an unscheduled priority train to pass from Rome to Ostia docks. This is most surprising...wait, I'm getting another report..."

More silent footage of the open track portal. I clutched Bane harder in mingled hope and fear. Any moment now we'd be going through that wall—but the points *were* set for Ostia.

Our coach door slammed and Eduardo appeared, easing his way through the crush. His eyes fell on the TV. *"Turn that off!"*

The layman looked taken aback. "The Holy Father—"

"I'm watching it, Eduardo," said Pope Cornelius mildly.

Eduardo scowled. "No need to frighten everyone with sensational EuroNews, surely?"

"Well, for some reason Veritas TV and Radio has temporarily stopped broadcasting." The Holy Father smiled slightly. He might well be sitting on some of the smaller transmission equipment.

The train jolted and began to move. I gulped in a breath and wrapped a hand over my mouth to try and keep any cowardly noises from escaping. Bane held me close.

"Yes, it's confirmed...this footage just in..." the newscaster was back again. "The Head of the Vatican Free State appears to be sitting in his vehicle in the middle of the Forbidden Square, holding some sort of switch in his hand."

"What?" bellowed Pope Cornelius, lurching to his feet and clutching the TV, staring at what it showed.

A little white popemobile parked in St. Peter's Square; inside it, a figure in white.

25

THE ALTERNATIVE

"Hans!" moaned Pope Cornelius, even as the camera zoomed in close enough to show the shiny red shoes—and the lined old face. He spun around to face his Head of Security. "Eduardo, you...you *heartless—*"

"All his idea," said Eduardo expressionlessly, spreading his hands. "Someone had to stay and hold the button—we've no way to detonate the charges from the middle of the Mediterranean. And letting them think they'd get *you* just sweetened the bitter pill of their losing Margaret."

Some people looked at me—my eyes were glued to the tiny screen. I was shaking again. The tally of lives laid down for mine was about to total one helicopter pilot, one dismantler, one commandant, a shift of bridge guards, two brave New Adults, an old man and his sons—and one cardinal.

One cardinal. It would be Conscious Dismantlement. Shudders shook me and I began, unstoppably, to cry. I buried my face against Bane's chest and clung to him and couldn't stop. Selfish, cowardly wretch that I was, I couldn't speak. Yet...he was dying in *my place.*

Somehow, somehow I unstuck my tongue from the roof of my mouth.

"Stop..." I cleared my throat and tried again. My voice was ragged. "Stop the train! I'll...*I'll* hold the switch..." My voice almost died away to nothing, but I got the words out. Getting down from the train to act on them might be another matter.

No one made any move to stop the train, anyway.

"Calm down, Margaret," said Eduardo. "Cardinal Hans was adamant he should do it. He has a very serious heart condition, if it makes you feel any better. He said and I quote, 'As for me, I fully intend to drop dead the moment the dismantler's needle touches my skin.' While laughing in their face, I imagine. I'm certainly quite confident that the imminent prospect of Conscious Dismantlement will be more than enough to bring on a nice fatal heart attack. So don't torture yourself. He's not doing it for *you*, anyway, he's doing it for the whole state."

It didn't help. Nothing would help ever again. Misery overload. Choking back a moan, I huddled deeper into the circle of Bane's arms. Bane clutched me tightly and made a snarling sound that said if I'd not been almost beyond reason distraught, he'd have words with me about my offer, and that anyone taking me up on it would need to go through him.

The Holy Father and Eduardo were arguing...the Holy Father wanting the train stopped so *he* could take Cardinal Hans's place...

"It's too late," I heard Eduardo reply. "Look, we're going under the wall. So let's not waste a brave man's sacrifice, right?"

The wall... EuroBloc territory... I clung tighter to Bane, shaking.

When Bane turned some time later to perch on the edge of Jon's box-bed and settle me on his knee I caught a glimpse of the pontiff, sitting again, his face twisted with grief. Old friends? And then I was sobbing again as if I'd never stop.

"Sedative?" suggested Kyle anxiously.

"Oh, shut up!" snarled Bane.

"She's my sister, I'm worried...!"

"She's my fiancée and I think I..."

Even in my choking world of tears I sensed the explosion of testosterone in the air and was glad to hear Father Mark's voice cut in, rather sharp. "You two, act your age. Kyle, she needs hugging not drugging, you twit. And Bane, could you even *try* to keep your temper?"

Kyle was right about one thing though, I was quite beside myself. Bane held me and held me until I'd cried myself into a stupor... Vaguely aware of him lifting me and laying me beside Jon, tucking the blanket over me and perching again to stroke my hair and rub my back. Jon's scent in my nostrils was almost as calming as Bane's and his hand closed gently around mine...

...The train stopped with a jolt. I sat up, my mind reeling and panic stirring.

"Where are we?"

"Ostia, Margo." Bane's arm slipped around me at once. "Ostia. Everything's okay."

Swallowing my heart back down into my chest, I looked around, head aching, eyes gritty with sleep and throat raw with weeping. But the fog of misery and unreason had lifted. Through the people packing the carriage I glimpsed warehouses outside the windows. Ostia docks. There should be a ship here. We were getting on it. Don't think about the fact you're on EuroGov territory and they know where you are...

Father Mark slipped out of the crush and placed a pile of clothing on Jon's legs. "Put these on over your things, Margo. The press'll be looking for you above all others, you need a better disguise." He saw my inquiring look and smiled slightly. "Oh, no one's tried to *deny* you're here, it's just that matter of bulls and red rags, again. Come on."

I swung my legs off the boxes and picked up the top item. Spread out a peculiar shaped garment. What...? Oh...a wimple: A nun's habit, the oldest type.

"I can't wear this. I'm not a nun."

"The Holy Father said to put it on."

"Oh. That's allowed, then."

"Pretend you're a Jew in the Great Wars," said Bane. "Went on all the time, didn't it?"

"I don't know about *all* the time, but there was certainly quite a bit of it going on," said Father Mark. "Especially in Rome."

"Yes, um, okay," I agreed. "I'm just not quite sure *how*..."

Laughing, a young sister with the wimple-style veil eased her way across the carriage and started to help me.

"Is your sister here, Jon?" I asked suddenly.

"Been and gone," said Jon happily. "One of the doctors found out for me." His face fell slightly. "'Course, I've no idea how she is by *now*. She made it, though."

"Well, that's good." I squeezed his hand and carried on

dressing, then paused to enjoy the sight of Father Mark yanking a friar's habit over the head of a protesting Bane.

"Trust me," he told him, "This is as weird for me as it is for you."

"I doubt it," snarled Bane.

Father Mark just laughed at him. "Hood up, Bane. Take these."

He handed us both a pair of glasses. Plain lenses, I discovered, obediently slipping them on. The wimple and veil covered my forehead completely, coming up to my chin below and minimizing how much of my Technicolor face showed. A laywoman crouched in front of me, took the glasses off again and began smearing makeup over my bruises.

From the expression on Bane's face as he looked me up and down once the glasses were replaced, the disguise was quite effective. "Don't go getting any ideas."

I hugged him but couldn't quite bring myself to kiss him with us both dressed like that.

"Ready?" Eduardo's voice came from the doors.

"Yes." Father Mark pulled the blanket up so it half covered Jon's face and plumped the pillows to hide most of his hair.

"Let's go. Persons of special interest to the EuroGov, *stay in the middle*. Jack, stick with them."

I found myself next to the Holy Father, the young agent who'd been put in charge of the anti-aircraft thingies hovering near us. Still wearing the coat, Pope Cornelius had added a hat and a pair of glasses.

"These are my reading specs," he told me, in an obvious attempt at cheerfulness, "so I'll probably trip and break my neck."

"I hope not," I said, just as falsely light-heartedly.

"Not on my watch, *please*," murmured Jack, half fervent, half joking.

"Hey, you're British!" His accent was unmistakable. Very upper class, in fact.

He flashed me a grin, giving me a glimpse of a pair of very blue eyes, then went back to professional-mode, those striking eyes never still. No time now for chit-chat.

We moved forward with the crush, Bane's hand clamped under my arm as though I were elderly and he assisting me. Once through the doors we buried ourselves deeper in the middle of the crowd as we moved across pavement. I hardly dared to look up, but I glimpsed a police barrier further up the dockside and a throng of people, many cameras... I looked at the ground again.

A gangway appeared before me. Head down, I started up it. Only room for one person on each side of me. The prow of the ship reared to the left, with a name, *Freedom II.* Did it belong to a safe town in some Free State? Jon hissed in pain as his stretcher was jolted behind us, the bearers muttered apologies, he quickly murmured reassurances...

Then we were moving over a deck, through doors into dimness, down stairs that clanged under our feet... Finally we were directed along a corridor and into a poky cabin with bunks up each wall.

"Think I'm off to the sick cabin," winced Jon, as he was borne past our door.

"Okay, see you," said Bane after him.

"We'll find you," I called.

Father Mark, Kyle, the sister who'd helped with my veil and the laywoman who'd done my makeup were all directed into the cabin, then the door was shut. The young British VSS agent had followed the Holy Father.

"For now, I think they just want us, er...stowed...as quickly as possible," said Father Mark, climbing up to a top bunk.

"That's all right." The sister took a bottom bunk.

I sat on the other, since the laywoman wore trousers— she took a middle one. Bane sprung up into the one above me, leaving Kyle the other high one. All quickly and amiably enough decided. There simply wasn't room for everyone to stand.

"Will they really let us go?" said Sister Mari, after we'd made introductions for those who didn't know each other. Hard to tell with her dark skin, but she looked pale to me.

"'Course they will." Kyle shot me a worried look. But I was all out of tears for the moment.

"I think they will," said Father Mark, more convincingly.

"Or they wouldn't bother letting us get this far. Unless something goes wrong, they'll let us sail away."

Unless something goes wrong. Such as Cardinal Hans dropping dead of the stress a little too soon? I swallowed.

"Was it actually a...what do they call it? A dead man's switch?"

Father Mark snorted. "Heavens, no. It will take us hours to steam out of EuroBloc waters: he couldn't hold a switch in for that long. Just a button he could push. But he's got it hanging around his wrist, tucked under a nice long, wide sleeve, so they can't be sure what it is. Just in case they're tempted to get a marksman to try to penetrate that glass."

"Or just bazooka the vehicle," muttered Bane.

"They won't dare," said Father Mark. "Could easily set off the charges."

"That's okay, then." Bane leant over the side of his bunk to hold hands with me.

A tremor ran the length of the ship. The engines had started.

"They've transferred the stuff already?" Sister Mari sounded surprised.

"There wasn't that much of it," said Kyle. "If everyone who wasn't acting as camouflage picked something up..."

But it was about another ten minutes before the slight movement of the ship deepened and changed and Kyle and Father Mark, who could see through the tiny, high porthole, announced we'd undocked. I tried to breathe slowly and deeply, but I was too drained to be very anxious. They reported on the dock and the coast dwindling behind us and finally disappearing from sight, then there was just the sound of the engines and the motion of the waves.

Someone announced on the intercom that anyone un-happy with their bunking arrangements should go and see Sister Eunice in the canteen where dinner would be served in half an hour and that, Lord willing, we'd be in Africa in twelve hours.

We'd no complaints about our bunking arrangements, so we said a rosary for our safe landfall in the morning and in thanks we'd got this far, and went to eat.

* * *

I woke with someone's hand over my mouth—drew breath to scream...

"Hush, it's Father Mark." The hand was removed.

"What's wrong?" My heart pounded painfully.

"Nothing wrong. Eduardo wants you and Bane. Quietly."

Prudently, he let me wake Bane. We slipped from our bunks and eased the door open. I couldn't see Kyle in his bunk. Where'd he gone? It was deep night. The ship still steamed steadily on its course.

Father Mark led us to another, slightly larger cabin. The only people inside were Eduardo and Pope Cornelius, both calm-faced. My heart rate slowed a little more.

"Ah, Margaret, Bane, sorry to disturb you," said the Holy Father. "This can't wait until morning." He waved us into two seats—Father Mark hadn't followed us in.

"Margaret Verrall," said Eduardo seriously, "am I under the impression you wish to carry on doing everything in your power to undermine the EuroGov?"

I swallowed. Nodded.

"Bane Marsden, you feel the same?"

Bane nodded. "Wanted to speak to someone about that, actually. But I expect now's not the time."

"You have an idea?"

"Yes. I want to empty some more Facilities. Using non-Lees, y'know."

Eduardo's head turned slightly to one side as he digested this.

Pope Cornelius's eyes lit up. "Spread hope."

"Yes..." From the gleam in Eduardo's eyes he'd immediately seen the progression from mere hope to outright social unrest. "Yes. That's an interesting one. But no, now's not the time. The point is, this ship's going to Africa, where you can settle in a free town and go on with your work as best you can from there, in safety. Is that what you want to do?"

On the tip of my tongue to say yes, but I paused. Something about the way he said it, something about this whole secret nighttime conversation...

"What's the alternative?"

Eduardo smiled slightly, as though I'd just passed some

test, and the Holy Father answered, "A small group of us will be leaving this ship within the next half hour and travelling to a new HQ much closer to the EuroBloc. Sorting and all the rest of the rot has spread to other blocs, but it started here. When you're getting rid of a weed, you deal with the roots first. So I'm staying on the scene if I possibly can."

I swallowed. "In EuroBloc territory?" Did my voice have to squeak like that?

"No. Close to it. Somewhere happy to have us so long as no one knows about it."

"Where?"

"If you choose to come," said Eduardo, "you'll be told when we arrive there."

Many island Free States were to be found in the Mediterranean—mostly dry, barren places, lacking sufficient freshwater for reforestation and of no interest to the EuroBloc. A number of them probably wouldn't mind sheltering the Holy Father, providing the EuroGov didn't find out. None of them would be able to put up any more resistance than a wet paper bag if the EuroBloc came to get us, mind you.

I looked at Bane, my heart thudding uncomfortably in my chest. This felt all too much like that moment when we'd left the deceptive safety of the bus to face a trek to a destination we all secretly feared we'd no chance at all of reaching. A cowardly part of me wanted Bane to insist we go to Africa, to refuse to consider this much riskier course. *How can I face this again? So soon? We just got here...and we only just made it this time.*

But we *had* made it.

We *had*. Against all the odds. The three of us had had no chance alone, but we'd not *been* alone, had we? The Lord had been with us on every step of that ghastly journey, and He was still with us now.

And the Holy Father was right. If the war was really for hearts and minds, then what we did spoke as loudly as what we said. If I wanted to fight, I had to stay.

Bane was, surprise, surprise, scowling. Weighing the risk to me against the temptingly positive response to his idea.

"Can Jon come?" I asked.

"If he wants to spend a night bouncing along in an open boat," said Eduardo.

"I dare say he will." Bane looked at me again. "Do you want to go?"

"Want" wasn't at all the right word. I actually *didn't* want to go, quite a lot. But I would *go*, providing he didn't absolutely refuse to go with me.

I nodded.

He sighed. "I s'pose we'll go."

"Marvelous." Pope Cornelius sounded sincere and I couldn't help a faint snort.

"I'm surprised you're even asking me after that meltdown on the train."

"I saw a brave woman grieving because she could not save a brave man," said the Holy Father very evenly. "What is there to be ashamed of in that?"

But I turned my head towards Bane and let him slip his arm around me.

"Well, anyway," said Eduardo. "You two go and speak to Jonathan—make it quiet and discreet, please. I'll send a couple of guards along in a minute to carry his stretcher, assuming he's up for it. Don't go out on deck until I give the word. We're waiting for the Eye of Sauron—sorry, Vatican slang—the EuroBloc satellite, I mean—to pass over. Then we'll have enough time—just-about-if-we're-lucky—to get where we're going before one of the USNA ones comes over."

Ah. Thank goodness most of the satellites from the turn of the century were no longer operational. And no question of replacing them, these days.

We tiptoed along to the sickbay and woke Jon.

"Fancy a boat trip?" Bane whispered in his ear.

"Aren't we having one already?"

"This is a ship, silly. D'you want to go bounce, bounce, bounce all night in a little boat to a rather-less-safe location than Africa to carry on stirring the pot?"

"No. Do I look mad? Are you two going?"

"Yes," I murmured.

"Okay, then. When do we go?"

"Right away, apparently. Here come your stretcher bearers."

Two Swiss Guards had just slipped into the sick bay.

"Okay." The guards lifted the stretcher he still lay on and he hissed slightly in pain. "Oh, I'm so going to regret this. Let's go before I change my mind."

By the time the stretcher had been maneuvered back up several flights of narrow ship's stairs, Jon had gone very white but not changed his mind. Eduardo was already directing two lines of people over the ship's side and down rope ladders into a large twin-hulled highPropulsion speed-boat. Lots of familiar faces from the briefing and the train carriage.

"Margaret, you *are* coming!" Sister Mari looked pleased.

Kyle...? There, just climbing over the side. My heart leapt with delight our reunion wasn't to be over so soon, then sank...he was going back into danger as well.

"Come on," Eduardo was hissing, "hurry it up, move."

We reached the side at last and Bane climbed down first, steadying me as I reached the boat, which went up and down in such a way one had to pretty much jump for it. We sat beside Father Mark, who looked utterly unsurprised to see us. "Made it, then?"

"Oh, very funny," growled Bane.

The Holy Father was seated in the middle of the boat, surrounded by anxious-looking guards. Jack was sitting near him too, clearly hyper-alert, but he returned Bane's and my smiles. Also looking forward to getting to know fellow refugees from the British department? The boat looked well overloaded to me, even before Jon's stretcher was lowered down and wedged into the foot well in front of us. One of the guards who'd carried him climbed down with a life jacket and wriggled a now grey-faced Jon into it.

Life jackets...

"No life jackets for the rest of us?" I muttered to Father Mark.

"No space. Just say a Hail Mary."

Bane snorted.

Father Mark added, "That is...there are life jackets for non-swimmers. You can swim, can't you?"

"I can swim," I assured him. "We both can."

"That's all right, then."

The cabin space below us and every locker and cupboard must be stuffed with equipment salvaged from the Vatican. We fifty or so seated passengers were packed together like sardines. Father Mark was right. No space for life jackets.

From the way Eduardo chivvied the guards loosing the mooring ropes, time was very much of the essence. All the same, ropes coiled, we floated silently until the black silhouette of the *Freedom II* disappeared entirely over the horizon. Only then did the engines spring into life.

The boat leapt forward under full throttle, smacking from wave to wave like an out-of-control toboggan. Definitely overloaded. Let's hope we didn't capsize.

I said that Hail Mary.

Then I took Jon's hand and held it. Every smack of the boat drew an almost choked-back whimper from his lips.

"Regretting it yet?" Bane took his other hand.

"Oh, shut up," gasped Jon, holding tight.

Eventually he either passed out or fell asleep. I huddled up to Bane in the nighttime chill and watched the stars, trying not to think about where we were going and why.

We'd left the ship. The *Freedom II* which even now steamed towards Africa and safety. Without us.

The immensity of the stars above mocked my little concerns. Bane's heart beating under my ear and Father Mark's warmth at my side and the gentle rise and fall of Jon's chest in the moonlight mocked the mockery. Everything truly precious in the universe was right here, and I was right to worry about it. To fight for it.

And if we made it to our destination, that's what we would do.

DON'T MISS BOOK 3

LIBERATION

The EuroBloc Genetics Facility where Margo was imprisoned stands empty…

…every other Facility is full.

Time to do something about it.

OUT NOW!

READ A SNEAK PEAK!

Paperback: ISBN 978-1-910806-10-4
ePub: ISBN 978-1-910806-11-1
ASIN: B0163DAICW

unSeen

Find out more at:
www.UnSeenBooks.com

I AM MARGARET
LIBERATION
NOMINATED FOR THE
CARNEGIE MEDAL AWARD 2016
CORINNA TURNER

LIBERATION
SNEAK PEAK from CHAPTER 5

Clouds hung heavy with rain overhead and the night was dark. With the trees looming around and the train tracks failing to gleam in front, there was a slight feeling of déjà-vu.

Everything was different, though. I held a fully charged nonLee and wore the bulletproof vest Bane and Eduardo had forced me into—it felt much like wearing an ancient corset. "Why me?" I'd protested, since there weren't any more, but they'd ignored me. Nasty feeling it might be the Holy Father's spare, or something.

Silent and resigned, Jon had stayed in the Citadel. Carla and Francesco were with him—safer for the train guards, if not for Jon. Avoided known Resistance members being caught with us if this got hairy, more importantly.

Hairy. My hands were shaking. I wrapped them more tightly around the butt of the nonLee. The plan was sound. Father Mark thought so. Carla thought so. Francesco thought so. Eduardo thought so. And Bane thought so. I thought so too.

All along the hundred meters of track before the signals lay our team, two by two, over half of them unarmed—Eduardo could only spare ten nonLees. Those lying where the front and rear carriages should stop had the guns, but the others all had their jobs.

My mouth was going dry. My hands still shook. Bane lay there beside me in the blackness. Despite agreeing in principle, he'd refused point-blank to allow me to come unless my hormones had settled down. But I'd managed four days now without bursting into tears or throwing myself at Carla's throat, so here I was.

A dark shape suddenly sprang up from where it'd been using a non-electric rail as a pillow and ran up the opposite slope, lay down, and was magically absorbed by the deep shadows.

"Little Lion can hear a moth," came Father Mark's voice on my earpiece.

The train was coming.

ABOUT THE AUTHOR

Corinna Turner has been writing since she was fourteen and likes strong protagonists with plenty of integrity. She has an MA in English from Oxford University, but has foolishly gone on to work with both children and animals! Juggling work with the disabled and being a midwife to sheep, she spends as much time as she can in a little hut at the bottom of the garden, writing.

She is a Catholic Christian with roots in the Methodist and Anglican churches. A keen cinema-goer, she lives in the UK. She used to have a Giant Snail called Peter with a 6½" long shell (which is legal in the UK!), but now makes do with a cactus and a campervan!

Did you enjoy The Three Most Wanted*? Please consider leaving a review at your favorite retailer. Thank you!*

Get in touch with Corinna...

Facebook: Corinna Turner - *Twitter*: @CorinnaTAuthor

or sign up for **news** and **free short stories**,
including several I AM MARGARET stories, at:
www.UnSeenBooks.com

DOWNLOAD YOUR EBOOK

If you own a paperback of *The Three Most Wanted* you can download a free copy of the eBook.

1. Go to *www.UnSeenBooks.com*
or scan the QR code:

2. Enter this code on the book's page:
MXB27377G

3. Enjoy your download!

All Free/Exclusive content subject to availability.

Pan-Worldly Things

Pan-Worldly Things

The Hermetic Realm of the Opposites

CRAIG MATHESON

RESOURCE *Publications* · Eugene, Oregon

Frances Mackie-Matheson
You will always be in our hearts.
Love, Kent and Craig

CONTENTS

SPIRIT TO THE WORLD

It can seem a sort of intoxicant,
such apparent Spirit to the World,
Thick with affair to collar intent,
leaving some dizzy in swirl.

Amid younger years, there's more innocence
being stirred by fantastical things;
With time, grows need for dark cognizance
if a goat-god uncannily rings.

What a monkey sees, a monkey may do
in the realms of mania and play,
Where games and tricks, such as switcheroo,
could raise higher urge for parlay.

As more experience is gained across time,
many patterns come naturally learned,
If heads then inflate by delusions of prime,
a good bridge more likely gets burned.

What's mine is mine . . . and I want yours too!
The Narcissist's Way in extreme;
always computing for how to accrue,
To Act Less Human Than Machine.

Anything eyed for complete control
can ironically seize hold of us;
Invest *ALL-IN* a dear prideful goal,
friends may get squeezed by the bus.

Them Pan-Worldly Things so ever abound
with bright spectacle full of impress,
resounding alarm and gripping astound,
Designing Flash to capture one's guess.

Where if such schemes delight the way,
quickened could be a Mental Debt
of resting assured, at the end of the day,
an Absolute Mind is wisely set.

Is there Spirit to the World of mania?
Planet Frenzy, Hysteria, or Crisis?
Can a pressure amass upon crania
to a point where conformity feels righteous?

Can freedom within define as we choose
despite a cloaked meddling from some other?
To journey inward per whatever muse
without fearing Orwellian Big Brother?

Does 'perfection' exist upon our Earth?
Is safety required to feel free?
Does life really test a spiritual girth?
¡There's a perfect score in a math bee!

A Spiritual Trap may so pull for 'perfection';
Many calls which tempt to the world.
Billionaires crave 'it' despite vast collection
of things they already have squirrelled.

So just as there's *two sides* to every coin,
worldly spirits seem but half the story,
as what's in between in concert can join
true giving with *the more predatory*.

FREEDOM VS. SAFETY

To jump from a plane in skydiving fashion
can wildly scream *freedom* for some,
But if the parachute fails to *safely* fasten,
a Great Adventure is all but done!

To *freely* imagine whatever one might
regardless of darkness within thee,
There's a *safety* in choosing against false-light
while striving to tame tranquility.

The *freedom* to learn a particular power
which simply thyself can serve,
Yet the *safety* of belief in a final hour
that soon will come just deserve.

Notions of *freedom* and *safety* are linked
by way of being opposite polarity;
although *such ends* are utterly distinct,
they're bound in abstract solidarity.

As *contrasting ends* to the same concept
—The Perception of Ranging "Risk"—
as night follows day it's there to accept,
what's idle does balance *what's brisk*.

Within such flair, when masses of air
hot-n-cold size the other up-n-down,
Two Ends there to a Mighty Affair
where "temperature" is the noun.

As North and South Poles to our dear rock
stage inversely blended through Earth,
as MJ danced into his moonwalk,
a push-n-pull of magnetic worth.

As Above, so Below—or—Yin and Yang,
differing walks to similar approach
for labelling well a Karmic Boomerang;
Reverse Ends to Hemispheric Reproach.

If *contrary forces* seem per a design
where *one pole* to *the other* offsets,
Freedom vs. *Safety* can thereby define
but one way to frame such vignettes.

Further, in seeing those *freely* empowered
by others' reaction to their presence,
Yet a *safety* to know that sweet turns sour
if to IMPRESS becomes one's full essence.

So, as far as the concept of ranging "risk,"
too much for *Either End* seems ill-advised:
Unchecked Freedom can snap in a whisk;
Absolute Safety may summon State spies.

MIGHT IS ALRIGHT

Where worldly ploys predict to ensnare,
a term often to show may be *might*;
Might one seek wager in truth or dare?
Will *might* be sought after through a fight?

When gauntlets are thrown to catch an eye,
it's a challenge to Know the best answers,
where certain displays may mystify,
such as glorified Militant Banners.

Before have many questioned such 'need'
for war—such horror, in summary;
Where not a belligerent intends to cede,
hence likely to bolster a gunnery.

Given 'paths to hell' can surge meaning well,
once compromise is nowhere in sight,
if under siege by storms of personnel,
it's been cried, "Lethal *Might* is Alright!!"

But prior to blood being spilled to a field,
could *might* be abandoned too early?
Might it be wise a bit more to yield
where impossible it seems so, surely?

If haven't all yet found 'heaven on earth',
might call we upon a Healing Guidance?
Can humans alone well measure our worth
when a tyrant coos for mass abidance?

Might a choice come around to walk or dance,
it physically takes two-to-tango;
In games, ever the element of chance,
especially if one's playing Rambo.

As we struggle along on our space rock,
Alas, where a child can pass from cancer,
rarely clear amid the absolute talk
what Almighty *might* reign Almighty for Good answer.

The apropos story of an ole Zen master,
whose legend's traversed the years,
Where others perceived a bad luck or disaster,
"Perhaps" he'd say to oncoming fears.

So, here we are (ourselves) always found
within, wherever thy *might* be.
If a good day to some is one above ground,
"Perhaps" it's okay to disagree.

Might one imagine other ways to be,
from-Zen masters to-royals: imperfect;
recall King Louis, who wasn't so free,
'shortened' by the French people's verdict.

Endless seems wonder by *might* upon *might*,
as hardly a head wishes to fall,
Where folks must (at least) be slightly alright
with impositions that clip wherewithal.

Might there plea One loving Creator force?
If so, what purpose for all the suffering?
Might it be alright to ask such a Source
if even thy answer is deemed puzzling?

DEAD PEOPLE DON'T LIE

A temptation to lie when one's alive,
There's wonder in wherefore it becomes:
At times, half-truths are sold to contrive
clever schemes to quell Warring Drums.

Most kids get taught that it's bad to lie,
and wrong to be Knowingly dishonest;
The elfish spirit, so playful and spry,
foretells whimsy and fanciful promise.

A winding road may run hard to discern
when good direction's up in the air,
Yet a proven path can turn more concern
if a scoundrel's caught, where not a care.

Therein a real trouble awaits to be
as some fools rush reckless into 'fun',
Within the midst being tougher to see
a damage manifesting once done.

Thus, when's it okay to cast a tale?
(or) When is what's said actually true?
An ancient book was cast to prevail
for leading so the likes of me and you.

The *Hermetica*, drawn up moons ago,
appears to examine such notion
of: What could be true? What could be faux?
(and) What could be imped a Magic Potion?

The Kybalion, a book more recently made,
spells out on the studies foregoing;
"Seven Hermetic principles," as so relayed,
sheds light on such old things *unknowing*.

Its "principle of polarity" (here in question):
"All truths are but half-truths," is read;
but is it gospel,.. or more of an expression?
Less concern when people are dead.

Once the curtains fall,.. does a Vortex still call?
Such urge may only be of a Temporal Surge;
such a Twisting System's call to enthrall,
Does the Spin keep pulling more than purge?

Yet, before the show's over (in time and journey)
life hardly sticks to a grand plan;
Hopefully not so bad to need an attorney,
going on as gracefully as one can.

As alive now, it's there to recall:
There ain't No perfect way To Be!
Whether in full sprint or down to a crawl,
most trauma's unlikely to foresee.

So, if weathered roads seem clocked by a trend
where *swift* and STARK action looks vital,
When worlds are awfully predicted to end,
may gurus tempt not upon *TIDAL.*

11

OPPOSITES, OPPOSITES, EVERYWHERE . . .

Opposites, opposites, everywhere,
and it washes over many to think,
That if we were all-the-way similar,
then whatever was *blue* would be *pink*.

If every great color were the same,
then fades any need for debate
on which of a pigment we get to blame,
as blandness would be more innate.

So colored a plan may thus be a goal
for robots to shrink down the spectrum;
by replacing the storied human's role
with something 'bits' short of a rectum.

Yet, could drones be fit for the famed adage?..
There are Two Sides to the same coin;
Opposite Ends to the flipping average
wherein Paradoxes conjoin.

Can a brain have but one hemisphere
when supported by universal law?
Would the other half need then disappear?
¿A Dark Magic of unipolar flaw?

A better idea seems to incorporate
that things tend to have their opposite;
In from Both Ends to coordinate
for making a counterbalanced composite.

As Darkness exists so a Light can beam
of difference between such polarity,
therefore to show a contrasting gleam
of theory tested in disparity.

As way up Above, so flows down Below;
ranging from One End to The Other:
from Start to Finish, Goodbye and Hello,
conceived too in Father and Mother

As wherever Yin, so cycles Yang;
an ancient grasp on the fact,
that alike the theory of Big Bang,
It seems of a cosmic pact.

Thus to speak geometrically:
¿Do opposites therein so exist?
Such inverse Polar Ends could there be
of a mathematical gist?

Are there shapes to such a notion?
¿Equilateral Triangle and Circle?
Is this talk of a Magic Potion?
Nah,.. that's parlance of purple!

Pan-Worldly Things

For thinking lit auras or round halos,
a more Circular Shape comes to mind,
while a Pyramid Symbol yet bellows
dark action of the ethically blind.

Wherever a pair, when formulas dare,
The Tandem comprises The Whole.
Not too much care to 'circle what's square'
and still figuring on anything droll!

So, clearly (as ever) it comes down to *the one*
for how *an individual* will think,
Where hearing another is easier done
than listening, which tests every link.

WISDOM VS. INTELLIGENCE

Yoda versus Vader—a tangled debate:
Who is of *truer power* in the end?
Was it the Jedi Master?—while more sedate
(or) was it Darth, the Sith Lord?—once a friend.

Anakin (later Vader) was in a spot,
so troubled by his past and future;
In chase of heroic feats, he hatched a plot
with Sidious — his Dark Side smoocher.

Yoda, ever-seeking a Force-filled light,
struggled long to lessen all disaster.
Anakin (or Vader), more pulled by spite,
went on despising his Jedi Master.

In the fullness of time,.. Yoda trudged *wise*,
as Vader grew *intelligently* deranged;
a Questioning Yoda sought little surprise;
an all-Knowing Anakin got led estranged.

Archnemesis Tales are fueled by unease
of clashing *dual force* across time;
enduring feuds; Moses-n-Ramesses;
Profound Strife upon What's Divine.

Lord only knows, "One Ring to rule them all,"
possessed by an *intelligence* for control;
whereas to 'un-Ring', in spite of its call,
demanded a real *wisdom* and tested soul.

As well so pictured playing out in nature,
from a sly serpent to the *wise* old owl;
Where the scorpion-n-frog settled a wager,
an *intelligence* may've steered it afoul.

In there, the scorpion showed *intelligence*
by convincing the frog so positively;
wiser at first . . . froggy leaped any sense:
A shared lunacy killed them both causatively.

¿Do all such creatures fail to understand?
"I think, therefore I am"
René Descartes (this quoted man)
echoing throughout time span.

Is *intelligence* a Mirror for others to See
what's designed for outward projection?
Yet, *wisdom* (as life can bring to a knee)
but gained through Depths of Reflection?

Where *intelligence* pulls upon one to gather
(or hoard) as much stuff as possible,
does *wisdom* serve to push against the latter?..
Anonymously philanthropical?

Two plus Two *intelligently* is Four.
Such calculation fetches small debate.
But as Life's Things add to throe a bit more,
a based *wisdom* smarts more for the grate.

The Left Hemisphere (of mathematical power)
ever surveys for *logical perfection*;
whereas (electrochemically more of dour)
the Right Half reports in *contrary direction.*

The proctor, the doctor, and the lawyer
all must *intelligently* master their knowledge,
yet to earn 'a shingle' in Tom Sawyer,
well,.. high 'degrees in *wisdom*' need not college.

Thus, sometimes it's awkward and not so clear
which narrative is best to heed;
while Socrates to many was very dear,
others hated he hardly agreed.

When the curious sage wandered Athens' streets
he was more led by questions than answers;
Where some sense history rhymes or repeats,
the State cried he spread social cancers.

Lest we forget about the ole Zen master
— The Keeper of Little Gossip to Sell —
If asked to contribute as a forecaster,
he'd mostly advise for time to tell.

So, each of us all into the future we go,
a bit *wiser* and more *intelligent* for our past;
In worlds which pressure us all to Know,
more seasoning cautions: not so fast!

18

WORTH THEIR SALT

Through spells, a seasoning's there to unfetter
the climate in state or within mind;
The Winds of Change—Vast Tempests of Whether
unsettling things locked up in time.

To weather many seasons, a vision refined;
tempered, as a dove's wing can treat a stone,
with each passing swipe finished more for the grind,
A curious pressure upon what's 'set in known'.

To unearth if somebody's Worth Their *Salt*
differs some from seeing one to Have Sand;
For *salt*, more matters of honor-n-fault
and integrity able to withstand.

As the universe comprises so many elements,
The most vital arguably is *Salt*;
without *it*, humans would have little relevance
internally decaying by default.

As an early commodity known to humankind,
long is *its record* being invaluable,
Where traditionally *such use* was surely *unrefined*,
nowadays,.. *refined salt* seems fashionable.

Pan-Worldly Things

Salt's oldest accounts originate in China,
as past Egyptians drew pictures of *its use*.
If there's more glow for scores of Princess Diana,
so tends for gold (not *salt*) if running a sluice.

Vintage societies found *salt* indispensable,
an *applied agent* routine for preserving trade.
Hammered out for salary, *salt* became sensible,
even *used contemporarily* to get paid.

But the right kind of *salt* is good to know,
depending for which 'seasons' are upon:
Refined Salt better for melting ice-n-snow;
Unrefined Salt better for curing anyone.

A mythology has spread that *salt* is bad
for hypertension and some other ailments,
Yet, the truth is, it's actually a bit sad
where the air's been fogged per such entailments.

Most *salt* is *tabled* from drilling deep holes
where companies dig down as they must;
Harsh Cleansers thus meet their 'purifying roles'
when combined with Brine cracked from the crust.

As aluminum makes clouds sprayed high-in-the-sky
across lofty lines to save our Mother Earth,
without *salt* in our bodies . . . each human would die . . .
begging: Which element conserves more worth?

From younger years we learn *salt* is unhealthy.
Shameful it's so misunderstood an element!
For the right kind of *salt* can grace a body wealthy
through regulating systems of development.

Table salt, *refined* in its most regular form,
increases a pH-level of acidity;
Whereas *unrefined salt*, like calm to a storm,
more balances the spectrum through alkalinity.

As goes with assorted things pulled off-the-shelf,
salt's packaged in differing lots and kinds;
Dr. Brownstein's good book, *Salt: Your Way To Health*,
shakes out many well-seasoned guidelines.

In any case, for getting *down-to-earth*
could be a treasure as the years come and go;
granted *salt's* long held various forms of worth,
is *it* clear a crystal gift Above, Below?

AS ABOVE, SO BELOW

"As Above, so Below" is the English translation
of a Hermetic phrase brought forth in Greek *text*;
From antiquity-to-today, such explanation
to a portion of longer *scripts,* which could vex.

The *scripts* go a very, very long way back,
Classic Cultures and the beliefs some held;
the *Hermetica* (such *scripts*) full of theory to unpack:
Mental Alchemy, . . . and else things spelled.

The schools of Astrology, Magic, and Medicine,
all included per its long-standing mystery;
"Occult Sciences" — a term set to roundly jettison
old subjects studied here in our modern history.

The defining *text* found ways to 'power through' today
across passages trailing back to Ancient Greece;
Within elite-circles, so alleged to 'have stay',
where legend has *it* held as a Golden Fleece.

The *Hermetica* (boiled down to the *Emerald Tablet*)
drew Islamic Scholars plenty toward its way.
Ahead in time, there formed a version less elaborate:
The Kybalion—was published for present-day.

As Above, so Below (the Hermetic *text* in question)
is considered to be a take on "correspondence";
for what's here Below is seen of Connective Suggestion
to what's figured Above . . . of One's extreme Preponderance.

The *script* says alikeness therein Polar Opposites,
"corresponding" but by a matter of degrees;
Not of a notion to need many doctorates,
yet perhaps just one in Life Expertise.

Thusly it's theory for framing All Things,
where No Thing is pictured *ALL* Good or Bad;
just varying rings . . . from Christ to kings,
Cosmic Duos made wholly upon add.

A college of Hermeticism keenly pursued
offsetting paths 'illuminating' moons ago,
where a Theistic Philosophy resolved to construe
whatever's 'allowed to occur' here Below.

Hermeticism's characters sprang from the *Iliad*,
such storylines titanically hurtled through.
If the primordial myth did raise an Olympiad,
it Uplifted from a Greco-Roman worldview.

Whence the Romans adapted such Greek dogma-n-creed,
a God could be renamed a colossal planet;
hence a Universal Ethos, from giving-to-greed,
full of precepts so plotted to game their gamut.

The pharaohs (at some point) were ergo tied in
through the mythical Hermes Trismegistus;
a Moses-like See for Hermeticists akin,
relative to thus a metaphysical-checklist.

The aged faith holds: Below distinct from Above,
yet likened through a measure of degrees;
so too for a contrast between Hate and Love,
"corresponding" affectionately in a breeze.

The doctrine has it, only Above "truly good,"
as here Below: undue temptation in the flesh.
Accordingly, such questions of Shouldn't or Should
ever involve Dual Degrees of intermesh.

To some, Hermeticism is civilized witchcraft.
Regardless, a mentalism seems at play;
despite whether or not folks see it mostly as daft,
whatever it is . . . appears here to stay.

Hence here so Below, within a temporal moment,
is Dual Polarity all about the world?
If upon ever urge pulls to tease for torment,
could also (from Above) push a grace less swirled?

BI-POLAR-ITY VS. DUAL-ITY

A Wilderness of Wonder within Open Thought,
where questions cut path to better concept;
Blessed Freedom in Ponder—to Wander in Aught
Hallowed Nothingness to Zen thine Mindset.

To brave Round Rambles, if testing the norm,
a trial of Mental Landscapes for compare;
as usual to a curious brainstorm,
a trendier voice may air, "Don't you dare!!"

Cognitive strolls (at times) pairs twos,
More or Less, Yea or Nay — so to say;
Wherein thereof only one can choose,
it's impossible to always see grey.

Whether that's Good—or—not so Bad,
there's innate Dual Structure for opposites;
Cosmic Bi Poles, from Happy to Sad,
despite what degree of its cognizance.

Decisions, decisions . . . such is the notion,
whether to query Less or More,
As whatever may stir within motion,
the concept splits by Two, not four.

Pan-Worldly Things

To consider a lead through Left or Right,
or whether something's Real or Fake,
To delve a Darkness in chase of Light;
A trade-off between Give and Take.

If such a split's sensed of Above and Below,
or of Bi-Speeds—Fast and Slow—to a race,
a *stage of reflection* sets in a Duo,
just as there are *two sides* to one's face.

Whether the mercury climbs Up or Down,
it's still part of the same thermometer,
in measure of the climate all around
changing more fluid than Him-to-Her.

If the concept becomes a matter of size,
the split can set between Big and Small;
Where "all things being relative" is no surprise,
of course . . . one can feel Short, and Tall!

In each such case there's Dual such Force,
such opposite Bi Polarity for choice,
Whether a sensation feels Smooth or Coarse,
there's an associated pair to invoice.

By that, which Giveth can Taketh away
in our realm of the Come and Go,
Within and throughout ever much to weigh
amid *cosmic ends,* To and Fro.

A *coincidence of opposites* within our realm,
it's long been of the great Human Mind;
therein a clear contrast can serve to overwhelm,
wherefore good reason may be Divine.

That being so, lasting books were created
(over time) for the transfer of keen theory;
questioned by some as reading grossly outdated,
was each *Origin Story* robust query?

Such a spanning library includes the *Bible,*
as well as the enduring *Quran,*
yet the *Hermetica* precedes both books in cycle,
of a rhyming Ancient Greek brand.

It was Roman Byzantines forwarding the *script,*
¿the *Hermetica* infused about the *Bible*?
Where certain Greek portions would surely have been clipped,
a true believer may consider this libel.

The Kybalion (much more recently published)
— A literary child of the *Hermetica* —
is translated *script* (some deem as rubbish)
through a shorter so-styled replica.

Per the modern work: "Seven Hermetic principles."
Each maxim goes back to the Greek philosophy;
today, such decrees heard less than a pope's papal bulls,
nevertheless,.. may All Power be used responsibly.

"The principle of mentalism" is firstly stated,
in essence: The Mind is everything-n-All.
To understand that is to get so illuminated
without needing join a Masonic Hall.

Next in order, "The principle of correspondence,"
As Above, so Below . . . in a nutshell;
More or Less mirroring any given instance
where folks reflect upon Heaven-n-Hell.

Then so addressed, "The principle of vibration,"
As molecularly . . . matters never stop . . .
even if a Thing appears of stagnation,
particles keep spinning wherever It's dropped.

Up then for review, "The principle of polarity,"
As everything so understood is framed as Dual;
whereby if this notion triggers a great hilarity,
even Earth gets measured in drifting from Hot to Cool.

"The principle of rhythm" next sways per the flow
along such Hermetic Waves of consideration;
Not much based upon which direction will go,
but more that Movement Begets Compensation.

For each-n-every action, an opposite-n-equal
— one of Isaac Newton's Three Laws of Motion —
"The principle of cause and effect," as if a sequel,
is Cosmic Theory so 'tide' to an ocean.

And last but not least, "the principle of gender,"
As both Feminine and Masculine make the whole;
in opposing degrees away from what's center,
each distinction combining from a Counter-Pole.

So, whether one wishes to affix the label
of someone being Bipolar or Dual,
the idea is: we're All Set upon The Table
cosmically: where Anyone can Play the Fool.

To that end, what goes Up spawns pull to come Down,
whatever Rises temporally must Fall,
More to the matter of when Things turn around,
as variations come by each catch-all.

Where 'cases' are noted in the scale of human minds,
could it be that 'some' more fully flux per Either End?
In any event, it dynamically takes all kinds,
otherwise . . . *would there be an offsetting amend?*

In that, Abraham Lincoln suffered bouts of depression
amid fight to reform justice in a broken world;
Abe honestly struggled to beat a wicked oppression,
enough for throwing a good breakfast roundly hurled.

Additionally, the aforesaid Isaac Newton
amounted equally of some Bipolar suspicion;
where his oddness may've cast images of a highfalutin,
most gravitated to his heady 'Apple System'.

For good measure note the mercurial Beethoven,
maker of the EU's anthem, *Ode to Joy*;
Renown for his mood swings and melodies so woven,
he seemed tuned-in to create more than destroy.

Today, from the likes of Ted Turner to Mel Gibson,
Jim Carrey, Russel Brand, and others of 'such friction';
where also is 'the case' with Catherine Zeta-Jones,
(in their bones) too Mariah Carey and Tyson Fury.

So, no matter if others feel it stranger than some,
we all Dually Range across Bipolar Force;
Within, one can accept as thy kingdom come,
the Mental Cosmos — despite onset to any course.

SOCRATES VS. THE STATE

'Twas the 5th century before our Common Era,
when alive in this time were three men:
Buddhic, Confucian, Socratic *sierra*
skyward ranging uplifted through Zen.

Therein India, China, or Athens,
Vigorous profiles shone for display;
The horizon of citizen passions
thusly broadened . . . to some dismay?

A Royal Pain felt for the great masses?
So annoying to imagine their struggle!
But a new icon for common classes?!
An elite could sense fortune or trouble.

As the Buddha mulled dharma in India,
debating the sanity of the System,
Confucius there reflected in China
upon ethics, morality and wisdom.

But perhaps the most tested of the three,
only Socrates did battle in war;
going on to perplex the Powers That Be
where They ultimately begged for no more.

Pan-Worldly Things

What had brewed within Socrates the Great?
Was it trauma from war's savage combat?
Renowned for legion defence of the state,
he survived to press 'the grand format'.

Widely viewed as a brave fighting hero,
He'd rescued fellow soldiers in battle;
The State eventually ground him to zero
for cerebrally moving 'the cattle'.

"True knowledge" he offered as "the best good,"
though bad for engineering hive mind,
By contending ALL was NOT understood,
some deemed he was rather unkind.

Where consulting with folks upon "true knowledge,"
an advisement to find in self-search;
Divine Inspiration, not mental bondage
so tied to blind faith in a State-church.

He cleared path for Plato and Aristotle,
but how much were the three Greeks alike?
Plato grew cautious and applied more throttle
seeing his mentor seized by the Reich.

Plato wasn't known as veteran to war;
Aristotle sought the class of a prince;
Such cherished visions of elite-adore
did swell upon Socratic Waves since.

The Wave Maker himself barely scribed his way,
He was more an Athenian to the streets;
Plato so classically moved to parlay
via dialogues written about *the peaks*.

The Big State-Plato penned his *Republic*,
twenty years beyond Socrates's death,
whereupon wished some forgotten the Lunatic,
the Greek Yoda had spread in social breadth.

Although ages have passed since an ancient year,
still standing are *Socratic opinions*,
despite *them* fielding much ridicule and jeer
from convinced gurus, or allied minions.

Into the Greek Forum he cut novel space
to openly question a State Actor;
Debate the new tool (not a spear or a mace),
Peaceful Arms for a civic 'detractor'.

Improve Women's Rights . . . he argued a duty,
where some saw him too ugly to ignore!
He challenged bold definitions of beauty;
was a good sport if lampooned as a boar.

He refused faith in any Greek deities,
yet praised phony Gods on a lark;
doing it all with few anonymities:
"I know that I know nothing," his mark.

He'd seen value to get lost in talking
through searching to scan one's lead;
Even if an endpoint stirred a mocking,
such banter germane to his creed.

Socrates and Jung both figured the same:
It's rare folks "knowingly" act wrong;
that if (by habit) there's others to blame,
grim shadows cast gladly along.

Impassioned not to rule upon a soul,
Liberty for each woman and man;
where the State preached about a Hero's Role,
he'd bless: seek your own Divine Plan.

(Both) scientific theory and common law
amend stronger for trial in open debate;
His rigorous style exposed previous flaw,
and without it . . . non-sense derives more innate.

Not so Magnificent alike Suleiman,
nor Great like the ravenous Alexander,
Socrates executed as a free-thinking man
of Promethean Fire, and candour.

Hence for this fellow, shall we raise a glass?!
An Athenian the State took to task.
Socrates the Good, or Socrates the Crass!?
From within, seems a kindred place to ask.

PAN-IC, PAN-DEMIC, PAN-GLOBAL, PAN-HERMETIC

Past conjurers gave chase to sciencey magic within Alchemical
spell,
Turning iron-to-gold — one of the tricks — it promised to serve
them well.
The metal-conversion thusly predicted high triumph and monied
prize,
but it was mental-chemistry that became more to charm their
shimmering eyes.

To succeed in transmuting tin-to-treasure whispered of fortune
untold,
Yet their metallic dreams fantastically dashed upon a reality to
behold.
Hence the Alchemical Tree branches out per various species of
nature,
where the humankind barked convertible through rhetoric and
nomenclature.

Hermetic Conversion (or Mental Alchemy) — electrochemical
train;
Neurolinguistic Programming to condition desired a brain.
Control the story—believe the narrative—the body's sure to
follow,
for if one becomes so beguiled, a con is easier to swallow.

The Mind-of-One is That-of-Many dead set in fearful contagion,
no matter if classified as Black, White, Rainbow, Hispanic, or Asian;
where the System excites Pan-ic, compliance can spread
Pan-global,
then dare to question a Pan-solution, you may get cast as acting
ignoble.

Institutions Unite! Fascistic Synergy? Consensus by way of The
Dollar;
Big Data, Big Tech, Big Media, Big State, Big Pharma, Big Bank
. . . Oh, Brother!
It baits on a hook, entices a nibble, then switches to sink in
mind-virus.
Infection resistant? Unmask the shrouded! Get blamed with vigor
and slyness.

But such massive conforming pressure: Is there nothing more
routine?
Temporal systems (alike our Milky Way) seem governed from in
between.
¿Are not such physical arrangements usually churned by a spun
inner-core?
Become too impressed by the vortex's force, systemic corruption's
in store.

¿So why bother with a grinding struggle? In the end all things
turn to dust.
Ancestors going before too struggled . . . and there's a story to trust!
Cosmic black holes (or warping mentalities) have not complete
control,
for if they did,.. any internal system wouldn't have a unique patrol.

Galileo was sentenced to house arrest for questioning 'the science'
of the Church;
¿Consent of the Vatican? The Sun follows Earth — the astrono-
mer dared 'besmirch'.
Freedom to think; such was the battle — Galileo was not to be
released.
Centuries later, vindicated by time . . . his presence had tamed the
beast.

Socrates was renown for valor during his time as an Athenian
soldier,
Praised for this by the Powers That Be . . . to only condemn him
when older.
In wiser years, he roamed to inspire more curiosity within
groupthink;
Corrupting the youth: the State levied charge—hemlock his sentence to drink.

Include Yeshua, Gandhi, and Martin Luther King: Establishment
unapproved;
Per each such account — beloved by so many — the Selects
wished them removed.
Whatever propelled these leaders to quest withstood Institutional
threat,
Ashes to ashes, dust to dust . . . as They piled up spiritual debt.

Some folks believe it's a righteous act to leverage Alchemical
discovery,
to Hermetically impress upon another for easing an adult's
recovery.
There, malevolent holds can harbor many a scared or spurned child
entrapped by a lure of spite in feeling abandoned to the world, to
the wild.

Time's the keeper of tragic tales for compassionating a heart;
Hansel and Gretel's parents deserted their kids, and thought it
smart.
¿Did Hitler and Stalin function seeking revenge for simply being
born?
As children, both were fiercely beaten by a family member in
'loving scorn'.

In younger years, a tyrant could accept an existential theory as
fact:
Power and love? Hand in glove! — a philosophy crescendoed in
attack.
Ancient Greek myths (of the pagan sort) tell of such similar sin;
Cronus the patriarch, Zeus his son, and Hermes—the next of kin.

The classical creed's full of sagas which played-out on a titanic
stage,
Such myths reveal family-struggle across a hierarchy cursed by
rage:
Cronus devoured his baby boy (Zeus) to preserve his own seat of
power;
a future fear that Zeus would *take 'em* as *he'd took* before his
father.

In dual contrast, the patriarch for Abrahamic story is the name-
sake sage,
Before he'd been taken—a hellish dark spirit—fooled so when
younger in age;
Almost nightmarishly killing his son, then . . . baffled . . . by the
grace of an angel,
Forever changed, a wiser path chosen over luminous occult fable.

Hermetic Paganism to Occult Elitism — imperious outlook
— age-old,
a world where mind-gaming charms had intrinsic value beyond
bricks of gold;
Greek and Egyptian mindsets anciently-linked in the study of
Alchemy,
in that, Hermes's goat-headed son (Pan) plays 'the devil' . . . so
goes mythology.

Published in 1908, *The Kybalion* — a Hermetic handbook of sorts;
Brims with theory metaphysically dear to past royal and ancient
courts.
Where some so liken the *script* to an Ancient Greek book,
the *Hermetica,*
Practitioners may see the *Bible* (in certain ways) as a Roman replica.

What in the world does Hermeticism have to do with Pan-demics
of stealth!?
Hermes's snakes-n-wings—the Caduceus—currently a crest for
public health;
His 'magic wand', as a medical symbol, was first modernized in 1902
when the U.S. Army (claiming blunder) instituted it for all, . . .me
and you.

The Kybalion (of Masonic publish) spells out ways to Alchemi-
cally Train . . .
"Seven Hermetic principles"— cosmic notions (with some for any
ole brain);
The "principle of polarity": All Things have poles (of dual, opposite nature).
but is *the Truth* a Thing? An absolute concept? Argued to settle
within chamber.

By the 1920's, a mental-virus had long been spreading Pan-global;
The U.S. Eugenics 'school of science' was elite-financed as noble.
Their monied-stewardship set the tone to receive institutional
graces,
then once Eugenics more normally socialized . . . it was off to the
races!

Kookily praised to serve the public, a 'high expert' may've gushed
of its need:
"Undesired genetics?!" . . . "A drain on society!!" — rhetoric for
all to heed.
The spooky vibes indeed did spread; U.S. precedent was set in
court.
Crux of the matter? Better procreation — 'the feebleminded' to
be cut short.

As the fabled Pan-creature played his flute, a spellbound hysteria
gave chase;
such affect could impress so deep and wide, vast others were
forced to face.
When Eugenics stirred in Nazi Germany, an imperiousness set it
on fire,
in tracking a myth to build a Super Man, such lunacy collapsed in
a pyre.

If humanity's bungling toward enlightenment, surely it's not a
done deal,
for when rapt ideology yet fails, a lifting fog can bare much to reveal;
Echoing over time, of rhyming concern, the trouble in so many
people,
be it of pharaohs, Malthus, or Gates today, some of us sectioned
'not-so-equal'.

The pulling convictions of a left hemisphere. It's necessary to feel
right!
Yet the right hemisphere—of a wiser push—offers temperance by
way of a fight.
To suffer a right-brain stroke is to be 'left' more myopic pulling
the strings;
Doctor Iain McGilchrist highlights such findings per *The Matter
With Things*.

¿Are the two hemispheres of dual-nature? ¿Would that mean
they're of bi-polarity?
If so, then perhaps Hermetic principles before touched on the
same disparity;
For if citizens ever Alchemically-align with polarizing tyrant leaders,
then social pathology's 'left' to spread fast-n-wild à la microscopic
creatures.

As Ancient Rome knew Hermeticism, it cycled back for a Renais-
sance revival;
the Medici-loyal, Ficino, translated the *Hermetica* — early modern arrival.
Granted the philosophy ties together so many empires
metaphysically,
perhaps the Medici-employed Da Vinci remarked as well, but
artistically.

Leonardo's timeless *Vitruvian Man* has asymmetry within his eyes,
The darker look to his left eyeball mightn't give too much
surprise.
Could a hint to a Hermetic principle be there embedded within
his classic?
If so: was it Medici-approved?—or—unknown to such elite Catholic?

Provided a Medici fellowship with the Church held establishment
sway,
Da Vinci's art, and Galileo's findings, pushed through at the end
of the day.
So just as balanced floors can build sky-high for structure of the
hidden joist,
could faceless Time scale a Supreme framing to level our main-
stream voice?

THE SEEKER'S PATH

While heavy may seem the load
along the burdensome taxing road,
If compassion remains the goal,
then freer releases the soul.